FATEFUL
DECISIONS

Enid O'Dowd

ORIGINAL WRITING

ISBNS
PARENT : 978-1-78237-365-0
EPUB: 978-1-78237-366-7
MOBI: 978-1-78237-367-4
PDF: 978-1-78237-368-1

A CIP catalogue for this book is available from the National Library.

Published by ORIGINAL WRITING LTD., Dublin, 2013.

Printed by CLONDALKIN GROUP, Glasnevin, Dublin 11

Dedicated to

Monty and Jamie

Acknowledgements

My English teacher at Stratford Grammar School in London didn't think writing was my forte as I was good at maths. Maybe he was right?

Writing fiction is a new experience for me.

Vanessa O'Loughlin of the Inkwell Writers Group gave me helpful feedback on the first 10,000 words. I took her advice on board. Helen Falconer gave me structural advice, and feedback on the draft after I made the changes she suggested. My thanks to them.

The following family and friends gave me advice and/or proofing assistance with later drafts: Annie Clements, Dr Anna Finnegan, Ciara Gillan, Johanna Lowry O'Reilly, my daughter Jess and my sister Jean. Again, my thanks are due.

If there are typos, bad grammar and apostrophes in the wrong place, the fault is all mine.

Author's Note

The cases mentioned in the book, apart of course from the babies Tommy and Rose which are entirely fictional, are real-life ones.

At the time of going to press there had been developments in several of them.

The fathers of Bianca Jones and of Ruth and Jose Breton have now been convicted of their murders despite in Bianca's case, her body not being found. The mother and stepfather of Kiesha Abrahams and the parents of Marina Sabatier were convicted of their children's murders in July 2013 and June 2012 respectively. Hailey Dunn's body was found in March 2013 but nobody has been charged. Jhessye Shockley's body has not been found but her mother Jerice Hunter is currently awaiting trial for her murder and for child abuse.

Scotland Yard, following a review of the Madeleine McCann case, said in July 2013 that there are 38 'persons of interest' to them and that they are working with the Portuguese authorities. This baffling case has led to the establishment of several websites discussing the mystery; one of them: http://mccannfiles.com/ contains a myriad of published material including the Portuguese police files and my own research 'A review of the background to setting up the limited company Madeleine's Fund: Leaving No Stone Unturned and a forensic examination of the company accounts.' The website http://www.mccannpjfiles.co.uk will take you straight to the Portuguese police files most of which were released in August 2008.

The French case mentioned by a character in Chapter 34 in which a woman left four children aged between 2 and 12 alone for a weekend while she attended an evangelical prayer meeting was reported in a local paper. I mention this as it is hardly believable that a parent would do this and the reader might think this was a creative device on my part to develop that character. In fact in researching for this book I was continually surprised how casual some parents are about their small children.

Readers may be interested to visit discussion sites such as The Complete Mystery of Madeleine McCann http://jillhavern.forumotion.net/ and Missing Madeleine http://missingmadeleine.forumotion.net/. These websites sometimes contain tetchy exchanges when members disagree. Occasionally a member flounces off after a disagreement despite intervention from a forum moderator.

The official Madeleine McCann website http://findmadeleine.com/ may also be of interest, and Dr Kate McCann's book *madeleine* gives a fascinating insight into the case.

The Missing Children Forum is of course fictional though it has been based in layout and headings on existing forums like the ones mentioned above. Forum members may post on one discussion thread only as Molly does, or on many. Molly was of course on the Forum every day while she was recovering from her accident but did not post unless she felt she could move the debate on. Her post numbers are consecutive while those for some other members are not as it is assumed they were also contributing to other threads.

Readers may also feel that it is unlikely that characters in the book would so easily accept requests to be a Facebook friend or a LinkedIn contact from someone they did not know. My own experience tells me otherwise. For example after appearing on Liveline talking about politicians' expenses I received about 12 requests to be a Facebook friend from people who had heard the broadcast, and after publishing my research on www.mccannfiles.com I received a similar number of 'friend' requests and from several countries.

By way of experiment about Facebook members' security concerns I picked a name at random, and googled it, preceded by Facebook. Of the first ten accounts in that name, six (60%) were completely open and the four that were 'closed' still gave limited access to pictures of family and friends plus some information about the holders. Not a scientific survey admittedly but I found a similar situation when I googled the name of one of the characters in the book.

In real life, as well as in fiction, it seems that people can be as careless about their own personal safety as they are in respect of their children's!

Contents

Prologue
Manchester
June 2011

Part i
August 2011 – November 2011

PART II

DECEMBER 2011 – APRIL 2012

PART III

WATERFORD 2010

PART IV

MAY 2012 – JULY 2012

Part v
August 2012
France

Part vi
September 2012-October 2012

Epilogue
France
October 2013

PROLOGUE

MANCHESTER
JUNE 2011

The worst thing was having no warning. One minute Jeff was there, fit and healthy; the next he collapsed training for a charity run on a sunny June day. He was dead by the time they got him to hospital.

Hypertrophic cardiomyopathy took my husband; something I'd never heard of then. In simple language it means sudden cardiac death and it can affect young people. Jeff never smoked, was seriously sporty and had completed two marathons. He was 34, the same age as me; we'd been married for seven years. I mean I was the one who smoked; not as much as I used to because he went on about it. I was the one who ate red meat every day and always had cream with dessert. He was always warning me about cholesterol. He'd have just one glass of wine with dinner at the weekends and tell me I should cut down on the vodka and tonics, yet he was the one who died. It didn't make sense.

As I came home from the hospital with tears flowing down my face I thought how unfair it was that he'd never see his unborn son.

'Molly, you must get bereavement counselling,' my GP had said when, after the funeral, I went to ask him for sleeping pills to get me through the first few weeks. In hindsight I probably should have taken his advice but I've always tried to sort out my own issues. Jeff used to say I was stubborn. So I tried to move on without counselling. Being on compassionate leave from my job as an IT consultant, at home with my only regular source of comfort being Jeff's distraught dog Pedro, a little black and white terrier, wasn't the best route to recovery. Jeff had tried unsuccessfully to restrict my home computer use on the grounds that I worked with them all day. He never understood my fascination with the internet and the information out there.

With him gone, I lived on the internet, initially obsessed with discovering more about the condition that killed him and whether there had been any warning signs I had missed.

Two weeks after Jeff died, on what would have been his birthday, I fell down the stairs breaking my right leg in two places, three lumbar vertebrae and my pelvis and bringing on a miscarriage. I had been five months pregnant and proudly showing my bump. We'd put off starting a family for the usual practical reasons; the size of our mortgage and career issues but three years ago we'd decided to try for a baby. We'd assumed it would be easy but nothing happened. We were both tested; the doctors found nothing. We actually had an appointment to discuss the possibility of IVF treatment when I discovered I was pregnant.

So I never saw our son either.

I was found unconscious by Lidia, my Polish cleaner, and the hospital told me later how lucky I was that she had arrived only minutes after my fall given how much blood I had lost.

Lucky? That's a matter of opinion.

In hospital I just wanted to die. Before the accident at least the baby had given me a reason to live.

Meanwhile, Lidia reorganised my terraced house to take account of my temporary immobility. With the help of her husband, who speaks even less English than she does, she turned the second reception room downstairs into a bedroom/office for me as I couldn't get upstairs without help. Thus I had an independent existence given the downstairs toilet and shower.

Back home, I became in effect a hermit, ignoring family and friends, and seeing only Lidia and Pedro. I moved on to sites about fertility issues. The hospital doctor had been evasive when I asked about having another child which I took to mean there was an issue. Hours on those sites did not lead me to any definite conclusions so I turned to other ones about lost babies which only made me feel more miserable even when some of the mums posting said there was life after miscarriage.

Every night I looked at the scan picture they printed out for us when we had that ultrasound the week before Jeff died. It's on the dressing table next to my favourite wedding photo showing me ever so slightly plump, with shoulder length glossy honey blonde hair good enough for a shampoo advertisement. I don't look like that now or how I did before the double tragedy that hit me. I used to dress smartly when I went out to clients, had a weekly blow dry and always wore make-up. Now I can't be bothered about my appearance and I know I'm not eating properly. I could do with gaining half a stone and sometimes I can't be bothered to wash my hair even though I've all the time in the world.

My internet research moved on to the separate issue of missing children.

How careless some parents are! Their needs come first. Shortly after my tragedy, two babies went missing thanks to fateful decisions made by their mothers. I became obsessed with these two cases with personal consequences for me and for the mothers that I could never have foreseen.

Like these two women, I made a fateful decision and I don't think I will ever know if it was the right one.

PART 1

AUGUST 2011 – NOVEMBER 2011

Chapter 1

Waterford Tuesday 9 August 2011

S he parks her old blue Micra close to the corner. The parking wardens don't usually go down this narrow side street. She used to park outside her hairdressers but got a ticket last month. She can't really afford this hairdo; she certainly can't afford another ticket. The bastard left a note on the car saying she shouldn't leave a baby inside her car; she wasn't even in there for ten minutes. She was just having her fringe trimmed.

She grabs her mobile from the dashboard and dials quickly.

She hears his voice yet again, saying, 'Hi, this is Dave. I'm busy; keep trying or leave a message.'

'How many more messages do I have to leave before that fucker answers?' There is no reply from her sleeping child strapped in the scruffy car seat.

She stands by the car smoking her last cigarette.

She tries another number.

'Well girl, it's me Carli. Dave promised to take Tommy today but he hasn't turned up and he's not answering his mobile. I'm parked round the corner from Hair-I-Am and Tommy's asleep in his seat. Can you come down and get him? I'll be ages. I'm getting extensions and my roots fixed for the show tomorrow.'

She shakes her head as she takes her last puff.

'No, I can't take him in. There's no room since they put that nail bar in. The buggy wouldn't fit. It's a nightmare to fold up. I can't have him on my lap the whole time. You know how big he is for ten months and he's trying to walk. They're really snotty about kids anyway.

'You'll do it? I'm really stuck.

'You're a star. I'll leave the car keys at reception. Text me when you've collected him. Thanks, I owe you one.'

She is relieved and thinks 'Thank God for Emer, she's a real friend.'

She flicks the cigarette end into the gutter then glances through the car window at her sleeping son. She'd changed his nappy and fed him just before she left; and he's sleeping so soundly. He'll be fine she thinks. She looks at her watch and swears; it's later than she thought. She almost runs round the corner, passing the charity shop, then the shoe shop next door to it and finally into Hair-I-Am. She enters the salon. It's busy as it always is on special offer days. Her appointment was for 4.0 pm but she's half an hour late, thanks to Dave. The receptionist is on the phone with customers waiting.

'Can I go through?' she asks.

The receptionist recognises her and snaps, 'Kevin's had to start on someone else. You'll have to wait.' Why is it, she wonders, that the receptionist always seems to look at her in a disapproving way? Perhaps as the woman is old, at least 35, she doesn't like Carli's tattoos. Well sod her, she thinks, it's nothing to do with her.

She considers returning to the car and asking the receptionist to ring her when Kevin's ready but decides against it. The woman doesn't like her and is clearly busy.

There's only one seat left in the new blue and gold reception area. She rather likes it though she's heard some customers saying it's crap.

The hairdo is a must because she has to look amazing for the local final tomorrow. If she makes it past the judges, she'll be in the national final and from there who knows? Star Search! She smiles to herself. It'll really piss Deirdre off when she sees her name in the papers. Assuming she wins, that is. She knows she should stop badmouthing her. But even though it's four years since her foster parents took Deirdre in, and two years since Carli moved out, she still blames her for turning them against her.

Her mobile rings. She can see that at last Dave has returned her calls.

She feels like screaming down the phone at him but restrains herself, considering the other women waiting in reception.

'Where were you lad? In the pub?'

'Look, Social Welfare rang me, said I had to go in for an interview. They'd have cut me off otherwise. I had to switch off my phone while I was in there. They had me taking tests and they're sending me on a course.'

That's a better excuse than last time, she thinks. It could even be true. She knows they're clamping down on scroungers. Dave has lost his job and isn't exactly looking for another.

She calms down.

'I was really stuck but I got hold of Emer and she's on her way now. So I don't need you. Bye.'

As she clicks end call, her regular hairdresser Kevin emerges looking for her.

**

Fifteen minutes later, sitting in the chair while her hair absorbs the colour, she's desperate for a fag, and then remembers she smoked her last one before she came in.

The salon has an area at the back of the building for customers who don't want the world to see them in their rollers while they have a puff. This is why she uses Hair-I-Am even though it's not the cheapest. It's the only hairdressers she knows in Waterford where you can smoke.

'Kevin,' she asks, 'can I borrow a fag. I'll pay you back.'

'You said that last time,' he says, offering her one anyway.

She goes to the smoking area where she meets another regular customer.

'I heard you're in the Waterford Final tomorrow. We've got audience tickets and we'll be rooting for you.'

She smiles.

'Yeah, I think this is going to be my year. I just missed out last time.'

She knows the customer and her boyfriend often come to the pub where she sings. It lifts her spirits to know she has a fan base, albeit a small one. Almost simultaneously both women remove their cardigans as the sun moves overhead.

'Great to feel a bit of sun,' the customer says.

'Yeah, you feel you can do anything when it's like this.'

The customer offers her a cigarette. She's in the middle of it when Kevin comes and insists she returns.

'Do I have to come right now?'

'You do, we're really booked up today.'

Reluctantly she returns with him.

'Julie was looking for you.' She takes no notice. She doesn't like the receptionist's manner.

'I really think you should have the shorter extensions given your height.'

They've discussed this before and she had argued for the longer ones. While the discussion is concluding with a win for Kevin, the receptionist appears.

'You left your phone in reception. I was looking for you.'

'Thank you,' she says begrudgingly. Then she notices a missed call and a text from Emer. She looks at her watch. It's now 5.25 pm.

Alarmed, she calls Emer. Before she can speak, Emer says, 'I'm really sorry. I was on my way when I got a call to say my mam was taken bad. I rang you but it was engaged. The salon number was engaged too so I sent you a text.'

She snaps, 'I told Dave I didn't need him as you were coming. I left my mobile in reception and only just got it back.'

Then she feels guilty. Emer's mum is a lovely person who'd fed her and let her stay over whenever there was trouble at home.

'Don't worry girl. I'll go and get Tommy now. Please God he's still asleep.'

Without thinking of her bizarre appearance, she dashes out of the salon ignoring Kevin's plea to stay in her seat. As she turns the corner she sees her car but can't see Tommy. Panicking she thinks OMG he's got out of the seat somehow, crawled into the back and trapped himself on the floor. She remembers she left the keys at reception but tries to open the front passenger door anyway. It opens. Fuck, she didn't lock it.

She babbles, 'Tommy, Mammy's sorry. I didn't mean to leave you on your own.' Then it sinks in. There is no Tommy. Just an empty car.

She wails. And wails again. The sun that had brightened her cigarette break has now been replaced by grey sky and a shower. Two cars pass her and ignore the small figure with the odd hair. But nobody comes as this is a narrow side street with few pedestrians. She's frozen like a statue. Then she hears a voice saying 'Your hair'll be ruined if we don't get the conditioner on.' It's Kevin, who's left the salon to look for her.

She pounds her wrists against his chest.

'He's gone, he's gone.'

'Who's gone?'

She screams, 'He's gone. He can't have.'

Kevin shouts, 'Who the hell are you talking about?'

She looks at him as if he's stupid. 'He's gone. My baby's gone.'

He almost drags her back to the salon where he orders Julie to get off the phone and call the gardai.

It is 5.35 pm.

She's still shaking and not very coherent. Some of the customers have left their chairs to investigate. They don't know what to do with the hysterical Carli and stand there gaping. Kevin steps in, ushering the women back to their places.

Carli is like a stuck record screaming the same sentences over and over again.

'My baby's gone. He can't be gone. He can't be. Not my Tommy. He's gone. He can't be gone. He just can't be.'

CHAPTER 2

Accrington Thursday 25 August 2011

Pacing up and down her living room Amy hears yet again, 'The mobile you are calling is switched off; please leave a message after the tone.' She can't understand why Teresa isn't answering or at least returning her calls. It just isn't like her.

She's told her to be back by seven o'clock so Amy can get to her meeting in good time. It's going to be a difficult meeting and she just has to be there early.

If only the meeting date hadn't been changed. She's still fuming about that. It should have been on Monday but the committee secretary changed the date and claimed she couldn't get through to Amy to check it with her. Utter rubbish! And she doesn't believe that several members couldn't make Monday so the date had to be changed. The meetings are on the fourth Monday of the month. Committee members know to keep that day free. She doesn't buy it; something is up.

Jimmy would have been here to mind his daughter if the meeting hadn't been changed and she wouldn't have needed to ask Teresa to come back early from her day off. She decides there's no point in ringing Teresa again and replaces her mobile in her cardigan pocket.

Amy is determined not to let her annoyance about the rescheduled meeting affect her evening. Everything is planned; Peter is at a sleepover with his best friend. She must stop fussing about Teresa. She will be back in time to babysit Rose.

**

Sitting in the rocking chair in Rose's room with her daughter on her lap, Amy wishes she hadn't given in on the room's revamp. Jimmy had insisted on getting in a designer to redecorate it when he knew she was expecting a girl. The only nice thing there Amy considers is the rocking chair and that came from her old family home. She could have organised Rose's room so much better; it would have been much more tasteful and half the price. Rose is reaching up to pull her mother's earring when her mobile rings. She just manages to change her hold on Rose to free up an arm so she can retrieve the phone from her pocket before it stops ringing. She doesn't recognise the number that comes up so she's very surprised to hear Teresa. She's not Irish as her name might suggest but Chinese, and had explained to Amy when she came for interview that English people can't pronounce her birth name so she is now known as Teresa after her favourite saint. The au pair speaks good English normally but she gets a little mixed up when she's agitated as she clearly is now.

'Amy, I think I late. The bus at 5.45 was full and I can't get on.'

Giving her no chance to explain, Amy interrupts, 'I need you back. What's the problem?'

'A man told me there was bomb scare at Manchester Piccadilly station and no trains running now so people they go to Chorlton Street bus station instead. They filled bus and I couldn't get on when it come to my stop. I wait for the next bus at the bus station. Very crowded here but I think I will get on this time. Sometimes bus takes one hour, sometimes little more but I should be back for half past seven. Have to go, I borrow this phone from nice lady in the queue because I leave mine at home.'

So now she has a problem despite all her planning.

Damn, she thinks. It'll take me 15 minutes to get to the hotel, so I'll have to be out of here by 7.30 pm to have a chance to talk to early arrivers. Rose has given up on her earring and she can tell she's ready to go to sleep. She stands up slowly and places her gently into her cot. As she pulls the blanket over her, the child gives a sleepy smile which melts her heart. She's a good sleeper; and she always has been, apart from the first two months. Amy knows she's been blessed with her. She pulls the plum velvet curtains closed and tiptoes out, leaving the door very slightly ajar.

She looks at her watch. 6.30 pm. She has time to shower, change and have a final run through her paperwork. Being an organised person she has already put out her meeting outfit. Her best jeans from a Victoria Beckham collection, a fitted grey T-shirt and a designer black jacket reduced from £300 to £100 in a sale. She had been so happy with that purchase. Getting a real bargain is almost as good as winning a case. A couple of the committee had complimented her on the jacket but had inferred how expensive it must have been. She hadn't let on about the sale as they can be a bit funny about things like that. They never have to worry about the cost of anything.

The jeans were a present from Jimmy after he pulled off a big deal with the help of some legal advice from her. It had been great to use her legal brain again. She isn't convinced her career break is a good idea especially as she was close to being made a partner when she reluctantly gave in to Jimmy's wishes for her to become a full-time mother for a while. She had argued with Jimmy about it and to her annoyance her mother had taken his side. She had given in, seething with resentment which she tried not to show.

At ten past seven she is in her meeting outfit, perfectly made up with her short blonde hair immaculate. She thinks how fortunate it was that Gareth was able to fit her in for a trim earlier in the day. He'd persuaded her to have more off than usual and she has to admit he was right. And she smiles at her reflection in the full length mirror in her bedroom which shows a flat stomach. She had agonised over the cost of the personal trainer but the sight of her perfectly toned body in the mirror confirms it has been money well spent to get back to her pre-baby figure. She needs to feel good tonight because she has bad vibes about the meeting. The date change has unnerved her if she's honest.

For a moment she regrets she ever got involved with the charity. The politics of the committee are unpleasant; her Vice Chair Davina hates her. She had gone for the Chair but lost out to Amy and has never forgiven her. So petty! The meeting tonight is going to be tough because Davina has got it into her head that Amy has acted improperly in some way. She doesn't really understand what the issue is, but she wouldn't put it past Davina to try a motion of no confidence in her.

She sits at her desk looking over the minutes. She knows Davina will challenge some items and isn't sure who will support her. Pre meeting lobbying will be vital. She has never got on with Davina, and Jimmy doesn't like her either.

Can I leave now she asks herself? Teresa will be here in a few minutes. She is momentarily worried as she rationalises what she is about to do. She knows that some of her friends leave their babies alone the odd time if they need an urgent prescription or are out of milk or something basic and need to run down to the corner shop. She has often discussed the practicalities of such domestic emergencies with friends and the consensus has always been that it's not worth waking up a baby, locking up the house when you're only going to be five minutes at the most. Out loud, as if to a friend, she says 'If I had a barbecue I wouldn't hear if Rose woke up crying. She never does anyway.'

She had noticed Teresa's house keys on the hall table just after she left for her day off in Manchester, but had forgotten that when talking to her about the bus problem. Should she leave the back door unlocked or hide her keys somewhere she might find them? She decides to text her, then remembers she left her phone behind. She decides to leave the back door unlocked. It'll only be for a few minutes. She wonders if Teresa made the bus. Surely she'd have borrowed another phone to let her know if she hadn't. She can see the number she used in her 'received calls' so she rings on the off chance that Teresa and the 'nice lady' are now sitting together on the Accrington bus. A friendly voice answers.

'Yes, I let a young Chinese girl borrow my phone. She was waiting for a different bus to me. It was due to leave ten minutes after she called you and she must have got on as she was at the front of the queue. Don't worry; I'm sure she made it.'

This reassures her. She goes upstairs for a final check on Rose who is sleeping soundly.

**

She drives into the hotel car park and finds a space easily. The hotel is a renovated Victorian mansion on the other side of Burnley, about eight miles from her home. It's convenient for the others on the committee and she has negotiated a nominal rate for the meeting room on the basis of regular business. She smiles at the receptionist and tells her she's here for the meeting in the Oak Room. She searches the bar to see if anyone has gone there before checking in at reception, but no luck. Damn she thinks, normally there'd be a couple of members here already.

She debates with herself whether to sit in reception to grab people as they arrive or to set up in the meeting room. Deciding on the latter course of action, she takes her seat at the top of the table and rings Teresa's mobile to see if she's back. No reply. She's not really worried because Teresa has probably checked on Rose first, then gone to the kitchen to make herself some tea.

Her mobile will still be in her bedroom where she left it. She tries the landline but gets the answering machine which she had put on as usual as she left. It's 7.59 pm. It's odd that nobody is here yet when the meeting officially starts at 8 pm. Three minutes later six committee members appear together which strikes her as odd. She notes that the normally very punctual Davina hasn't arrived. She switches off her mobile as she always does for meetings and asks the others to do the same. Davina's mobile had once gone off in a meeting and she took the call not even bothering to leave the room. Amy rarely loses her temper but had blown her top on that occasion.

**

Davina arrives at 8.15 pm just after she has opened the meeting. Every committee member is now present, unusual given that it's late August and still in the holiday period. Her earlier feeling of unease increases when she notices that some members seem unwilling to make eye contact with her.

**

As she had suspected things are not going well.

At 8.45 pm Davina calls for a motion of no confidence in the Chair and a normally placid member seconds it. She cannot believe it. She starts to say the motion is out of order but while she is arguing her point a porter comes into the room.

'Can't you see we're in a meeting,' she snaps. 'We'll call you when we want some coffee.'

The porter stands his ground.

'There's an urgent phone call in reception for a Mrs Amy Blake,' he says.
'Take a message and say I'll ring them back,' she snarls.

The porter pulls himself up to his full height, which is only about five feet seven.

'Mrs Blake you have to come. It's your au pair. She's insisting you speak to her. She tried to ring you but your mobile's switched off.'

She hears Davina mutter something under her breath.

Amy hesitates. Surely Teresa wouldn't interrupt her meeting if it wasn't important she asks herself. No, she wouldn't.

'I'll be back in a few minutes,' she informs the meeting, trying to sound calm.

**

She barks down the phone, 'What's wrong?'

'Amy, is Rose with you? She's not in her room.'

'She's not with me. She must be there. She could have got out of her cot. Her door was ajar. And remember she's walking a little now.'

'Amy, I search the house. She not here.'

She cannot believe this but Teresa has no reason to lie.

'Call the police,' she screams. 'I'll be back in ten minutes.'

**

She drives home like a maniac. Rose can't be gone. She can't be. Could her mother have called and taken her? No, she'd have phoned first. And anyway she plays cards on Thursdays.

Pulling into the drive she sees a police car already there.

CHAPTER 3

Since Jeff died, my Aunt Bernie in Waterford rings me twice a week to see how I am. I have such lovely memories of all the holidays I spent with her when I was younger. Though she's my mother's twin sister, they're like chalk and cheese. To be honest I don't really get on with my mother which is why when she offered to come and stay with me after Jeff died, I politely rejected her offer. When I was in hospital after the fall, Bernie rang every day and the nursing staff affectionately referred to her as 'Molly's mad aunt.'

This week after Bernie's asked what the consultant said about my various injuries at my latest hospital appointment, she can't stop talking about a missing baby taken from a car left near a hairdressers in the Waterford city centre. Normally, after asking about my recovery, I get a polite lecture on a sociable person like myself shutting myself off from the world apart from a dog, and a cleaner with limited English! Bernie isn't being insensitive in telling me about the case as she knows how interested I have become in this subject. Coincidentally, her daughter, my cousin Sandra, goes to that salon. Bernie says she has posted me some cuttings from Irish papers about the case. She doesn't do computers and telling her I can read most papers online doesn't impress her.

The cuttings arrive; I do know about the case from Sky News but I have been behaving totally irrationally whenever that item comes on, sometimes turning the TV off as I can't cope with hearing about that stupid young girl, and other times I'm glued to the set. I've been having a bad time with the pain; the pills don't seem to be working even when I up the dose which I'm allowed to do. When I'm in bad pain, I become angry with her. Nonetheless I read the cuttings which have me spitting feathers. How could this young woman have been so casual about her baby?

Later in the month another baby goes missing after being left home alone. Not in Ireland but here in the UK in Accrington, a small town about 30 miles north of Manchester where I live. This mother is quite different to the young one in Ireland, older and professional.

Despite or perhaps because of my own tragedy, my interest in these two missing baby cases becomes an addiction and I read everything I can about them. I lost my baby from that stupid fall and I still don't know what caused it. The doctor said I shouldn't have been living alone in the house, at least in the month or so after Jeff died. I think I must have fainted near the top of the stairs. I just remember coming to with blood running down my thighs, in terrible pain and with my legs hurting so much. I was in hospital for three weeks and for the following month I was only allowed up for brief spells when I used the wheelchair. Now I'm in the wheelchair most of the day, my laptop on my knee and Pedro at my feet. Later I'll be on crutches for a while. It's going to be several months and lots of physiotherapy before I walk normally again. If it wasn't for Pedro I'd go out of my mind. Fortunately as a terrier he doesn't need a lot of exercising and I have a decent sized garden. My neighbours take him out for walks so he doesn't lose out. In fact he's never had so much attention.

I've never been in a situation like this before where the simplest little thing requires planning. For example if I was low on milk in the past I could run down to the corner shop and get some. It opens until nine; it has to in order to compete with the local supermarket. Now I have to watch stocks carefully and keep a list of what is running low so Lidia, now promoted to housekeeper, and relief dog walker when the neighbours are unavailable, can replace stocks. My house wasn't intended for the handicapped, having three steps up to the front door which makes getting in and out with a wheelchair difficult to say the least. At least my habit of writing lists is useful. My elder sister used to tease me about that; she's quite disorganised. I have to say it's been great to have her support and to know that I can cry down the telephone to her. She's been married for twelve years and no sign of a baby so she has really empathised with my loss.

Before I became interested in the missing baby cases I just used to scan newspapers the way I think most people do and I certainly wouldn't read tabloids, so I'd never realised how papers can use the same facts, or maybe I should say assumptions, differently.

The Waterford local paper quotes the Irish mum Carli as saying Tommy was only in the car for 20 minutes though *'sources at the salon state she was there for an hour without once checking on him.'* The salon manager claims that babies are welcome in the salon; which means either Carli or the manager is not telling the truth.

An Irish Sunday tabloid then implies Tommy's dad is no good, quoting an unnamed friend.

The newspapers didn't ask how Carli was able to perform the next evening with her child maybe in the hands of a paedophile and win the final of that competition. She is quoted as *'doing it for Tommy because he would have wanted me to appear.'* Hmm, not sure I believe that. Did the competition organisers want her to go on in the circumstances? Probably not. But they couldn't stop her because presumably they wouldn't have had a rule to cover her situation. She seems very determined and perhaps the only way she would have agreed not to perform would be if they gave her a pass into the national finals; but if they did that they could have faced legal actions from the other competitors. These competitions can be the passport to stardom. I can recall competitors occasionally being removed from them but that was when they were under the age for entry or had breached some other rule.

Judging by a text poll in the local paper, I'm not the only person critical of her. 74% believe she should be prosecuted for child neglect. Her friend who apparently let her down on the day has criticised the poll and says, '*Carli is a good mother and I feel bad because I couldn't get there and maybe it mightn't have happened if I'd been able to.*'

I get annoyed with a councillor in Waterford using missing Tommy to raise his profile. He blamed cutbacks for the police – they call them gardai in Ireland - not finding Tommy. It goes without saying that the police will work any hours they need to, even if they're not getting paid, to find a missing child.

This councillor said,

'*This happened when a lot of the gardai were on annual leave. The first 24 hours are crucial yet from what I hear the overtime ban was adhered to rigidly. The gardai are doing their best but it's not good enough. Money shouldn't be the deciding factor in a case like this. We're supposed to be having a referendum about children's rights. We can afford that, but we can't afford some gardai overtime to look for a child.*'

However, a gardai spokesman refuted his claims.

'*In fact,*' the spokesman said, '*leave was cancelled and all available manpower was put on the case.*'

So just who do you believe?

As well as reading everything I can find about the babies, I also watch internet sites, more precisely those about missing children. I 'lurk', meaning I read the posts but do not contribute myself. I consider registering so I can join the debate on what happened to these two missing babies, but I don't. For some reason it seems like a commitment, and that's not what I want with the way I am now.

In August, the month when the two babies went missing, most of the comments are critical of the mothers:

Missing Children Forum	
Portal Home Register Log In	every child matters
August 20 2011 at 4.45 pm	GoodMum
Am I the only person who thinks that Carli set up the 'abduction' to get publicity for herself since she's in that talent competition? I don't believe she couldn't have taken the kid into the hairdressers and the salon manager told the papers there wouldn't have been a problem. Or she could have parked the car outside the salon, not round the corner. In a busy street it'd have been harder for the baby to be taken.	Posts: 372 Join Date: 4.1.2011 Location: UK
August 20 2011 at 5.20 pm	MaryT
Well the hairdressers would say that wouldn't they? Not good publicity for them that they don't look after their customers with kids.	Posts: 561 Join Date: 7.5.2010 Location: Birmingham

August 21 2011 at 6.05pm How come an 18 year old on single parents' money has a car?	Taxpayer Posts: 192 Join Date: 22.11.2010 Location: London
August 22 2011 at 8.05 am Don't go for the bleedin' heart stuff Suzy. She should be prosecuted for child neglect.	Supernanny Posts: 301 Join Date: 21.10.2010 Location: In the nursery
August 22 2011 at 11.01 am And who's paying for all those fags? You'd think she wouldn't let them take a pic with a fag in her hand, but she does.	Taxpayer Posts: 193 Join Date: 22.11.2010 Location: London

August 22 2011 at 8.10 pm The poor baby must have inhaled a lot of smoke. Disgusting!	Supernanny Posts: 302 Join Date: 21.10.2010 Location: In the nursery
August 22 2011 at 9.44 pm You're all very judgemental. You can't believe everything you read. I don't but some of you clearly do.	Suzy Posts: 60 Join Date: 27.2.2011 Location: Bath
August 22 2011 at 11.06 pm The FACTS are clear. She left Tommy in the car in a laneway.	Supernanny Posts: 303 Join Date: 21.10.2010 Location: In the nursery

August 23 2011 at 3.22 pm Have to agree with that councillor said in the paper. You'd think they'd relax the overtime ban with a child missing	Declan Posts: 286 Join Date: 2.4.2011 Location: Dublin
BREAKING NEWS....ANOTHER BABY MISSING.......	
August 26 2011 at 10.08 am Another missing baby, two in one month. On Sky news last night. The mother left the baby on her own to go to a MEETING. Can you believe that! If they'd prosecuted the McCanns this kind of thing wouldn't happen....	Mags Posts: 344 Join Date: 2.9.2010 Location: Liverpool
Will posters please watch what they say? Unsubstantiated allegations/innuendos will be removed.	Moderator

Amy, the other mother, also has a hard time in the media. A headline in the Daily News implying that 'socialite' Amy was living it up in a 'luxury hotel' probably isn't fair. She was attending a meeting of a cancer charity to which apparently she gives a lot of time.

A friend who asked not to be named said, '*Amy did what we all do occasionally. She left her child for a few minutes in what she thought was a safe situation. She's absolutely distraught.*'

Now did a friend say that or did the paper make it up?

On the Forum the theories get a little off the wall.

August 29 2011 at 2.13 pm Anyone notice the resemblance between the babies?	Christine Posts: 43 Join Date: 3.8.2011 Location: Dorset
August 29 2011 at 4.04 pm All babies look alike; don't know how maternity nurses manage to return babies to the right mother!	Carol34 Posts: 109 Join Date: 15.1.2011 Location: all over the place

August 29 2011 at 4.31 pm That's a bit cynical, maybe Christine has a point?	Mags Posts: 345 Join Date: 2.9.2010 Location: Liverpool
August 29 2011 at 7.31 pm It's coincidental because both are about the same age	Taxpayer Posts: 194 Join Date: 22.11.2010 Location: London
August 30 2011 at 8.44 pm Babies change all the time; my youngest was the image of the boy next door when they are both one but now they're four they couldn't be more different.	Supernanny Posts: 304 Join Date: 21.10.2010 Location: In the nursery

'Christine' doesn't post again, maybe put off by Carol34's sarcasm. Over the following months I learn that posters can be very sensitive.

** **

I hear first about a real development in the case on Sky News. Amy's au pair has gone missing. She's the one who discovered the child had disappeared, but if she and an accomplice are responsible why didn't she leave with the baby? I suppose, if she's guilty, it was to give her accomplice time to get the baby out of the country. Maybe she didn't intend to go so soon but felt the police suspected her. She must have been on their list of prime suspects. In all the crime novels I've read the person who finds the body or whatever is always looked at closely. I saw Detective Inspector Hargreaves who's in charge of the case on the news appealing for her to come forward.

While Carli carries on with the competition, Amy according to media reports is, to quote her housekeeper '*too upset to talk to the press.*' Which may be true but then again she may want to avoid the hard questions.

The local paper says -

'*It is understood that Mrs Blake employed Teresa from a supermarket notice board*'

and that

'*Ms Liu had only begun working for the Blakes in recent weeks after their nanny left suddenly.*'

That's a polite way of saying that she was paying her cash and saving on National Insurance contributions. And I wonder why the nanny '*left suddenly.*'

I try not to let my own sadness cloud my judgement, but it's so hard. I feel sorry for the difficult life young Carli has apparently had but it doesn't excuse what she did, and as for Amy, on some days, depending on how much my injuries hurt, words fail me.

CHAPTER 4

I don't have to wait long to find out why Amy Blake's previous nanny left. In September she goes public and explains her sudden departure, no doubt helped by a big fee from the tabloid that got the 'exclusive.'

I read the 'exposé' three times, feeling a bit guilty for intruding into the Blakes' private life.

Exclusive - Nanny Gemma tells all in missing baby Rose case

'My year of hell....

Blonde Gemma Andrews sobbed as she told the Sunday News about her year with high flying couple Amy and Jimmy Blake.

'It was my first job after I got my diploma. The agency got me several interviews and all the families I met offered me a job. I decided to go for the Blakes and how I wish I hadn't. I had a lovely room and the use of a car, but it wasn't what I'd hoped for.

Initially I only had Peter. I met him before I took the job but he was probably bribed to behave. Amy doted on him and never saw how spoilt he was. I tried to tell her nicely but she snapped at me. She seemed happy to be having another baby but after she came home from the hospital, I never got the feeling there was any bond there. Now Rose had colic and didn't sleep well at first. Which is quite common. Amy'd taken a career break so she didn't have to go to work but she really resented losing her sleep. I mean I took over Rose in the mornings so she could sleep. Then she decided to give up breast feeding so I could go to Rose in the night and give her a bottle. I didn't like that. I told her nicely that breast is best. They emphasised that in my

33

training. You'd think someone like her would know that, but she told me to mind my own business.

She also had me cooking dinner on the days the housekeeper didn't work. That wasn't my job but I happen to like cooking so I did it.

Jimmy, that's Mr Blake wasn't around much. He's got offices in London as well as Manchester. She complained to me about him being away so much. I heard them having a row about it more than once. I think she really regrets taking the career break; it was his idea apparently. She was involved with lots of committees but I think she found some of the people on them a pain in the neck. She once told me that some of them wouldn't be capable of holding down an ordinary job. They just happened to have a husband with money. When I was interviewed by her, she seemed nice and friendly. But working for her was a different story. She's cold and self- obsessed.

One day this June she was particularly rude to me. She said I never bothered to make an effort with Peter's school lunch box. It wasn't true and he had probably told her a lie because I'd made him tidy his room. I told her exactly what I usually put in it but she just screamed at me. It was over the top. I picked up Rose who was in the baby
bouncer and took her up to my room where we stayed until we heard her drive off a couple of hours later. Much later that night after Rose was asleep, I heard shouting. It was another row. When I thought the coast was clear I went down to get myself something from the fridge. Jimmy was sitting there with a whisky bottle. He insisted I join him. He wasn't very coherent and I didn't understand most of what he was saying. He got up and put his arm around me. He squeezed my breast. I didn't like it and pulled away. Then he said, 'You're as cold as that bitch' and he staggered up the stairs.

I packed my bags that night. In the morning I told Amy I was going. She started getting all legal on me but I wouldn't take any crap. I had booked a taxi and I left.

I heard she replaced me with a Chinese girl. I doubt if she had anything to do with Rose being taken. She probably left for the same reason I did. Amy refused to give me a reference and I'm taking legal advice about that. I worked bloody hard for her and put up with a lot. My advice to anyone before taking a job as a nanny – talk to the last one and find out why she left!'

How embarrassing for Amy. As she's a lawyer I'm wondering why there wasn't apparently a confidentiality agreement.

After the nanny exclusive the internet debate hots up. I stop 'lurking' and join the Missing Children Forum. I register under the name 'Miss Marple', the amateur detective in Agatha Christie's books. I had given some thought to the pseudonym I would use as an internet blogger. Some people think up witty names, others use their first names while others choose names that are simply bizarre. I've read all her books and enjoyed the complicated plots. While she's an elderly spinster and nothing like me, I couldn't find a younger female detective in fiction that I could relate to, so Miss Marple it is, and not Ms Marple. I don't go along with this politically correct nonsense.

I decided on the name a week ago but I held off registering. I don't really know why. My sister thought it would be better if I made an effort to get friends round rather than communicate in this odd way with people I don't know who could, in the real world, be the sort you wouldn't touch with a bargepole. Maybe it was because my sister annoyed me a bit with her conservatism about this that made me decide to go ahead. What harm can it do, and it'll help to pass the time until I can walk again and return to work. I didn't know then how my apparently harmless online detective activities would change my life.

Missing Children Forum Portal Home Register Log In	 every child matters
September 1 2011 at 5.43 pm Hey, did you see the au pair in the Accrington baby case has gone missing	Fairplay Posts: 33 Join Date: 5.5.2011 Location: Ireland
September 1 2011 at 6.06 pm Looks odd, but you'd think if she's involved she'd have gone off with the baby at the time	Luke Posts: 14 Join Date: 3.6.2011 Location: Glasgow
September 2 2011 at 9.26 am Jeez, she lost the baby and now she lost the au pair, what kind of a woman is Amy Blake?	GoodMum Posts: 373 Join Date: 4.1.2011 Location: UK

September 2 2011 at 11.01am A pretty careless one by the looks or it, another nanny Gemma ran for the hills. Did you see her story in the Sunday papers?	Declan Posts: 287 Join Date: 2.4.2011 Location: Dublin
September 2 2011 at 1.15 pm But it was the au pair that raised the alarm. If she hadn't, her accomplice would have had more time to get away because Mrs Blake could have stayed on after the meeting for a drink and she mightn't have got back till after 11 pm – which means the au pair could have got out of the country	Luke Posts: 15 Join Date: 3.6.2011 Location: Glasgow
September 3 2011 at 11.07 am I don't buy Gemma's story. If two people behaved like that she could take a case for bullying & harassment in the workforce. Why didn't she, they'd have paid her off rather than face publicity? She just wanted money and the papers pay for stuff like that.	MaryT Posts: 562 Join Date: 7.5.2010 Location: Birmingham

September 3 2011 at 2.38 pm If my childminder told me what to do like Gemma did, I'd tell her where to go! Breast feeding doesn't suit everybody. I know, it was really painful so I gave up and that doesn't make me a bad mother.	Michelle Posts: 42 Join Date: 2.7.2011 Location: Yorkshire
September 3 2011 at 3.50 pm I don't get why Jimmy spends so much time away from home. The juniors do the audit and he can easily do all of the meetings via skype these days. Up to no good I reckon.	Taxpayer Posts: 195 Join Date: 22.11.2010 Location: London
September 4 2011 at 8.05 am Can't say I blame him, she does seem like "one cold bitch".	Columbo Posts: 73 Join Date: 6.3.2011 Location: New York

September 4 2011 at 10.10 am	Fairplay
I don't get Amy Blake. When you google her you see some very impressive history on her career. She's an associate in a law firm, qualified in record time too. She's traded all that in for a few stupid gigs on committees? She has a full time nanny and a housekeeper. What a waste of talent.	Posts: 34 Join Date: 5.5.2011 Location: Ireland
September 4 2011 at 12.19 pm	Mags
They say Jimmy's a control freak. Maybe he forced her to give up work, wanted wifey at home.	Posts: 346 Join Date: 2.9.2010 Location: Liverpool
September 4 2011 at 4.11pm	GoodMum
Only she's rarely home and neither is Jimmy.	Posts: 374 Join Date: 4.1.2011 Location: UK

September 4 2011 at 9.09 pm Not much coverage now on the Irish case.	Declan Posts: 288 Join Date: 2.4.2011 Location: Dublin
September 5 2011 at 6.07 am Now that you mention that, there's very little on Baby Tommy now.	Sherlock Posts: 92 Join Date: 29.6.2011 Location: Baker Street
September 5 2011 at 7.18 pm Hey, has anyone thought there might be a connection?	Fairplay Posts: 35 Join Date: 5.5.2011 Location: Ireland

September 5 2011 at 11.22 pm Very unlikely, someone happens to spot a baby in a car in Ireland, grabs him and runs off, two weeks later they happen to "know" that a baby is home alone in the UK, dash in and steal it?	Columbo Posts: 74 Join Date: 6.3.2011 Location: New York
September 6 2011 at 9.02 am The only connection could be murder by one or both parents	Declan Posts: 289 Join Date: 2.4.2011 Location: Dublin
September 6 2011 at 11.33 am And that both mothers should be behind bars.	Supernanny Posts: 305 Join Date: 21.10.2010 Location: In the nursery

September 6 2011 at 2.46 pm It'd be hard to prove anything without a body. It's very easy to hide a baby's body. Forensics solve so many cases nowadays but without a body....?	Declan Posts: 290 Join Date: 2.4.2011 Location: Dublin
September 6 2011 at 4.46 pm Sniffer dogs can indicate cadaver/cadaverine presence. There's two amazing springer spaniels Eddie & Keela who work with the police. They've never been proved wrong and have cracked lots of cases.	Fairplay Posts: 36 Join Date: 5.5.2011 Location: Ireland
September 6 2011 at 5.12 pm How do we know it's not the father? Did anyone check whether he actually was outside the country? Even if he was, he could have paid someone to do it. Maybe he was going to look for a divorce but he knew she'd get custody so he takes the child now. Keeps her safe outside the UK. The man has money. Then he gets a divorce, leaves the country to start a new life – with little Rose and maybe a new woman.	Taxpayer Posts: 196 Join Date: 22.11.2010 Location: London

September 7 2011 at 7.03 am Could the new woman be the Chinese au pair? Only a suggestion.	Mags Posts: 347 Join Date: 2.9.2010 Location: Liverpool
September 7 2011 at 9.19 am Didn't like the father on the news last night. Too much fine food and wine, he had quite a paunch.	Liam Posts: 10 Join Date: 2.8.2011 Location: Belfast
September 7 2011 at 11.03 am What's that got to do with anything? Lots of men his age have a paunch. You might just as well say that you don't like Amy because she hasn't had breast implants and doesn't use a lot of make-up. I mean we're trying to debate what happened to those poor kids, not bitch about their parents' appearance.	Suzy Posts: 61 Join Date: 27.2.2011 Location: Bath

September 7 20 11 at 3.32 pm I think Dave the Waterford father is kind of cute. Saw him interviewed on the news.	Jenny Posts: 65 Join Date: 5.5.2011 Location: Slough
September 7 2011 at 3.40 pm That's as stupid as Liam's post. Whether Dave is cute or not is irrelevant.	Olive Oil Posts: 23 Join Date: 13.4.2011 Location: Kent
September 7 2011 at 8.08 pm I don't get it, why would an unemployed father abduct his own child, where would he hide Tommy? Unless, oh no, they don't mean that he murdered him? But how could that be? Carli was the last person to see Tommy. Unless people think both parents are involved?	Declan Posts: 291 Join Date: 2.4.2011 Location: Dublin

September 7 2011 at 8.55 pm I just said Dave was cute. I never said he took Tommy.	Jenny Posts: 66 Join Date: 5.5.2011 Location: Slough
September 7 2011 at 9.06 pm The standard of debate is deteriorating fast.	Sherlock Posts: 93 Join Date: 29.6.2011 Location: Baker Street
September 8 2011 at 10.04 am Folks, I met Julie Farrell from Hair-I-Am in a pub last Sat night. She was pretty well on; she's convinced that Carli is a seriously bad mother. She said a traffic warden called into the salon some weeks ago before Tommy went missing wondering if any of the customers had left a baby in a car. Sound familiar? Hey guess who was having their fringe cut at the very same time. Julie's told the cops everything. *Source verified by Moderator*	Fairplay Posts: 37 Join Date: 5.5.2011 Location: Ireland

September 8 2011 at 10.52 am	Mags
Wow, wonder if they were setting the stage then, and planning for the warden to come forward with a statement?	Posts: 348 Join Date: 2.9.2010 Location: Liverpool
September 8 2011 at 11.16 am	GoodMum
OK so either she's a serial child neglecter or is setting the stage for abduction opportunity, very sad.	Posts: 375 Join Date: 4.1.2011 Location: UK
September 8 2011 at 1.03 pm	Liam
Maybe one did it and the other's covering up? Two unemployed people with a baby too many?	Posts: 11 Join Date: 2.8.2011 Location: Belfast

September 8 2011 at 5.33 pm Something strange here. It's just not natural she'd leave the child in the car for an hour without checking he'd been picked up	Fairplay Posts: 38 Join Date: 5.5.2011 Location: Ireland
September 9 2011 at 9.22 am They say she gave a great performance. She was singing to Tommy, there were tears in her eyes. I think she's innocent.	CoolDude Posts: 9 Join Date: 4.7.2011 Location: Bahamas
September 9 2011 at 9.45 am She was probably crying because she knows they'll arrest her soon	Sherlock Posts: 94 Join Date: 29.6.2011 Location: Baker Street

September 9 2011 at 3.16 pm Does anyone know when Tommy was seen last? By an independent party that is?	Supernanny Posts: 306 Join Date: 21.10.2010 Location: In the nursery
September 9 2011 at 3.55 pm Not sure, apparently the police are still working on that	Fairplay Posts: 39 Join Date: 5.5.2011 Location: Ireland
September 10 2011 at 11.09 am Just a thought, could the friend, Emer be in on the action? She's been very quiet; just saw one quote in a paper supporting Carli but nothing since. Strange she didn't look for her 15 minutes of fame.	Declan Posts: 292 Join Date: 2.4.2011 Location: Dublin

September 10 2011 at 2.33 pm What's her motive? And how could she take him when the car was locked, she had no keys.	Liam Posts: 12 Join Date: 2.8.2011 Location: Belfast
September 10 2011 at 4.04 pm Does anyone know if the car was actually locked? I read somewhere it wasn't. That would make sense. If she'd leave a baby in a car like that, then she could easily not lock the car, whether deliberately or she just forgot.	Sherlock Posts: 95 Join Date: 29.6.2011 Location: Baker Street

September 10 2011 at 8.56 pm	Miss Marple
Hi there – I've just registered, been following this site for a bit and here goes. I wonder if they did any forensics at her place or what showed up from the car? Strange nothing's been reported. How about opportunity? If both children were actually where the mothers say they were it's far more likely that baby Tommy was abducted than baby Rose. Anyone who was passing by the car might have taken him. But in Rose's case only Amy Blake knew that she was home alone. That gives an abductor a window of less than an hour to try the door, find it open, turn on all of the lights, find the baby and make a getaway without causing the dog to bark. Hard to believe that despite other events involving missing children – like the McCann case for example - two mothers can still choose to be careless to say the least regarding their small children in favour of a hair appointment and a committee meeting. I'm finding it very hard to get my head around how either of them could justify their actions. Sometimes I think lock them up and throw away the key. I must be getting old (although I'm only 34) but I sometimes despair for our society. Doesn't anyone take responsibility for their actions anymore?	Posts: 1 Join Date: 10.9.2011 Location: St Mary Mead

September 10 2011 at 9.54 pm Both of them must have broken some law about child neglect surely? But neither of them apparently has been prosecuted.	Nora Posts: 19 Join Date: 15.7.2011 Location: Grimsby
September 10 2011 at 10.25 pm I was stunned to read that Carli already has a solicitor. Surely her first priority (apart from getting her hair done, smoking cigarettes and the singing competition) would be to focus on finding her child, not trying to defend herself. It makes no sense. Why are both women not out looking for their children, putting up posters, talking to the locals, begging for help and information? I might be totally unfair but that's what I'd be doing in their position.	Miss Marple Posts: 2 Join Date: 10.9.2011 Location: St Mary Mead

September 10 2011 at 11.01 pm Gosh Miss Marple. Welcome to the Forum. That's a lot of points. You don't like those mothers! One point, my granddad lives in Waterford and he says that solicitor is an ambulance chaser. Well known for it. Probably acting for free for now until she hits the big money. If she's telling the truth and I'm not sure if she is, she's very vulnerable to creeps like him.	Declan Posts: 293 Join Date: 2.4.2011 Location: Dublin
September 10 2011 at 11.34 pm Welcome from me to Miss Marple, Impressive first posts	Fairplay Posts: 40 Join Date: 5.5.2011 Location: Ireland
September 10 2011 at 11.57 pm Thanks everybody. Back tomorrow	Miss Marple Posts: 3 Join Date: 10.9.2011 Location: St Mary Mead

I'm surrounded by half-empty coffee cups. Ever helpful Lidia set up a tea and coffee station in my bedroom/office which encourages me to make drinks which often go cold while I check for a post responding to mine. I bought a mini fridge so I can feed myself here if I can't be bothered to make the effort to go to the kitchen which to be honest isn't a big effort as there aren't any steps on the way. Even though the room's quite big, it's a bit cluttered now which normally I would hate. But my life isn't normal anymore, and the convenience of having everything in one room suits me while I'm like this.

Have I really been on this site for the last three hours? I must have as I switched on after the evening news. The stuff I've posted is really harsh. Am I a sad person for sitting at my computer writing this way? And what about the other people who post here? Are they sad too? Do they make stuff up? You just can't know.

No, I am not a sad person. In fact I feel proud of myself and I'm going to put some make-up on. That may seem crazy given that it's midnight but I've decided I don't like the mess I see in the mirror. And I'll sleep in the make-up but I won't tell my sister. She'd be utterly shocked.

As I lie in bed, the title of one of Agatha Christie's books comes into my head, '*The 4.50 from Paddington.*' Change Paddington to Manchester and you'd have the train that would have got Teresa into Accrington station in plenty of time to babysit if only there hadn't been a bomb scare just as rush hour started.....

CHAPTER 5

After my first evening as Miss Marple I sleep surprisingly well and wake up looking gorgeous. Why wouldn't I as I applied the make-up very carefully before I went to bed! I brush my hair vigorously and resolve to get the home hairdresser in.

I feed Pedro and let him into the back garden. I wonder if he notices the new me? I love to talk to him and he seems to read my every mood.

Today I want to find out more about both Amy Blake's background and her husband Jimmy's. He sounds a sleazebag from what the nanny was quoted as saying but that paper regularly publishes exaggerated interviews.

I start with the professional networking site LinkedIn. Amy's page sets out her impressive academic and work record. I wonder what her employers feel about her new fame. It hasn't exactly helped their image. Even though she's on a career break from the company, their name has been mentioned a lot. Will they want to take her back when the career break ends? They'll have to because she'll sue them if they don't!

Jimmy's LinkedIn page shows he's a director of a number of companies. Interestingly he doesn't seem to have a degree. He has an accountancy qualification but he's not a chartered accountant which is apparently the best qualification to have.

Next I move to Facebook. It's always amused me how some people don't seem to understand about security settings, that you need to limit access to the 'friends' you have accepted. I search for Jimmy Blake and after a morning clicking on over a hundred of them I finally come to the one I want. I could have got there faster but some of the wrong Jimmy Blakes I 'meet' on the way have not used the security settings so I read the ones that catch my interest.

When my employer recruits staff, he checks the interviewees' Facebook pages and stuff he's found there has on occasion lost the person the chance of the job. It says something about a person if they put personal material up that anyone with basic computer skills can access. Naïve certainly, and a risky employee?

Will I be lucky with the *right* Jimmy Blake? I am; his page is open. There's lots of pictures of Rose and adoring text and just one picture of Amy at their wedding. Jimmy looks rather handsome I have to admit; he'd have been around 40 then. A few pictures of their son Peter, but Rose is the star of the show. Some new information; he's a football fan. There's a section of pictures of recent West Ham matches and lots of comments from Jimmy about their form and his belief that they'll return to the Premier League after being relegated at the end of the last season.

He seems to have a lot of 'friends' and quite a few are very attractive, but that doesn't necessarily mean he is a sleazebag as the tabloid exclusive implied.

People often mention where they were educated on their Facebook page. Jimmy's says University of Life.' Hmm. I wonder if that was ever a source of conflict at home. Amy is a first class honours graduate; he was at the University of Life and has done well financially from it.

Studying his online profile has been helpful. I think the best way to proceed is to invite him to join my LinkedIn network. Before I do that, I'll have to change my picture which is very businesslike to a more glamorous one with the help of some photoshopping. Maybe he isn't watching his email regularly with his daughter missing but he'll see my request at some time and why wouldn't he respond. He only has to press *accept*. Why wouldn't someone with his business interests not be interested in 'linking up' with an IT consultant?

**

After lunch I attempt to find Amy on Facebook. Unfortunately as Amy is a popular name and Blake a common surname there are hundreds of Amy Blakes there. And by that evening I haven't found the one I want. It doesn't really surprise me. Her LinkedIn page gave concise information useful to anyone wanting a lawyer in her field of expertise. How would a Facebook page help her career? Though I have one myself, I don't use it much and with Jeff gone I can't bear to look at it as it has pictures of us; at our wedding, on holiday....I get weepy thinking about it.

I feel a bit annoyed as I've really learnt nothing new about Amy from hours of research. Then I have an idea, what about old newspaper articles. There could be something about her earlier life perhaps in her local paper, or in a university magazine that might help me to get a more rounded picture of her. In the past, finding old articles would mean hours in the library but nowadays you can get a lot of archived material on the web for free.

Not that having to pay for it would be an issue. When we got married and took out that big mortgage, Jeff who wasn't normally the most practical person with money, insisted we took out life insurance on each other. It seemed a lot of money at the time when cash flow was so tight but he had insisted. 'You just never know Molly what life will bring,' he had said. He was so right. I burst into tears. Oh dear, I thought I was doing better today. Having £100,000 in the bank from that policy will never make up for losing wonderful Jeff. Pedro senses my pain, and tries to jump on my lap but I have to stop him as it would be too painful given my injuries. But Pedro's concern for me just about manages to divert my sadness.

**

After my Marks & Spencer ready meal and a large glass of red wine I set off on the trail of Amy's past. Initially not much success. Her common name is again a problem. I spend the first half an hour looking under the name Amy Blake before I realise that old material would be in her maiden name which fortunately I know. It's Browne and I remember thinking when I saw her mother Edith Browne being interviewed about her missing granddaughter on TV that Amy's initials didn't change when she got married. In fact you would think a high flier like Amy would have kept her name on marriage.

It's almost eleven when I find something and I wish I hadn't. It's in her college magazine in an article about a successful fundraising event students had organised. Accompanying the article is a large photograph of the organising committee at the charity ball and Amy is captioned as the Chair of the committee. The picture was obviously taken late in the evening; the committee members look tired and emotional as they say. The young man next to Amy has his arm round both her and around the girl on the other side of him.

The affectionate and probably drunken guy looks like Jeff. My coffee cup goes flying and the tears start. Perhaps my sister was right. Maybe I shouldn't have started on this road. But I have and that's down to my personality; when I start something, I like to finish it.

I take a sleeping pill and retire to bed. The pill doesn't work and I toss and turn all night unable to erase the memory of that face in the student magazine. It's as though a knife's been put through my heart. Maybe I'll feel better in the morning.

CHAPTER 6

Two months on and neither baby has been found. In Waterford the police have been asking a woman in a burka to come forward for several weeks now. Apparently she was seen in the side street that day around five o'clock by a woman going to the salon where Carli Walsh was having her hair done. Needless to say the local paper spices up the story by saying that unnamed 'sources' have suggested that the 'woman' was actually a man and the traditional dress was to hide that fact.

And the story continues,

'Rumours continue to circulate that Tommy's dad, unemployed Dave Nevin, had fallen foul of a drug dealer to whom he owed money. The car was registered in Mr Nevin's name but had been used by Carli after they split earlier this year.'

Here in the UK the media coverage is getting dirty. They're implying Jimmy Blake cares more about his affairs, well his alleged affairs, than his missing daughter.

It gets worse when a Sunday tabloid prints a much redacted article about an unnamed businessman's extracurricular activities explaining the gaps by citing threatening legal correspondence it had received. It's obvious to whom the article referred; well it is to me anyway.

'According to our sources, the businessman who has recently been in the news over a family tragedy, has been consoling himself in the Parkview Hotel in Chelsea with a stunning woman who is apparently not his wife.

The woman is described as statuesque with long dark hair; his wife is (redacted). She remains at home keeping a low profile, looking after their (redacted) and coming to terms with the recent tragic event that befell the family.

Apparently, the meetings in the hotel were going on before the event that put his family on the front pages though there is uncertainty as to whether his most recent companion is the same as the one on previous occasions.'

The following week, its sister paper doorsteps Amy Blake and asks if the businessman is her husband Jimmy. The journalist (if you can call the scumbag that) gets a 'no comment' and the door slammed in his face. The intrepid reporter then shouted through the letter box, 'Is it true that you and Mr Blake are sleeping in separate rooms?' He claims the response was 'F...off or I'll call the police.'

What an exclusive! I actually felt sorry for Amy when I read that.

Carli stories are everywhere with the competition hotting up with the public eliminations. I find an interview in the magazine Hot Pop revealing. It uses her 'style secrets' in the headline as though they are as important as finding her child. I have to say I soften a little towards her after reading the feature. Even if she exaggerates her time in care homes, losing loving parents when you're five is absolutely dreadful.

The Big Interview – Carli Walsh talks exclusively to Hot Pop and reveals her style secrets

As told to our Show Biz Editor Beccy Bates

'BB: *You've been through hell in the past two months Carli. How have you coped?*

CW: *It hasn't been easy and sometimes I cry myself to sleep. But the support I've been getting from people, it's been amazing, and that keeps me going.*

BB: *What kind of support?*

CW: *Letters, emails, texts, tweets. It's been unbelievable. People have sent me presents for Tommy. It was his birthday last week and I got so much stuff for him. I couldn't tell you the number of people who say they are praying for Tommy. I'm not really religious but this means so much to me. I haven't mentioned this to anyone before but I've been going into any church I pass to light a candle for Tommy.*

BB: *People can't believe how you picked yourself up and went on stage for the Waterford finals the day after your little boy was taken.*

CW: *But I did it for Tommy. When he's back, how could I face him if I hadn't gone out there and sung for him? He's my biggest fan. I couldn't do anything useful. Nasty people have said I should have been out looking – but where was I supposed to look? It's a mystery. Poor Tommy mightn't even be in Ireland. Should I have spent all day in the station crying and annoying the gardai?*

BB: *But some people have criticised you for......*

CW : *(interrupting), Look I've explained that so many times. It was a total mix- up. I thought my friend Emer had collected him. I only did what other mums do. I'm being judged by women who need to get a life. I don't believe they've never left their kid for a minute. It's easy to attack someone you don't know. If they had any idea about the life I've had....*

BB: *I was just getting to that. Tell us about that life...*

CW: *Well I was nearly killed when I was five. This mad driver smashed into our car and killed my mum and dad who were in the front. They never caught the bastard. He must have been blind drunk. I was badly hurt, but I did recover. But there wasn't anybody in the family who could take me in. So I ended up in a home, then another one, then with foster parents. I just got moved around. It was terrible. In one place the manager was touching me up. Know what I mean. But nobody believed me. So I ran away from there. When they caught me, the manager wouldn't have me back; claimed my place had been filled which was a load of cobblers. He couldn't risk me being back and talking. Maybe somebody would have believed me.*

Anyway, finally they found me long-term foster parents and that's when I moved to Waterford.

BB: *So life got better for you then?*

CW: *Well it did and it didn't. It was nice to have my own room and be in the same place. But I didn't ever feel I belonged. Then, they took in another foster child and they preferred her. Everything revolved around her. I just tried to pretend it wasn't like that. I stayed in my room writing my songs.*

BB: *One of the judges in the Waterford final said you had the potential to be a major songwriter...*

CW: *Yeah that was so exciting. I've quite a few written and I've got a solicitor to look after my copyright and all that sort of stuff.*

BB: *You've split up with Tommy's father. Is there any chance of a reconciliation?*

CW: *Who knows? I was mad with him on the day when he let me down. But he's done his best to support me through this. He misses Tommy too. I have to concentrate on the competition to make a future for me and Tommy.*

BB: *So you believe he will be found?*

CW: *I have to believe it. There's no proof that anything bad's happened to him. He's gorgeous. Nobody would hurt him.*

BB: *Well hopefully the pictures we're doing with this interview will help the search for him. We know our readers would love to help.*

Now we've had some questions from readers about that amazing outfit you wore in the show last weekend. Can you tell us where you got it ...'

**

Then the tabloids start again about the 'businessman's indiscretions' querying why Amy hasn't spoken out if Jimmy isn't the man involved. Then, as the tabloid campaign is getting really nasty, Amy releases a letter from her missing au pair which temporarily at least stops the tabloid vendetta. The letter, if it is genuine, opens up new possibilities.

The Sunday News gets the exclusive -

Exclusive – New Lead in baby Rose case

Amy Blake releases letter from her missing au pair

'*Distraught Amy Blake, mother of baby Rose who vanished from her home two months ago has released a letter received from her missing au pair Teresa Liu. The young Chinese woman vanished 24 hours after discovering Rose missing. Exhaustive police inquiries have failed to locate her.*

In the letter, exclusively released to the Sunday News, Teresa claims she is innocent of any involvement in Rose's disappearance and that she went into hiding realising she could be deported when it was realised her student visa had expired. As a Catholic she claims she faced persecution in her home country.

The letter reveals that a man befriended her in the supermarket the day before Rose vanished. A man she thought she had seen before. And, a woman chatted to her in the local dog grooming parlour three days before Rose vanished and she told her about her planned day off in Manchester.

So was this man stalking her? And could the original plan have been to snatch Rose at the supermarket?

Or did the woman in the dog grooming parlour deliberately befriend her to get information about the house?

Detective Inspector Hargreaves who is leading the investigation told the Sunday News that the police are examining the security tapes in the supermarket to try to identify the man. And they are again appealing for Ms Liu to come forward to answer questions. He declined to comment on whether she would be safe from deportation.

Have you seen Teresa? – call the Sunday News Hotline at 1 890 444222.

Hmm. I'm in cynical mood today and wonder if Amy sent that letter to have the police looking for two innocent people to take the pressure off her.

And Carli it appears is setting up a fund which reinforces my suspicion that she is involved, that ultimately it's all about making money. I'd heard that from somewhere and wasn't sure if it was just a rumour but her local paper confirms it:

'Padraig Mahoney, solicitor for Waterford songstress Carli Walsh, says he is looking into setting up a fund to search for her missing son Tommy.

'Carli', he claims, 'is very concerned that budget cuts will force the gardai to limit their work. She has been contacted by a number of individuals asking if they can help financially and I am currently talking to them on her behalf. They have asked that their names be kept confidential.'

Carli sings this weekend in the second national elimination heat of Star Search and is temporarily based in Dublin until the final in December. Bookmakers have her at 25/1. Donegal rapper Jackie Gallagher is the current bookies favourite at 4/1.

Carli remains in daily contact with Inspector Dan O'Rourke and his team who are investigating Tommy's disappearance.'

The internet debate hots up with me posting away and Forum members obviously devouring the media coverage as I am. Like me, they find Carli's interview fascinating. I'd mentioned the rumour about a Fund in an earlier post.

Missing Children Forum

Portal   Home   Register   Log In

every child
matters

October 5 2011 at 10.19 am Declan, thanks for the info on Carli's solicitor. Setting up a fund, don't like the sound of that, manipulating her maybe.	Miss Marple Posts: 4 Join Date: 10.9.2011 Location: St Mary Mead
October 5 2011 at 11.39 am Wonder if she was really abused in that home or simply playing the sympathy card in the interview?	Liam Posts: 13 Join Date: 2.8.2011 Location: Belfast
October 5 2011 at 3.11 pm I'm keeping an open mind on that one, there are so many stories these days, and would be surprised if it didn't happen.	Mags Posts: 349 Join Date: 2.9.2010 Location: Liverpool

October 6 2011 at 2.32 pm I find it interesting that despite the life that she had, the constant letdowns and abuse attempt she still believes that nobody could possibly hurt Tommy.	GoodMum Posts: 376 Join Date: 4.1.2011 Location: UK
October 6 2011 at 4.15 pm It's refreshing to see a bit of optimism but IMHO this points to 2 distinct possibilities. Either she was abused as a child and has blocked it from her memory or she's lying about it. Society has always provided opportunities for paedophiles. In the past it was the church, schools, hospitals, orphanages, boy scouts and even the local swimming & soccer coach. Nowadays children are taught about abuse at a very young age, how to spot the attacker, how they will try to groom and manipulate and exactly what to do.	Miss Marple Posts: 5 Join Date: 10.9.2011 Location: St Mary Mead
October 7 2011 at 7.06 pm Are you saying children are being held captive and being abused? Where could they be, who's holding them and why doesn't anyone notice? That's just too hard to believe.	Luke Posts: 16 Join Date: 3.6.2011 Location: Glasgow

October 7 2011 at 7.22 pm	Miss Marple
Sadly it's been proven that in the Catholic Church the people at the top were responsible for the cover-ups so they were also in on the action. These people don't just stop. If it happens in the church I firmly believe it's also commonplace within the police, the Government etc. There are various rumours and insinuations coming from both Ireland and the UK. Plenty of empty buildings available to the clergy & the government financed unfortunately by you and by me.	Posts: 6 Join Date: 10.9.2011 Location: St Mary Mead
October 7 2011 at 8.23 pm God, that makes me feel sick.	Taxpayer Posts: 197 Join Date: 22.11.2010 Location: London

October 7 2011 at 9.06 pm Changing the subject for a mo, I can't get Carli's comment out of my head "There's no proof that anything bad's happened to him. He's gorgeous." What a strange thing to say. Is she implying that all the proof has been cleaned away and what about the throw away comment "he's gorgeous"? If he wasn't gorgeous, would that explain something bad happening to him?	Miss Marple Posts: 7 Join Date: 10.9.2011 Location: St Mary Mead
October 7 2011 at 11.34 pm Wow Miss Marple you are cynical. She's just sticking to her optimism, probably been looking on the bright side all of her life, she's a gutsy survivor. I just take her comment to mean she loves little Tommy with all of her heart.	Fairplay Posts: 41 Join Date: 5.5.2011 Location: Ireland
October 7 2011 at 11.58 pm I'd like to believe that, Fairplay, but can't help wondering about this interview. I think it was spun in Carli's favour to boost the show's ratings. In fairness, Hot Pop just did a complete U turn on their earlier reports on her.	Miss Marple Posts: 8 Join Date: 10.9.2011 Location: St Mary Mead

October 8 2011 at 9.10 am It's possible, however I'm a firm believer in human nature, I can spot a crook a mile off. When I look at Carli I see a very honest girl who is upbeat & caring and beats herself up about a dreadful mistake that she made.	CoolDude Posts: 10 Join Date: 4.7.2011 Location: Bahamas
October 11 2011 at 7.16 pm I'm suspicious about the Fund she's setting up. Don't see the point.	Fairplay Posts: 42 Join Date: 5.5.2011 Location: Ireland
October 11 2011 at 9.23 pm Carli's not definitely setting up a Fund. The solicitor is looking into it. No harm in that.	GoodMum Posts: 377 Join Date: 4.1.2011 Location: UK

October 11 2011 at 10.02 pm You're very suspicious, Fairplay – what's your problem with that. Other people have done that. Mitch Winehouse has set one up for his daughter.	MaryT Posts: 563 Join Date: 7.5.2010 Location: Birmingham
October 11 2011 at 11.47 pm But Amy Winehouse is actually dead.....and his charity is to help other addicts.	Miss Marple Posts: 9 Join Date: 10.9.2011 Location: St Mary Mead

Some people are so trusting like GoodMum and MaryT. No matter how well people argue a point, they still believe in the two mothers. It's as if parents are automatically good people in their eyes; parents can never harm their children. That's a very naïve view IMO.

At least my Amy Winehouse comment about the proposed Fund shuts them up for a while.

CHAPTER 7

Three weeks after the Carli interview that did influence me just a little in her favour I read an interview with Amy in the National Independent written by Carol Jennings, a journalist whose work I like.

The Saturday Interview - Amy Blake breaks her silence

'*As I walk up the path to Amy Blake's door I am apprehensive about the woman I am to meet. In research for the interview I had discovered a tough woman with a formidable legal reputation. 'If she's on the other side, you know you're in for a fight' one person told me on condition of confidentiality. 'I'm not saying she bends the rules. No way. But if there's a loophole she'll find it for her client. She certainly did in the case I was involved in and it cost me a packet. But then maybe I should have hired her and not the guy I did.'*

This is the first interview Amy has agreed to give since her daughter Rose vanished from her home eight weeks ago. Despite extensive police activity there are no leads. Amy's behaviour in leaving her daughter home alone has been widely criticised and even raised in Parliament. And others have attacked her calm demeanour in the aftermath of the disappearance.

I ring the doorbell and hear yapping. I remember that, when I phoned to make the appointment, Amy said she had a dog and warned me that Sammy can be snappy. I am wearing thick leggings and hope I will be safe. The door opens and I recognise Amy. She's holding a King Charles spaniel. 'I'll put him in the garden while we chat,' she says smiling. 'It's unusually warm for October. He'll be happy especially if he finds my neighbour's cat and can chase it out.'

We go into her living room which I recognise from the TV appeal she did with her husband Jimmy the first weekend Rose was missing. I'd noted how the mantelpiece was full of pictures of Rose and her big brother Peter. Amy has lost weight since the appeal. Her face looks pinched and her cream blouse seems a size too big. I decline her offer of tea and take out my notebook and recorder.

I start by asking her about her schooldays. Were they the happiest days of her life as the cliché goes?

She looks thoughtful. 'I loved studying but I didn't really have any close friends.'

I ask why that was.

She hesitates, then replies, 'My parents ran a newsagents shop and scraped the money together to send me to boarding school. They thought it was the best for me though I would have preferred to go to the local school. They were great admirers of Margaret Thatcher and my second name is Margaret after her. She was a shopkeeper's daughter too; they said she'd go far and weren't they right? She was Education Secretary when I was born, Leader of the Conservative Party four years later and Prime Minister in 1979. Most of the other girls at the boarding school were from professional families and some of them really teased me about my northern accent. And I made a mistake; I said my father was managing director of his own company which was true. The newsagents shop was set up as a company but when I was asked what sort of company I had to admit it was only a corner shop and there were some bitchy comments. So I started off on the wrong foot, so to speak.'

I move on to her university career and ask how she decided to become a solicitor. I ask was there a legal tradition in her family?

'Actually no. As I said my parents had a small business and none of my other relatives were in the legal profession. I did very well in my 'A' levels and I could have done anything really at university. My form teacher thought I had a really analytical brain and encouraged me towards law. We used to get talks from different people coming in and I just thought law would suit me. And it did.'

'There were rumours that you were quite the wild child at university?'

Amy frowns. I can feel her thinking; I was promised no hard questions. She responds.

'Well you know the tabloids can be creative. Somebody I had never met apparently claimed I could drink anyone under the table. But I can't remember anyone of that name in law in my year or even as part of the group I hung around with. My course was really demanding. You couldn't be out drinking every night and get first class honours like I did.'

'There were also claims that you were a popular girl,' I say.

This doesn't go down well either. I had been wondering how to phrase the question and it hadn't come out too well.

'What exactly are you implying? Surely not those crazy stories about me being the law faculty groupie? I considered suing over that. But you know what they say, there's no smoke without fire so I didn't. Sometimes it's better to ignore rubbish like that, and not fuel it by constant denials.'

I ask whether there was anyone special in her student days.

She pauses and I wonder if she's about to reveal something.

'Well a few dates. Then I did go out with one guy for over a year, nearly two years actually. He was a medical student. That's a really tough course too. We'd stay in and study together and drink a bottle of plonk. Sometimes we might start a second bottle. Maybe that's what the tabloids meant by my drinking sessions. You can get quite a hangover from cheap wine so I suppose it is true that I had the odd one now and again.' She smiles at the memory.

I sense her relaxing a bit.

'What happened to that relationship?'

I see her stiffen and I feel the lawyer in her choosing her words carefully.

'We drifted apart as you do. We both moved on. He was in a different faculty so after we split, our paths didn't cross really. Medicine is a long course so I graduated in 1992 before he did. I heard later that he qualified. I've no idea where he is now.'

As I'm reading the article an image of the young man in the photograph at the charity ball comes into my head. Is he the old boyfriend the interview refers to? Not necessarily; after all he had his arm round another girl too. And he mightn't be connected to either, just a member of that student committee celebrating a successful event. What a pity the magazine photo wasn't captioned. I've been thinking about that young man a lot and it's probably not healthy though understandable in my situation. If I'm honest there was nothing very unusual about Jeff's looks and any number of men of similar age and colouring could be said to resemble him.

The interview continues:

'And after you qualified?'

I can see she's happier with that question. She tells me about the offers she got with her first class honours degree, and the firm she went to work for in London.

When I met Jimmy through my work I wasn't interested in him at all she says.

My editor had warned me that she is very sensitive about the fact that Jimmy was married when they met. But she raises this herself.

'*I want to put the record straight on this. Yes Jimmy was still married to Brenda when we met. They'd drifted apart and were living separate lives then but stayed under the same roof for the children's sake. For the first six months I knew Jimmy it was a business relationship. He's ten years older than me, and I've never had a thing about older men. And, she laughs, 'He's 5' 9" which is only three inches taller than me. I can't wear my Jimmy Choos out with him.*'

I know in making this remark, she's joking and getting a dig at a downmarket paper that claimed she is obsessed with designer shoes.

'*Six months after we met, Jimmy and Brenda decided to divorce and he was very generous to her. That was when he asked me out. The cases I had worked on for him were completed and I have to say successfully. Our first date was at a big charity fund raising dinner at the West Ham United Hotel. Sir Alex Ferguson was there. Jimmy's a football fanatic and West Ham is his team. We got married a few months later. Jimmy is very decisive, that's one of the things I like about him.*

I interject to ask how her parents felt about the marriage.

Again, she considers her reply carefully.

'Initially they were apprehensive, with him being older and having children from his first marriage. But they liked him being a successful businessman when he didn't come from money.'

She returns to the subject of football.

'Actually football is one of the things we have in common. Not the same team mind you, but we both support teams that are not what you might call fashionable. My dad used to take me to see our local team Accrington Stanley every week and I loved it.

'Jimmy grew up near the West Ham football ground and he's always supported them. I think a couple of their players are tax clients of his. They were relegated last season but they're doing well now. Hopefully they'll be promoted back to the Premier League.'

Seeing her face become animated, I have to say that I'm surprised the sophisticated
Mrs Blake is a football fan.

Hmm. This ties in with Jimmy's Facebook page and the West Ham pictures. Might be a way to establish a relationship with him.

I read on:

'I miss London, but we had to move back north when my dad had a stroke. We had Peter then and London isn't the best place to bring up children.'

Her face lights up when she mentions her son.

'He keeps asking me when his sister is coming back. He waited so long to have a brother or a sister. I haven't said this

before but I had two miscarriages before I had Rose. Peter was as devastated as I was.'

'That's dreadful,' I say, 'you lost two children and now you've lost a third.'

'Well I almost lost Rose at her birth. I had to have an emergency caesarean; but I don't accept I've lost her now. She's out there somewhere. There's no evidence that anything bad has happened to her. Information comes in all the time and the police are following it all up. But we are going to get our own detective to back up the police investigation.'

'Won't that complicate things?'

She shakes her head. 'I've heard unofficially that the search is being cut back. Budget cuts. It's happening everywhere. So this has to be done. I've talked to Detective Inspector Hargreaves about this. And he understands.'

We don't go into the specifics of that night as it's been rehashed in paper after paper.

'I had planned to go back to work when Rose was a year old. But I've put that off because Peter needs me, and Jimmy is away a lot. And I need to be available in case anything crops up. If there is a sighting I'd have to travel at short notice. That's happened a couple of times already but it wasn't her.'

'There were stories that you and Jimmy were splitting up because he blamed you.'

She interrupts. 'Lies. Lies. He was angry when he got the news. He was abroad. And when he got back he was jetlagged and naturally upset. He adored her. His only daughter after three boys. Yes there was a row but it would have been odd if

77

there hadn't been. He's accepted now that the guilty person isn't me; it's the person who took Rose.'

I ask how she got through Rose's first birthday on September 3, and then feel guilty about asking the question.

'I just don't know how I did. Sometimes I just stared at the unopened presents I had already bought or I'd go into her bedroom and look at the rocking horse mum and dad had made especially for her. They insisted on bringing it over after she vanished and putting it her room. The police asked me to do another appeal on the day which was really hard, and it didn't bring in any good leads.'

Finally I ask Amy if she has any theories about who took her daughter.

'I lie awake at night going over it all. I think it's related to our business life. We've both made enemies. We could have been watched. Maybe someone in Jimmy's office or my housekeeper were targeted and they innocently given out information. There were five people in the house the day before for a viewing as it was for sale then. Now the police have followed them up and eliminated four of them. There's one man they haven't been able to find and I'll get my detective to look at everything again. This person wants to make us suffer but I don't believe they would harm Rose. Why would they hurt an innocent child?'

She dabs at her eyes as the tears start. Then she adds, 'I'm starting a blog to let people know how the search is going, and to correct any lies that are printed.'

I assure her I'll give details of her blog in the article. I thank her for agreeing to talk to us and say how hard it must have been and that our readers will appreciate her talking so frankly.'

I pour myself another cup of coffee and reread the article. Do I feel differently about her after reading that? Maybe a little. But that was a soft interview and it didn't go into her motivation on the evening she left Rose. I am annoyed by the references to her college days; absolutely irrelevant to what happened. I am admittedly interested in the young man who may have been a college boyfriend but my interest in him has nothing to do with solving the case. Much later I discover that I was right to be interested in him if for the wrong reasons.

After that soft interview, the tabloids start on Amy again and watch her comings and goings from their cars parked outside her house.

One tabloid journalist even had the neck to bang on the door and ask to use her bathroom. Amy refused. For want of anything better to photograph, his photographer took shots of her dog Sammy piddling in the front garden and actually published them with a headline '**Amy's Pedigree Pooch takes a leak.**'

Absolutely disgraceful behaviour.

Then another paper ran the headline '**Social Services Swoop on Amy.**'

Apparently a social worker will always visit a family where one of their children has gone missing. It doesn't mean the family is under suspicion; it's routine. However, the paper didn't say that. The social worker seemingly refused to talk to the journalists outside Amy's home so they followed her back to her office, realised she was a social worker and then came up with that misleading headline.

This coverage was followed by other 'exclusives' quoting parents they had cornered at her son's school waiting to collect their children. This led to harmless comments being taken out of context and making her seem a really inadequate mother. One parent had obviously said something like Amy was very well qualified and doing well in her legal career and this had become a headline '**Ambitious Amy's Career more important than the School Run.**'

But the headline '**Peter's Bed Wetting Crisis over Missing Sister**' deserves an award for nastiness. Apparently Amy's housekeeper Mary Bristow, not used to the media, told a journalist who knocked on the door to 'go away as he was frightening Peter who was so upset about the loss of his baby sister that he was wetting the bed.' How poor Peter must have suffered at school over that.

Not surprisingly Forum members dissect the interview with Amy Blake.

Missing Children Forum Portal Home Register Log In	 every child matters
October 25 2011 at 10.13 pm My ex-gf went to school with Amy Blake, swears blind that Amy was up to all sorts. Apparently she sewed her wild oats very young and then settled down to her career	Liam Posts: 14 Join Date: 2.8.2011 Location: Belfast

October 25 2011 at 11.33 pm Yes, I have read similar stuff but hey, who cares, that was a long time ago, we all go off the rails for a while when we reach a certain age.	Fairplay Posts: 43 Join Date: 5.5.2011 Location: Ireland
October 26 2011 at 11.37 am Hang on, conduct unbecoming of a lady, for a solicitor is a pretty serious allegation. Wonder how many skeletons might fall out of her cupboard?	Miss Marple Posts: 10 Join Date: 10.9.2011 Location: St Mary Mead
October 26 2011 at 1.33 pm I'd imagine she's got enough issues with a missing child, a missing au pair and a super angry husband.	Fairplay Posts: 44 Join Date: 5.5.2011 Location: Ireland

October 26 2011 at 4.16 pm Speaking of which did anyone notice the stories in the tabloids about a businessman playing away? I reckon it's Jimmy Blake.	Miss Marple Posts: 11 Join Date: 10.9.2011 Location: St Mary Mead
October 26 2011 at 5.01 pm You mean the story about the businessman who had a 'recent family tragedy' to quote the papers. You're assuming it's Jimmy. They can't print who it actually was.	Declan Posts: 294 Join Date: 2.4.2011 Location: Dublin
October 27 2011 at 8.39 am Saw that but isn't that related to the abduction?	Liam Posts: 15 Join Date: 2.8.2011 Location: Belfast

October 27 2011 at 11.33 am He does spend a lot of time away from home. And heard one or two stories of a mistress not so far from home. Makes me wonder who she is. Heard she's one of Amy's charity circle.	GoodMum Posts: 378 Join Date: 4.1.2011 Location: UK
October 27 2011 at 12.21 pm Hang on, we have a pattern here. If one leaves a woman in favour of a younger more interesting model then history will repeat itself, right? Hardly much keeping him home these nights. I can only imagine the tension in that house. Very obvious on that TV appeal too, they couldn't even pretend.	Miss Marple Posts: 12 Join Date: 10.9.2011 Location: St Mary Mead
October 28 2011 at 9.32 am Remember what James Goldsmith said, 'if you marry your mistress, it creates a job vacancy.'	Declan Posts: 295 Join Date: 2.4.2011 Location: Dublin

October 28 2011 at 2.33 pm I don't buy that story of their celibate "friendship" before his divorce. It sounds like a story you'd spin to your parents.	Fairplay Posts: 45 Join Date: 5.5.2011 Location: Ireland
October 29 2011 at 11.07 am I'm beginning to feel a bit of sympathy for Amy. She's had two miscarriages, baby is abducted and now finds out her husband is cheating.	Mags Posts: 350 Join Date: 2.9.2010 Location: Liverpool
October 29 2011 at 12.03 pm It's funny, she almost appears human when she talks about "Accrington Stanley FC"	Sherlock Posts: 96 Join Date: 29.6.2011 Location: Baker Street

October 29 2011 at 2.43 pm Wow, is it true about the police cutbacks, she has to hire her own detective?	Taxpayer Posts: 198 Join Date: 22.11.2010 Location: London
October 30 2011 at 10.29 am Apparently so, those big investigations are a thing of the past. The McCann case review is using up a lot of their budget.	Miss Marple Posts: 13 Join Date: 10.9.2011 Location: St Mary Mead
October 30 2011 at 11.48 am You're wrong, Miss Marple. It's the Met who are doing the McCann review. Their budget is separate to the police budget in the Blake case.	CoolDude Posts: 11 Join Date: 4.7.2011 Location: Bahamas

October 30 2011 at 3.32 pm Amy thinks that a business enemy of theirs is responsible, wonder if they suspect someone in particular.	Columbo Posts: 75 Join Date: 6.3.2011 Location: New York
October 30 2011 at 5.15 pm I find that hard to believe. It's easy to know who your enemies are, I am sure the police have already chased down all those leads.	Liam Posts: 16 Join Date: 2.8.2011 Location: Belfast
October 31 2011 at 9.17 am It's a very bizarre story, that's for sure and still no sign of the missing au pair.	Mags Posts: 351 Join Date: 2.9.2010 Location: Liverpool

October 31 2011 at 10.23 am	Fairplay
Hey, speaking of which, did you see they published a letter she sent to Amy Blake, had forgotten about that.	Posts: 46 Join Date: 5.5.2011 Location: Ireland
October 31 2011 at 11.22 am	Declan
I don't buy that she was involved why would she write a letter? It sounds like she's genuinely concerned about Rose and racking her brains to help. Really thoughtful of her to have sent that information.	Posts: 296 Join Date: 2.4.2011 Location: Dublin
October 31 2011 at 1.12 pm	GoodMum
I think she's another victim; I would honestly do anything to help her out.	Posts: 379 Join Date: 4.1.2011 Location: UK

October 31 2011 at 3.13 pm	Sherlock
The poodle woman sounds innocent enough to me but I wonder about supermarket guy. Wonder if he'll come forward, I'm sure they'll have no difficulty tracking him down.	Posts: 97 Join Date: 29.6.2011 Location: Baker Street

I can't object to being corrected by CoolDude because he/she has a point. Silly name though. And silly location. The Bahamas. I don't believe he/she lives there. So far I think I like Declan the best. He seems to have an open mind.

My next move will definitely be to check out Amy's blog though whether I'll believe what she writes is another matter.

CHAPTER 8

The first entry in Amy's blog reads:

'Thank God, the weather has improved. At least the rain kept the photographers away for a while. They made me feel like a prisoner in my own home, on trial by the tabloids without bail. A couple of them have come back, but hopefully their expense budgets will run out soon.

I don't know how I got through Rose's first birthday on September 3rd. All the presents I bought are unopened in her wardrobe. All wrapped except for the rocking horse mum and dad had specially made for her. Mum insisted on bringing it over after the disappearance and putting it in Rose's room.'

I've read that before; it was in the Jennings article. She's really going for the public sympathy vote. I bet she's got PR people helping her with this. In fact she probably had PR people set up the Jennings interview given that she wasn't asked about the evening Rose vanished and why she made the choices she did.

'People can be so cruel. The paper that published Gemma's story never asked for my side of it. Yes I did refuse to give her a reference; that was because she walked out on me and ignored the period of notice in her contract. She also broke the confidentiality clause she signed. I considered suing her but I mightn't win because the article is all innuendo and the paper will have someone good arguing that I'm seeing things that are not meant. Gemma implied that my husband might be unfaithful but he told me he wouldn't sue as saying someone is monogamous is almost libellous nowadays.

'Peter's teacher asked to see me and it was really upsetting. She told me that some parents have been complaining about the press being down at collection times. She suggested that as

Peter was being targeted, it might be a good idea if I kept him away from school until this all blows over.

'*I argued that I wanted life to go on as normal, well as normal as it can be in the circumstances. But the teacher persuaded me otherwise. 'The reality is that children can be cruel and not realise it. Their parents are discussing this at home. The children are hearing it and sometimes getting the wrong end of the stick. I honestly think it would be better if he was with you and his dad for a while.'*

Yes, I do feel sorry for the child. He is innocent. The press shouldn't be allowed to intimidate parents at school gates but here's what confuses me, why is she so supportive of the missing au pair?

'*I wish the police could find Teresa. They regard her as a prime suspect but I know they're wrong. If she was guilty she knew I wouldn't have been back until at least 10.30 pm so she'd have had plenty of time to get away. The police don't seem to understand that after my bad experience with Gemma, I preferred to try Teresa out before formalising the arrangement. Detective Inspector Hargreaves suspects her but I think she just got upset by the whole thing. She feels guilty. She told me that if she hadn't got so engrossed in shopping she would have got an earlier train before everything was disrupted. Then all of this wouldn't have happened.'*

She makes a case of sorts for Teresa going but I'm not sure I buy it. The next bit is interesting because I thought ransom was a motive.

'*There's been misleading stories in the press about the ransom notes. What actually happened was that I gave them to the police though the notes warned me not to. They had the drop, a waste bin in the Trafford Centre in Manchester, staked out but somehow the press got hold of it, and an ambiguous*

story appeared
nobody turne(
Rose if this t
number and
parents not
hold of it,
the call w
When the
week aft

'Jim
but nc
other
baby .

Amy's blog comments:

'Don't believe what you r
generously to Brenda and

She is right to be
believe Amy and a
Brenda on her b
whooshed prett

Ever
week
kno

'With all the offic...
breakthrough by now.'

Just as the media is moving on to other stories, Jimmy Blake's ex- wife, decides to speak to the press. She must have gotten the idea from reading Gemma's story. Maybe she's not happy with the maintenance she gets but most probably she believes that Amy was the reason why her marriage to Jimmy broke up.

She claims she was a devoted wife and mother foregoing her own career allowing Jimmy to develop his business. But she doesn't mention specifically the career she 'gave up.' I read somewhere she was a hairdresser. Judging from the photograph accompanying the article, she can't have been a very good one. She claims she was pressurised into the divorce, the maintenance payments are inadequate and that she has been forced to go public for the sake of her two sons' education. She describes Amy as a 'cold calculating bitch.' She doesn't do herself any favours in my opinion by being so nasty. Didn't Gemma use a similar phrase; I think she did?

ead. Jimmy has always contributed
his two sons.'

dignified but some people clearly don't
e posting nasty comments in support of
g, but the ones that use bad language are
quickly.

**

week new members register on the Forum. In the first
of November, two interesting ones register. One claims to
w things about the Waterford case. He/she is called Alro. Funny
ame and I don't think it's an old Irish one. I'm going to assume
it's a 'he' as Alro doesn't sound like a female name to me. And the
other posts a 'hello' opener as some people do and informs us she
works with babies hence her pseudonym 'Babydoc.'

Missing Children Forum	
Portal Home Register Log In	every child matters
November 2 2011 at 7.17 pm Hi folks. I've got friends in Waterford and they're telling me no-one other than Carli saw Tommy on the day he vanished.	Alro Posts: 1 Join Date: 2.11.2011 Location: MYOB

November 2 2011 at 7.24 pm So are you implying he was never in the car?	Declan Posts: 297 Join Date: 2.4.2011 Location: Dublin
November 2 2011 at 7.45 pm Didn't say that but it's a possibility. Another thing I heard that the story about the mix up, the friend Emer letting her down, mightn't be true.	Alro Posts: 2 Join Date: 2.11.2011 Location: MYOB
November 2 2011 at 8.02 pm You 'heard', yeah right. You'd need to be more specific than that. We try to discuss facts here.	Declan Posts: 298 Join Date: 2.4.2011 Location: Dublin

November 2 2011 at 8.17 pm I can't say too much, have to protect my sources.	Alro Posts: 3 Join Date: 2.11.2011 Location: MYOB
November 2 2011 at 8.55 pm Are you a journalist?	Declan Posts: 299 Join Date: 2.4.2011 Location: Dublin
November 2 2011 at 9.19 pm No. One of my friends could get into trouble if it came out he was talking to me.	Alro Posts: 4 Join Date: 2.11.2011 Location: MYOB

November 2 2011 at 9.56 pm So why is he telling you stuff, if it could be trouble for him?	Declan Posts: 300 Join Date: 2.4.2011 Location: Dublin
November 2 2011 at 10.20 pm Because he feels that the police investigation isn't going anywhere, and the longer this goes on the less chance there is of the kid being found alive.	Alro Posts: 5 Join Date: 2.11.2011 Location: MYOB
November 4 2011 at 11.04 am Hi, I'm a new member. I work in a London hospital with babies so am very interested in discussing parental attitudes to caring for them.	Babydoc Posts: 1 Join Date: 4.11.2011 Location: Emergency Ward 10

November 4 2011 at 11.42 am	Miss Marple
Welcome, Babydoc. Your perspectives will be interesting.	Posts: 14 Join Date: 10.9.2011 Location: St Mary Mead

If Alro is genuine he could be connected to the police, not necessarily a policeman but maybe working in the station or a family member. That would explain why he is being so careful and won't even indicate where he is located while at the same time he is throwing out clues for us to discuss. I try to draw him out.

November 4 2011 at 11.59 am	Miss Marple
Alro, do your friends have a view on Tommy's dad, Dave?	Posts: 15 Join Date: 10.9.2011 Location: St Mary Mead

November 4 2011 at 12.32 pm They were suspicious at first, but it seems he's a decent guy, loves the kid. There were stories about him doing drugs and upsetting a drug dealer but nothing was proven.	Alro Posts: 6 Join Date: 2.11.2011 Location: MYOB
November 4 2011 at 1.05 pm And the friend Emer?	Miss Marple Posts: 16 Join Date: 10.9.2011 Location: St Mary Mead
November 4 2011 at 2.32 pm Like I said, can't say too much. Emer and Carli go back a long way, at school together, but hadn't been so close since she met Dave.	Alro Posts: 7 Join Date: 2.11.2011 Location: MYOB

November 4 2011 at 2.52 pm Are you saying Emer might have resented Dave?	Miss Marple Posts: 17 Join Date: 10.9.2011 Location: St Mary Mead
November 4 2011 at 3.02 pm Could be. Might have felt used, being asked like that to collect the baby.	Alro Posts: 8 Join Date: 2.11.2011 Location: MYOB
November 4 2011 at 3.56 pm I don't believe she would have left the baby in the car. If she did feel used, she could just refuse to help in future.	Mags Posts: 352 Join Date: 2.9.2010 Location: Liverpool

I was going to switch off feeling I've got as much as I'm going to get for now when another recent member posts something interesting. She's Italian and tells us about an unusual case there.

November 4 2011 at 4.05 pm	Guilia
Hi. Please excuse my bad English but I am Italian. I want you to know what an Italian family do.	Posts: 7 Join Date: 3.10.2011
They are old parents; they use the IVF to get baby. He is 70 and she is 57.	Location: Italy
But they leave her in a car like the Irish baby but outside their house.	
Neighbours tell the police and they take the baby away.	
The court in Turin, today say the baby girl should be adopted because the parents are selfish and not good parents.	
November 4 2011 at 4.45 pm	Declan
Wow, seems sloppy parenting is everywhere. Maybe we'll get an EU directive saying we can't leave babies in cars. That'll sort it!!!!	Posts: 301 Join Date: 2.4.2011
	Location: Dublin

While I'm looking up that Italian case another worrying story is posted, and this one is not far from where I live. How did I not know about this one?

November 4 2011 at 6.02 pm	Nancy
Did you see the story about the mother who left two children in her car in Rusholme while she was drinking? The car wasn't locked either. One child was 3, and the other 9 months, almost the same age as Tommy Walsh. They were in the car for over an hour while she was drinking and dancing in a local bar. The poor children would have been there longer if someone passing hadn't called the police. The car was parked in a side street just like Carli's car was. Apparently the car stank of wet nappies and vomit.	Posts: 23 Join Date: 3.9.2011 Location: Manchester
November 4 2011 at 7.01 pm	Supernanny
Disgusting! What happened to the mum? Was she very young?	Posts: 307 Join Date: 21.10.2010 Location: In the nursery
November 4 2011 at 7.39 pm	Nancy
She's 21, not much older than Carli. The children are now with foster parents. She got a 4 month jail sentence but it's suspended for 2 years and she has to do 200 hours community service.	Posts: 24 Join Date: 3.9.2011 Location: Manchester

I just have to know more about both these cases which does not please Pedro who's been sniffing at my feet for the last fifteen minutes. I pat him and tell him I won't be much longer. Is talking to your dog a sign that you're losing it? As I freely admit, he is my confidante.

It doesn't take long to confirm the two cases. The couple in Italy appear to be middle class; she's a librarian and he was the mayor of a town in the Piedmont region in NW Italy. The father, Luigi de Ambrosis, claims he was merely unloading shopping and his daughter was never out of his sight; but neighbours say on another occasion the baby was left alone and crying in the car at 10 pm because they believe the parents were trying to make her sleep. Expert reports on the couple found they had not established an emotional bond with their daughter and that her father had not shown enough concern for her well-being. The Turin court did not believe the parents who are now appealing. Ultimately, they can take their case to the Italian Supreme Court.

I have to say it's weird. They were turned down for adoption because of their age. They go through IVF and then are indifferent to their miracle child.

The UK case is quite different but just as shocking. If a member of the public hadn't been in the side street at 3 am and called the police, how much longer would they have been there? The court was told the mother Kayleigh McNaughten was 'unsteady' on her feet when she finally returned. Presumably she would have driven home in that state with her children in the car. The older child whose age varies from two to three depending on the report you read was not strapped in when the police came. So would she have driven home drunk with him just sitting in the back? The children have different fathers and there is no mention of them in the reports except that her lawyer claimed she had been in a violent and abusive relationship – whether both fathers were violent is not clear. Her lawyer also claimed she had gone out intending to buy painkillers as the baby had been crying all day. Yet she ended up in a bar and video footage showed her dancing. Apparently the young woman is now living in a refuge.

One report on this case mentioned another incident earlier in the month where a young mother locked three children aged 2, 5 and 8 in a 'sweltering car' for 45 minutes with the temperature inside 40^0C to go into a store. Thankfully the oldest child alerted passers by sounding the horn. This mother received a suspended sentence after admitting ill treatment and possessing class B amphetamine.

It's definitely time for bed. I switch off the PC, let Pedro out for a last piddle and retire to bed. Switching off the PC is easy; switching off mentally is not. I have been telling my sister about the Forum but not how many hours I spend online. I know she wouldn't approve. She's just had her first pregnancy confirmed after years of hoping for a baby. I'm delighted for her but she was almost embarrassed to tell me after what happened to me.

When I was younger I wasn't particularly interested in having children. I don't mean I didn't want them eventually; it just wasn't high on my agenda. Jeff was from a large family and he always wanted children; it was me putting them on hold and we'd had the odd row about it. When I did realise three years ago that I was ready, I read everything I could about childbirth and parenting even though I wasn't pregnant. Every month when my period came I'd be miserable for days. Will I ever have my own child now? As I said I feel the doctors haven't been straight with me about the implications of my stupid fall.

Adoption isn't apparently easy because so many women abort their unwanted babies so there's very few available for adoption. That's another way I've changed – twenty-something Molly supported the right to choose, but widowed and possibly infertile Molly doesn't. Why should a baby in the womb be killed just because it is inconvenient to the mother? I don't mean where there is a serious threat to the health or life of the mother. I have to admit I've been researching abortion numbers in the UK and there were over 180,000 last year. How many of those were medically necessary and how many a matter of convenience? I must send a personal message to Babydoc and ask about her experience. Has she ever performed a social abortion I wonder? I am becoming so judgemental. I wasn't like that before.

CHAPTER 9

As I suspected even in sleep I can't switch off. I dreamed about Alro. I see a young man on a mobile talking about Carli's friend Emer. He's saying he thinks she hasn't been completely truthful but it's not clear about what. I drift into deeper sleep and when I come out of it, Alro is still there on his mobile saying there's a discrepancy regarding the hospital.

In the morning I struggle to recall Emer's surname; then I remember the expanding pile of Irish press cuttings. Yes, her name is there. Emer Flynn. I google 'Facebook Emer Flynn.' Only a few and easy to identify which one of them is her as one of the newspaper cuttings pictures her with a quote supporting Carli.

I send her a friend request. Surely she won't accept; I mean she doesn't know me. Before sending it I edited my Facebook page a little, changed my photograph to the youngest looking one I have and added a picture of Pedro. I have also posted about Carli saying she was suffering enough for her error of judgement and people should be less vindictive. And of course I change my security settings so she can see my page if she wants to before accepting me as a 'friend.' I hate my Facebook account being open, but it's a necessary evil if I am to progress my investigation.

The next day her ACCEPT message lands in my Inbox. So easy!

I send her a message.

'How is Carli holding up? It must be great for her to have a friend like you who isn't selling stuff to the papers. I had something bad happen to me this year and I couldn't have coped without my friends.'

This is the truth in that what happened to me this year couldn't be worse but it's not friends that have helped me; it's my obsession with these two missing babies which keeps my mind off my own tragedy.

Emer replies two days later.

'She's holding up but the gardai keep asking more questions. There's this lady garda who's really persistent. She talked to people on Carli's estate and she came to see me. We just feel she doesn't believe us. She was round the other week and with Tommy's first birthday just having passed, Carli was feeling emotional.'

'Yeah, tough. I used to live in Waterford. Family had a problem and weren't impressed with the gardai.'

Yes I did stay with Aunt Bernie when I did my degree at Waterford Institute of Technology but the problem with the gardai is fiction. Clearly I'm playing a blinder as the messages flow over the following days. I can't ask her yet about the specifics of the day Tommy vanished as she might suspect something. I do ask her about Dave and she's quite forthcoming. She doesn't seem to like him much. I encourage this topic by telling her about a fictitious girlfriend who would not listen to me about a boyfriend I was sure was bad news.

'The gardai suspect him but they can't prove anything. He was with social welfare like he said, but I suppose he could have got someone else to take Tommy. He's trying to get back with Carli now. He's texting her every day. I told her to be careful and she slammed the phone down on me. She rang me back half an hour later apologising. She knew I was trying to protect her. I'm used to her being like a volcano.'

'Is it true that Carli's got a solicitor?'

'About a month after Tommy went missing her doorbell rang close to ten o'clock at night. Carli was reluctant to answer. It could have been a nosy journalist. She half opened the door so she could slam it if it was. This plump guy in a crap suit clutching a briefcase thrust a card into her hand, said he was a solicitor and offered to help her. Carli's no fool, except where Dave's concerned. She asked the guy why she needed him and he said to stop all the lies the papers were printing, and to look after the money people were sending in. So she let him in. She said he had his foot in the door anyway. Apparently he was very persuasive. She had been upset by the lies printed about her so she agreed he could deal with the media for her and she'd only have to pay him if he got libel damages for her. He reminded her that the McCann couple got over half a million damages from the UK papers for their lies about them when their kid was snatched. He told her it would be worth some nasty untrue articles to get that much!

'He wanted to set up a Fund for Tommy but she didn't buy that. There wasn't nearly as much money coming in as the media implied and she put it into the Credit Union account she opened for Tommy when he was born.'

'What do you feel about this solicitor guy?'

'Well I suppose she does need someone like him. He's in touch with her most days and the papers are much better. Did you see the interview she did in Hot Pop? He arranged that for her. They'd been nasty. He came round to her place with a bottle of whisky just before she did that interview to help her prepare for it. That's what he said anyway. She's not used to drinking whisky and she told me she can't remember much about the evening. She just remembers them both getting drunk and him telling her that there's lots of things he'd like to have done differently in his life and then him falling sideways on the settee and passing out. She covered him up with an old blanket and went to bed. In the morning she had a mega hangover and *she found a note from him – 'Got a client meeting at 8.30 am. Had to use the last of your coffee. Sorry.'*

'She says he's written quite a few letters to editors. I asked around about him, and people say he's an ambulance chaser whatever that is.'

I explain that means a solicitor who goes looking for business in a less than ethical way, and that she should advise Carli to be wary of him and to watch what she signs. She promises to pass on my warning. So now I am advising Carli. Hilarious!

Should I feel guilty about 'befriending' Emer? I'm ambivalent. Yes I've told a couple of lies and I've been a bit creative with the truth, but surely it's motive that matters. I want to find the truth, and if you have to tell the odd lie to find it, then it doesn't really worry me. We all tell lies and often with the best of motives – so as not to hurt someone else's feelings. That's acceptable so why can't you lie and spin for an ultimately good motive?

Like Amy, Carli has a blog. It opens with a quote (allegedly) from a supporter:

'I say prayers for your Tommy every night, he reminds me of my grandson sadly now in heaven. Don't mind what people say. You made a mistake. Somebody took a chance, I'm sure they didn't mean any harm, and the police will find him,'

Sligo grandmother.

'I keep this note under my pillow and read it every day. If only all my post was like that.

But it isn't. Lots of it is cruel and the stuff online can be sick. Spiteful tweets.. Have the fuckers nothing better to do? Some people post hateful things on my Facebook page. I've got a solicitor now – Padraig Mahoney –and if anyone lies about me, they'll hear from him.'

Another entry, October 13,

'It's Tommy's first birthday today. Some kind people sent cards and gifts. I don't know how I'm going to get through the day. I couldn't sleep at all last night.'

October 14,

'My best mate Emer was round last night. That kept me sane. And Dave came later on. We are getting close again.'

Later in the month she blogs:

'Inspector O'Rourke keeps in regular touch with me. His wife is expecting their first baby in the New Year. He says the stories about cutbacks are not true and they're working lots of overtime on my case.'

And of the competition she says -

'I collapse into bed each night. Have to stay focussed on getting through to the final in December. Have to get through the quarter and semi finals and the public vote to get there. I want to win but I don't want to be a one hit wonder.'

An interesting piece in her blog later in the month – pregnancy advice!

'People have said why wasn't I on the pill? Well I was, and I hadn't missed any. I didn't know that if you're on antibiotics, which I was for an eye infection, the pill isn't so safe. When Tommy arrived, a week early, I just loved him. I felt so guilty about the resentful thoughts I had before. But having a baby in a bedsitter is no joke and Dave and I survived only another

four months. I fled to Social Services. They put Tommy and me into a damp hostel. But I had the local TD hound them, so they fixed me up with something better.'

I wonder if the blog is vetted by some PR person or the solicitor, though some of it seems to this cynical reader quite genuine.

Flushed with my initial success with Emer, I decide that tomorrow I will follow up my LinkedIn request to Jimmy Blake.

CHAPTER 10

It's funny but when you write a list of things to do the next day, following up unanswered emails and the like, it can happen that you get a reply the next day rendering part of your list irrelevant.

So it was with Jimmy Blake. In my inbox at 9.05 am was an ACCEPT from him for LinkedIn, a week after I sent him the original request.

I spend the day drafting and redrafting an email which I hope will start a correspondence such as the one I have been having with Emer.

'*Good morning Jimmy*

I hope I can call you that. I read about the mysterious disappearance of your daughter and hopefully there are now positive developments that the papers cannot print. It must be difficult to run your business with the strain of all this. I thought that perhaps you might be able to use some computer expertise to deal with some of the problems all businesses face which at least might free you up a little to work with the police to find out what happened.

I looked at your Facebook page and see that you are a West Ham supporter. What a small world! My mother grew up near their ground and converted me to the cause! Not the most fashionable side; but they are always entertaining. When I can, I try to get to Upton Park to see them.

Sometime soon, I'm hoping to go out on my own as a self employed IT consultant. My present company has been a good one to work for but it's time to move on to develop my own business.

Please get in touch if I can be of help.

Regards

Molly Carter'

My finger nervously presses the send button.

I'm certainly gaining experience as a liar. It's fun! I know quite a bit about some sports thanks to Jeff. Certainly I can hold my own on rugby and athletics, those at which he excelled. But football no! However, I have research skills and have compiled a history of West Ham United. Originally, that's back in 1895 they were called the Ironworks but took their present name in 1900. The club moved to its present home in Upton Park in 1904. Their glory days were in the 1960s when they provided the captain Bobby Moore and two other players to the English national side that won the World Cup in 1966. But in 2011 they were relegated from the Premier League to the Championship League.

Jimmy must have been devastated. Amy mentioned this in the Jennings interview; she was positive though about them getting back into the Premier League.

**

For many weeks after Jeff died I rely on sleeping pills. My doctor is reluctant to prescribe more because they are addictive. He is right I know but natural sleep is hard to come by particularly when I can't exercise normally with my damaged back and leg which are healing slowly. So I use fewer pills and sometimes have a large glass of brandy before going to bed on a night I don't take a pill.

Whether it was the brandy, the media reports about the philandering businessman that I believe relate to Jimmy or the creative email I sent to him that day, I don't know, but that night I dream about him in the West Ham strip chasing me round a hotel bedroom! And the crazy thing, in the dream I let him catch me. I don't go for older men and he's around 50 now but the Jimmy Blake in my dream is the good-looking toned 40 year old one in the wedding picture on his Facebook page.

**

Next day I get a reply.

'*Molly, thank you so much for your email picked up after a dreadful day.*

A difficult VAT inspector, a client planning to make half his employees redundant and wanting me to find a way out of paying them anything, and a meeting with a whingeing client telling me the tax avoidance scheme I created for him wasn't going to work. People don't really understand what it's like being an accountant in practice these days. Most of your clients are struggling, or they say they are to delay paying you. Even the celebrity clients can be tight; records not selling, films flopping at the box office and other excuses. People don't realise accountants are the last to get paid. They think accountants always have money.

Would love to meet up to discuss business possibilities but very tied up now as you can understand.

Kind regards

Jimmy'

I email back:

'I'm very busy too. Know what you mean about the accountancy scene. My cousin is an accountant and he says the same about the profession. Will be in touch. Molly.'

Me busy! That's another lie. I have nothing to do. My only commitments are to feed Pedro and let him out into the back garden. The housework is done for me. I order my shopping online and Lidia gets a few basics from the local shop when I run out. But a lie in a good cause is OK with me, and I suspect with most people.

But one thing is true. Aunt Bernie's eldest son Brian is an accountant. He may be helpful later if I need to look into Jimmy's business affairs.

**

Over the next two weeks we exchange emails via LinkedIn and his emails become friendlier. It's tricky judging how far I can go without him realising he is being investigated. I discuss strategy with Pedro and providing he's been fed he'll listen!

One line in his most recent email gives me an opening:

'Can't wait to meet you Molly but the press stalk me; Amy is like a jailer at the moment and the bloody deadlines for the clients. So I can only dream about meeting you at the moment......

So I respond:

'Jimmy, funny you should mention dreaming. Would you believe I had a dream the other night about meeting you in a hotel? Maybe it was the one on the West Ham ground? Please

don't take this the wrong way but you were chasing me round the hotel room, I was in a shortie nightie and wearing claret and blue socks like the West Ham team do; you were in a tracksuit and blowing a whistle. It was quite bizarre, but fun. Must have been the brandy I had to help me sleep that night.'

His reply comes in as I'm about to go to bed.

'Molly, I think you could be my soul mate. Must clear my desk and escape from the press and get to meet you. Let's act out that dream of yours. I'm in bed thinking about you; the photo on your LinkedIn page is a real turn on.'

So he's in bed thinking about me. What about Amy?

The email continues.

'I've moved into the spare bedroom. Can't bear to sleep in the same room as Amy after what she did. I'd like to discuss a new IT system with you but don't bother about the nightie, just keep the West Ham socks on! We won't spend too much time on the IT system. You bring the contract and I'll sign it. Then we'll have the whole night to fuck our brains out. And I hope you'll want LOTS of replays! Jimmy xxx.'

Now while this is not evidence that would stand up in a court of law it does in my eyes confirm that Jimmy plays away to use the football anology. It's not clear from the tabloid stories whether Jimmy has a regular woman or a series of one night stands. Now if it's the former, this gives him a motive.

Must have another look at the women on his Facebook page. If he wants a new life with somebody else he won't get custody of his darling Rose. A bit drastic to kidnap her but all the evidence is that he dotes on her. Even though Amy is not exactly a candidate for Mother of the Year, no court would award custody to him and she's unlikely to agree to shared custody in the circumstances. In the Jennings' interview, it said that he was in New York on a business trip, but he could have had help. Maybe the au pair was being blackmailed into helping over her immigrant status. Somebody suggested online that Teresa could be his girlfriend. I think that unlikely as she's less than half his age and more relevantly she's a devout Catholic - or is she? In that letter to Amy released to the papers she said she was afraid of being persecuted in China for her beliefs. But an illegal would say that!

I retire to bed wondering how to respond to the sexy email. Perhaps better to ignore it for a day or two. Let him get anxious and maybe reveal more. This man is obviously very clever in some ways. He has to be to have built up a successful business with offices in London and Manchester from a relatively humble background. But he's naïve at the same time. He's a married man in the public eye and he sends sexy emails to a person he doesn't know via a business network. I mean if you joined an online dating service you might expect some conversations to get sexy but this is a serious business networking site! Yes, I did lead him astray with my mention of a dream but he should have ignored my comment or made a joke about it.

**

The next day I pick up a magazine in my physio's waiting room. This is a new one I haven't seen before, a current affairs magazine called Life Today and a feature promoted on the cover attracts me, '**How charitable are charities?**' I'm reading how some of them spend a huge amount of money on their CEO and management salaries when I notice that they have some interviews with people who sit on charity boards on a voluntary basis and I recognise one of them. She's on the board whose meeting was more important to Amy that night than her child. I remember her face on the BBC news the day after Rose disappeared, essentially saying nothing, that the meeting had been adjourned and how the board were all praying for the child's safe return. I recall thinking she didn't sound very sincere. Her name is Davina Marsden and she's a striking looking woman, though not conventionally attractive.

After explaining how she came to be on this board due to her favourite aunt getting cancer she has some interesting things to say:

'*I do think some people sit on boards because they have time on their hands, and sometimes it's part of a career plan. It can look good on a CV.*'

'*That's a little cynical,*' the interviewer comments.

'*I'm not talking about the board at St Jude's,*' Davina had responded, '*I've sat on a lot of boards and quite honestly you get the 'ladies who lunch' who want to keep their names in the social pages. Helping at a fund raising function for a charity gives them great PR, and when it's a big charity sometimes they get the chance to put lucrative contracts the way of their friends.*'

Strong stuff from Davina. The interviewer queries this.

'*I wouldn't stay on any board where I felt my colleagues weren't bona fide. I'd just say to anybody considering donating to a charity, ask to see the accounts and if you aren't financially literate, get someone who is, to advise you. If the charity spends most of its income on salaries and administration, that's a very bad sign. And if they don't put their accounts on their website and give updated figures, forget them. If they needed the money they would be open and transparent.*'

'Molly, I'm ready for you now.' My physio is calling me but I've read enough. Interesting. I think Davina is sending out a coded message; look into Amy's charities.

CHAPTER 11

The taxi drops me back from the physio's. She told me at our last session that I'm now well enough to drive the short distance from my house to her clinic but I prefer to use a taxi. At least with the insurance money, taking taxis is not a financial issue for me. I always chose a cake, and sometimes two, from the shop below her clinic, to take home as a reward for surviving the discomfort of the session. I can't say I enjoy her manipulations but I'm making progress and it'll be great to walk without needing a stick. I finished with my crutches two weeks ago.

After a welcome back from Pedro, I make a cup of coffee and put in dollops of cream. I've managed to put back some of the weight I lost in the two months after Jeff died.

I turn on the PC. It seems the Accrington police held a press conference while I was out.

Missing Children Forum	
Portal Home Register Log In	every child matters
November 13 2011 at 12.21 pm Did you see the police press conference?	Declan Posts: 302 Join Date: 2.4.2011 Location: Dublin

November 13 2011 at 12.34 pm Yeah, they seem to be spending lots of our money and getting nowhere	Taxpayer Posts: 199 Join Date: 22.11.2010 Location: London
November 13 2011 at 12.41 pm That's a bit harsh. They've so many calls to follow up. It takes time.	Sherlock Posts: 98 Join Date: 29.6.2011 Location: Baker Street
November 13 2011 at 12.56 pm Well, it's over 2 months since baby Rose vanished. Chances of getting her back can't be good.	Suzy Posts: 62 Join Date: 27.2.2011 Location: Bath

But what did the police say? I'm learning nothing. I join the debate.

November 13 2011 at 1.03 pm Hi folks. Missed the conference. What exactly happened?	Miss Marple Posts: 18 Join Date: 10.9.2011 Location: St Mary Mead
November 13 2011 at 1.08 pm Not like you Miss Marple to miss anything to do with missing children! They can't trace the Chinese girl. They've followed up the leads in her letter to Amy. They've reviewed the supermarket tapes and are putting them out but they're not good quality. Showed them at the press conference. Could be anybody really. That woman Teresa chatted to in the doggie place has been identified and eliminated from the case. Remember the Jennings interview and the man who viewed Amy's house the day before Rose vanished. They're appealing for him to come forward to be eliminated from their inquiries. The other people who viewed have been followed up and eliminated but they can't contact this guy.	Declan Posts: 303 Join Date: 2.4.2011 Location: Dublin

November 13 2011 at 1.42 pm What's the problem with the mystery viewer?	Miss Marple Posts: 19 Join Date: 10.9.2011 Location: St Mary Mead
November 13 2011 at 2.02 pm He rang to ask about the house which was on the estate agents' website – there was a viewing in the afternoon so he was booked in by the receptionist who then lost the contact phone number he gave. The agent dealing with the property was with a client at the time of his call which was why the receptionist dealt with it. Then they had the estate agent describing him. Late 30's about 5'10 or 11". Brown hair. Well spoken. Had a good tan and she asked him where he got it but he didn't answer. Told her he might be moving to the area and was starting research on houses. Said she had several others viewing that afternoon and couldn't give any of them much time. She thinks he mentioned having a couple of children but she could be confusing him with another viewer. She remembers him patting Amy's dog.	Declan Posts: 304 Join Date: 2.4.2011 Location: Dublin

November 13 2011 at 2.10 pm	Taxpayer
Sounds like genuine guy looking for bigger house who likes dogs. Big deal! How much money will they waste looking for this man? That estate agent doesn't sound very experienced; should have taken notes about his requirements and of course his phone number. Quite cheeky to ask him where he got his sun tan, that's nothing to do with selling a house. I wouldn't answer a question like that.	Posts: 200 Join Date: 22.11.2010 Location: London
November 13 2011 at 2.46 pm	Olive Oil
Bet that receptionist is embarrassed, losing his contact number. If she hadn't, he could have been eliminated like the other viewers were.	Posts: 24 Join Date: 13.4.2011 Location: Kent
November 13 2011 at 3.04 pm	Nora
She probably never took it down at all. It's an excuse because it'd be policy to always get a number.	Posts: 20 Join Date: 15.7.2011 Location: Grimsby

November 13 2011 at 3.11 pm A thought, that sun tan might not be a holiday tan. Maybe he lives abroad in a warm country and is considering relocating home? His contract might have ended and he wants his children educated here. That would explain why he hasn't come forward if he doesn't live in the country.	Declan Posts: 305 Join Date: 2.4.2011 Location: Dublin
November 13 2011 at 3.29 pm The question I'd like to ask is whether the police have got even one independent sighting of Rose on the day she vanished. From all I've read it seems not. The housekeeper was there that day but Rose was asleep in her room and she didn't go in to clean. Amy apparently took Rose out in her buggy that morning but the only people who saw her were on the other side of the road and couldn't see whether Rose was actually in the buggy.	Miss Marple Posts: 20 Join Date: 10.9.2011 Location: St Mary Mead
November 13 2011 at 3.40 pm You're sharp, Miss Marple. Obviously you know that statistically the villain in most missing children is a parent, relative or someone else known to the child.	Columbo Posts: 76 Join Date: 6.3.2011 Location: New York

November 13 2011 at 3.47 pm Another thing. The au pair had a car supplied with the job. Why didn't she take it to Manchester? Then the problems caused by the bomb scare wouldn't have delayed her.	Miss Marple Posts: 21 Join Date: 10.9.2011 Location: St Mary Mead
November 13 2011 at 3.52 pm Can answer that one. A car in a city is bad news especially when you're moving around shopping. Makes more sense to use public transport. She couldn't have predicted the bomb scare.	Suzy Posts: 63 Join Date: 27.2.2011 Location: Bath
November 13 2011 at 4.04 pm You'd think Amy would have told her to get a taxi when she rang about the delay?	Declan Posts: 306 Join Date: 2.4.2011 Location: Dublin

November 13 2011 at 4.12 pm A taxi could be slower. There'd be a rush on them anyway.	Suzy Posts: 64 Join Date: 27.2.2011 Location: Bath
November 13 2011 at 4.22 pm I expect there are a lot of things the police aren't telling us. I just wonder what. We don't know if Rose had a passport and if she had, whether it went too. We're not sure exactly when Amy left that night so the window of opportunity is unclear but it seems to me the abductor – if there was one – had an hour to strike.	Miss Marple Posts: 22 Join Date: 10.9.2011 Location: St Mary Mead
November 13 2011 at 4.51 pm 'If there was an abductor' – don't you think there was one? Do you think Amy is responsible?	Columbo Posts: 77 Join Date: 6.3.2011 Location: New York

November 13 2011 at 5.05 pm	Miss Marple
We have to consider that as a possibility. We have a story that's hard to believe for Rose being left alone. We have a bomb scare on that day of all days. We have an altered meeting date creating a 'babysitting difficulty' and now vague suspects who really could be anybody like the man in the supermarket. I'd like to know what those women on her committees think of Amy. Read an interview today with her Vice Chairwoman on that cancer charity – wasn't about the baby but about charities in general. Got the impression the woman was really saying something about Amy.....	Posts: 23 Join Date: 10.9.2011 Location: St Mary Mead

And with that cryptic comment I switch off and turn to Sky News to catch up on the police press conference which they'll repeat throughout the rest of the day. At the conference they show a photo fit of the house viewer they want to come forward. OMG it's a bit like Jeff. I thought I was getting better. I'd managed to remove the drunken young man from Amy's university magazine from my mind, and now I'm seeing Jeff in this photo fit. Yes, I should have accepted the bereavement counselling but it's too late now.

**

Though it's mid November it's quite mild and the autumn leaves are still very much in abundance. So I do as my physio says I must, and get controlled exercise. Pedro is delighted to spend the afternoon in the garden chasing the balls I throw for him and watching me do a little pruning. The neighbours have been helping with the garden so it's in quite good shape and only a little work is needed. After a cup of tea with the blueberry muffin from the shop, the Danish pastry having been consumed with the coffee on my return, I make the big decision to venture outside and attempt the short walk to the corner shop. I didn't intend to take Pedro as he had lots of exercise in the garden but he creates so much fuss as I'm leaving that I relent.

I'm nervous that he'll pull, affect my balance and I'll drop my stick. Fortunately he doesn't. I feel like I've climbed Everest when I get to the shop. I don't actually need anything; the shop was just a realistic target to start with. The owner knows me but looks surprised when I limp in. After all I've been like a hermit since Jeff died. She recovers her composure, pats Pedro and tells me how well I'm looking. We exchange pleasantries; I buy some magazines and set off for home.

∗

I'd taken a chance and sent a personal message to Alro five days earlier. Internet forums normally permit secure personal messaging between members. It read:

'Hi Alro,
I get the feeling you are genuinely trying to get information out there but you have to protect your sources. I'm really keen to get the truth. Can you tell me anything you can't post online? Email me at missmarple@gmail.com or send me a personal message via the Forum.'

As I hadn't heard anything I thought I'd scared him off but after dinner I found a long email in my inbox.

'Miss Marple

This is what my sources tell me. There are no independent sightings of Tommy on the day he vanished, though it's known that Carli had left him in the car there on at least one other occasion but for a much shorter period. There've been rumours about Dave dabbling in drugs and annoying a dealer but there's no proof of that. Forensics tests at Carli's place came up with nothing suspicious and mobile phone records back up her story. But the story about the friend Emer letting down Carli is dodgy but not enough to take further. Witness saw a woman in a burka with buggy around 5 pm in the side street but witness seemed unreliable. There's also a rumour about the kid being in the traveller camp in Waterford. Dave Nevin's from a settled traveller family. Father fecked off years ago and mother drinks too much. Not surprising he left home as soon as he could get work. Nothing being done about the traveller camp rumour. Bloody political correctness.'

And the email ends:

'You'll agree sloppy parenting isn't confined to the Irish!'

Regards

Alro

Very interesting. Alro has to be a policeman or the partner of one. The message I'm getting from him is that the police believe Carli and Co are behind it but don't have enough evidence to prosecute.

Alro has mentioned Emer again. I continue to post on my Facebook page in support of Carli to keep up my cover, and I send Emer the occasional friendly message and click 'like' for things she has posted on her page. She responds to my messages but I can't ask her directly the questions I really want to ask. The only way I can do that is to meet her; she knows I have Waterford connections so a visit to Aunt Bernie wouldn't be suspicious. Yes, once I am fully mobile again I'll go there and follow up this lead. And I'll visit Accrington which is not far from where I live.

CHAPTER 12

I'd meant to follow up Jimmy's sexy email the next day. It was on my daily list of things to do but I didn't send a reply, and I'm not sure why.

Five days after that email, I hear from him again:

I'm shocked. There's a picture attachment of him in the West Ham kit with what looks like a glass of whisky in his hand. The shorts are tight and he appears to be having an erection. The email reads:

'Molly, don't tease me. I'm dreaming about you every night, can't wait to taste your wetness...I've found out where you live and if I don't hear from you I'm going to call over..'

The sleazebag! And yes it wouldn't be hard to find my address as I used my real name in our correspondence. It had seemed the only way to make contact with him was to use my real business profile. Imagine him turning up here. Yuck! I need a cigarette. I really do. I wish I didn't as I'm so close to giving them up altogether. I keep a packet in a high cupboard which I can't reach safely without Lidia's help. She's not due in for over an hour and I can't wait that long. I take a chance and stand on a chair. I know this is crazy; if I lose my balance and fall I could undo all the progress I've made thanks to my medical team.

Pedro is whining, his way of telling me to get down. I ignore him. The cigarettes are at the back of the cupboard to make it hard for me to reach. I lunge forward to pick up the packet trying to support myself with my other arm. I wobble but regain my balance.

An hour later I'm calmer and busy hiding the cigarette stubs where I hope Lidia won't find them. I've opened all the downstairs windows, not what you'd normally do in November even when it's relatively mild. Lidia thinks I'm eccentric so when she arrives hopefully she won't detect the real reason for the open windows.

The cigarette cover-up completed, I email back:

'Sorry. This has all been a mistake. I've had time on my hands recently as I'm in a wheelchair after an accident and I don't know if I will ever walk properly again.'

Back comes an email and it isn't nice.

'You fucking bitch. I wouldn't want to meet you like that!'

I delete him from my LinkedIn contacts.

Thankfully I hear nothing afterwards. It's left a nasty taste in my mouth but I'm glad I did it as it moved the story on. He's definitely someone to go on my suspects list. For a brief moment I pity Amy.

CHAPTER 13

Though the police conference told us about the mystery house viewer, and they still have to eliminate him from the inquiry, I'm getting the vibe that they suspect Amy. I can't wait to see the latest news on her blog. She's not happy.

A long entry dated 25 November 2011 reads:

'This is my annus horribilis.'

Yes, 2011 has certainly not been good for her but it annoys me. That phrase was used by the Queen after the scandals in the Royal Family. Is Amy comparing herself to Her Majesty?

But the next entry does move me:

'One month left in this year. Surely it can't get any worse? I thought it couldn't but then they killed Sammy. They killed a defenceless animal. I remember watching that film Fatal Attraction years ago when the mad woman killed the family pet rabbit. It gave me nightmares. And now someone just as mad has poisoned Sammy. They threw poisoned meat into the front garden sometime in the night and poor Sammy found it when I let him out in the morning. They left a note in the letter box saying I could be next.'

I had already read about this despicable act but seeing her pictures of poor Sammy, a gorgeous King Charles spaniel, has the tears trickling down my face. I had a King Charles when I was a child who died when I was nine. And I remember that film Fatal Attraction too. I couldn't sleep the day I saw it. I couldn't even look when the family pet was found boiling in the saucepan. The woman who did it was obsessed with the husband in the family and it was her way of dealing with rejection. I glance at Pedro sleeping at my feet. Scary that there are people out there who would do something so evil.

She continues:

'My poor darling Peter found him and didn't realise he was dead. I'll never forget him screaming for me to get the vet, but Sammy wasn't breathing. Peter said 'Mummy how can people do things like this' and I couldn't answer. I thought of telling him Sammy just ate something bad he found in the garden which was true in a way but it wouldn't work. He's nearly eight. He can read. I did keep him home for two weeks after the school suggested I did. He's back now. He's already hearing things in the playground about Rose. He bottles things up and then it all comes out. He said some boys told him that their mums say I'm a nasty bitch. I said I wasn't, I tried to hug him but he pushed me away. I don't know those women and I certainly don't want to. How do they judge someone they don't know? And they really shouldn't say things like that when their children are around.'

Then she moves on to the police.

'I met Detective Inspector Hargreaves last week but there's nothing new. They're following up all the calls from the Press conference but so far there's nothing useful. He asked me again why I didn't ask my parents to help when Teresa rang about the delay. He just doesn't seem to understand me when I say there'd have been little point. Thursday is their bridge night and they would have been out. I gave mum a mobile for Christmas last year but she doesn't switch it on, and Dad refuses to have one. So I wouldn't have been able to get hold of them. I think the problem was because he went to see them and they told him their bridge night was Wednesday. I thought it was Thursday. Maybe it was and the night changed. They wouldn't necessarily tell me. They know I hate cards and would never want to go with them.'

Is she trying to cover herself for a lie she told? Of course you'd ask your parents to help and by all accounts they are the most devoted of grandparents. But then again some older people aren't into mobile phones so not being able to contact them could be true.

She doesn't say whether she even tried to ring their landline. Hmm, maybe suspicious. She surely should have tried.

Amy continues her complaints.

'The Law Society informed me that a few people had written to them about me, asking that I be struck off for child neglect, but that's not professional misconduct as far as the Law Society is concerned. You'd think people would have better things to do than be so vindictive.'

After my LinkedIn experience with Jimmy I'm naturally curious to know about her relationship with him so I skip ahead and find:

'I came home from the doctor yesterday to find a hall full of flowers from Jimmy. He knows how much I've been suffering from all the negativity about me in the media, and how the rumours in the tabloids about an unnamed businessman having an affair upset me. I advised him to sue as the articles clearly referred to him although they didn't name him. I had a journalist call to the house looking for a comment, just when I thought journalists at the door were a thing of the past. The stories are lies.'

OMG - a hall full of flowers. I'm not clear from her dates whether that was before or after Jimmy told me he didn't want me in a wheelchair!!!

The blog is getting boring and I'm almost relieved to be interrupted by a call from Aunt Bernie. There's news from Waterford; Dave Nevin has been attacked and is badly hurt. I tell her I'll look the up the story online. She is starting to understand that she doesn't need to send cuttings. The local paper reports:

'Mr Nevin was rushed to Waterford Regional Hospital. A spokesperson described his condition today as 'serious but

stable.' It is understood that the gardai are anxious to talk to him as soon as his condition allows as this incident may be related to the disappearance of his son Tommy on August 9th.

Rumours had circulated that Tommy's disappearance could be related to a debt the young father owed to local undesirables. This vicious attack appears to confirm that. A neighbour who asked not to be named said, 'Dave's not a bad kid and he seemed to love that baby. He was upset when Carli left him. But I have seen some dodgy looking characters calling to his flat.'

I wonder how Carli feels about this. The paper said she had no comment. Carli has new problems as Celebrity Now exclusively reveals. Apparently she's doing the diva bit. She has insisted that Kevin her regular hairdresser does her hair for the competition.

To quote the magazine, 'A source told Celebrity Now that Carli's antics are not endearing her to her fellow contestants but management is going easy on her because she's under stress from the abduction of her baby.

'Carli was annoyed by comments from the judges on her new look in last Saturday's show and later by others in the fashion press. She didn't return our calls but it's understood that she will look after her own styling for the rest of the competition.

'This weekend the eight remaining contestants again face the public vote. Carli is now second favourite at 5/1.'

But more importantly, Aunt Bernie says there is a new lead. A woman who did not realise the possible significance of something she saw has come forward. She was in the street where the car was parked but she left Ireland on an early flight the next morning before she heard about Tommy vanishing.

According to the Irish Tribune:

'Bernadette Carroll has told the police that she parked in the side street from which Tommy vanished at around 4.40 pm that afternoon. She was doing some last minute shopping for a trip to Italy where she was to stay with her sister for three months helping with her new baby.

Police sources say that Ms Carroll passed a well dressed woman of around sixty years of age, standing by an old car parked near the corner. Ms Carroll suggested to the woman that she move her car back a bit as she was too near the corner. The woman indicated that she would do this. Ms Carroll remembers thinking that she would expect such a smart woman to have a better car. She says there was another car parked about 50 metres behind this one and she thinks a youngish man was sitting in the driver's seat. After completing her shopping she returned to the side street about 45 minutes later. The old car was still parked there and she is sure the second car had gone then.

While Ms Carroll had heard a child had gone missing in Waterford she did not know the location of the incident so it wasn't until she returned to Ireland that she realised the possible implications of what she had seen. She had been staying in a small town in Italy with no Irish papers available.

The police are appealing for these two people to come forward so they can be eliminated from their enquiries.'

Now will this woman come forward? Why would she 'indicate' she would move the car when it wasn't hers? I suppose she could have been taken aback by the request to move it away from the corner. After all most people complain about bad parking but rarely have the courage to ask the owner to move the car. She might have thought it easier to do nothing. She didn't say she would move the car. If this woman took him, could Tommy be safe? Could she be someone whose child rearing days are over, who never had a child and who acted on impulse seeing Tommy inside and alone? And Tommy is an adorable looking child.

The day after this hopeful news the media return to the story of Sammy's death. One paper headlines their article:

'You cared more about your pedigree pooch than your baby – watch yourself Amy is warned.'

I empathise with an editorial in the Daily Record:

'How low can society sink when an innocent animal is poisoned to 'punish' a woman whom the perpetrators feel did wrong? And some people are supporting this evil act on the internet. Have we lost all our values?

We refer to Amy Blake, mother of missing baby Rose. Our letters column over the past weeks show that opinions differ on Mrs Blake's decision to leave her daughter 'home alone' as she thought for a matter of minutes.

But whatever you think about what she did, no-one can doubt her suffering since. She has to come to terms with the fact that she may never know what happened to Rose and why? She has to try to help her young son Peter cope with the loss of his sister and now of his beloved pet.

*The person who killed the Blakes' dog should be tracked down and jailed, whatever it costs. This person is evil and a danger to **anyone** he or she decides has transgressed against their twisted values.*

We hope our readers' thoughts are with the Blake family at this difficult time.'

I'm grateful that the Daily Record has condemned the killing of Amy's dog; I don't think I could ever have read another tabloid if it hadn't.

And the media finishes the month with another exclusive Carli story.

Celebrity Now reveals that Carli, according to her, hasn't had a 'fling' with a young man in a boy band I've never heard of.

'Single mum Carli Walsh has denied she had a fling with Jay Murphy, lead singer with boy band 'The Edge.' The couple met when the Star Search finalists were taken to the Point for a concert in which the popular boy band was performing. All the finalists were invited back stage after the gig to meet the group.

Carli told Celebrity Now:

'Yes we all had a few drinks with the boys after the show and I went outside for a smoke with Jay. That's all it was, a chat. He has a kid who he doesn't see cuz his ex gives him grief with access. He understood what I'm going through, missing Tommy. I gave him a hug and we came inside. Some fucker saw that and told the press and they made out I'd had a night of sex with him. My solicitor is thinking of suing them.'

She continued, 'I'm concentrating totally on the competition. Relationships are out for now. I made a mess of the last one with Dave, Tommy's dad. He was beaten up by some thugs and the competition organisers let me off for a couple of days to see him through the worst provided I kept a low profile which I did. The papers said I couldn't be bothered to go to see him but it wasn't true. They didn't even ask me.'

What an exclusive! The sad thing is that it probably sold lots more copies of the magazine.

On the internet I start a long rant.

Missing Children Forum

Portal   Home   Register   Log In

every child
matters

November 26 2011 at 9.17 am

I'm very concerned about the effect budget cuts will have on the investigations into the disappearance of these two babies. Granted, they're gone because of the direct negligence of their parents but the police are the only ones who are acting in their best interests. What if the parents are guilty and have harmed the babies, no private detective they engage to make it appear as if they are really looking is going to find anything.

I don't feel that the parents or family or any interested party in a missing child case should be allowed to hire their own investigators. It could mess up the police investigation. I'm also dead against a fund for the same reason. I understand people like to donate to a fund because it's the one thing they can do to help. But I think that we've reached a stage in our culture where if your child is missing you can become an instant celebrity and that means money. I'm not for a moment implying that this is the situation here but what happens if a parent simulates an abduction? In today's world they get instant fame and money. Look at the Shannon Matthews case. At least that mother was caught.

Miss Marple

Posts: 24
Join Date:
10.9.2011

Location:
St Mary Mead

I think that a separate body should be set up to deal with all aspects of child abduction comprised of representatives from the media, the police, social services and independent members. Donations should only be made to this body so they can help all missing children equally. I don't see the need to parade the parents and family members, they have enough to be doing and they don't belong in the spotlight.	
November 26 2011 at 9.25 am Miss Marple, I think you speak for many people. But I have to say 'set up a separate body' rings warning bells for me. Another quango! In Ireland we have far too many useless state bodies costing a fortune. Maybe this isn't the case in the UK? I would worry that this body would be another gravy train for incompetent people.	Fairplay Posts: 47 Join Date: 5.5.2011 Location: Ireland
November 26 2011 at 9.45 am Loadsa useless state bodies in the UK too....	Taxpayer Posts: 201 Join Date: 22.11.2010 Location: London

November 26 2011 at 9.55 am	Miss Marple
Fairplay, thanks for keeping me in check; I can get a bit one dimensional sometimes.	Posts: 25 Join Date: 10.9.2011 Location: St Mary Mead

Maybe I was a bit over the top here? Anyway the members move on.

November 26 2011 at 10.43 am	GoodMum
Just seen the latest news in the Waterford papers, wonder if it's really possible Tommy was abducted because of Dave's drug debt?	Posts: 380 Join Date: 4.1.2011 Location: UK
November 26 2011 at 10.58 am	Columbo
If he was abducted to do with drugs, Dave would have to know. I don't buy it, how would they know the baby was in the car alone on that particular street? Coincidence?	Posts: 78 Join Date: 6.3.2011 Location: New York

November 26 2011 at 11.14 am Similar coincidence to anyone else taking him, drug dealers do hang out on side streets, could already be on the lookout for his car. Remember Dave gave his car to Carli when they split as she had the baby.	Declan Posts: 307 Join Date: 2.4.2011 Location: Dublin
November 26 2011 at 11.39 am No wonder the cops were so interested in Dave, none of us saw that attack coming.	Liam Posts: 17 Join Date: 2.8.2011 Location: Belfast
November 26 2011 at 12.02 pm Wonder if the drug dealer disguised himself in a burka?	Mags Posts: 353 Join Date: 2.9.2010 Location: Liverpool

November 26 2011 at 12.14 am	Miss Marple
People in burkas are usually not noticed, very clever if you ask me, a little less conspicuous than a nun's habit these days.	Posts: 26 Join Date: 10.9.2011 Location: St Mary Mead
November 26 2011 at 12.56 pm	Luke
It sounds like a bit of a stretch to imply it was a man, doesn't sound like the witness was sure about that	Posts: 17 Join Date: 3.6.2011 Location: Glasgow
November 26 2011 at 1.31pm	Mags
Hum, now Carli is turning into a Diva, wonder if she should be allowed to have her own hairdresser. Who does she think she is? I don't believe contestants should be allowed to have their own team; wouldn't it put others at a disadvantage?	Posts: 354 Join Date: 2.9.2010 Location: Liverpool

November 26 2011 at 1.42 pm He'd have to be working for the same pay as the others, maybe doing it at a knockdown rate cos it's raising his profile.	Taxpayer Posts: 202 Join Date: 22.11.2010 Location: London
November 26 2011 at 2.03 pm You two are believing what you read in those tabloid rags, they have to come up with a scoop every week and last week it was – shock horror – Carli's sacked stylist	Supernanny Posts: 308 Join Date: 21.10.2010 Location: In the nursery
November 26 2011 at 2.41 pm Sacked stylist. Thought it was only the hairdresser she changed.	Jenny Posts: 67 Join Date 5.5.2011 Location: Slough

November 26 2011 at 2.57 pm Depends which rag you read!	Declan Posts: 308 Join Date: 2.4.2011 Location: Dublin
November 26 2011 at 3.13 pm I don't think this show should be about advertising or hairstyles, anyway how is this new hairstyle going to help her in the grand scheme of things, it's about singing.	Mags Posts: 355 Join Date: 2.9.2010 Location: Liverpool
November 26 2011 at 3.19 pm You are NAIVE. It's not about singing; it's about the whole package, how you look, what you wear, personality, who you're dating. It was about singing in the OLD days.....	Fairplay Posts: 48 Join Date: 5.5.2011 Location: Ireland

November 26 2011 at 3.48 pm Gawd you guys are hard, her son is missing, her ex is in hospital, she must be in bits, surely it's not too much to ask that she has a friendly face from home helping her out	Suzy Posts: 65 Join Date: 27.2.2011 Location: Bath
November 26 2011 at 4.02 pm Wonder if the beating has anything to do with the abduction? Maybe Dave might know where Tommy is at after all	Miss Marple Posts: 27 Join Date: 10.9.2011 Location: St Mary Mead
November 26 2011 at 4.11 pm Em, I doubt there's any connection. A beating up will cause a police investigation, would lead a trail to your door. Anyway he seems pretty cut up about the missing baby. Losing your child, that's got to be worse than any beating	Sherlock Posts: 99 Join Date: 29.6.2011 Location: Baker Street

November 26 2011 at 4.20 pm	Columbo
Ok, this is a truly baffling case. A missing baby, a wannabe star, a beaten up father, a silent friend, a man/woman in a burka, an older woman, a younger man seen at the key time..	Posts: 79 Join Date: 6.3.2011 Location: New York
November 26 2011 at 4.34 pm	Declan
And don't forget a gay hairstylist and a snog with Jay	Posts: 309 Join Date: 2.4.2011 Location: Dublin
November 26 2011 at 4.55 pm	Mags
Who said her hairdresser was gay? That's a stereotype!	Posts: 356 Join Date: 2.9.2010 Location: Liverpool

November 26 2011 at 5.06 pm Saw him pictured in a magazine. Looked as camp as a row of tents.	Declan Posts: 310 Join Date: 2.4.2011 Location: Dublin
November 27 2011 at 5.14 pm Strange that woman by the car hasn't come forward yet if she had nothing to hide.	Miss Marple Posts: 28 Join Date: 10.9.2011 Location: St Mary Mead
November 27 2011 at 5.21 pm Could have been a tourist. It was August. Mightn't even know about it depending on where she was from.	Pam Posts: 1 Join Date: 27.11.2011 Location: York

November 27 2011 at 5.28 pm OK, a couple just happened to pull in and park behind Carli's car. Woman gets out of car, passes Carli's car and just happens to see Tommy and suddenly decides to take him? Does that make sense?	Miss Marple Posts: 29 Join Date: 10.9.2011 Location: St Mary Mead
November 27 2011 at 5.39 pm What if there is some connection between them all? Carli was fostered, right, she has to have relations somewhere.	Luke Posts: 18 Join Date: 3.6.2011 Location: Glasgow
November 27 2011 at 6.01 pm The word on the street is that she was adopted in London as a baby. Moved to Ireland when she was about five and then her adopted parents were killed.	Declan Posts: 311 Join Date: 2.4.2011 Location: Dublin

That's interesting. Adopted. I must have missed that earlier, but she didn't say that in the Hot Pop interview. Declan is a good poster, so I wonder where he heard it. They continue on the real mother theme.

November 27 2011 at 6.13 pm I'm pretty sure the detective will have checked this out. If it's true, wonder if Carli has met her birth mother?	Mags Posts: 357 Join Date: 2.9.2010 Location: Liverpool
November 27 2011 at 6.18 pm I doubt it's the birth mother, she'd never be an old woman by now. Hey unless the mother disguised herself as an old dear?	GoodMum Posts: 381 Join Date: 4.1.2011 Location: UK
November 27 2011 at 6.29 pm Now there's an idea. Her birth mother disguises herself as an old woman and just finds her grandchild in the car, so she takes it....pull the other leg	Suzy Posts: 66 Join Date: 27.2.2011 Location: Bath

November 27 2011 at 6.47 pm What a tough situation, given away at birth, losing your new parents young, being shunted from home to home after that, leaving final home, breaking up with BF and then losing your baby. It's heartbreaking.	Fairplay Posts: 49 Join Date: 5.5.2011 Location: Ireland
November 27 2011 at 6.55 pm This is ridiculous. Somebody mentions a rumour she is adopted. A rumour not fact and some people here are posting as if that's true. Let's stick to the facts.	Pam Posts: 2 Join Date: 27.11.2011 Location: York
November 27 2011 at 7.17 pm Those two who they want for questioning could be from any of the homes she'd been through in her childhood	Supernanny Posts: 309 Join Date: 21.10.2010 Location: In the nursery

November 27 2011 at 7.26 pm I doubt it, she would have recognised the police photofit of the woman	Fairplay Posts: 50 Join Date: 5.5.2011 Location: Ireland
November 27 2011 at 7.44 pm What I don't get is why would an old woman have any interest in a baby? Not being funny but a baby is also for life, the woman in the photofit looked to be in her mid 60's, maybe older.	CoolDude Posts: 12 Join Date: 4.7.2011 Location: Bahamas
November 27 2011 at 7.47 pm Mid 60s is NOT old. One report I saw said around 60.	Pam Posts: 3 Join Date: 27.11.2011 Location: York

November 27 2011 at 7.51 pm	Fairplay
Babies fetch a pretty good price in the marketplace. I'm pretty sure paedophiles would pay top price for a blond haired cutie like Tommy, he's adorable. Not to mention childless couples.	Posts: 51 Join Date: 5.5.2011 Location: Ireland
November 27 2011 at 8.01 pm	GoodMum
It's a sad thing to see, a defenceless baby being reduced to nothing but a commodity to be sold on the open market. What's the world coming to?	Posts: 382 Join Date: 4.1.2011 Location: UK
November 27 2011 at 8.05 pm	Miss Marple
It's simple commerce, the marketplace responding to the selfish actions of a mother who puts her hairstyle above her son's safety. Crisis & opportunity	Posts: 30 Join Date: 10.9.2011 Location: St Mary Mead

November 27 2011 at 8.09 pm The same opportunity the mother takes to use the abduction to further her chances in the talent show	Declan Posts: 312 Join Date: 2.4.2011 Location: Dublin
November 27 2011 at 8.15 pm Perhaps you're right but from the looks of it the poor mother was almost as vulnerable as the child.	Pam Posts: 4 Join Date: 27.11.2011 Location: York
November 27 2011 at 8.26 pm Speaking of vulnerability did you see that Amy Blake's dog was poisoned, spooky that.	Luke Posts: 19 Join Date: 3.6.2011 Location: Glasgow

November 27 2011 at 8.44 pm Ouch, what an incredibly cruel thing to do. Shocking blow after your child is abducted, I feel desperately sorry for the family, especially the poor son.	Suzy Posts: 67 Join Date: 27.2.2011 Location: Bath
November 27 2011 at 8.58 pm Our Amy doesn't have much luck looking after things does she?	Fairplay Posts: 52 Join Date: 5.5.2011 Location: Ireland
November 27 2011 at 9.16 pm Oh, come on, you can't watch a dog 24/7	CoolDude Posts: 13 Join Date: 4.7.2011 Location: Bahamas

November 27 2011 at 9.22 pm In what world can you criticise a woman for neglecting her child and retaliate by killing a dog? People like that deserve prison.	Mags Posts: 358 Join Date: 2.9.2010 Location: Liverpool
November 27 2011 at 9.31 pm It's not looking good for either investigation; they seem to be scaling both down. Good thing as they're going nowhere it seems to me.	Taxpayer Posts: 203 Join Date: 22.11.2010 Location: London
November 27 2011 at 9.39 pm I saw a very interesting clip on BBC last night now don't laugh, they were also discussing a possible link. Psychic Breda Ross claims they're both alive and the answers lie in Waterford.	GoodMum Posts: 383 Join Date: 4.1.2011 Location: UK

November 27 2011 at 9.46 pm There's rumours going round Waterford that Tommy is in the traveller camp.	Declan Posts: 313 Join Date: 2.4.2011 Location: Dublin
November 27 2011 at 9.56 pm Absolute racist rubbish you're spouting	Suzy Posts: 68 Join Date: 27.2.2011 Location: Bath
November 27 2011 at 9.59 pm No, Dave's family are settled travellers. His dad's not so settled. Did a bunk years ago leaving Dave's mum with four kids. Where would you hide a baby where the gardai wouldn't dare to look?	Fairplay Posts: 53 Join Date: 5.5.2011 Location: Ireland

November 27 2011 at 10.03 pm But why would Dave use his traveller connections to do that?	GoodMum Posts: 384 Join Date: 4.1.2011 Location: UK
November 27 2011 at 10.09 pm What if the abduction is all a scam? To raise Carli's profile and get her that recording contract? Like someone said being a star now is not just about being a good singer. You have to be constantly in the news and it doesn't matter really why you're in the news. Have they really split up? Why would he be babysitting if they hate each other? Tommy'll turn up when she's got enough cash in the bank... Just a theory.	Miss Marple Posts: 31 Join Date: 10.9.2011 Location: St Mary Mead
November 27 2011 at 10.16 pm Warning – please be careful about unsubstantiated allegations	Moderator

Hmm, better watch what I say. The moderators on this site are quite fair. I did go a bit too far.

November 27 2011 at 10.18 pm Miss Marple, do you think Rose's disappearance is a scam too?	CoolDude Posts: 14 Join Date: 4.7.2011 Location: Bahamas
November 27 2011 at 10.19 pm No comment. Look I went a bit too far with Tommy.	Miss Marple Posts: 32 Join Date: 10.9.2011 Location: St Mary Mead
November 27 2011 at 10.22 pm Come on now, you're a great one for theories. Do you think the two cases are linked?	CoolDude Posts: 15 Join Date: 4.7.2011 Location: Bahamas

He is being persistent. I think CoolDude is a he. But I mustn't let him bait me. Keep calm Molly.

November 27 2011 at 10.26 pm I really don't know but I'm open to discussion on it.	Miss Marple Posts: 33 Join Date: 10.9.2011 Location: St Mary Mead
November 27 2011 at 10.29 pm How about friends, could they have any friends in common I wonder	Fairplay Posts: 54 Join Date: 5.5.2011 Location: Ireland
November 27 2011 at 10.40 pm Only Carli's friend Emer has been mentioned. Amy seems to have more acquaintances than friends, all those charity do-gooder types	Columbo Posts: 80 Join Date: 6.3.2011 Location: New York

November 27 2011 at 10.52 pm Why would a working class single mum in Waterford have friends in common with a lady lawyer in the UK twice her age? Give me a break, Fairplay	CoolDude Posts: 16 Join Date: 4.7.2011 Location: Bahamas

He's being rude to Fairplay now. Hope she'll stand up to him. Anyway GoodMum goes off on a tangent about Amy's boyfriend from student days.

November 27 2011 at 10.59 pm Amy dated a medical student for over a year and left him with a gigantic broken heart.	GoodMum Posts: 385 Join Date: 4.1.2011 Location: UK
November 27 2011 at 11.05 pm Ah, yes, the college relationship the reporter Carol Jennings referred to. Bet the tabloids would pay a fortune for an interview with him.	Liam Posts: 18 Join Date: 2.8.2011 Location: Belfast

November 27 2011 at 11.25 pm Amy had a boyfriend at university – shock/horror. Alright, you guys badly need to get a life. This discussion is going nowhere.	CoolDude Posts: 17 Join Date: 4.7.2011 Location: Bahamas
November 27 2011 at 11.31 pm I disagree, all we're doing is looking for links. Detectives do that all of the time.	Miss Marple Posts: 34 Join Date: 10.9.2011 Location: St Mary Mead
November 27 2011 at 11.42 pm It reminds me of the link they tried to find in the Kerry babies case in the 1980s in Ireland. Hammering in those pieces won't necessarily make them fit.	Fairplay Posts: 55 Join Date: 5.5.2011 Location: Ireland

November 27 2011 at 11.58 pm	Miss Marple
Laugh all you want, CoolDude there is an answer here somewhere and someone's got to find it.	Posts: 35 Join Date: 10.9.2011 Location: St Mary Mead

I was going to switch off the computer when a PM arrives. It's from Babydoc. When she joined the Forum she announced she had a professional interest in babies but when she didn't post I contacted her and we've been exchanging PMs discussing the case. I assume this message is responding to my last one but get a surprise when I read it.

'Miss Marple, I sense from our private messages and your public posts that you've had a tragedy in your life involving a child. You must have done to feel so strongly about these mums. Maybe it would help to talk about it. I have a professional background in this area as you know and would love to help you. Be strong and contact me at the number below if you need me.'

I start to cry and sit there in my pyjamas sobbing away. She is right. Every day I think about the son I never saw except in the ultrasound picture.

I know I need counselling but something inside me has stopped me from getting help. Now an internet acquaintance has copped my problem and I should listen to her. I send Babydoc a thank you message together with my phone number and switch off my computer. I dry my eyes and go to bed. It's after midnight. Tomorrow I vow to take a day off from the case. But it doesn't work out that way as Amy's 'annus horribilis' gets even worse and I'm glued to breaking news.

CHAPTER 14

The next day's headlines scream:

Missing Baby's Dad Fights For His Life

Jimmy Blake had crashed his car only a couple of miles from his home on a road he knew well. A hospital spokesman said he had suffered multiple fractures in his spine, a broken leg, several broken ribs and other impact injuries from the crash, and was in intensive care. Later editions had pictures of Amy leaving the hospital putting a brave face on things and saying *'The doctors say he could make a full recovery in time.'*

I have to feel sorry for her but certainly not for him. My online flirting with him had revealed a very nasty side to him. The next day it gets worse for Amy with a tabloid exclusive; the story behind the car crash. It occurred after Jimmy had been thrown out of the family home when Amy discovered he was having an affair. And not just with anyone but with Davina Marsden, Amy's fellow director on the board.

It seems that when Amy found out, she packed up his clothes and sent them by courier van to Ms Marsden's house. The suitcases were dumped at her gate all bearing the same message in thick black marker pen - 'Jimmy Blake is shagging Davina Marsden.' A neighbour must have seen the suitcases and tipped off the papers.

Of course both Amy and Davina Marsden had 'no comment' to make. Needless to say the tabloids managed to find pictures of the two women in the same group at a charity ball and ran that photograph on the front page together with a pile of suitcases outside Davina's gate. Obviously a set up picture with suitcases obtained for the shot; how could the paper have got a photographer there in time? Unless it was Amy who tipped off the paper – would she have done that even though the story meant public humiliation for her?

Of course the tabloid story fuelled rumours about the crash. One quality paper ran an editorial:

'We do not believe the conspiracy theories circulating about the crash. But we do believe the stress Mr Blake was under was added to by the killing of the family dog and that this may have caused a momentary loss of concentration which was probably a major factor in this accident.'

Online, Forum members have their theories.

Missing Children Forum Portal Home Register Log In	 every child matters
November 28 2011 at 7.33 pm It's not the only problem our Amy's having right now, did you read about Jimmy, that crash seems pretty serious. It's unbelievable. How much more can the family take?	GoodMum Posts: 386 Join Date: 4.1.2011 Location: UK

November 28 2011 at 7.43 pm It's mighty peculiar, a car accident so close to home. Wonder if he'd been drinking?	Declan Posts: 314 Join Date: 2.4.2011 Location: Dublin
November 28 2011 at 7.49 pm Not necessarily, bound to be a difficult time for him, maybe he was distracted, thinking about little Rose.	Fairplay Posts: 56 Join Date: 5.5.2011 Location: Ireland

But then the news of the affair broke.

November 30 2011 at 8.11 am OMG, what bad timing, poor Amy. I really feel sorry for her. She's lost her daughter, au pair, dog & husband all in three months. It goes to show, there's more to life than status & money.	Suzy Posts: 69 Join Date: 27.2.2011 Location: Bath

November 30 2011 at 9.13 am There are mixed reports about the accident and hey, they're not ruling out foul play.	Miss Marple Posts: 36 Join Date: 10.9.2011 Location: St Mary Mead
November 30 2011 at 10.12 am I think the cause is probably the least of their worries right now, it's still not clear if Jimmy will live and even if he does, he mightn't ever work again.	Liam Posts: 19 Join Date: 2.8.2011 Location: Belfast
November 30 2011 at 11.01 am A missing baby, a missing au pair, a stranger in the supermarket, a dead dog, a cheating husband, a serious car accident. Sounds like a film script	Supernanny Posts: 310 Join Date: 21.10.2010 Location: In the nursery

November 30 2011 at 1.09 pm	Miss Marple
The parallels to the Waterford cases are interesting. Both fathers badly hurt for example. The supermarket man fits the general description of the house viewer who hasn't come forward. The supermarket CCTV image is very grainy. Could they be the same man?	Posts: 37 Join Date: 10.9.011 Location: St Mary Mead
November 30 2011 at 1.44 pm	Fairplay
Funny you should talk about connections. I was looking at some images of Tommy & Rose side by side, though it may be a trick of the light, thought they look very similar.	Posts: 57 Join Date: 5.5.2011 Location: Ireland
November 30 2011 at 2.14 pm	Suzy
Somebody raised that likeness issue before I think?	Posts: 70 Join Date: 27.2.2011 Location: Bath

November 30 2011 at 2.19 pm You're right, the eyebrows & cheekbones do look similar but maybe we're grasping at straws. But then again, Rose looks like my niece. Look at this picture of her when she was the same age as Rose. Maybe all babies look alike?	Columbo Posts: 81 Join Date: 6.3.2011 Location: New York
November 30 2011 at 2.40 pm Hey, I wonder if the detectives have joined forces, it'd be interesting to see if there's any DNA link.	Sherlock Posts: 100 Join Date: 29.6.2011 Location: Baker Street
November 30 2011 at 3.53 pm What a waste of space some people are on this site. You'd waste police time on DNA of the two missing kids. The only thing these cases have in common is (1) babies went missing this summer and (2) both mothers made a mistake and have paid for it. Columbo, you really shouldn't be posting up your niece's photo – did her parents give you permission?	CoolDude Posts: 18 Join Date: 4.7.2011 Location: Bahamas

November 30 2011 at 4.23 pm	Declan
Does anyone think it was Amy who tipped off the papers? I heard she had a private detective following Jimmy after all those articles about a well known businessman playing away? She could have opted for a discreet divorce but instead she throws him out and wrecks his designer luggage with a marker pen!	Posts: 315 Join Date: 2.4.2011 Location: Dublin

Declan's reading my mind. I also suspect it could have been Amy. But another thought occurs to me. If Davina and Jimmy had an ongoing relationship, was Davina involved with the change of meeting date that left Amy with a babysitting problem?

You have to remember that statistically in missing children cases it's generally someone close to the child. Keeping the original date on the Monday of that week would have lost her a night with Jimmy who didn't leave for his business trip to the States until Tuesday. She could have known about Teresa being off on Thursday if she was the woman in *Pampered Pooch* but she couldn't have known there'd be a bomb scare. Unless she made the call...... Why would Davina want Rose? She doesn't have any children of her own and she's on husband number three according to the media.

I have to admit that Columbo's niece does look like Rose; but so does Lidia's baby! She was showing me pictures taken at little Alicja's first birthday party last week. I don't think this resemblance issue is a runner.

The accident generates support for Amy. I am feeling uncomfortable about this new development.

November 30 2011 at 6.06 pm Did you see women are posting messages of support for Amy on her blog? Saying she's inspiring them to kick their own cheaters out!	Mags Posts: 359 Join Date: 2.9.2010 Location: Liverpool
November 30 2011 at 6.31 pm That woman Davina has resigned from the charity board apparently.	Sherlock Posts: 101 Join Date: 29.6.2011 Location: Baker Street
November 30 2011 at 6.52 pm Yes, read that – she said it was due to 'pressure of other commitments.' Pull the other leg!	Declan Posts: 316 Join Date: 2.4.2011 Location: Dublin

November 30 2011 at 7.06 pm	Suzy
Not really very nice of those women to support what she did IMO – whatever he did, Jimmy is fighting for his life and it must be dreadful for his little boy	Posts: 71 Join Date: 27.2.2011 Location: Bath
November 30 2011 at 7.42 pm	Liam
Amy hasn't posted on her blog since the accident. Hardly surprising. Let's wait until she does to hear her side of things.	Posts: 20 Join Date: 2.8.2011 Location: Belfast

A week after the accident Amy breaks her silence and blogs:

'Telling Peter was bloody awful. He wanted to go to the hospital but I said he couldn't because daddy was too ill. I didn't think he could take seeing Jimmy on the life support machine. He cried and I felt guilty. Will those horrible mums tell their sons that this was my fault too, and it'll get back to Peter?

I've been spending hours at the hospital. I try to avoid the photographers but they seem to be everywhere. The tabloids are implying it wasn't an accident but I can see they've had their libel people checking the copy. I mean if it wasn't an accident, the readers can only think it was me.'

The medical news is serious:

'The consultant tells me Jimmy was lucky. He has serious impact injuries from the crash. The fractures in his back came close to severing his spinal cord but the paramedics managed to stabilise him in time though it will be a while before his mobility will return. The real problem is the head injury. There's extensive swelling around his brain which has led to an increase in his intracranial pressure. Early tests have indicated that there is decreased brain function but there is no way of knowing the extent of the damage at this stage so it's impossible to be definitive about recovery. Jimmy will be in hospital for some time.'

Amy then thanks people for the 'hundreds' of cards and good wishes she's received from the public. She's stretching my credibility.

Coincidentally I'm due at my physio's today so I ask her about injuries like Jimmy's.

'In theory he could make a full recovery. He appears to have suffered significant damage to the frontal lobe of his brain. That area's concerned with personality and emotion so you can see personality change and even aggressive behaviour after an injury like that. If he also suffered damage to his temporal lobe he'll experience both expressive and receptive dysphasia.'

She sees my blank look and explains, 'It means he's unable to give meaning to anything people say and can't articulate what he wants to say; which is really frustrating for any patient.

'The spinal fractures alone will involve a hospital stay of at least six weeks but the head injury could involve rehab for three to six months, possibly more. It may take years to know the extent of recovery.'

How ironic! Jimmy didn't want to meet me when he thought I was in a wheelchair. Now he'll be in one, possibly for the rest of his life. Then I feel guilty; not even a sleazebag deserves that. And his son certainly doesn't deserve to, in effect, lose his father. I'm so preoccupied with his gloomy prognosis that I don't initially hear the physio tell me I'm discharged.

'Molly, aren't you pleased? You've made a really good recovery; you don't need that stick anymore. You can take that dog of yours for walks every day.'

I apologise. This is great news. I can now move from being an armchair detective and get out into the field.

PART II

DECEMBER 2011 – APRIL 2012

CHAPTER 15

Before I start making the most of my new found freedom I realise from Carli's blog that the final of Star Search is on this weekend. I can't watch it live here in the UK but I'll watch the pod cast on my PC as soon as it's available.

On Monday Carli's blog records her account of the final. Interesting reading and very detailed. It seems too literate for someone who dropped out of school so perhaps the PR people helped her.

'I hear my name called. I take a deep breath, clutch my microphone and pray that I won't trip walking down the stairs onto the main stage. This is the Final and I'm singing my own song against the advice of my mentor. I've also changed my entire look. My hairdresser Kevin wasn't pleased when I told him I wanted to go back to my original colour and abandon the hair extensions. The papers printed rubbish about me sacking my stylist. I didn't; she went on maternity leave but her replacement hasn't been listening to me. I explained that I was singing my own song about losing Tommy and there'd be a backdrop of pictures of him and I didn't want to look like an over-made up half-naked member of a crap girl band.

So I'm wearing a simple cream dress just above the knees with my naturally fair hair hanging softly just below my shoulders. My make-up is understated and I let them spray me lightly so I don't look white, but not as if I'm just back from baking myself in Ibiza.

I've had so much post this week. Most of it supportive including good luck cards from my old foster parents and a teddy from Deirdre. I couldn't believe it. Some hate mail too but very little really.

My fans are chanting Carli, Carli and I can't start for a minute or two.

I look to the right and see the huge poster of Tommy. I hold back a tear. I nod at the guitarist telling him to start the opening bars of **One Mistake** *my own song.*

Should one mistake

Be all it takes

To wreck a life?

I was wrong

Yes I was wrong

But to lose my son

For what I've done

Is so hard to bear

And just not fair

I know I was wrong

So very wrong

But at the time I thought it would work out fine

But someone took my boy

They took my lovely boy

Where is he now?

With a new mum?

I made a mistake. Just one mistake. I'm only young.

Tommy I love you. Please forgive me.

Don't let one mistake keep us apart.

After singing the last line I break down. I don't mean to. The Carli haters online will say I did it deliberately. The presenter comes out and leads me to the judges' table. The audience is on its feet cheering. The two women judges are crying and the two men look as though they're about to. It's unbelievable. The noise from the audience gives the judges a chance to compose themselves.

*Judge Suzy, a former girl band member, dabbing her eyes says 'Babe, you **are** amazing, you moved the entire audience... you deserved that standing ovation.'*

Judge Charlie, a top manager, says he's backed me from the start (not true) because he knows a star when he sees one.

Judge Jenny, a successful solo singer, says my bravery in continuing in the competition has always amazed her and that I've put my soul into the song and win or lose tonight it'll be a No.1.

Finally Rory, Chairman of the judges, who I've had some arguments with, says it was the performance of the evening. But then he totally surprises me, he makes an appeal to the kidnapper or to anyone who has information, to come forward and says he's personally putting up a reward of €100,000. Now he's a wealthy bastard. He was in a band for years with more No.1 hits than I can count. According to the press he's invested the cash well. But it's still brilliant that he's doing this when we don't really hit it off.

I start crying again and hug him. The audience is still noisy. I almost feel sorry for the next finalist.

Back in the studio the last contestant has sung and all of us finalists come on stage, smiling nervously and waving to the audience. The presenter repeats that it's now all down to the audience at home and gives out the numbers to ring again.

Behind us are videos showing us at home with our families. Well not in my case. They had a problem with me, with dead parents, no known relatives and most of all with a kidnapped child. So they did some filming with me in the rehabilitation place with Dave. He looks better now that the bruises have almost gone but he needs regular physio on his broken leg. The men who attacked him broke it in two places. We talked to camera about how we're trying to work things out and how we believe that Tommy will be found one day.

A final wave and we leave the stage. We'll know tomorrow which of us gets the recording contract. I'm not really worried. Padraig who's now my agent as well as my solicitor says he's getting lots of inquiries about me, and win or lose, I'm made. I know that some people who didn't win have done better than those who did. Like One Direction; they were only third in X Factor and Simon Cowell signed them up for a £2 million record deal.

Surprisingly I sleep soundly, I suppose because my emotional performance took it out of me. And I enjoy a big breakfast in the hotel where we're all staying. It's going to be a busy day with rehearsals. We have to sing again as lines don't close until 8.30 pm so they make even more money.

The day flies by and almost before I know it, I step out on stage with the other finalists. Tonight I'm wearing the Waterford colours; a draped blue blouse with white palazzo trousers. Like last night I've gone for a simple look and I know that the papers today have been commenting on my new look, generally favourably, though some tweeters are saying it's to get the granny vote. Tonight I'm singing another of my own songs and we all have to sing the one we have to record if we win. I don't like it but I have to do what I can with it.

* *

My songs are over and we wait back stage while they play edited versions of our performances. The presenter keeps telling the viewers how close it is and that their vote could make a difference. I doubt it, but who really knows? I'm not the bookies favourite but when I started I was the rank outsider and now I'm about 6/1 I think. I just want it to be over. Dave has just texted me and I'm wondering if we'll get back together. He insists Tommy is still alive and I want to believe that.

We are called. We troop onstage, trying to look as if we all love each other. I don't mind any of them to be honest. They're just like me. This is their chance to get a life.

The presenter announces there's been a record vote and that he has the results and he's going to announce the first three but in reverse order. I know that second and third means a holiday and some cash but the real prize is the recording contract and representing Ireland in the Eurovision next year.

The third prize winner goes to the rapper from Cork. He looks disappointed. The second prize goes to the boy band from Finglas.

The drums roll. The presenter says, and the winner is.........................

At first I don't believe it's my name. I can't move. Then some of the other contestants push me forward. Oh my God......'

**

It'll be interesting to see how the pod cast compares with her blog. I settle myself down with Pedro at my feet and a cup of coffee, then press start.

Carli looks so different. As she said in her blog she changed her look and ignored the stylist. There's something familiar about her but I can't put my finger on it. I like the new look as she's a really naturally pretty girl but you didn't see that with the old look, or old looks to be more precise. You never knew what colour her hair was going to be. Her performance is really emotional and I feel a tear starting. She even made the crap song she had to sing on the second day sound classy. Yes, she deserved to win.

And will that reward the judge offered lead to a breakthrough? I hope so. It's bugging me that I can't think who she reminds me of. Maybe it'll come to me in the middle of the night. That's the way I usually remember things that initially elude me. But inspiration doesn't come and I lie awake most of the night annoyed with myself for obsessing over it.

CHAPTER 16

It's time for action. I put my stick in the back of my wardrobe alongside the redundant crutches that I had to use when I made my tentative move from the wheelchair. A trip to Waterford is overdue. Aunt Bernie has been on the phone about Carli's victory.

'We're so proud of her here. Apparently they had hundreds of calls after the show to the Hotline; the gardai couldn't cope.'

I point out that while callers will be well meaning the chances of a breakthrough are slim particularly as Tommy will have changed a lot in the four months he's been missing.

'You know Frances next door, she works in the canteen in the garda station. She told me they've had a lot of tip-offs about the traveller camp. Dave Nevin's from a settled traveller family. Frances reckons it'd be an ideal place to hide a child but says they're too afraid go in.'

'Why would the gardai be afraid of going in?'

'Frances says it's all about political correctness; they don't want to be accused of racism if they don't find him.'

'Look,' I say trying to sound tactful, 'maybe she's exaggerating. I'm sure they'd act if they had serious tips. I mean this is about a missing child not a missing bike.'

Bernie agrees Frances does tend to exaggerate so we move on to family matters. Putting down the telephone I return to my *to do* list. At the top is Alro. He hasn't posted for a while. I send him a private message and I get a reply later in the day.

'Yeah, like I said before, rumours about the traveller camp and PC reasons why nothing might happen. Carli's friend Emer did not tell the truth. She claimed an emergency to do with her mother stopped her collecting Tommy but Waterford Regional Hospital deny that. Mrs Flynn was booked into outpatients that day but they're not aware of any crisis with her. Now they say that as it was August they had agency temporary staff in so they can't say for sure that none of them phoned Emer about her mother. Apparently after a second interview Emer changed her story a bit. She claims she was told they couldn't justify an ambulance to bring her mother home. She was apparently feeling groggy after an outpatient procedure. What she initially said was that there was such an emergency that she had to drop everything and go to her mother. The gardai were led to believe Mrs Flynn was actually in the hospital. Now she admits her mother was in the Outpatients Department and could be monitored, meaning there was no panic to collect her. Emer could have helped Carli out and then picked up her mother.'

Mm. I wonder did Carli phase her out of her life to some extent after she moved in with Dave? And did she use her with Tommy? A free babysitter whenever she needed one? Could she even fancy Dave even though she claims to be suspicious of him? All questions I can't put to her by email but when I meet her I can suss this out.

I suspect the most likely explanation is that she did get a call from the Hospital, or it could have been from her mother looking for collection, and she decided to put her mother first even though it wasn't an emergency. She was probably a bit annoyed getting asked at the last minute to help Carli given she could have been asked in the first place. Maybe resentment had been building up over being used? And she would have presumed Carli would get her message and bring Tommy into the hairdressers even though she didn't want to. The salon couldn't have refused in the circumstances.

I email Alro.

'*The traveller camp makes sense if Carli and Dave are in this together. Tommy reappears when they can't milk the 'abduction story' anymore. Now that Carli's won the competition the money should start rolling in. So I wonder if Tommy will turn up in time for Christmas. I can imagine her PR people writing the headline 'Carli's Christmas present...'*'

He responds:

'*Maybe he'll turn up in a crib inside her local church?*'

Alro is being very communicative. I ask what he knows about the attack on Dave.

'*He got a terrible beating . Might have a limp after the way they broke his leg. Two men arrested but they've said nothing useful about this case. Dave says he can't identify them; but I hear the gardai have enough evidence to convict without him. A patrol car picked them up later with a baseball bat which had Dave's blood on it. They were as high as kites; had stayed out looking for more entertainment. No drugs found on them but they can be put away for a good while for the attack.*'

**

Two days later an Irish paper headline reads:

Broken Promises to Traveller Families causes Heartbreak before Christmas.

Aunt Bernie and Alro had been correct about the traveller tip-offs. The gardai had visited the Ballybeg camp in Waterford and found nothing. Social workers also went along and allegedly promised some items for families but what a ridiculous headline!

How could they already have broken promises if the visit was only a few days before the article appeared?

Another article was quite amusing. It said that one old traveller woman claimed to be psychic and told the gardai that Tommy was alive, living in the sun and didn't want to come back to his mother. How can a 15 month old child have an opinion anyway? Should I talk to this psychic on my trip to Waterford? Maybe she could tell me something positive about my future. I chuckle to myself. And a long letter to the Editor appears in one paper from the Travellers Rights people complaining about the gardai's visit.

I quote, '*It was totally wrong of the gardai to respond to an anonymous tip-off claiming that the missing baby Tommy Walsh was there. That tip-off was obviously motivated by racism and prejudice. They didn't find anything. It's quite ridiculous to think that a missing settled child would be in a traveller camp.*'

Another paper headlines the garda visit as a 'raid'. Over the top but that's the media for you. They called there and asked questions. That's not a raid. The headline was pure drivel.

But at least the paper gave the gardai a chance to respond.

'*A garda spokesman explained that there had been a number of calls about the camp, not all of them anonymous, and those calls together with other information in the gardai's possession meant it was a lead that had to be followed up. The spokesman added that the gardai were still following up the hundreds of calls following the appeal made on the Star Search final.*'

And Babydoc starts posting again

Missing Children Forum Portal Home Register Log In	 every child matters
December 10 2011 at 1.03 pm Think we need to give more consideration to Amy's past.	Babydoc Posts: 2 Join Date: 4.11.2011 Location: Emergency Ward 10
December 10 2011 at 1.13 pm You mean, people she dealt with in business?	Declan Posts: 317 Join Date: 2.4.2011 Location: Dublin

December 10 2011 at 1.46 pm Police are following up that surely, and Jimmy's ex clients. Some fights in the past I gather.	Sherlock Posts: 102 Join Date: 29.6.2011 Location: Baker Street
December 10 2011 at 3.17 pm And do you think we should look into Carli's past too?	Pam Posts: 5 Join Date: 27.11.2011 Location: York
December 10 2011 at 3.57 pm Come on Pam, Carli's only 19. Amy's close to 40, maybe there is something there. Tell us more, Babydoc.	Jenny Posts: 68 Join Date: 5.5.2011 Location: Slough

December 10 2011 at 4.19 pm I can't say anything specific, I just have a feeling the answer lies in the past in Amy's case, and I think Rose is alive.	Babydoc Posts: 3 Join Date: 4.11.2011 Location: Emergency Ward 10
December 10 2011 at 5.04 pm Are you psychic or something?	CoolDude Posts: 19 Join Date: 4.7.2011 Location: Bahamas
December 10 2011 at 6.03 pm Just saying what my intuition tells me.	Babydoc Posts: 4 Join Date: 4.11.2011 Location: Emergency Ward 10

December 10 2011 at 6.44 pm I believe in following your instincts. It's always worked for me.	Miss Marple Posts: 38 Join Date: 10.9.2011 Location: St Mary Mead

CoolDude's sarcasm doesn't annoy Babydoc. Since Babydoc correctly spotted my need for help from the emails we were exchanging about the cases, we've talked on the phone about my situation. She's a gynaecologist and has given me hope that I might be able to have a child some day though as she says, she hasn't examined me and can only go on the information I've provided. Anyway the members move on to psychics generally.

December 11 2011 at 7.16 am That old woman in the traveller camp said Tommy was alive and living in the sun. He can't be in Ireland if he's living in the sun.	Columbo Posts: 82 Join Date: 6.3.2011 Location: New York

December 11 2011 at 7.38 am Very funny Columbo	Declan Posts: 318 Join Date: 2.4.2011 Location: Dublin
December 11 2011 at 8.18 am 'In the sun' – could be anywhere! Australia, India, Brazil........Can't you just see the kidnapper taking a baby everyone was looking for on a plane to any of those places?	CoolDude Posts: 20 Join Date: 4.7.2011 Location: Bahamas
December 11 2011 at 9.05 am Does anyone watch that programme on late on TV3 Psychics Live?	Columbo Posts: 83 Join Date: 6.3.2011 Location: New York

December 11 2011 at 11.03 am	Declan
Occasionally flick channels to get a laugh from it. It's a money making racket. Keeping vulnerable people on premium rate phone lines.	Posts: 319 Join Date: 2.4.2011 Location: Dublin

Life doesn't get any better for Amy Blake. Jimmy's still alive but it's not looking good for him having much quality of life. And the rumours about the crash must be adding to Amy's stress. She's aged ten years in the pictures taken after the accident.

One neighbour apparently said *'Jimmy knew that road well and was an experienced driver. He was driving his BMW which is a good solid car. I don't believe the rumours that he'd been drinking.'*

However another neighbour insisted *'Jimmy was devastated by Rose going like that. He worshipped her. He's been fighting with Amy. He blamed her. The child's been gone for three months; the police have got nowhere and I think he'd given up hope. He does like a drink and with all that stress maybe he had one too many.'*

But for Carli Walsh, life is looking up. She won the Irish talent competition. She easily could have opted out when baby Tommy went missing. In a way, I admire her tenacity but then in another way I can't understand how she could have continued with him missing. With a record number voting, Carli received 61% of the vote. As the winner she gets a recording contract, a cheque for €100,000 and will be Ireland's entry in the 2012 Eurovision Song contest.

As her local paper said:

'She has been criticised for going ahead with the competition, while others have called for her to be prosecuted for child neglect. Her hair and outfits have been either slated or praised to the skies. But nobody denies her raw talent and the great career that lies ahead of her.

Can Carli end Ireland's Eurovision drought and woo the Eastern European voting bloc?

For all the exciting prospects that lie ahead for her in the New Year, Carli's son Tommy has now been missing for over four months. As she faces Christmas without him, our readers will no doubt be thinking of this young woman.'

Coming up to Christmas, Carol Jennings did interviews with both mothers. I used to like her work but I think she's lost her critical faculties.

National Independent December 17, 2011

Saturday Review - No Christmas Joy for Missing Baby Mums

'Two months ago I met Amy Blake whose daughter Rose went missing after she was left home alone after a childminding mix-up. Since I met with Amy further tragedy has befallen her. Her son's beloved dog Sammy was poisoned by vile people as 'revenge' for what she did, and her husband Jimmy was severely injured in a car crash. And vile people have been at work again, claiming that Jimmy's car crash was not an accident.

I'm using the word 'vile' deliberately because that is what these anonymous people on the internet are.

Amy is a private person and rarely gives interviews but in a long telephone conversation this week she told me that Jimmy will be home for Christmas though needing a live-in nurse for a while and probably facing further surgery. She told me how she's going back to work in the New Year but not to her former law practice but to manage Jimmy's accountancy practice until he can return. She told me 'People think we're rich. We're not. We've a mortgage like anyone else. There's the staff to pay in his business. And we've spent money on our own search for Rose.'

I've also met tragic Irish mum Carli Walsh. When Carli's son Tommy was snatched from her car over four months ago, she was unknown except in the pub in Waterford where she sang two nights a week. Now tipped to have the Christmas No.1 everyone knows her. Like Amy Blake, Carli has been heavily criticised both for the mistake she made that resulted in her baby being taken and for her actions afterwards.

How could she go on stage the next day and win the Waterford final people have asked? But we all react to tragedy in different ways. She chose to go on and leave the police to do their job. What is so wrong with that? Amy tells me some local people are criticising her for returning to work to run her husband's business. But what choice does she have if she wants to keep a roof over her family's head? Jimmy Blake will probably never work again. If he had been killed in the car crash she'd have had a substantial life insurance payout but as a very sick man there's only a modest payment from a health policy.

Both mothers face a very sad Christmas. Carli tells me she often thinks about Amy and hopes to meet her one day.

It's time those self-righteous people who post poison online about these two mothers stop. They made a mistake for which they have paid dearly. Christmas is the season of goodwill. I suggest a prayer for their missing children and a card of good wishes is better than another internet rant.

In the words of Carli's no.1 song 'Should one mistake be all it takes to wreck a life?'

So I'm a 'vile' person. She's entitled to her opinion I suppose.

But then Carli's good fortune changes. On December 19 the media reports:

Solicitor Missing with Carli's Cash

'Following a Law Society inspection the gardai were called to the offices of Waterford solicitor Padraig Mahoney. It is understood that there is a substantial deficit on his clients' account. Mr Mahoney's most high profile client is singer songwriter Carli Walsh, currently at No.1 in the UK charts.

A Law Society spokesman confirmed that another client had raised concerns with them and an inspection had revealed 'irregularities.'

The gardai want to question Mr Mahoney but his office says he is out of the country enjoying a Christmas break.

While there was criticism of Ms Walsh's conduct in the disappearance of her son, members of the public contributed generously to help fund the search for him. It is understood that Mr Mahoney may have handled these donations, many of which were in cash. He received on Carli's behalf the cheque that was part of her winnings from the Star Search contest she won earlier this month.

Both the gardai and the The Law Society refused to comment.

Carli faces an even bleaker Christmas with both her son Tommy and her money gone.'

Not exactly the Christmas present you'd wish for, having your money stolen by a dodgy solicitor. I'm not that sorry for Carli to be honest. I'd be more concerned about the other clients he robbed.

CHAPTER 17

The Forum is very active in the week before Christmas and I'm getting flak. One of my critics, Paul12, is a new member, which makes me suspicious. Has he an agenda or just someone with nothing better to do? Christmas can bring out the worst in people.

Missing Children Forum	
Portal Home Register Log In	every child matters
December 20 2011 at 6.27 pm	Paul12
I've been watching this Forum for a while and I'm becoming very uncomfortable with some of the material being posted which is why I've decided to start posting. This used to be a place where you could come to sympathise with victims and express your feelings. Lately it seems like we're ripping the victims apart, it's uncalled for. It seems to have become worse since Miss Marple started posting. Maybe she's a troll winding us up?	Posts: 1 Join Date: 15.11.2011 Location: Leeds

December 20 2011 at 6.38 pm I have to agree, Paul12. There are all kinds of unsubstantiated allegations here. Accusing the victims, attacking their good names, even looking for links between them when there quite obviously couldn't be. When is this going to stop? It's going too far.	CoolDude Posts: 21 Join date: 4.7.2011 Location: Bahamas
December 20 2011 at 6.43 pm Wow, guys, do you think that's fair comment? There are 3 things that I care passionately about. 1. A parent is responsible for the safety of their child. If their actions place their child in danger then they should be held to account. 2. Having neglected their child the parent should not be in a position to gain financially. (Remember Shannon Matthews). 3. If a child is missing then it's up to the whole community to help find the child, not just the police and the parents. (remember Jaycee Lee Dugard)	Miss Marple Posts: 39 Join Date: 10.9.2011 Location: St Mary Mead

December 20 2011 at 6.52 pm Paul12, what if the answers are right here and we refuse to see them because we're just too nice? We can't cope with the fact that the mothers may be involved? You can't make an omelette without breaking eggs. Lots of theories have been raised here like the Chinese Au Pair and the Traveller connection. We still don't know if the au pair was involved though the travellers seem to be out of it.	Fairplay Posts: 58 Join Date: 5.5.2011 Location: Ireland
December 20 2011 at 7.17 pm So are you saying that we're now armchair detectives?	Paul12 Posts: 2 Join Date: 15.11.2011 Location: Leeds
December 20 2011 at 7.21 pm We're no different to the people in the street who meet and discuss possibilities, everyone does it. It's a good place to share information and discuss possibilities no matter how unlikely. What if it leads to the safe return of the babies?	Columbo Posts: 84 Join Date: 6.3.2011 Location: New York

December 20 2011 at 7.59 pm	Declan
Guys, the traveller camp rumour has been rampant in Waterford for months. The Gardai and social services had no choice but to check it out, we're talking about a missing child. It's a win/win situation, don't you get it. So now the traveller community are known to be innocent. It's a pity that the Gardai got attacked for doing it.	Posts: 320 Join Date: 2.4.2011 Location: Dublin
December 20 2011 at 8.09 pm	Fairplay
Carli won the Irish Final, she was amazing. But realistically her odds at the start were abysmal; the question had to be asked. Let's not take the win from her, she worked hard and deserved it. But would she have won if Tommy hadn't gone missing? I guess we'll never know the answer. But I think in fairness that's all Miss Marple is trying to say.	Posts: 59 Join Date: 5.5.2011 Location: Ireland
December 20 2011 at 8.18 pm	CoolDude
I think part of Paul12's problem and mine too is that Miss Marple's trying to create a link between the two cases. To me it's ludicrous, they're worlds apart.	Posts: 22 Join date: 4.7.2011 Location: Bahama

December 20 2011 at 8.27 pm And yet the newspapers tell us that Carli wants to meet Amy. I wonder why.	Noelle Posts: 8 Join Date: 3.10.2011 Location: Bradford
December 20 2011 at 8.36 pm It'd be unnatural if they didn't want to meet up if you think about it. Both have lost a child, must feel dreadfully guilty, partners in hospital, slated by the press and the people, so much in common. Yet very different at the same time.	Suzy Posts: 72 Join Date: 27.2.2011 Location: Bath
December 20 2011 at 8.49 pm I just can't explain it fully but my instincts tell me there is a connection between both cases. I've said it before and I agree it sounds unlikely, but I trust my instincts.	Miss Marple Posts: 40 Join Date: 10.9.2011 Location: St Mary Mead

December 20 2011 at 9.01 pm Hi all, I've been following your posts with great interest. Miss Marple, keep the faith, don't forget we're still entitled to freedom of speech and exchange of ideas. I see life returns to normal in Accrington, Amy's going back to work but in Jimmy's accountancy business and Jimmy's coming home to be nursed.	Noelle Posts: 9 Join Date: 3.10.2011 Location: Bradford
December 20 2011 at 9.13 pm Makes me wonder exactly why a good solicitor would wish to run an accountancy firm.	Mags Posts: 360 Join Date: 2.9.2010 Location: Liverpool
December 20 2011 at 9.25 pm It sounds very logical to me; she had already put her professional life on hold, what's wrong with helping your husband through a difficult time? Not much good if he recovers and has to build up his business again from scratch. As she says, it pays the bills.	Taxpayer Posts: 204 Join Date: 22.11.2010 Location: London

December 20 2011 at 9.37 pm After Jimmy's shenanigans I'd be inclined to run it into the ground	Sherlock Posts: 103 Join Date: 29.6.2011 Location: Baker Street
December 20 2011 at 9.52 pm Sherlock, what do you say we'll bury the hatchet for these two families for Xmas, they've been through enough. A very thought provoking piece in the Saturday Review by Carol Jennings. Miss Marple, I suppose you won't like it though?	Paul12 Posts: 3 Join Date: 15.11.2011 Location: Leeds
December 20 2011 at 9.59 pm Yes, it looks like Jimmy has a long way to go yet. Fair play to Amy for standing by him.	Liam Posts: 21 Join Date: 2.8.2011 Location: Belfast

December 20 2011 at 10.06 pm A bleak Christmas for all. And now it looks like Carli's solicitor has run off with Tommy's fund (if there ever was one? What the media says what she blogs isn't always consistent!) and Carli's winnings too.	Declan Posts: 321 Join Date: 2.4.2011 Location: Dublin
December 20 2011 at 10.29 pm That solicitor stitched her up right from the start. Claiming to be her friend when she was vulnerable, looking out for a lucrative libel payout, a Fund for Tommy and her recording earnings. The bastard!	Fairplay Posts: 60 Join Date: 5.5.2011 Location: Ireland
December 20 2011 at 10.32 pm Welcome to the Forum, Noelle and thanks for your kind words. Does anyone know if the Gardai checked Padraig Mahoney out? Talk about motive.	Miss Marple Posts: 41 Join Date: 10.9.2011 Location: St Mary Mead

December 21 2011 at 1.59 am I've just been reading through the article, seems libellous. No proof he ran off with Carli's money. The investigation is about another client's account. It is suspicious though that he can't be contacted.	LegalEagle Posts: 1 Join Date 20.12.2011 Location: Law Library
December 21 2011 at 2.33 am You're working late Mr LegalEagle. Maybe you're in a different time zone like me? I agree, that paper could be in trouble for that piece. Padraig will never be able to work as a solicitor again if it's true. Where could he hide?	Columbo Posts: 85 Join Date: 6.3.2011 Location: New York
December 21 2011 at 2.57 am Maybe he's in the traveller camp too!	Paul12 Posts: 4 Join Date: 15.11.2011 Location: Leeds

December 21 2011 at 7.59am The word on the street is it's about bookies & loan sharks. The same loan shark that put Dave in hospital.	Declan Posts: 322 Join Date: 2.4.2011 Location: Dublin
December 21 2011 at 8.33 am Simple, he bleeds some accounts dry and heads for sunny south America, buys a business and lives happily ever after.	Mags Posts: 361 Join Date: 2.9.2010 Location: Liverpool
December 21 2011 at 9.02 am So all the time that people were saying Dave was a drug dealer he was actually trying to support Carli & Tommy on money borrowed from a loan shark?	Miss Marple Posts: 42 Join Date: 10.9.2011 Location: St Mary Mead

December 21 2011 at 10.06 am And the questionable people that Carli mentioned in an interview I heard on the radio hanging around were the debt collectors?	Fairplay Posts: 61 Join Date: 5.5.2011 Location: Ireland
December 21 2011 at 10.19 am Wow, poor Dave, then he gets accused of kidnapping & hiding Tommy. All the time he's just trying to support his family.	Pam Posts: 6 27.11.2011 Location: York
December 21 2011 at 10.27 am They're all saying that Carli is broke again. She's keeping a very low profile. Why wouldn't she? It's a rotten end to her year.	Declan Posts: 323 Join Date: 2.4.2011 Location: Dublin

December 21 2011 at 12.03 pm You should hear some of the stories that've been bandied around here. Like Amy tampered with Jimmy's car, a certain woman kidnapped Rose, an ex bf of Amy tried to kill Jimmy, an ex client tried to kill Jimmy, Jimmy's been drinking, it's endless.	Liam Posts: 22 Join Date: 2.8.2011 Location: Belfast
December 21 2011 at 2.34 pm It should be interesting to see what comes back from forensics. I think Davina has enough on her plate trying to save her current marriage. Why would she kidnap her lover's child? Amy Blake had no affairs. To me it leaves just two possibilities, driver error or client revenge. Using the same logic as the Waterford case, why would an abductor try to kill Jimmy, surely it would lead the police right to their door. Unconnected I think.	Fairplay Posts: 62 Join Date: 5.5.2011 Location: Ireland
December 23 2011 at 3.33 pm Here are the results of my online poll, what do you think? The question was: Who is responsible for the disappearance of Tommy & Rose:	Miss Marple Posts: 43 Join Date: 10.9.2011 Location: St Mary Mead

Waterford Suspects:	Accrington Suspects:	
• Carli (21%) • Dave (9%) • Burka Tranny (14%) • Older woman seen by car 4% • Man in car in side street who may or may not have been with the older woman (2%) • Solicitor (28%) • Passing opportunist stranger (22%)	• Jimmy (16%) • Amy (24%) • Au Pair (19%) • Supermarket Man (14%) • Poodle Woman (6%) • Passing Stranger (10%) • House Viewer (11%)	
December 23 2011 at 4.05 pm Wow, interesting stats. It's not surprising in the Waterford case that the vote for the solicitor is quite high at this point. He's a close second, only 2% behind Carli and Dave added together, and passing stranger is third. What's interesting I think is the older woman seen by the car who never came forward and the younger man sitting in a car only get 6% between them.	Taxpayer Posts: 205 Join Date: 22.11.2010 Location: London	

December 23 2011 at 4.16 pm	Declan
Probably people feel that the older woman was a tourist who never knew anything about a kidnapping. People doubt the relevance of this sighting because it came in so late and nobody other than the woman who reported it can confirm it.	Posts: 324 Join Date: 2.4.2011 Location: Dublin
December 23 2011 at 4.46 pm	Fairplay
I understand the logic of what you're saying Declan but obviously the detective in charge took it very seriously. He organised photo fits of the two of them and held a press conference. Though the photo fits could really be anybody...	Posts: 63 Join Date: 5.5.2011 Location: Ireland
December 23 2011 at 5.16 pm	Pam
I know the parents are obviously the first suspects but I'm really surprised at how high they both rate, very interesting. Why would either of them kidnap their own child, where could they hide her, what's the motive?	Posts: 7 Join Date: 27.11.2011 Location: York

December 23 2011 at 5.51 pm In Jimmy's case, marriage difficulties, something that began innocently enough and spiralled into something he couldn't get out of?	Mags Posts: 362 Join Date: 2.9.2010 Location: Liverpool
December 23 2011 at 6.30 pm 24% blame Amy; we're obviously back to the theory of accidental death here. It's quite high. Why do we think that Amy murdered Rose whereas Carli didn't murder Tommy?	Paul12 Posts: 5 Join Date: 15.11.2011 Location: Leeds
December 23 2011 at 7.11 pm Because Dave probably would have had to have been in on it whereas Jimmy wouldn't. He was in the States. If something happened to Rose it gave Amy loads of time to hide the body and fake the abduction.	Columbo Posts: 86 Join Date: 6.3.2011 Location: New York

December 23 2011 at 7.18 pm So are you saying that Amy also phoned in the bomb warning? Be careful what you're implying!	LegalEagle Posts: 2 Join Date 20.12.2011 Location: Law Library
December 23 2011 at 7.53 pm It's immaterial, all she had to do was make sure Teresa didn't enter Rose's empty room before she left, then she was in the clear.	Noelle Posts: 10 Join Date: 3.10.2011 Location: Bradford
December 23 2011 at 7.59 pm If you think about it, she's not the main suspect; Supermarket man is the main suspect as far as I'm concerned.	Fairplay Posts: 64 Join Date: 5.5.2011 Location: Ireland

December 23 2011 at 8.03 pm Supermarket man and the house viewer the police couldn't contact combined are 1% ahead of Amy in the Poll. Can't understand why they polled so high. Is it because people can't bear to think a parent could be involved?	Columbo Posts: 87 Join Date: 6.3.2011 Location: New York
December 23 2011 at 8.11 pm Can anyone answer this one, have sniffer dogs checked out both homes and cars?	Miss Marple Posts: 44 Join Date: 10.9.2011 Location: St Mary Mead
December 23 2011 at 8.26 pm Interesting, poodle woman only scores 6%	Pam Posts: 8 Join Date: 27.11.2011 Location: York

December 23 2011 at 8.57 pm LOL she was guilty of sinning but not guilty as sin. I think Poodle woman is Davina who was on the receiving end of Jimmy's belongings	Liam Posts: 23 Join Date: 2.8.2011 Location: Belfast
December 23 2011 at 9.12 pm In Waterford the man in car & passing stranger make up 24% of suspects. In Accrington supermarket man, house viewer and passing stranger make up 35% of suspects. Photofit man is low in the rankings because only one witness. Could they all be the same person? The descriptions in as far as we have any are not dissimilar.	Miss Marple Posts: 45 Join Date: 10.9.2011 Location: St Mary Mead
December 23 2011 at 9.17 pm It's a bit of a lame point, Miss Marple. You can manipulate statistics to make any point really.	Taxpayer Posts: 206 Join Date: 22.11.2010 Location: London

December 23 2011 at 9.26 pm Miss Marple, I think you're on the Xmas drink and it's still two days to go. Come to think of it I wonder if drink is your problem? They're all the same person! You're just obsessed with finding a link.	Paul12 Posts: 6 Join Date: 15.11.2011 Location: Leeds
December 23 2011 at 9.58 pm Many thanks everyone for stimulating conversation and intriguing ideas. Wishing you all a happy Xmas.	Miss Marple Posts: 46 Join Date: 10.9.2011 Location: St Mary Mead

Wow. A difficult time but some people like my ideas. Wonder if the members supportive of the mothers are genuine? Could they be their family or friends?

That was a nasty comment from Paul12. I've a drink problem! But Christmas is meant to be the season of goodwill and I'll forgive him for that and his other mean comments.

CHAPTER 18

The online and telephone counselling from Babydoc has been helping me to feel more in control of my life and now that I'm mobile again I'm considering going away for a New Year's break. I had almost put down the phone on my sister when she said it would be an opportunity to meet some new people.

'Nobody can replace Jeff,' I had snarled; then I backed down because all she was saying was that there comes a time to move on. Babydoc has been giving me similar advice.

Babydoc's parents live in Wexford and she'd told me she normally comes home to Ireland for Christmas. I don't know how much leave she can take but it would be great to meet up with her at New Year and also do some research in Waterford. It's only about 60 kilometres from Wexford to Waterford so it wouldn't be far for her to travel to meet up with me.

I text Babydoc – *'wld u b interested in New Year hotel break in Waterford for a couple of days.'*

Ten minutes later she texts: *'So you listened to what I said. I'm on. Book me 3 nights Dec 30, 31 and Jan 1. Wish I cld stay longer but on duty Jan 2.'*

I spring into action. I call on my neighbours; they are happy to look after Pedro. He'll be so spoilt. A few phone calls later and I've got the last two single rooms in the Clonee Strand Hotel in Dungarvan for the New Year. I did plan to book somewhere in Waterford; then I remember previous holidays in Dungarvan which isn't far away and change my mind.

It's my first Christmas and New Year alone since Jeff died and usually I love this time of year. We'd visit both sets of parents on Boxing Day and there'd be lots of invitations and catching up with friends in the week after Christmas. But when you're no longer part of a couple the post Christmas catch up week could be dreadful.

My parents want me to spend Christmas Day with them but I can't face it. I just want to be on my own that day. I mightn't even get dressed. My sister is still fussing about my obsession with the missing babies and she doesn't know the half of it! She's asked me for Christmas as well but I've turned her down too. She's expecting her first baby and it'll be her last Christmas with her husband before life totally changes. I feel she's embarrassed about her own happy situation given what happened to me, and I suspect she's glad I rejected her invitation.

Pedro has helped me survive this dreadful year. When I got back from medical appointments I looked forward to the welcome I always received from him. Dogs can tell when their owner is coming. I'd hear him barking before I even opened the front gate. Unconditional love is wonderful.

I know South East Ireland quite well thanks to Aunt Bernie. When I was younger I used to spend summers in Dungarvan which has beautiful beaches; there's something special about this part of Ireland. Bernie has asked me to stay with her but her house'll be crowded with my cousins home for the Christmas so I decline her invitation too. I've told Bernie I need some time to myself, but I'll be in and out to see them all. Now that Babydoc is coming too, Bernie will stop trying to persuade me to stay with her.

I tell Bernie I intend to pamper myself in the hotel's spa and leisure centre which is true. But another plan, which I don't mention to my aunt, is my intention to pump her for her local knowledge and to get my hair done in the hairdressers Carli was in when Tommy vanished.

**

Pedro and I survive Christmas. I consider going to the carol service at the local church but decide against it and stay in my pyjamas all day. I ring my parents and my sister and exchange Christmas pleasantries. I assure them I'm fine and looking forward to a relaxing day in front of the TV. Having made the duty phone calls, I switch off my mobile. My PC also gets a day off. I hear my neighbours knock late morning and I know they are asking me in for a drink but I can't face it. Nice people but not today. My Christmas dinner is a heated ready meal and a bottle of Australian Shiraz. I watch TV with Pedro on my lap; fall asleep for part of the Christmas schedule, wake up feeling mildly drunk then go to bed where I sleep through to 10 o'clock on Boxing Day. I would have slept in longer only Pedro wanted his breakfast and climbed onto my bed.

I'm booked into the hotel on the 30th December so I have four days to continue as yesterday or to do something completely different. I decide on a compromise, a late start but then a purge on the house which has become disorganised over months with a semi-crippled hermit owner and a demanding dog. Clean it is, thanks to Lidia but there's work to be done sorting and mending clothes, dealing with paperwork and going through Jeff's possessions, something I'd obviously put off doing. I think about some serious blogging but keep my resolution to take a few days break from the case.

**

December 30th and I'm feeling better with an organised house. Three black sacks for the charity shop dominate the hall but it's not open again until the New Year. I look good too, having managed to find a hairdresser open yesterday and had my highlights done.

Feeling excited, I board the 13.10 Aer Arann flight at Manchester airport heading for Waterford, the nearest airport to Dungarvan. A bus takes me from there to the hotel, and a late afternoon session in the hotel leisure centre revives me. I feel great and ready to start my fieldwork.

When I arrive in the dining room feeling glamorous in the sparkly green top my sister gave me for Christmas, the waiter informs me my friend has already arrived. He escorts me to a corner table where a good looking red-headed woman is sitting. She's more attractive than her Facebook photograph suggests.

'Liz. I'm Molly. Nice to finally meet you.'

I'm dying to discuss the case but for a while we talk about our work, usually a safe topic to break the ice. Liz has a rewarding career as a gynaecologist working in the NHS. She's Irish but she trained as a doctor in London because she couldn't get into an Irish medical school.

She explains, 'You need incredible exam results to get into medical school in Ireland because the number of places for Irish students is limited. They keep places for overseas students because they'll pay huge fees. At least it didn't really cost much more to go to England because there were college fees here until 1997 and they were free in the UK then. And my parents would have had to pay for accommodation anyway as we live in the country.'

She says she comes back to Ireland often but decided to make her career in the UK. She's hearing horror stories about the Irish health service from medical colleagues and feels she's made the right choice location wise. After all this information about her, I have to reciprocate.

When I tell her I'm an IT consultant, she giggles. 'I can just about cope with email. They're trying to make us doctors use them so much more. I can see the potential but I just have a block about it all and I try to delegate that stuff to my assistant.'

I disagree that computers are not her thing.

'Liz, we wouldn't have met if you hadn't joined the Forum and exchanged personal messages with me.'

She has to agree she puts herself down where computers are concerned.

'You might even get addicted to them,' I laugh. I tell her how I left school with good 'A' levels, and got a job in the civil service.

'In those days you could get good jobs easily. I fell in love with computers then but not with the civil service. You served your time, didn't rock any boats and got your increments regardless of how competent you were or weren't. I just got frustrated when I suggested changing things and my manager wasn't interested. So I left. People thought I was mad to give up a permanent job. Then I went to Waterford Institute of Technology and did a degree in computing, and stayed with Aunt Bernie while I did it.'

She asks why I didn't study in the UK.

'I loved Ireland from visiting my aunt there, and as I'd been working for a few years I had money saved and could finance myself. I stayed with my aunt which cost very little. Two of my cousins were studying in Dublin then so their room was available.'

The conversation becomes more personal. Liz explains why she was happy to extend her Christmas stay in Ireland to meet up with me. She split up with her boyfriend in the autumn after a five year relationship and hasn't met anyone new. She wanted a break away from her usual crowd to see the New Year in, a year she hopes will be better for her. So we are both needing some space in order to move on.

By this stage, we've finished our starters and the main course has arrived. Liz fills up my wine glass. We both prefer red which is convenient and I suspect we'll need a second bottle.

We move on to getting over heartbreak. From our earlier conversation it's obvious that work is part of healing process for her. She admits there can be great rewards from her work and says she still gets a thrill when she sees each healthy baby she delivers. Then she realises what she has said and apologises.

'Don't apologise,' I say. 'I'm so much better now than I was earlier in the year. I got really interested in those two babies that went missing in the summer; I'm so angry with the mothers.'

Then I pause as she knows that well. After all she had intuitively known from our online communication that there was a serious issue in my life involving a child.

'I can understand why you felt upset after losing your own son. But those two mothers are grieving too.'

I tell her I don't agree; that neither have shown any real signs of grieving.

'The thing that really gets me in both cases is the decision to leave the child in the first place....'

Liz interrupts me. We've started our second bottle of wine by this stage.

'Molly, I have to tell you. I knew Amy Blake at university. The worst decision she ever made was then.'

'You mean when she broke up with the medical student? I read about that in the papers.'

'Yes, we all thought they were made for one another.'

'Did you know him well?'

'I did. Thought she was so lucky. Peter was devastated after they split. I saw him at a reunion nearly four years ago.'

OMG. Amy's son is called Peter. Out of all the names she could have chosen for her son she chooses that one. Must mean something.

'I presume he's married now?'

'No, he's not. Well, he wasn't then. He's been working all over the world. It was quite a coincidence that he was even there. He just happened to be staying with his parents when the letter about the reunion arrived. The guy who was organising it sent the invites to the old home addresses he had.'

'Are you still in touch with Amy?'

'I lost touch with her after university but I did see her recently.'

'I suppose that was after she was in the news. You wanted to commiserate with her?'

'Well it wasn't exactly to commiserate.'

She hesitates. I fill up her glass.

'The police weren't getting anywhere. There was an implication in the papers that she was involved, I don't mean because she left her daughter alone. I mean the papers were hinting, not all of them, that something happened earlier that she was covering up. I knew she wouldn't do anything like that, and I did have information I thought she should have.'

This must be what she has hinted at on the Forum.

'Go on, so you had an idea to break the case?'

'Well something that ought to be followed up but Amy doesn't agree with me.'

'What was it?'

'Look, this has to be confidential.'

I assure her it will be.

'Well Amy had Peter's baby and she gave it up for adoption. She told him she had an abortion and he believed it. She intended to have one but the counsellor made her realise it wasn't the right thing to do so she had the baby adopted instead. But at the reunion Peter and I were talking and something I said annoyed him and one thing led to another and he guessed what actually happened. I was really upset. I'd promised Amy I'd never tell him. I didn't tell him; he just realised the truth from my silence. I never would have told her but when Rose vanished this year and then when the police couldn't find her I started thinking what if Peter took her...'

This is unbelievable. I try to conceal my excitement.

'But the reunion was a good while ago so why would he have acted only recently...?'

'Yes I know, it's not logical but I think he should be followed up just in case. I left it with Amy. It's her call. She treated him so badly and she doesn't want to have the police down on him. He's probably nothing to do with it. Amy thinks someone in the police is leaking stuff to the media. She's afraid of trusting anyone in case it gets into the papers. So she doesn't believe that any police review of Peter's possible involvement will be confidential and I can see where she's coming from. It wouldn't be fair for his name to be in the papers over this if he's nothing to do with it.'

I ask if she knows anything about Amy's first child.

'All I know is that it was a girl and named Catherine. Amy only had the baby with her for the few days she was in hospital then it went to social services for the adoption. I saw the baby when I visited her. Gorgeous little thing. That was the bad decision she made. She should have kept the baby and Peter.'

We're interrupted by the waiter asking us about dessert. This totally breaks the atmosphere but I've got the information I need. This could solve the baby Rose case and as I'm here until January 6, I'm going to Hair-I-Am to see what I can discover about baby Tommy.

Actually it's good that the waiter came then. We move on to other topics, and finish the second bottle of wine. I don't think she would have told me anymore, and she may not remember how much she told me which would be good.

**

The hotel has a special dinner on New Year's Eve with a band and dancing. Most of the single guests are female which doesn't bother me. I'm not on a manhunt. Liz and I meet in the sauna in the afternoon and chat about harmless things. I want to distance her from that conversation last night. I don't want her telling Amy she let that out. I suppose it's possible that Amy has told the police but Liz is certain that she hasn't.

**

New Year's Day is a brilliant crisp day. Liz and I walk on Ardmore beach and later we take the cliff walk which has a breathtaking view. We talk about changing jobs and I may have persuaded her to give the Irish health service a try. But maybe not. She's leaving first thing in the morning as she has to get back to work or I'd have invited her to join me on a trip to Lismore Castle which was built in 1185 by King John but of course has been added to since then. I've seen it before when I was studying in Waterford but I've heard it's been recently renovated and I'd love to see it again. I'd arranged to borrow my cousin Sandra's car for the day; it's a lovely drive. And I fit in Mount Mellory Abbey run by the Cistercian monks on the slopes of the Knockmeaden Mountains.

I'll be going into Waterford tomorrow for a wash and blow dry with Kevin, hairdresser to 'diva' Carli Walsh. It wasn't easy to get an appointment with him and they charge a supplement for him now even though he's not the owner. Of course he hasn't been there much because as the papers told us she insisted on having him for the competition.

* *

The receptionist tells me Kevin is running a little late so she's really sorry but I'll have to wait. That suits me as I may be able to talk to her. I say, trying to sound casual, that I suppose his name being in the papers for doing Carli's hair has been good for business.

Julie sniffs. 'It has and it hasn't. We've had journalists annoying us. Kevin was away for weeks and that annoyed his regular clients. Some people blamed us for that baby going missing, when there never was a 'no baby rule.' We don't encourage buggies in here, that's for sure, we don't have the space but Carli made the call to leave him, not us.'

'Does she still come here?'

'Haven't seen her since it happened.'

'What do the customers think happened?'

'Nobody knows. It's all really weird. There were rumours going around about the traveller camp. That they'd been slipped a few bob to keep him there but the gardai went in and found nothing. Heard they found a few other things though.'

She lowers her voice and says, 'You know, stolen fags, stuff like that.'

Then Kevin comes in looking for me while Julie takes payment from his departing client.

Initially Kevin is suspicious of me. You can't blame him when new clients may be journalists or just nosy parkers. After he's inspected my hair and criticised the person who last cut it, which was only last week, we agree on the style I want.

I explain that I'm Sandra's cousin and that he did her hair once though she normally goes to Michelle. This reassures him. I decide to be honest and tell him that I'm interested in the case and also thrilled that a Waterford person has done so well in the competition.

He's obviously a Carli fan and why wouldn't he be as he's now a celebrity hairdresser? I tell him I saw his picture and an interview in a style magazine and he smiles.

'Yes, Carli's brought me luck. She smoked my fags but she did the business for me.'

I ask if she talked much about Tommy. He laughs and says no, she didn't but suggests that was because she thought a gay guy wouldn't be interested in babies. He says they did chat about their partners though. I suspect he has a soft spot for Dave. He tells me Dave has been to him a few times though not recently.

'Are they really split up?' I ask. 'I get the impression from the papers that they might get back together.'

'Yeah, I think they could,' he agrees. 'He told me that the bedsitter they lived in would split anyone up. When he was in the last time, that was about ten months ago he told me he really misses her and the little boy. Ridiculous that some people said he was involved.'

'What do you think about the solicitor going missing with her money?'

'Carli was a bit suspicious of him but she didn't have time to check up on him. He came to her when Tommy went missing and believe me she really needed help then. And he kept the papers in line more or less. They were printing terrible things about her. She said he got her some out of court payment from one of the tabloids for some lie it printed. Suppose he's run off with that as well. Met the fucker once in the Outpatients Department down at the hospital. Touting for business.'

My fair hair is fine and normally doesn't hang well. He's persuaded me to have a little cut off even though I'm only booked in for a wash and blow dry. I'm impressed with the way it's looking, glad I took his suggestion of a trim.

I thank him and say I'll be back.

* *

A most productive visit to Ireland. 2012 should be interesting.

As I enter my hall Pedro cannot stop licking me. Surprisingly he hasn't upended any of the black sacks waiting for the charity shop to open. I know my neighbours will have spoilt him rotten, but he still wants me. As I said before, unrequited love is a wonderful thing. Only dogs and babies can give you that.

CHAPTER 19

I had wanted to see both Emer and Alro while I was in Waterford but it wasn't to be.

'Sorry can't meet you, Molly. You were right; I've been doing too much overtime at work so I'm taking a week in the Canaries. Can't wait to go. Won't be back until after you've gone. See you next time you're over. Emer.'

Ironic! Emer has taken the advice I've been offering in the emails we've been exchanging and unknowingly I've foiled my own plans!

And Alro refused to meet me.

His email read, *'Sorry, can't risk a meeting. Waterford's a small place relatively. Would be just my luck for someone to see me with you.'*

I'd emailed back, *'Look I'm just an average looking 30 something woman, not a celebrity; why shouldn't you be having a coffee with me?'*

His reply, *'Believe me, I can't risk it.'*

So I had to give up. I turn to Carli's blog to see her perspective on her new status, on the way to stardom but broke thanks to the solicitor.

'The first I knew about my money being missing was when a journalist rang me just before Christmas.

Nobody will believe me but I can't even remember exactly how much the cheque was for that's missing. Padraig told me to tell the Star Search people to make the cheque out to Padraig Mahoney Clients' Account. He explained that solicitors have special accounts to look after their clients' money. I was photographed receiving the cheque a week before he went missing; he took it as soon as the shoot was over. I suppose I should be crying about my missing money but I'm not. As I told the journalist who rang me, 'I've never had money so how can I miss it and I'd give away everything I have to get Tommy back.'

Padraig turned up on my doorstep three months ago offering to help me. I'd never met a solicitor before and he persuaded me to take him on. But I didn't agree with everything he suggested.

He wanted to get some Tommy toys made. Said he had a friend who could give me a good deal; he insisted it'd be a good marketing idea as I had to keep my profile up. Well I told him to 'fuck off. I'm not making money out of Tommy.'

He was always going on about setting up a company to deal with the money people sent. I said no lots of times, but maybe he did it anyway. He often gave me forms to sign and to be honest I didn't always read them; I couldn't be bothered. I assumed he knew what he was doing. He'd send emails to my iphone saying everything was fine. And he was good with the papers when they went too far. He got money off one of the tabloids and the paper hasn't been as bad since. I suppose that money is missing too?

So I need another solicitor and this one I'll choose more carefully!'

Carli's website permits you to blog on her posts and some fans try to advise her.

'Carli, you can pick a name out of the yellow pages but they could be more dishonest than him for all you know.'
Bethany

'*See what solicitors other stars use*'.
Lulu

And an interesting suggestion:

'*That woman in Accrington with the missing baby is a solicitor. And a bloody good one apparently; like one of those lady lawyers in the TV soaps. Why not get in touch with her. She'll understand what you've been through.*' XXX
Angela

Carli responds to her fan.

'*Thanks Angela but Amy Blake has her own problems and isn't looking for clients. She's more or less lost her husband as well as her baby. He's in hospital for God knows how long and he may never be all there mentally according to the papers. Now I know you can't believe all the papers say, as I know from the stuff that's been printed about me, but I saw the photo of his smashed car on the front pages and he must have been hurt really badly. Some people are implying she did it when she found out about the affair. That stinks. She wouldn't kill her own son's father.*'

Angela persists.

'*Carli, true, she's got her own problems but you two have a real bond. She'd help you, Carli I just know she would.*'
Angela

Hmm, will Carli follow the fan's advice? She moves on to tell us about her new life.

'*I can't believe I made the Christmas No.1 in Ireland and in the UK. Thanks so much everybody for buying it. It's been manic since I won the competition with photo shoots, interviews and personal appearances to promote it. The record company pushed the official A side, the competition song we all had to sing in the final. But the other side is my song One Mistake and that's why I believe it's selling so well. I've been so busy it sort of takes my mind off my Tommy at least in the day. There was a live TV appearance on Christmas Day. But that night I was crying in my hotel room; miserable until 3 am when I took a sleeping pill. If I hadn't had the madness of the competition and the promotion of my record I could have been crying all the time.'*

I move to the section of her website where fans can ask questions:

'How is Tommy's dad doing after the attack and are you getting back together?'
Michelle

'He's doing OK. We text every day.'

'How are you managing with all your money missing?'
Paula

'The record company is covering my expenses for the time being and I get lots of free stuff.'

'Are you really dating all the people mentioned in the papers?'
Tracey

'It's a laugh reading about all the people I'm shagging, Tracey. I can't even remember meeting some of them. I suppose I might have been introduced at some of the events I've had to go to since I won. And then a picture gets taken and the paper doctors it to make it look as though something is going on. Dave gets annoyed about these stories but it's really nothing to do with him.'

And someone actually asks about Tommy.

'Are there any new leads that might get your baby back?'
Gary

'Inspector O'Reilly had great hopes after the new witness who left Ireland the day after it happened came forward in November, but nothing came of it. The police really tried to find the woman seen standing by my car. But that was two months ago. I think she was probably only a tourist. My solicitor was supposed to be using money that came in to put a private detective on the case. That's what he told me anyway.'

And the final question, a really serious one!

'Is the rumour true that you're changing your look again though lots of people loved the natural one you had in the final?'
Kitty

'You can't stay the same in this business, so yes but can't tell you more now'.

Over to Amy's blog, not expecting happy posts.

'The medical team had hoped he could come home for Christmas and New Year if I organised medical back up, but in the end they had felt it was too risky. They'd operated for the back fractures when they felt his condition was stable and they'd told me that went well; and that they were confident he'd walk again eventually though maybe not as well as before.

Jimmy seems to recognise me now, and Peter too. I suppose that's progress, but he still can't talk properly. I don't think he understands what I say to him. He tries to talk. He seems to be trying to say he's sorry. Peter gets upset visiting him and doesn't want to go. Jimmy seems to be wondering where he is, which makes me feel guilty.'

I do feel sorry for the child. He's innocent in all this. He's lost his baby sister and his father will never be the same. Jimmy may be a crude womaniser but who's to say he wasn't a good father? There's a picture of him in a wheelchair with Amy standing behind it looking solicitous. To me it shrieks PR spin but then I'm still bitter about his cruel comment when he thought I was permanently in a wheelchair.

Amy refers briefly to a newspaper article I'd seen relating to Brenda, Jimmy's ex-wife and an alleged scene at the nursing station in the hospital. She says it was all a misunderstanding.

Hmm. I felt the article was set up by the ex-wife. I mean why would a journalist just happen to be near the nursing station the one time Brenda visited? Apparently her maintenance hadn't been paid for a couple of months and she was 'worried sick' about her sons' education. Aren't the sons in their early 20s? Brenda claimed she had come to show her 'respects.' But other papers have trashed that claim and suggested she look for a job – probably because they resented her giving the exclusive story to one paper. They actually back Amy for working hard to keep Jimmy's business going while Brenda creates scenes near a very sick man. One paper described Brenda as 'tacky.' And another pictured her with her hair looking a mess with the caption 'former hairdresser Brenda Blake.'

The blog shows signs of professional help. Obviously Amy would be articulate given her academic and professional background but I suspect there's a PR advisor in the background. There used to be a facility to blog in response to her posts as there is on Carli's but that's not available now. Must have had problems with libellous posts and decided to take the safe option.

I'm wondering if Carli will contact her as her fan suggested. The PR people would love it but I suspect Amy wouldn't.

Interestingly Amy has commented on Carli's solicitor.

'Remember you are innocent until proved guilty and the reports on this case all imply the solicitor in question is guilty. The Law Society investigation will be fair and reveal the truth and until it reports, it's inappropriate to comment. I know this is a worrying time for his clients but as a former practicing solicitor I have to stand up for my profession, we are highly regulated and really try to do our best for our clients.'

Why would she say this? He is a one man band solicitor in a different country regulated by a different body. If she had specifically mentioned Carli and expressed concern for her I could understand it but this brief post is almost a defence of him. Peculiar? I must try not to see conspiracy everywhere.

I ask Pedro what he thinks about this top lawyer's unusual concern for a professional colleague she doesn't know. He wags his tail. What does that mean? I repeat the question and he wags his tail again. Eureka! He's telling me Amy does know him. You idiot Molly! It was obvious. She would not comment on a public blog about this man in such a way unless she knew him – and – she in some way owes him one so she makes a subtle legalistic defence of him.

Thank you Pedro, you deserve a treat. I'll follow that up with Emer when I finally get to meet her. She may know whether Carli and Padraig Mahoney have met Amy. Maybe he was negotiating some sort of lucrative book or interview deal with the two of them involved? Or has she had a professional contact with him unrelated to Carli? Definitely worth looking into.

CHAPTER 20

At school I was teased for being methodical. I'd take down homework details carefully for example, which seems to me a sensible thing to do. And one of my tormenters would sometimes ask for my help clarifying what assignments had been set! I haven't the world's best memory so listing things and ticking them off is the way I work. I've gathered a lot of information over the last few months about the missing babies; it's definitely time to focus my research which means lists. Making lists of domestic issues was so useful when I was immobilised back in the summer and autumn and had to rely on Lidia and the neighbours to help me.

Now it seems to me that in both cases the police have their doubts about whether the children were actually abducted, no doubt because the statistics on missing and/or dead children show that in the majority of cases the culprit is a parent, relative or someone known to the child.

Is fake abduction something that happens much? A day of internet research produces interesting material which like the nerd I'm accused of being I tabulate below.

Child	Age when 'abducted'	Country	Year	Details
Bianca Jones	2	USA	2011	Father claimed his car was 'carjacked' with Bianca in the back seat. No body found. Media coverage indicates father is suspected.

Jhessye Shockley	5	USA	2011	Body never found. Mother had history of child abuse. No charges yet.
Jose and Ruth Breton	2 and 6	Spain	2011	Father claimed they disappeared in a park. This month their mother claims in the Spanish media that their father knows where they are.
Hailey Dunn	13	USA	2010	Mother's then boyfriend declared 'person of interest'. No charges brought yet.
Kiesha Abrahams (or Wieppeart)	6	Australia	2010	Mother and stepfather claimed she disappeared from her bedroom. Now on trial for murder.
Marina Sabatier	8	France	2009	Beaten and abused all her life by her parents who claimed she was abducted from their car. Both charged with her murder.
Shannon Matthews	9	UK	2008	Found alive. Mother and uncle charged with kidnapping and jailed for 8 years.

Caylee Anthony	2	USA	2008	Mother tried for murder. Cleared in 2011 but verdict controversial.
Harmony Creech	11 months	USA	2007	Mother convicted of 2nd degree murder in 2011, sentenced to 11-15 years. Father away fighting in Iraq at the time.
Leonardo Sendejas	2	USA	2007	Mother claimed killed by burglars. Later admitted she made up this story and charged with murder.
Riley Sawyers	2	USA	2007	Beaten to death by mother and stepfather. Both convicted of her murder. The mother had claimed it was an accident.
Joana Cipriano	8	Portugal	2004	Mother convicted of murder

Samuele Lorenzi	3	Italy	2002	Mother claimed he was attacked when briefly left alone. Mother convicted of murder.
Zoe Evans	9	UK	1997	Vanished from her bed. Stepfather convicted of murder.
Michael and Alexander Smith	3 and 1	USA	1994	Mother claimed carjack when she had driven into a lake and left them to drown.

And then there are cases where children have vanished, no-one has been charged but suspicion hangs over the parents which is really unfair. A few weeks after Tommy and Rose vanished; eleven month old Lisa Irwin vanished from her bed in Kansas City, USA. No body has been found but the parents appear to be suspects. Dr Kate McCann reported her daughter Madeleine missing from their holiday apartment in May 2007. Nearly five years later she hasn't been found and nobody has been charged. There was a body found in the case of Jon Benet Ramsey in 1996 in Colorado, USA but no-one was charged despite significant concern about the possible involvement of her parents or her brother.

So fake abductions do occur. I make a mental note to follow up the open cases in my list to see if charges have followed, or convictions obtained. But did Amy and Carli fake the abductions of their children? I try to sum up the pros and cons:

AMY

Motive	Pro	Con	Comment
Accidental death covered up	No independent sighting of Rose on the day she vanished as far as we know	Why cover up an accident?	Does Amy have any relevant history eg temper?
Kidnap by parent (Jimmy)	Affair with Davina and fear of lack of custody if divorce	No evidence divorce imminent	What would Davina feel about taking on a child? Could have blackmailed au pair into helping given her immigrant status
Kidnap by parent (Amy)	Opportunity but meeting date changed on her not by her	No motive	
Kidnap by outsider	Window of opportunity. Family have money	No serious ransom demands Too young for paedophile?	Taken for childless couple? Any other possible motive?

If not the parents, who are the suspects?

Suspect	Comment
Teresa	Has to be serious contender if the child was kidnapped but why did she not leave on the night? And why did she send the letter? Could be to send police on wild goose chase?
Man in the supermarket mentioned in Teresa's letter.	Possible. Could have been stalking her.
Woman in pet grooming place	According to police she is ruled out but not clear who she was. She may have gleaned valuable information about the house from Teresa.
Man who viewed the house the day before	Definitely of interest. His name not revealed. Description is similar to the man in the supermarket but it's a description that would fit many men in that age group (late 30s/early 40s).
Person who has been crossed in business by Amy or Jimmy	Motive to hurt them, rather than ransom. Baby sold to childless couple. At least child safe in this scenario.
Amy's medical student boyfriend	Motive but why leave it for four years before acting?

It has certainly helped to write this down. Now I need a list of people to speak to.

First, the police are only telling us what they want us to know. I've been lucky with the information from Alro but I need a leak at the Accrington end. I'm pretty certain Detective Inspector Hargreaves' wife is in the golf club a friend of Jeff's belongs to. I can get him to take me there.

Pedro is sitting at my feet as I write these notes. I look at him affectionately and say aloud, 'Yes, you need some grooming. I'll book us into that dog salon and see what we can discover.'

And I'll talk to the estate agency which was handling the sale of Amy's house. Her housekeeper and her immediate neighbours could be helpful but they'll be reluctant to talk to strangers so I'll need to come up with a strategy. And those charity board ladies could provide an insight, again if I can get to meet any of them.

When I was a student I used to get summer work doing marketing surveys, sometimes knocking on doors and sometimes cold calling on the telephone. I rarely got a refusal whereas colleagues often had bad days when very few people would co-operate. My supervisor loved me. 'Molly,' she said, 'some people are natural communicators and you're one of the best I've ever had. If you want a permanent job when you finish college, there's one for you're here.' Hopefully I haven't lost my touch and the 'actors' in the missing babies drama will be co-operative.

When I'll get to meet these people isn't clear as I'm due back at work next week.

I'm in two minds about the medical student boyfriend. If he'd learnt about his daughter Catherine say a couple of months before Rose vanished he'd be my number one suspect.

One odd thing. Amy called her first child Peter. Surely it's unusual to call your first child after a former serious boyfriend? Even if she just liked the name, there must have been others she liked as much? It could mean that early in her marriage, she already regretted her decision and thought of her first love. Using that name certainly says something about her, but I'm not really sure what.

Maybe Peter did contact Amy at the time he heard of his daughter? Maybe they met, argued but he decided to move on. Now Amy never told Liz that Peter contacted her, but does that mean he didn't? Amy could be annoyed that she innocently let out the secret and her decision returned to haunt her? She stays quiet, feeling sure in her own mind that he's accepted the past. Another thing he could have met someone since the reunion and have his own family. That would surely help him to move on. For now, Peter's in my pending file.

Now to look at Carli.

Motive	Pro	Con	Comment
Accidental death covered up	No independent sighting of Tommy on the day she vanished as far as we know	Why cover up an accident?	Does Carli have any relevant history eg temper?
Faked kidnap to raise profile (Carli & Dave)	Carli ambitious and streetwise. Went on stage the day after as if nothing had happened.	Believable? Where is the child?	

Faked kidnap to raise profile (Carli & Emer)	See above. Emer's story changed re mother's health on the day.	Why would Emer get involved in such a crime for a friend?	
Kidnap by outsider	Window of opportunity.	Too young for paedophile?	Taken for childless couple? Any other possible motive?

I research parents leaving children in cars and discover that in the States an average of 37 children per year die in cars because their parents have either forgotten they are there or how long they have been there. These deaths happen on a typical summer day. Unbelievable! Other cases record children left in cars in shopping centres but fortunately not with fatal consequences as members of the public intervened.

Now Carli had apparently left Tommy alone at least once before. I believe she did leave him on that fateful day and thought it would only be for a short time before he was collected. So eliminating her, the suspects are:

Suspect	Comment
Emer	Resentment against Carli for being used. Maybe fancied Dave. Not enough motive surely?
Person in the burka	Seems unreliable sighting.

Woman seen by Carli's car (witness Bernadette Carroll)	She hasn't come forward. Description is limited. Most likely tourist
Youngish man sitting in car (witness Bernadette Carroll)	Didn't come forward. Not clear if the older woman was with him.
Unknown person taking child to get at Dave	Rumoured Dave knew some dodgy people, but no hard evidence, and no body
Deirdre	Emer says serious friction between Carli and Deirdre but not enough motive for this. Presumably the police have interviewed her and the foster parents
Solicitor	Reputation as ambulance chaser. Got 28% in poll. Moved in on Carli after Tommy vanished as her blog reveals. Aunt Bernie says solicitors have poor reputation in Ireland so is this high vote partly prejudice?

I'll have to get to meet Emer. I'll tell her I'm coming over on a family matter. Shall Aunt Bernie celebrate a 25th wedding anniversary or cousin Sandra get engaged? Which story would be better as a reason for coming over?

If the police can't find the solicitor then I doubt I can; but I'll call in to his office and see if I can get any information out of someone working there.

Chapter 21

I return to my office in mid January and a mountain of work. I feel guilty about having taken so much time off. I shouldn't because I was genuinely unable to work. I put in long hours every day so my research progresses slowly and I don't get round to media review until the end of the month. It's been a quiet month for coverage of the missing babies though Carli's new life is getting plenty of column inches. Jimmy Blake is still very ill but progressing slowly. Does Amy blame herself for that accident, I think she must? That's a lot of guilt to be carrying because she has to feel guilty about Rose too.

Good news for the policeman in charge of the Waterford case; he's become a dad. Aunt Bernie sent me the birth announcement in the local paper. He must have found it hard dealing with Carli with his own child on the way.

Births Column

O'Rourke, *Dan and Ellen (nee Byrne) are delighted to announce the birth of their first child, a son (Patrick Daniel) on 15 January. Our thanks to the wonderful nurses at the Waterford Regional Maternity Unit.*

And magazines are full of interviews with Carli -

At the end of January HOT POP carried a typical but not exactly penetrating interview:

Our Show Biz Editor Beccy Bates catches up with Carli Walsh

'BB: *Life's been hectic lately for you Carli?*

CW: *You can say that again. I'm working 24/7. It's great meeting the fans. I was back in Waterford last week. It seemed like the whole place came out to see me.*

BB: *You got the Christmas No.1 in the UK. Did you expect that?*

CW: No *way. Back in August nobody apart from the regulars in the pub where I was singing had heard of me.*

BB: *As the winner of Star Search, you get to sing for Ireland at Eurovision. Tell us about it.*

CW: *They're commissioning six songs from a number of songwriters. I sing them on a TV show in March and the viewers choose the one they like best.*

BB: *Wouldn't you rather sing one of your own songs?*

CW: *Yeah, I would. I'm talking to my management about that.*

BB: *Ireland used to win a lot but things have been pretty bad lately..?*

CW: *Jedward were amazing last year. I'd be thrilled to get 8th place like they did. I'm planning to sing part of whatever song I get in Polish to try to get their vote. There's lots of Polish people in Ireland with family and friends back home who might vote for me.*

BB: *I suppose it's too early to talk about your look for Eurovision?*

CW: *(laughing) You could say that! First I have to find something amazing for the evening when the viewers pick the Irish song for Eurovision. Let me get that over with. Eurovision's not until May. But I do want to wear something from an Irish designer.*

BB: *Lots of rumours about your love life. Can you fill us in?*

CW: *(laughs) I don't have time for love. People shouldn't believe what they read.*

BB: *Carli, now for the really tough question. How are you coping with your son still missing? Is there any news?*

CW: *Yeah, it's hard. I was crying quite a bit over Christmas. The gardai keep in touch. They thought they had a breakthrough when a woman came forward in November. But they haven't been able to find the woman the witness saw standing by my car, and the description they have is very vague. I'm working on an album and I'm writing a song for Tommy and his picture will be on the sleeve. I have to keep his face out there.'*

No new information in that interview!

The internet debate is quiet in January maybe because there isn't much media coverage, and maybe because like me the regulars feel the need of a break. I get a PM from Declan who is one of the most prolific bloggers asking me if I'm still alive. I email back to assure him I am and explain that work commitments are taking up my time; tempted to tell him more but better to be discreet.

I've been emailing Liz since we met up at New Year but her replies are short. I rationalise this communication deficit on the grounds of her work pressures. She's pleased I have returned to work which was her suggestion. I think she regrets telling me about Amy's baby and I note she hasn't posted on the Forum this year. I ask her for Peter's surname and that request is ignored in her next email. I ask again, trying not to make it appear a big deal but she doesn't respond. I'm afraid she may realise I intend to find this man and that seems to have scared her off. At the dinner when she dropped that bombshell I didn't get any information about what he looked like so I'm no nearer knowing if the drunken guy in the old college picture was Peter. That student's image comes into my head whenever I feel down which isn't healthy. Concentrate Molly. Get a list going. I draw up my interview timetable for the next three months.

Location	Timeline 2012	Target	Strategy/Objective
Accrington	February	Pampered Pooch staff	Investigate Teresa's chat with customer the day the meeting changed. And to be honest give Pedro a makeover!
Accrington	February	Estate agent who met the mystery house viewer	Get better description from her to help track him down.
Accrington	February	Amy's elderly neighbour.	Get picture of the Blake family from her perspective. Who had she seen around in the days before Rose vanished?
Accrington	March	Golf Club Policeman's wife a member, and Davina Marsden. Any member willing to chat.	Find a social occasion to attend and talk to anyone but obviously Mrs Hargreaves and Davina Marsden.

Waterford	April/May	Staff in pub where Carli sang. Staff in solicitor's office.	Staff may have noticed an over keen fan/stalker. Need story for solicitor's staff to justify questions.
Waterford	April/May	Emer Flynn and her mother	She is Carli's confidante. Are Carli and Amy now in touch? What was the truth about Emer's mother's health on the day Tommy vanished?

Presumably all these people, with the exception of Mrs Hargreaves, have been interviewed by the police. They don't seem to be anywhere near solving this. Am I being arrogant to think I could find something they missed? Yes, I was good at interviewing for those marketing surveys but to get the information I want now I'll need acting skills and I'll have to tell lies. To be honest I should say tell more lies. I haven't exactly lost any sleep over my lies to date. They were after all told in a good cause.

CHAPTER 22

It's not possible to implement my interview plan until late February as I'm so busy back at work. I try to book Pedro into the dog grooming parlour Amy used but they are fully booked on the day I manage to get off. Then I think a visit probably won't lead to any new information, as Amy's dog has been poisoned and she has said on her blog that even though her son Peter wants another one, she isn't ready yet. And the customer mentioned by Teresa in the letter released to the press wasn't described so it would be unlikely that the staff could tell me who she was.

I'd actually been looking forward to going but perhaps for the wrong reasons; to spoil my Pedro a little as he's been a lifeline for me. And to meet some other doggy people!

When I watched the repeat of the police press conference appealing for the man who'd viewed Amy's house to come forward to be eliminated from the inquiry, I'd made a note of the estate agency's name and also of the woman handling the sale who appeared at the press conference. She's my first challenge today. I've an appointment with her and my story is prepared: I'm thinking of selling my house to escape from my sad memories and moving maybe a little outside Manchester to a house with a bigger garden for my dog. I had in fact thought of moving but discarded the idea quickly so my story is not a total lie. Hopefully the chance of commission on both selling and purchasing will loosen her tongue.

Emma the estate agent is young, not more than 25, and gives me the impression she is not very confident. She takes copious notes about my house and wants to make an appointment to view.

I hope I sound convincing.

'I haven't made a decision to sell. Friends tell me it would help me move on but I'm not sure. I just want some advice on its value and what I might have to pay for something with a bigger garden. I don't want to waste your time going out to my house when I mightn't sell it.'

'It's no bother,' she says eagerly but I move the conversation on to my new house. Trying to sound casual I say, 'I saw you were selling Amy Blake's house. I read an interview with her in a magazine once and it had lots of pictures of the house. It looked lovely. And I saw how nice the garden was, well the front garden anyway, from all the TV coverage.'

'They took it off the market. You can understand why.'

Again trying to sound innocent, I ask, 'It's six months since her baby vanished, do you think she might reconsider selling?'

'I suppose I could ask her,' she says doubtfully.

I pluck up my courage and say sympathetically, 'It must have been difficult for you, having met the person who maybe took her baby. You must have been mad with the receptionist not getting his number.'

I've hit the right note as she smiles sadly.

'Yes, it was dreadful. I wouldn't have been handling that sale normally. It was late August and my boss was on holiday so I was just covering for him. Our receptionist was on holiday too and we had an agency temp in. I didn't tell her to get phone numbers from anyone she made a viewing appointment with. I mean it's obvious you'd do that. Anyway she wouldn't normally make the bookings, she'd just put the call through to me. When this man phoned I was on a call and he didn't want to hold so she told him about the viewing and just got his name.'

'Do you think he could be the one?'

Without hesitation she replies, 'No, I don't. Like I said at the press conference he seemed a nice man. He told me he might be moving into the area and was researching the market, seeing what was available suitable for a family. I think he said he had two children. There were other people viewing the house and they had lots of questions so I didn't spend much time with him.'

'Why do you think he hasn't come forward? That must put him high on the police suspect list.'

She looks thoughtful. 'I've been going over it in my mind a lot. I did remember something a couple of weeks ago which might be relevant.'

I interrupt, 'What was that?' Then I regret my eagerness which may put her off. Fortunately it doesn't.

'When I was in the kitchen talking to two of the other viewers, he was there too but not in our conversation. His mobile rang, and he answered in French and then left the room to take the call in private. I couldn't sleep one night recently and I was going through it all again in my mind as I've often done and I thought that could be why he didn't come forward. Perhaps he lives in France. He never said where he worked and the police assumed it was in the UK and he'd see the appeals. If he's based in France it's unlikely he knew about them.'

'That's very interesting. Did you tell the police?'

She shakes her streaked blonde hair. 'No I didn't. I don't think it would help them, and I suppose I worried they'd ask why I didn't mention it at the time. I just didn't think of it.'

There seems to be nothing more I can learn so I try to bring the meeting to a close but she insists on showing me an empty house 'just round the corner' which she feels is 'perfect' for me. I agree to keep her happy, feeling guilty about wasting more of her time and promise to ring her when I've decided whether to sell. To keep up the pretence I collect a pile of brochures of properties for sale as I leave.

Her new information is interesting. It may explain why the house viewer never came forward. A thought comes into my mind; didn't the psychic say the Tommy was alive and living in the sun? France is a sunny country…No, that's ridiculous. The psychic was talking about Tommy and if the viewer is the kidnapper, he took Rose not Tommy. And anyway, not all France is sunny. I recall a wet and cool summer holiday in North Brittany.

**

My next target is Amy's next door neighbour, Matilda Askworth, an old lady whom I've seen on the news and quoted in the papers which suggests she's open to talking. She's not in the phone book which doesn't surprise me and anyway I think it's better just to turn up. I've given some thought to my story and poured through my old cuttings to see what I can learn about her. She's a widow and seems to have been friendly with Amy's housekeeper Mary Bristow. Being in all day she may have noticed things that have not appeared in the media because the police may want to hold some information back.

After my second ring Mrs Askworth finally comes to the door. She apologises for the delay explaining that her hearing isn't the best. Oh dear, this interview could be tricky.

'You must be the lady from social services. They promised to send someone to look at getting me a stair lift?'

I feel bad preparing to tell lies to this old woman.

'Actually, I'm not. I hope you don't mind my calling but I need your help with something.'

She looks surprised.

I continue, 'You don't know me. My name's Molly Carter. I read about you in the papers and I saw you on TV...'

Mrs Askworth interrupts, 'You mean about baby Rose? Are you a journalist? You don't look like one.'

She had asked about my being a journalist in an excited way, not in an 'I'll slam the door on you if you are' kind of way. That makes me feel more confident so I explain, 'My husband died last year. My family encouraged me to join evening classes to keep busy and to meet new people. Well, one class is a writing class and we're doing interviewing this month. We each had to put an interview idea to the tutor, get it approved and then the best ones will be put into a book for teaching purposes in the college. I was fascinated by the baby Rose case especially as I live not too far away and I thought you would be able to tell me about how the family is coping.'

She almost drags me inside. As I'd hoped; she is lonely and happy to ask in an unknown person who appears friendly and unthreatening.

Her living room is cluttered but clean and homely. Before we start I open my large handbag which holds a multitude of things and produce the Marks & Spencer fruitcake I'd bought in Accrington Shopping Centre.

'I bought this for you Mrs Askworth. I hope you like fruitcake.'

You'd think I'd told her she'd won the Lotto. She can't stop thanking me. To try to get the interview started I take out my new shorthand notebook and a borrowed pocket dictaphone. She insists on making tea and vanishes to the kitchen but this at least gives me the chance to look out of her living room window to check the assumptions I'd made from using Google Earth to check out her house. As it had appeared, there's a good view of Amy's garden and carport from her house. I'm lost in Amy's front garden metaphorically speaking when I realise she's asking me how much sugar I take in my tea. My plan is to take her through the week leading up to the disappearance but she wants to talk about me being a widow.

'Molly, you look too young to be a widow. My Henry died when I was 70 and these past ten years have been so lonely. What happened to your husband?'

So I tell her the story and get weepy at the end of it. She produces a monster box of tissues. I ask her if she has any children; she doesn't and when she tried to adopt she was deemed too old.

'When I was younger I used to do some babysitting for the Andersons. They're the people on the other side of Amy's house.'

I sense the opportunity to get back on track.

'The Andersons. Weren't they on holiday when Rose vanished?'

'Yes, they always take August off. They have a holiday home in Spain.'

'Did you ever do babysitting for Amy? With her son perhaps?'

'I never did. I was 73 when Peter was born and she had live-in help anyway. And her mother would babysit the odd time.'

'I've often wondered why she didn't ask her mum to help her that night.'

'Well her mum's getting on now and she has to look after Amy's dad who had a stroke a couple of years ago. Mary, that's the housekeeper, told me Amy felt her mother wasn't up to minding such a young baby. Now she doted on her grandchild and would have helped. I don't know exactly where she lives but maybe it could have taken her a while to get here.'

I move on to ask about Teresa.

'I was so sorry she left. She used to visit me most days and bring Rose in. It was like having a daughter and a grandchild.'

'Do you think she had anything to do with it?'

Mrs Askworth is indignant. 'How could you even think that? She was a lovely lass. Not like the stuck-up one Amy had before. She never called here and she'd hardly give you the time of day if you passed her in the street.'

I protest that I don't think Teresa is guilty but it's just that the police seemed to believe she was involved. This mollifies her. Then it occurs to me, if Teresa regularly visited her, then she might know something about her background. Amy apparently knew very little having taken her on without references as she'd been left in the lurch when nanny Gemma walked out.

'Did Teresa ever talk to you about her family or any friends?'

'Not really. She said she wanted to see them but there would have been a problem getting back here if she went home. Something to do with visas. I didn't understand that. She mentioned a boyfriend at home but I don't think it was on any more.'

'Did she mention the course she was doing before she came to Amy?'

'No. I did ask her. It was something to do with computers. She was really clever. She helped me with a problem I was having with the electricity people. She rang them up for me and it's all sorted now.'

Hmm. Teresa seems to be just as has been portrayed; caring and helpful. I try a new tack.

'How has Mary the housekeeper coped?'

'She was really upset. She left about four o'clock that day. She never even saw Rose because she was asleep in her room when she arrived and Amy told her not to clean in there. She didn't see Rose the day before either because the estate agent was having an afternoon viewing and wanted Amy and Rose out all afternoon.'

'Did she see the people who came? Aren't the police still trying to trace one of them?'

'She did want to see them, but the woman asked her to keep out of the way so she brought some ironing into my house.'

A pity. There could have been a second witness to the mystery man. I presume the police asked the other viewers about him. The others have all been eliminated; but probably they didn't take much notice. After all, why would they?

I try to get her to talk about that evening and she tells me she now finds it hard to remember and she may accidentally tell me something different to what she told the police. I tell her not to worry and try to start her off.

'Did you know Teresa was on a day off?'

'Yes, she told me and asked if there was anything I wanted in Manchester. She mentioned she'd be looking for a present for Rose as her birthday was coming up.'

'And Mary?'

'I didn't see her that day. I did the day before like I told you because the agent wanted her out of the house, so she was busy that Thursday afternoon catching up on the housework.'

'Did you see Jimmy and Amy that day?'

'I rarely see Jimmy. He's away a lot. Mary told me he was in the States. Amy, she comes and goes. I'd usually hear her car if I'm in the front room. I might see it if the curtains were open. I have a small sitting room at the back with a TV and I'm normally there in the evenings so I wouldn't hear that much at the front. '

'I read that you heard a car at around seven thirty and then two hours later you heard cars and had the police at your door. And did I read that Amy's dog didn't bark?'

Mrs Askworth agrees. 'Yes, it was after nine because I looked at my clock when the police called. The dog was yapping then because it had been put out in the garden but I don't remember hearing it earlier. I did hear the car; it must have been seven thirty because Amy told me she left then. I was a bit confused and upset when the police turned up. They collected me the next day to make a proper statement in the station. Amy came to see me in the morning before I made the statement and asked me what I'd heard and I mentioned a car and she said it must have been her.'

Interesting. Is this interfering with a witness; calling on an elderly person and helping her recollection? Is this covering up that she left earlier than she said and it wasn't just a matter of minutes before Teresa would arrive – or is it more sinister? And the dog? It would have barked if an unknown person came into the garden and the house. Sometimes dogs bark when they know a person because they are excited. Now given where the old woman would be at any time she might not have heard it and she is hard of hearing anyway but it may indicate no intruder.

I am thinking it's time to go when I have an idea.

'Perhaps whoever took Rose was around earlier that day watching for an opportunity. Can you tell me what you did that day? There could have been someone you passed in the morning say, and you had no reason to think anything of it?'

Mrs Askworth looks slightly worried.

'My memory's not what it was, dear.'

'You probably have a routine, maybe you do a little bit of shopping every day?'

She agrees. 'Yes I would do that. And I usually have a cup of tea in the café next to the supermarket in the shopping centre when I've finished my shopping. Sometimes I meet someone I know there and it's lovely to have a chat.'

'Have you ever met someone there you didn't know and got chatting?'

She pauses and after what seems an age she says, 'Well I did once and it might have been that day. I'm not sure. A lovely woman with a baby asked me if I minded her joining my table. Of course I didn't. She was so nice to talk to. She doted on her grandson, little Greg. Or was it Garry? Something beginning with a G anyway. She didn't really look old enough to be a granny I thought.'

'Did you ever see her again?

'I didn't and I've looked out for her there. But I don't think she was from around here.'

'Why did you think that?'

'Well, her accent. She didn't talk like me. Sounded as if she was from down south.'

I don't think I can get any more information but this is interesting.

I'm wondering how to get away tactfully. She's offering me more tea and cake which I don't really want but she has been so kind I have to accept. I'm glad I did because she really trusts me now and the next thing she tells me confirms my instinctive feeling that the cases may be connected.

She leans forward and says, 'I shouldn't really tell you this. I promised Mary I wouldn't but I'm sure you'd like to know.'

I smile and compliment her on the tea.

She continues, 'That Carli Walsh who lost her baby too was here last week. I didn't see her myself but Mary met her.

'Mary told me she took a phone call and she never puts a call through to Amy before getting a name; and the person just said Carli. She thought she recognised the voice and Amy took the call. The next day Amy told her that Carli Walsh was coming to dinner. Mary cooked dinner for her and was invited to eat with them. She said she thinks Amy is going to do some legal work for Carli. They didn't talk about that at dinner, it was all Peter asking Carli questions. He's a fan and has her CD.'

'That's fascinating,' I say sincerely.

Mrs Askworth is now looking a bit worried. 'Perhaps you wouldn't put that in your article. I shouldn't really have told you.'

I promise not to. I finish my fourth cup of tea, thank her profusely and say I have to go.

'Will you come and see me again?'

I say I'll try to, feeling guilty because I know I won't.

A most interesting day. I now know that it appears nobody other than Amy saw Rose on the day she vanished or the day before. Where were Amy and Rose the afternoon of the viewing? And could Amy's mother have helped on that evening? That isn't clear, but certainly my doubts about Amy have increased after today.

The really big issue – are Amy and Carli in touch because she needs a new solicitor? That's a possibility certainly. But maybe the mention of legal work was deliberately made in the housekeeper's hearing to disguise the real reason for their contact. Surely Carli's management would have suggested a new solicitor and one based in Ireland? And Amy isn't practicing now and has her hands full running Jimmy's businesses. A call to Padraig Mahoney's office is on my agenda; hopefully it may throw some light on this.

And another line of inquiry – the friendly woman in the café. If only Mrs Askworth could be sure of the date! And how old was the woman she met? She said the woman didn't look old enough to be the grandmother of the child, but to an 80 year old, a 60 year old could look young. Now this woman had a child so why would she want another one? Mrs Askworth is both chatty and trusting. She would be a mine of information about her neighbour's routine; a godsend for someone planning to steal, whether property or a baby! A small point, Mrs Askworth was sure she was not a local woman, not in itself suspicious but my instincts are working overtime and I wonder....perhaps I should add the woman in the cafe to the list of Accrington subjects?

I get into my car absolutely exhausted by my day. Mrs Askworth had shown me all over her house and I could not refuse, while Emma had insisted on taking me round one property which she said was 'round the corner' and it wasn't. Having lied to both of these woman I had gone along with their wishes. My doctor has warned me to take things easily and since I've been back at work I haven't been doing that. When I get back, Pedro will expect a walk and I can't let him down.

CHAPTER 23

Heartened by my success in Accrington, I organise a 'chance' meeting with other players in the Rose saga. I've persuaded my friend Steve to take me to the golf club where Davina Marsden and Cathy Hargreaves, wife of the policeman in charge of the case, are members. He was more a friend of Jeff's than mine but he's the only contact I have in that place. I don't tell him my real motives. I just tell him I'm trying to move on and meet some new people like my family and friends are suggesting. And indeed that's not a lie. I'm under pressure to do just that. I'd checked out the club website and seen there's a table quiz at the weekend for the new clubhouse and Davina is listed on the organising committee. Cathy seems to be a serious golfer as she was lady Captain two years ago. I've told Steve I used to go to a lot of quizzes; I haven't been to one in years so I hope I won't embarrass myself.

**

Our team has been up with the leaders all through the quiz. I can't take the credit really as my team mates have all played their part. Last round coming up; haven't a clue what the prizes are and I don't care. This has been fun. The room is packed and they had to call for help with the bar. Our team is well lubricated other than Jenny, Steve's wife, who is the designated driver. A woman who looks like the tabloid pictures of Davina sits at the table at the front helping mark the answer sheets.

They take away our answer sheet for the last round and Steve goes to get more drinks.

Then an announcement from the quizmaster, 'We have a tie for first place and we have to go to a tie breaker between table 7 and table 15.'

'That's us,' Jenny screams. 'We must have got the last round all right to catch up with table 7. We have to get Steve back.'

It's chaotic. After a long evening people are tired. It's noisy. Steve is back by the time the quizmaster has quiet.

The question comes:

'This is in three parts: what was the title of the first Miss Marple book written by Agatha Christie, when was it published and who was the murder victim?'

OMG. I know it. The rest of my team have blank faces. They see the eureka look on my face. I write down the answer, and it is collected.

The quizmaster looks at the two answer sheets.

'The winner is table 15.'

We scream. I hug the guy next to me that Steve and Jenny have brought along for me. I don't fancy him but I'm on a high and he's the nearest person.

'The answer is Murder in the Vicarage published in 1930 and Colonel Protheroe was found dead in the vicarage. Can we have a representative from team 15 up here? The chairman of the fund raising committee Davina Marsden will present the prize.'

Steve pushes me forward. 'Molly you won it for us, get up there.' To loud applause I walk to the front of the room and collect the prize from Davina.

'Well done. I knew that question too.'

I give her a big smile. I ask her to join our table which she does. I can't ask too much as the others are there. I say, trying to sound casual, 'I read an interview with you in *Life Today* about charities. I thought it was really interesting. I've had some experiences with charities that leave me questioning them too.'

Davina likes that.

'People are too trusting and can attack you for raising uncomfortable issues.'

I respond, 'Yes, that's true. Independence of mind is threatening to some people. I've had that problem too.'

'I haven't seen you here before.'

'You haven't. I'm not a member. My friends are, the ones I'm with tonight. They invited me as I'm thinking of taking up golf.'

'I'm on the committee. I can propose people for membership. Give me a ring sometime.' She hands me her card and is called away to another table before I can make an arrangement to contact her.

I'm thrilled. The evening couldn't have gone better. Now the only problem is to tactfully get rid of the guy Steve and Jenny asked for me. Kind of them but I'm not looking for a man. Or am I? I'm still seeing that Jeff 'look-alike' in the college magazine. I tell myself it's because he could be Peter who is high on my suspect list. But to be honest, he's not high on the list. After the information gained from Mrs Askworth, Amy is my number one suspect at the moment.

∗∗

I resist ringing Davina for a week; can't seem too anxious.

'Hello, is that Davina? This is Molly Carter. We met last week at the quiz.'

I had wondered if she would even remember meeting me but she does.

'Molly, the Agatha Christie fan. Of course I remember you. Are you still interested in joining the club? Good. Thursday afternoon?'

We fix a time. Maybe I'd better do some research on golf to keep up the pretence.

* *

I'm feeling really nervous as I walk into the clubhouse. There's no sign of her or of anybody other than a cleaner. Not surprising I suppose because it's been raining all day. I sit down and look at my notes. I had looked into Davina's background for our meeting. She inherited money and appears to have invested it wisely in a number of businesses in which she takes an active role. She's been married three times and was separated – depending on which paper you read - from her husband when her affair with Jimmy was revealed. Judging from the local paper reports, she's active on the social scene as well as on the business one and is known to be outspoken. In fact one report I read about her was headed 'Davina takes no prisoners.'

The week after the table quiz I'd heard a local radio interview with her about some charity event she was organising. The interviewer was saying innocently, 'Davina it's wonderful you're able to give so much time to this charity' when she cut in quite aggressively saying, 'Yes I can because I was forced off the St Jude's Hospital committee because of the biased coverage about a relationship I had. The man involved was informally separated from his wife at the time...'

The interviewer had then interjected almost as energetically as she had.

'We have to go to an advert break now.'

When the show resumed, the interviewer apologised for Davina's absence and said she had had to leave for another appointment. Pull the other one! Clearly the station was afraid of libel. Should be interesting to talk to her.

I get lost in reviewing my copious notes and don't hear her come in.

'Sorry, I'm late. Had trouble starting the car. It doesn't like dampness.'

Though casually dressed and wearing little if any make-up she has something about her. I can understand why she would attract attention.

We exchange pleasantries and then she chats about the club. I nod appropriately and ask if it's possible to have a short term membership to see how it goes. Apparently it isn't, you join for a year or not at all. Then Davina makes me a generous offer.

'The committee can have guests play; I'm here a lot so I could sign you in until you made up your mind about joining.'

'That's so nice of you,' I say, really meaning it. 'I'd love to do that.' Official business over, I tentatively move to the real business of the meeting.

'I hope you don't mind my asking this; like I said at the quiz I read the interview you gave to *Life Today* about charities. Weren't you involved with one of Amy Blake's charities? I've been wondering if you were trying to say there was something wrong with that one.'

Davina looks thoughtful, and then says, 'I suppose you read about my relationship with Amy's husband?'

I admit that I did and add, 'I thought at the time that Amy probably tipped off the press. Your neighbours wouldn't have done it.'

Noting her appreciative look I continue, 'A rotten thing to do considering she has a son. He'd get teased at school about it.'

'I have good neighbours. I wouldn't insult them by asking them directly if they did it. Yes I was Vice Chairman of the board of one of her charities. We had a meeting the evening her baby disappeared, and a very controversial one it was too. I had just proposed a motion of no confidence in her when the meeting was interrupted because her au pair was on the telephone. Amy rushed off and in the circumstances we had to adjourn the meeting until another day. She didn't attend the next two meetings which people put down to her difficult situation, and then the papers ran the story about me and Jimmy. I had no choice. I had to resign from the board.'

Wow! She's been amazingly frank to someone she's only meeting for the second time but my research did establish that's her style. Obviously a difficult meeting but what was it all about?

As if reading my thoughts she continues, 'About two years ago Amy proposed that we change the auditors as we could get the hospital audit done for a nominal fee with the firm she had in mind. Everyone thought that was a good idea. Then it turned out that Amy and the Treasurer who's 80 and semi senile in my opinion had already indicated to the current auditors that their appointment was being terminated. That's not the way you do things. But guess who she was proposing as the new auditors - Jimmy Blake's firm! Now I argued there would be a total conflict of interest but she said Jimmy would have no involvement in the audit. One of his partners would oversee it so we'd get an independent audit. That satisfied the others.

Some of the Board are not the brightest; they saw it as a way of getting a cheap audit and saving money for the hospital.

'As we don't get on too well and she'd defeated me for the Chair, the rest of the Board thought I was just being bitchy so I had very little support.'

I make sympathetic noises.

'I couldn't let it go. I just knew something was wrong. I wasn't involved with Jimmy then but later when I was, I found out that he was involved with the audit despite what she said.

'I raised this at the meeting before the one when Rose went missing. It got pretty heated and I had quite a lot of support. But Amy is a master of procedure and said we couldn't vote on it as it wasn't on the agenda.

'Afterwards I discovered that she had censored the minutes. As Chair, the Secretary of the Board sends the draft minutes to her for approval before they're issued. It's just routine; for correcting typos and so on. I rang the Secretary and she explained that this time Amy had sent back the minutes with major deletions saying that they only needed to record decisions and that there'd been no decision on the audit.

'I was so mad that I emailed my version of the minutes to the whole Board and said I would be raising the censorship of them at the next meeting.'

'Shocking,' I say.

'There's more,' Davina adds eagerly. 'The accountant at the hospital is Amy's cousin.'

I don't see the relevance of this.

'None of us knew they were related. He's a cousin on her mother's side. I only knew because my husband overheard a conversation at the golf club. Thank God he told me. The accountant used to attend the meetings when we approved the annual accounts and discussed awarding new contracts. Everyone thought he was a pleasant efficient man. In fact we were glad to have a competent accountant in attendance as our Treasurer Hattie is very trusting, very old and should have resigned years ago. Now Amy never told us about him being her cousin and I discovered they are quite close. In fact I heard a rumour that they went out for a while years ago but I can't prove that.

'Amy goes on about us being accountable and transparent. She quotes her legal qualifications when she's on that bandwagon. She's unbelievable.

'Anyway when I found out about her cousin being the accountant, I emailed her and said it was to go on the agenda for the next meeting. I didn't want to tip her off, but if I didn't tell her she'd say it had to be put off to the one after. I also separately emailed the secretary about putting it on the agenda. I phoned all the other directors who weren't brain dead and I found that the original date Monday 23rd didn't suit some of them whereas Thursday did. So I got the Secretary to change it. She was concerned about the issue and agreed with me that it was important to have a good turnout. She told Amy she had tried to consult her about the date change but couldn't get through to her.

'Now I knew Amy would do her own lobbying but I got mine in first. She would have known from her own lobbying that she was in trouble. So what did she do, she arranges for her baby to vanish. That Chinese girl was an illegal and has to do what she's told. She probably took Rose to Manchester the day before when she left. Nobody but Amy saw the child after Wednesday. The bomb scare was a godsend to Amy as there was a reason why the au pair was 'delayed.' She could have taken Rose to the meeting and some of them would have clucked over her, but that mightn't have saved her. She would have anticipated I'd put down a motion of no confidence and probably had the numbers to win it.

'People say that she never wanted Rose. I mean she hadn't had a child for seven years. Peter is quite a handful apparently. But Jimmy wanted another child; he really wanted a girl. He may have been away a lot but believe me he phoned home every night and he always had Rose brought to the phone so he could hear her gurgle away. I'd say she could have sold the baby; money motivates her. There's lots of desperate childless couples. Or maybe Rose'll turn up when she feels safe.'

I'm gobsmacked. 'Have you been to the police about this?'

'I have but they don't seem to be doing anything about it. In fact I did a lot of research into companies who were getting contracts from the charity. It stank. I gave all that to the police too.

'I went through the minutes for the two years since we changed the auditors and I found the same companies getting contracts. Both the hospital and the Research Centre are expanding. The accountant would tell us about the tenders received and recommend the cheapest one. We all went along with that. I trusted him. I didn't know then about the accountant being Amy's cousin and that he would have been involved in sending out tender requests. So I did company searches on these successful companies and guess what, they were all fairly recently formed and we usually look for a track record when awarding a contract. One of the contracts was for a new computer system which was badly needed but you'd want to know the company record for support and maintenance. But we were never told the companies were relatively new.

'Generally the companies had the same two directors, Brenda Barry and Rosemary Freedman and their occupation on the annual return is listed as company director. That's what you state when you don't want to give information on what directors do or don't do.'

I look puzzled.

'But you don't know who they are,' she says triumphantly. 'Brenda is Jimmy's ex-wife and he keeps her sweet by paying lots of maintenance. She was a hairdresser when they met and she hasn't worked since they married as far as I know. And Rosemary is Jimmy's mother. Freedman is her single name. According to the companies annual return her date of birth is 1927. Who'd be starting up companies at 84? Jimmy controls these companies. Probably the contracts go on to clients of his accountancy business via the dummy companies and that keeps them happy and paying his fees.'

'Did Jimmy admit any of this to you?'

'Not exactly. He'd said, or rather he hinted, that there was some sort of set-up which meant work for local companies and that was a good thing.'

I'm in a state of shock after hearing all this. I mutter lamely, 'That's an incredible story.'

'That's only part of it. The hospital stands on acres of beautiful grounds and I discovered Amy was going to sell some of it to one of Jimmy's bogus companies at a knock-down price. It may be too late to stop it. She's had a free ride lately. She'll make a million at least out of that.

'And,' she adds, 'I've got copies of her expenses from the time she was Chair and they make interesting reading. In her book, charity begins at home.'

She laughs loudly at her own joke.

I'm stunned and amazed by her frankness.

'My friends told me the wife of the policeman in charge of the case is a member here. Could you get any indication from her if your information is being followed up?'

'Cathy Hargreaves is a member here but I don't know her very well. She hasn't been seen much recently and there's a rumour that she's pregnant. She hasn't any children and she's been married for close to ten years.'

'Must be difficult for her husband dealing with Amy Blake if he's had problems having a child?'

'Probably. He's a decent sort but I don't think he can cope with the idea of a mother being responsible for kidnapping her own child.'

'What are you going to do?'

'I'm going to give him some more time before I go back to him, and I'm going to talk to people like you who have an open mind and might have their own ideas and contacts.'

'Would it be possible to have copies of your research?'

She looks delighted to be asked.

'I hope you have journalist friends, Molly. I'll arrange to send you copies.'

**

Two days later a package arrives and keeps me reading into the early hours. It stops me, for a while at least, pondering the implications of the Amy/Carli linkup. I keep changing my mind about that.

CHAPTER 24

I'm in the middle of reading one of the documents in Davina's package when I'm interrupted by a phone call from Aunt Bernie. She's asking me about the latest cuttings she's sent. Now I've read everything from her and to be honest there was nothing of interest in the last batch. But there must have been something I missed because Bernie is going on about how sad it is, and how she went to the funeral. I don't understand what she's on about and to add to the confusion Pedro is sniffing energetically at the back door, wanting to go out. I ask her to hold on, let him out and return, now able to listen to her.

'Who did you say had died?'

'Our local TD; he was only 38. People here were really pleased when he was made a Junior Minister when the new government came in last year. I voted for him. Think your uncle did as well and all your cousins. He promised to bring some jobs to Waterford. Met him when he called canvassing. He was really charming.'

So she attended the funeral because she met him once on her doorstep. I always find it strange the way the Irish do funerals. I wouldn't attend the funeral of a politician just because he'd given me a leaflet on my doorstep.

Then Bernie has my 110% attention.

'It was shocking the way Carli Walsh was asked to leave his funeral. I saw it myself, the papers weren't exaggerating. It's in the cuttings I sent you.'

I can't wait to re-read the cuttings but can't understand how I missed it. Nothing in the cuttings as I thought. Got it; the current postman is temporary and a little careless with delivery.

It turns out my neighbours, the ones who helped with Pedro when I couldn't mind him, have the envelope and had forgotten to give it to me.

March 20, 2012

Minister found Dead in Bed

'The gardai were called to the Waterford home of Junior Minister Michael Moriarty this morning after his wife found him dead in bed. Mr Moriarty (38) was elected to the Dail for the first time last year and was a surprise choice for the Junior Ministerial post in Transport.

It is understood the Minister was in good health and that foul play is not suspected.

Tributes have poured in across the political divide. The Dail will stop for a minute's silence in respect when it resumes next week.

He leaves a wife Fiona. The Taoiseach is expected to attend the funeral.'

I've never heard of him but from reading his obituary he sounds as if he had a great career ahead of him. It's not exactly usual to be made a minister when you're first elected.

His obituary reads:

Michael Moriarty, Junior Minister for Transport

'Michael Moriarty was the son of Sinead and Fearghal Moriarty of The Manor House, Co Waterford. He attended

St Patrick's Community School, Waterford and held a B Sc Engineering from University College Cork.

He joined Young Fine Gael as a student and was Deputy President of the Students' Union.

His grandfather Patrick Moriarty was a senator, and Michael followed the family tradition when at the age of 24 he was elected to Waterford City Council on his first attempt. He stood unsuccessfully for the Dail in 2007, being eliminated on the 8th count but performing very creditably.

He combined working in the family engineering business with his role as a city councillor.

The issues with which he was most connected were the campaign to give the Waterford Institute of Technology university status, improved services at Ardkeen Hospital and support for small businesses in Waterford.

In the 2011 general election he topped the poll, bringing in his more experienced running mate Vincent O'Connor. His promotion to Junior Minister was unexpected but no doubt his outstanding election success played a part.

Michael's premature death at the age of 38 after only a year in his new role, and with a bright future before him, is a tragedy for his family, his constituents and the country.

This is the second tragedy in a year for the family. Last April Michael and his wife lost their only child to a cot death.

He leaves a wife Fiona, a former Waterford Rose, two brothers, Paul and Seamus, and his parents Sinead and Fearghal.

Michael Moriarty Born 12.2.1974. Died 20.3.2012'

So this family has also lost a baby. A cot death. How absolutely tragic! My sister had her baby last month and worries all the time about cot deaths.

But nothing about Carli at the funeral. At the bottom of the pile I see the Daily News.

The headline reads - **Carli ordered to leave Minister's Funeral.**

I read on:

'Waterford singer songwriter Carli Walsh was ejected from the funeral of Irish Junior Minister Michael Moriarty.

Mr Moriarty died suddenly earlier in the week and Carli, a constituent of his, was attending the funeral.

She told our reporter at the funeral,

'I knew Michael. He was my local councillor and he really helped me when I needed housing for my son Tommy and me. He used to hold his constituency clinic in the pub where I sang. He helped so many people. It's so sad that he has died. I'd just taken my seat when two security men came up to me and said I had to leave. I asked who said so, and they said it was Mrs Moriarty. I refused to go. I said there must be some mistake and I would go and talk to her. But they refused to let me; they just took hold of my arms and almost dragged me out. It was really embarrassing in front of all those people.'

Mrs Moriarty did not return our calls.

An inquest into Minister Moriarty's sudden death will be held next month.'

Absolutely weird. Why would poor Mrs Moriarty have Carli removed from the funeral? On the Forum, needless to say, suggestions are being made. I haven't posted for a while but other regulars obviously have judging from the number of posts logged. I can't resist joining in.

Missing Children Forum	
Portal Home Register Log In	every child matters
March 27 2012 at 7.11 pm I can't believe that Carli Walsh would turn up at a funeral just to keep her profile up. Has she no shame?	Noelle Posts: 51 Join Date: 3.10.2011 Location: Bradford
March 27 2012 at 7.23 pm You have to understand the funeral culture in Ireland. It's different to the UK. My aunt's from Waterford. She was at the funeral because she met him on the doorstep when he was canvassing. She says he was a good guy.	Miss Marple Posts: 47 Join Date: 10.9.2011 Location: St Mary Mead

March 27 2012 at 7.31 pm Surprised you're not putting forward a conspiracy theory Miss Marple – seeing a connection between this poor man's death and Carli's missing baby. By the way, have you worked out yet what the connection is between the Tommy and Rose cases!!!!	CoolDude Posts: 69 Join Date: 4.7.2011 Location: Bahamas
March 27 2012 at 7.43 pm You're not provoking me CoolDude. I'm here to debate not to insult other members.	Miss Marple Posts: 48 Join Date: 10.9.2011 Location: St Mary Mead
March 27 2012 at 7.52 pm But you have to admit it's really odd that someone so young would die in their bed and then Carli is ejected from his funeral.	Liam Posts: 31 Join Date: 2.8.2011 Location: Belfast

March 27 2012 at 8.06 pm	Mags
Did you see it said that the politician's wife lost a child to a cot death last year? Probably suffering from depression and didn't know what she was doing. Got upset when she saw the cameras and journalists concentrating on Carli?	Posts: 381 Join Date: 2.9.2010 Location: Liverpool
March 27 2012 at 8.32 pm	Sherlock
Wasn't he mentioned a couple of weeks back in one of the papers about some expenses; something about excessive mileage claims?	Posts: 112 Join Date: 29.6.2011 Location: Baker Street
March 27 2012 at 8.57 pm	Declan
Think you're right about that. But nobody cares about dodgy expenses claims. Nobody ever resigns. Irish politicians feel they're entitled to get everything they can from the system. Doubt if a newspaper article about suspect claims would have caused him much angst.	Posts: 472 Join Date: 2.4.2011 Location: Dublin

March 27 2012 at 9.12 pm The inquest will be next month. Hopefully that'll explain things.	Liam Posts: 32 Join Date: 2.8.2011 Location: Belfast
March 27 2012 at 9.27 pm Did anyone see the film on TV last night – Gone Baby Gone	Declan Posts: 473 Join Date: 2.4.2011 Location: Dublin
March 27 2012 at 9.38 pm Yeah, great film, and Casey Affleck's a really good looking guy	Suzy Posts: 89 Join Date: 27.2.2011 Location: Bath

March 27 2012 at 9.59 pm	Declan
It reminded me of Carli. It's about a 4 year old girl going missing in the States. She's left home alone and her mother is what they call white trash. A bit unfair to compare her to Carli maybe. Great twist at the end – won't mention it here for those of you who haven't seen it!	Posts: 474 Join Date: 2.4.2011 Location: Dublin

I resolve to get that film out on DVD.

CHAPTER 25

Ican't wait for the results of the Inquest on the dead Irish
politician from Waterford but in the end it leaves unanswered
questions as inquests so often do.

Daily News April 25, 2012

Inquest returns accidental death verdict on Minister

*'A packed court heard Coroner James Farrelly return a verdict
of accidental death on Junior Minister Michael Moriarty.*

*Close friends spoke of the long hours worked by the Minister
following his surprise promotion. His wife Fiona Moriarty said
she had begged him to ease up and see his GP. She said he had
been very upset by the loss of their first child in a cot death last
April. They had been for counselling and she thought he had
moved on, as she had done. She insisted he was not depressed.*

*A tearful Mrs Moriarty told the court, 'Our doctor told us
there was no reason for it to happen again and we were hoping
to have another baby. Michael had everything to live for and
the nasty speculation about suicide is disgusting; rumours
put about by political opponents and people who need help
themselves.'*

*She continued, 'Michael had a particularly important
meeting in Dublin the next day. I think after reading his brief,
he succumbed to the temptation of hoping that a mixture of
brandy and sleeping pills would help him. He wasn't much of a
drinker. I think the brandy made him quite tipsy and affected
his judgement so he didn't appreciate how many pills he had
taken. They were my pills, prescribed for me after our baby*

died. He'd no idea how strong they were. How I wish I had thrown them away when I stopped taking them, but they were in our bathroom cabinet.'

Coroner James Farrelly said the death was a tragic accident, a warning of the dangers of mixing alcohol and prescribed medication. He expressed his sympathy to the widow and the deceased's family.'

No mention of Carli in the inquest report and there hasn't been anything else about the funeral incident. You'd think some enterprising journalist would ask questions but then again there must be huge sympathy for poor Mrs Moriarty. She lost her first child to a cot death after apparently waiting for a child for years and then she loses her husband. And it's her sleeping pills he took. I'm glad my GP refused to keep prescribing them for me. Sometimes I was so sad I could have done something stupid.

I suppose Mrs Moriarty was just overwhelmed with grief and it was simply because she recognised Carli that she acted the way she did. If Carli had only been a pub singer whom her husband helped, she wouldn't have known who she was. But Mrs Moriarty has lost a child. Could she, or indeed any mother, who had had a similar loss while depressed from the death, take a baby on impulse if the opportunity was presented? There's no evidence that she did. She was probably just furious that someone who lost her child due to pure selfishness turned up at the funeral.

Should I put her in my list of suspects? I'm not sure.

CHAPTER 26

Nothing in the papers about Amy other than the odd inside page piece about her husband making slow progress. But my own research into Liz's revelation is progressing albeit slowly.

I'd like to find out more about Amy's first daughter, the one who was adopted. She'd be 18 or 19 now. Could she be involved in any way? She's old enough now to access her adoption records. She could have tracked her mother down, seen her living in affluent circumstances and asked why she gave her away. Maybe the daughter didn't get a good deal from the adoption. Could she have punished Amy for giving her away by taking her baby? Probably wild speculation on my part and there's no way of finding out about the daughter as I have no status in the matter. Liz doesn't know any more than she's told me and it's unrealistic to think I could befriend Amy as I have some of the other actors in this drama.....

**

I am making limited progress with tracking down Peter. Without his surname it's difficult to say the least. I thought it would be relatively easy as I had Liz's name and could use the Medical Council database which is open to the public to find when she trained; from that I could draw up a shortlist of doctors who might be Amy's former boyfriend. As his first name Peter, is a common one, I knew it wouldn't be immediately obvious but nonetheless possible.

But I hit an unexpected problem. I can't find Liz in the database. For one crazy moment I wonder if meeting her was a dream! Then I remember she said she hated her original name and had insisted on being called Liz. She'd refused to tell me what it was saying it was embarrassing. I tried using just the surname she had given me, but still couldn't locate her. Maybe her parents had split up and she had taken her stepfather's name but her medical training was in her original name. I had her telephone number and email address but I couldn't exactly ask her for clarification now that she has politely told me to 'back off.'

So I had to work on the name Peter only and the database revealed so many of them that sometimes I thought I'd be on my old age pension by the time I had a shortlist. Fortunately I was able to rule out lots of names on the basis of their age but that still left many to be followed up as I didn't know whether Peter started medical training straight from school or had changed career in later life which quite often happens. So I had to allow for some flexibility in his age when editing the list. If only I could have asked Liz these questions when she had dropped the bombshell in the hotel restaurant but I couldn't let her suspect what I intended to do.

After several frustrating months, and many embarrassing phone calls to the wrong Peter, I am down to nineteen names, all based outside the UK. I have obviously worked through the UK based doctors first. I use different stories to explain my call; sometimes I am a journalist trying to track down the trainee doctor the Jennings interview mentioned, sometimes I am a solicitor trying to track a deceased client's nephew. The story is that due to a family dispute the nephew Peter has changed his family name and is using another which is unknown to us as it doesn't appear to have been formally changed. The hint of a possible inheritance usually gets a relatively positive reaction, but none of these doctors fit the facts as I know them.

It was actually one of the doctors I tell the journalism story to who is helpful. He vaguely recalls a student called Peter in the year below his he'd seen around with a girl fitting Amy's general description. He remembers because he 'liked the look of her. She had great tits.' He can't recall the surname; he thinks it began with a 'B' and was fairly common like Barlow.

I'm going to have to take a break from the Peter research for a while as I've a trip to Waterford coming up. Sometimes I think the time spent on finding Peter shows I've lost it. He's probably married now with children of his own. That reunion was almost four years ago. If he's married, he couldn't possibly have taken Tommy. And if he's married even if he turns out to be the spitting image of Jeff what's the point of finding him? There is no point; get real Molly!

PART III

WATERFORD 2010

CHAPTER 27

Carli   Wednesday January 6, 2010

Not a great start to the New Year; they'd been fighting on and off since Stephen's Day. She tells herself that anyone sharing a bedsitter and kept in by freezing weather would fight. And Dave is really being selfish. She is practising her new songs for tonight when he has the neck to ask her to turn her volume down as he can't hear the telly.

Fucking prick! She swears under her breath. She is bringing in as much money as he is; not that it's much though, his dole and her gigs.

Just before she leaves for the pub another row erupts. She isn't even sure what sets this one off but she shouts not to expect her back; she'll go to Emer's. True to her word she doesn't return that night or for the following six days.

**

When she arrives at the pub around nine o'clock it's quite crowded. She's surprised as it's a cold night but then she supposes people are bored with being in over the Christmas period. She notices a few of her regulars who sometimes send drinks over after she finishes singing. Tonight she's certainly not rushing home. She'll be more than happy to accept some drinks and keep them company. They appreciate her. She notices one man in the group whom she talked to last month; some sort of politician. He'd said he'd just finished his clinic and had come downstairs for a drink. She'd asked why would a doctor have a surgery in a pub; said she never saw a surgery sign. He'd laughed and said he wasn't a doctor.

'I'm a councillor and I have a constituency clinic upstairs every fortnight.'

Seeing her blank face he had continued, 'People come to see me with their problems and I try to help them.'

He had asked with a grin whether she had voted for him.

And she had responded that he must be joking as she wasn't old enough to vote until the end of the year, but that anyway she wasn't interested in politics. She didn't ask him what party he was in. Dave had told her all politicians were the same.

Over Christmas she'd written a new song and she tries it out. It goes down well. The whole gig goes particularly well. She's just finished her set when Shay the barman says the guy over there wants her to join him. It's her politician friend now on his own. Why not, she thinks? She's accepted drinks from him before and he's a problem solver; maybe he can solve hers.

She joins him and jokes, 'Did you solve many problems tonight?'

'A few,' he responds. 'But do you remember my name?' He had told her when they first met and she tries unsuccessfully to recall it. Her face tells him the answer so he spares her embarrassment and introduces himself once more.

'Michael Moriarty.' He thrusts a card into her hand. Then he says, 'I loved your new song. You're really talented you know.'

That puts a smile on her face. Dave used to be supportive but lately he's been dismissive. He'd said the new song was crap which sparked the big row, though it had been coming for a while. Michael tells her that he used to play the guitar but he doesn't have time now because he's working to get elected, and can't wait for a general election to come. He sees the look on her face when he mentions elections.

'I wish young people like you could see that politics matters.'

She points out that there's no work in Waterford whether you're young or old.

'That's because the boom was wasted. We have to get rid of this government to change things. Then there'll be opportunities for talented young people like you.'

She asks what about young people without talent; don't they deserve a job too? He's impressed with her reply she thinks. He orders her another vodka and tonic. She wonders how old he is. In his 30s she reckons. She likes his smart haircut. Really good jeans and a long navy sweater. Good looking for an older guy. And he's also wearing what looks like a wedding ring.

'Excuse my ignorance,' she says, 'but what party are you?'

'I'm Fine Gael,' he says proudly.

'My foster father Paddy used to say they were as bad as Fianna Fail.'

'Well, he didn't know what he was talking about. Have you heard of Enda Kenny our leader?'

'Yeah. Paddy said he's just a rural school teacher; not suited to be a leader.'

'Promise me you'll consider voting if I promise to buy your first album.'

He's won her over.

'Do you know anyone who can help me get a record deal?'

'Maybe. It's hard but I could introduce you to a few people.'

He orders another drink for both of them. This is her third vodka on a relatively empty stomach. There wasn't much food in the house and she hadn't felt like cooking for Dave as she was so annoyed with him. So she'd just made herself a sandwich before dashing out.

She is enjoying herself but she hasn't had a cigarette for over an hour.

She asks him to excuse her while she has a smoke. He says he'll keep her company. They go outside to the smoking area at the back of the pub; it's empty given the freezing night. They chat and as she tosses the cigarette butt into the bin he suddenly pulls her close and kisses her on the lips.

'I've wanted to do that all night.'

It's a corny line she thinks cynically.

'You're really different, so talented and I'd do anything I could to help you.'

She has seconds to decide what to do, slap his face, push him away gently or respond in kind.

Maybe if it had been any other night she would have gone for the pushing away gently option but she'd left the bedsitter after a blazing row and said she wasn't coming back tonight. Here is a guy appreciating her. So she kisses him back.

'Carli, let's get out of here, I'll take you home with me.'

They gulp down the remainder of their drinks and get into his car. She is too light-headed to point out that he must be over the limit, but they get to his place safely, a bungalow a mile or so outside the city.

He takes off her coat, sits her on the settee and asks what music she would like. Whatever. She doesn't care; this is bliss. The warmth after her draughty bedsitter. The luxury of the leather couch. He pours out drinks. Hardly giving her time to take a sip he kisses her. She has to put down the drink. He tries to unbutton her top but they are fake buttons. He laughs. 'Take it off Carli,' he pleads. She does. Despite the cold night all she's wearing under her top is a bra which he removes deftly. She's quite full busted for her height which is 5' 3". He sucks on her nipples for what seems ages but in reality it's only a few minutes. Then he picks her up and carries her naked from the waist up into the bedroom.

**

Afterwards she asks him what if his wife comes home.

'You didn't ask that before,' he accuses her with a grin on his face.

'I didn't care,' she admits and kisses him.

'She's abroad for the week on business. She does her own thing. She wouldn't mind.'

She believes him because it suits her to believe him. Obviously the wife isn't here; and she likes him so why not?

There's a missed call from Dave on her mobile so before she forgets she texts Emer, *'If Dave rings, I'm with you. Talk to you in the morning.'*

**

She stays with Michael for the week. He runs an engineering business as well as being a councillor so he's out all day and she can write and practice without worrying about the noise. He's warned her not to answer the phone or the door. The next day she tries to find out more about the wife.

'I've been married for ten years.'

'Why don't you have any children?'

'Fiona didn't want any at first which suited me then. But she keeps putting it on the long finger and it's pissing me off.'

They're lying in bed one night and she says, 'Would you like a baby with me Michael?' He doesn't answer; he just rolls over and makes love again. She hadn't meant it seriously. She's never had so much sex in a week. If all politicians are like this she thinks, young women could get seriously interested in politics.

She hates leaving. She's spoken to Emer to check that she's been covering for her. She's ignored calls from Dave until now but she's going to ring him and say she's calmed down and coming home tonight.

**

Dave is so sweet to her tonight. Loving, and asking how her writing went at Emer's. He says it must be so much easier to work there than in a bedsitter. He knows Emer's family have a second reception room they don't use much. She feels a right hypocrite. She'd got used to the comforts at Michael's house. The proper power shower, not like their one with weird temperature controls, the lovely kitchen not like their two ring Belling in the corner, and the soft carpets everywhere. When she makes it big, she'll have all those things. Yes, she will.

**

Two months later she discovers she's pregnant, which doesn't make sense as she's on the pill. Her GP sees her disbelief at the news she has just given her.

'Don't you remember that when you came to see me with that eye infection and you needed antibiotics I warned you that they can affect the pill's reliability. I suggested you took other precautions to be sure'

She remembers now that the doctor did say that, and it was a couple of days before she'd met up with Michael again. She's almost sure he is the father. She'd had sex with Dave the first night she was back but she had managed to put him off for a while claiming that she didn't feel well. But she can't be sure.

That September she read a story in the local paper.

First baby for Waterford Councillor Michael Moriarty

Local FG Councillor Michael Moriarty, tipped for a seat in the Dail when the general election is called, is now the proud father of a 9 lb baby boy Eoin Darragh who was born yesterday to his wife, former top model Fiona Moriarty. Councillor Moriarty told the Observer 'This is the best day of my life; we've been waiting for a baby ever since we got married ten years ago'.

The happy parents are pictured in a private room at Waterford Memorial Hospital.

So Mrs Moriarty, ex top model, was pregnant when he fucked her, though he probably didn't know it at the time. All that crap about her doing her own thing....

When the baby comes, she'll be able to find out whose it is, and he'll have to help her if it's his.

**

She's got lots of information about blood groups from the library. She's told the librarian she's doing a project at school and the woman has been so helpful.

In the hospital she had asked the nurse what Tommy's blood group was. She knows Dave's as well as her own because he needed a transfusion when he had an accident on his bike two years ago. Both she and Dave are group A and Tommy is B. She knew from the library research that it's not possible for two people with blood group A to have a baby with blood group B. It might not have been conclusive if Tommy had been either type A or O, but the position was quite clear with him being type B. Michael was his father.......

**

As soon as she's out of hospital she checks the times of Michael's clinics. He no longer holds them at the pub. They had stopped shortly after that week in his house which doesn't surprise her. She had thought of contacting him but hadn't, given that Dave was being so nice to her. The details of the new clinic are on his website. The helpful librarian had checked that for her too.

She takes Tommy with her; the woman ahead of her is drooling over him. She tells her she's come to get help getting a medical card because her friend told her he (Michael) can fix anything. 'I've always been Fianna Fail,'she confides, 'but the Fianna Fail councillor we've got now is a rude bastard and this fellow is lovely and good-looking as well'.

One of the helpers asks for her name and address which she provides. 'What's the nature of your problem?' she asks. She is tempted to say, 'Your boss fucked me.' But the helper is a pleasant girl, presumably giving up her evening for nothing to help the party. Could he have fucked her too she thinks cynically?

'I'd prefer not to say,' she says, 'it's personal.'

'That's OK,' the helper says.

Twenty minutes later she is sitting in front of Michael. He has had sixty seconds notice of her arrival as the assistant has only just handed in the inquiry form she completed for her. But there is no mention of Tommy on the form.

'Nice to see you again,' he says not sounding very sincere.

'Here's your son,' she says. 'He's looking forward to playing with Eoin.'

He gets up and opens the door to see if the assistant is in earshot. She isn't. He shuts the door.

'You're joking?'

'I'm not. Tommy was born on October 13. I was with you for that week in January and after I was back I avoided Dave for the first week or so apart from the first night I was back.'

'So he could be the father?' he interrupts.

'What's your blood group?'

He ignores her.

'What's your blood group?' she repeats loudly.

Obviously scared that his helper will overhear, he reluctantly answers to stop Carli shouting the question. In hardly more than a whisper he says, 'Group B.'

'Tommy,' she says, 'is Group B. Dave and me are both Group A so Tommy can't be Dave's. It's that simple. The father has to have blood type B and you're the only person I slept with at that time.' She says that emphatically before he tries to suggest she'd been fucking around all January.

'You should have come to me and I'd have given you the money for an.......'

Carli interrupts angrily.

'For an abortion? You fucker. You were in the papers talking about family values when your baby was born.'

He looks embarrassed as well he might.

'Look, this has been a shock but we can work something out.'

She is surprised he doesn't mention getting a DNA test which the librarian had told her about, but then he'd be terrified of it getting out. She suggests getting a solicitor to draw up a maintenance agreement.

'No, that's not necessary. Waterford's a small place. We need to keep this quiet. Dave and Fiona don't need to know this.'

She'd expected this would be his attitude and had brought in her credit union account details.

'I want €1,000 a month paid in for now, and we can talk about more when he gets older.'

He looks pale. 'That's a ridiculous amount. You must be getting benefits.'

She retorts angrily, 'Dave gets the reduced rate of dole because he's under 21, I don't get single parents money as I live with him and our rent allowance has been cut. We can't afford to insure the old car we have....'

He sees she means business.

'OK,' he says, 'I'll pay but this'll be really hard. Fiona's given up her job to look after our baby. And I'll have election expenses when the government falls. The party pays for damn all.'

'I don't fucking care,' she retorts. She sweeps out forgetting to say goodbye to the assistant who looks slightly hurt by her abruptness.

PART IV

MAY 2012 – JULY 2012

CHAPTER 28

C arli has been in the news a lot after that funeral incident, but in a more positive light.

Sunday News   May 13, 2012

Carli 4th in Eurovision

'Ireland's Carli Walsh singing 'Nowhere to go' which she co-wrote came in 4th last night in the Eurovision Final, Ireland's best performance for years. Last year Jedward came 8th ending a run of disastrous Irish results.

She sang her heart out but couldn't beat the Eastern European voting bloc even though she sang part of her song in Polish.

Lithuania won with 137 points, with Carli eleven points behind. It was the closest Eurovision for years. Carli arrives back this evening at 6 pm at Dublin airport and is expected to get a tumultuous reception from fans.'

I have to admit I watched the Eurovision final against my better judgement. She's certainly an outstanding talent but I can't help wondering how she would manage her new lifestyle if she still had a 19 month old child as he would be now. Reading an interview in Celebrity Now confirmed my thoughts that perhaps Tommy is better off without her, providing he's now with a loving family. But you just don't know that.

Celebrity Now w/e May 23, 2012

Suzy Simmons our Show Biz Correspondent catches up with Carli Walsh

'SS: *Congrats on Eurovision Carli.*

CW: *Thanks. I had an amazing time.*

SS: *You were one of the favourites. Did that put pressure on you?*

CW: *Yes it did, but a bit of pressure is good. To be honest I never thought I'd win and I was over the moon with getting 4th. Unreal. The record got to No.1 in Ireland and No.3 in the UK. I've a tour of Eastern Europe starting soon.*

SS: *You've been quoted as saying you haven't time for love. That must be even truer now?*

CW: *Well it is and it isn't.*

SS: *Tell us Carli.*

CW: *Dave and I are hoping to get together again. It's not easy with all the travel I do. He's feeling very positive about his future. He'd been unemployed for a good while and that helped to break us up. He wants his own career. He doesn't want to live off me (she laughs). I don't have that much anyway as that solicitor ran off with my money at Christmas and I had to start again.*

SS: *Our readers will wish you all the best with making your relationship work again. It's so good of you to find time to talk to us.*

CW: It's a pleasure Suzy. I've an album coming out next month and I hope the readers will love it.'

Not one question about Tommy. It makes you ask about journalistic standards but I suppose Celebrity Now is not where a decent journalist would work. I don't normally buy it but because the cover promised an exclusive interview with Carli, I bought it, in the interest of research you understand! Is she trying to change her image by getting back with the father of her child? But she doesn't even mention the child and she could have even if the journalist didn't ask!

**

I've been wondering about contacting Alro as his silence has continued but don't want to scare him off. Then just when I'm about to give up, I get an email from him.

'Miss Marple, you need to look into the connection between Minister Michael Moriarty and Carli Walsh. It was more than fixing her up with housing.'

A bit cryptic. I email back.

'I read that that he had a constituency clinic in the pub where she sang so she could have known him apart from meeting him over her housing problem. And isn't it usual for politicians to fix things for constituents? That's how they get re-elected. What other connection could there be? I hear that nobody needs an excuse to attend a funeral in Ireland!'

He replies.

'They say here that Mrs Moriarty hates her, and you'd have to ask why. She did give one interview recently and this is what she said about the funeral incident:

'She was there to get photographed. She knew the Taoiseach would be there and lots of important people. And TV cameras. It was all about her and her profile. I didn't want someone like her demeaning Michael's funeral. You know how she left her baby in a car. I just wanted her out.'

'Now later she denied she said that, in fact she claimed that the journalist printed other comments that were off the record but you would wonder why she'd say anything about the funeral incident other than to say she was stressed and it was all a mistake.'

I'm getting a message. Moriarty was not the stereotyped career politician; late middle age, getting a paunch and hair thinning. In fact he was in his late thirties, looked younger, was a snappy dresser, tweeted and had hundreds of followers. So is Alro saying the ambitious Carli and the equally ambitious politician were 'an item' as the saying goes? Mrs Moriarty is glamorous and a former Waterford Rose but that doesn't mean her husband wouldn't stray.

A final cryptic PS from Alro –

'Moriarty might have had money problems. And he wasn't good at picking solicitors.'

The only solicitor I know of in Waterford is the one who did the bunk at Christmas with Carli's money. Bingo! If Padraig Mahoney also acted for Moriarty then that is a possibly significant link between them.

I can't get anything more out of Alro so I concentrate on organizing another trip to Waterford. I've been back at work for almost five months and I'm due time in lieu for all the overtime I've been doing.

**

I had called into the Black Swan during my New Year trip to Waterford but hadn't gleaned any useful information as the regular staff were on leave. What a difference on my second visit; a major revamp has taken place. I comment on this to the barman on duty who explains that the publicity about Carli Walsh singing there brought in customers even though she doesn't sing there now. Which meant the pub owner could afford to do the place up.

'Does she ever drop in here now? I'm a big fan of hers.'

'She did a couple of times but she's based in London now. You should talk to Shay over there. He's the barman who knew her best.'

Shay is delighted to be asked about Carli. He explains he's been working in the bar since 2006. We chat about the Eurovision result and agree she was robbed thanks to the Eastern European bloc vote. Then I bring up the funeral incident.

'Did you know Minister Moriarty, Councillor Moriarty as he was when he held his clinic upstairs?'

'Yeah, he was here every fortnight. It was good for business because some of the people would come into the pub for a drink after seeing him. Sometimes he came down himself. You'd see him with a group of regulars; we'd say he was getting the drinkers' votes. When I think about it, he'd usually stay on when we had live music. Think he once said something about playing a guitar when he was young. Jesus, he was only in his 30s.'

'Did he know Carli?'

'I remember him sending her over a drink the odd time. He wasn't the only one who did that. The regulars usually look after the musicians. But now that you mention it there was one time he spent a good lot of time with her after she finished her set. I remember because he suggested I ask her over to join him and she did. Me and Derek, the other barman on that night were laughing about it; saying these politicians don't miss a trick. Carli would have been eligible to vote next time round, though whether she would have bothered is another matter. I think they left together but I can't be sure. He might have given her a lift home.'

'Do you remember when that was?'

The young barman reflects.

'Probably a couple of years ago. Was about a month before Mr Moriarty closed his clinic here.'

'Why did Mr Moriarty close the clinic?'

'I think he said party HQ didn't want clinics in pubs; gives the wrong impression. The anti drink lobby had been getting at the political parties. The manager was disappointed. Gave him the room free because he's a Fine Gael supporter. We heard he paid a fancy rent somewhere else.'

**

My next call is to Padraig Mahoney's office. I'd contacted the Irish Law Society claiming to represent an elderly client of the firm. Apparently a trainee solicitor who had worked there had stayed on to help the gardai and an accountant had been sent in by the Law Society. I deliberately leave my visit until the lunch period in the hope that I find someone like a secretary manning the office who may be persuaded to reveal a thing or two.

I'm in luck. A rather plain woman in her 50s is eating a cheese and coleslaw sandwich in the dingy office. A piece of coleslaw falls out of her overfull sandwich onto her blouse. Deftly I retrieve a tissue from my handbag and offer it; she gratefully accepts.

'Sorry to interrupt your lunch, I'd hoped to get here sooner but the bus was late.'

Her mouth cleared, she's able to speak.

'What can I do for you?'

I call on my acting skills and start apologetically.

'I read about the problem with the clients' account. My granddad's pretty old and confused now and granny thinks he made a will with Mr Mahoney but can't find a copy in the house. She's worried about it and I promised I'd call in personally to sort it out.' I give her a common name and a vague address in a village outside Waterford.

She says she has a list of wills but it's in the safe which is locked at the moment but if I can wait until the Law Society man is back from lunch she can help me.

'Do you remember the name?'

She admits she doesn't. Not surprising really as I made it up.

'Have you worked here long?'

She beams. 'I worked for Mr Mahoney's late father and I stayed on when he took over the practice.'

'So you'd be familiar with all the clients. Perhaps my granny got it wrong?'

'Generally I'd know all the clients' names, but I had quite a bit of sick leave one year and your granddad could have been in then.'

'How much longer before that man gets back?'

'I'd say about half an hour.'

So I have a bit less than that to get information. She's finished her sandwich now.

I say sympathetically, 'It must have been dreadful for you when the press printed that story especially with you working here so long.'

I think she is going to cry. I continue.

'I don't believe everything I read. Maybe it's all a terrible mistake or a set up and he just felt he had to get away? I'd read about him before that story at Christmas. Carli Walsh wrote on her blog about the great work he was doing for her.'

I get the impression she doesn't know what a blog is. Anyway I continue, 'And didn't he act for poor Minister Moriarty? A smart man like that wouldn't get involved with a dishonest solicitor.'

She nods in agreement.

'Padraig looked after Mr Moriarty's business. He was often in here; a lovely man. I voted for him.'

'Poor Mrs Moriarty,' I say, 'how will she ever get over it?'

The secretary's expression changes.

'She was in here several times before all the trouble and she wasn't very polite to Padraig. I heard an argument the last time she was in. Don't know what it was about but she flounced out shouting, 'I don't believe there's no money.' Afterwards Padraig told me it was all a misunderstanding but he seemed really shook up.'

I sense I'm not going to get any more information about Moriarty so I ask if she's met Carli.

'She never came here, but of course I typed lots of stuff to do with her. We had to stop the papers printing all the lies.'

'Doesn't look hopeful for finding her son? It's been nine months now.'

She looks as if she's about to tell me something and I'm aware that time's ticking away. I take a risk.

'I read that Padraig was helping her with a private search. Maybe that wasn't true?'

'No, we talked about it but never did. We trusted the gardai but I'll tell you one thing. Just before Christmas I took a call from a woman who said she was Amy Blake. I put her though to Padraig and they were talking for some time. I'm sure it was the one who lost her baby too. And I know from the phone bills he rang her after that.'

Very interesting.

'He didn't tell you anything about the call?'

'No he didn't but he was always very confidential; he didn't tell me things unless I needed to know.'

One last question.

She clearly doesn't like Mrs Moriarty so I mention the funeral incident and how shocking it was when Carli was only showing her respects.

Bingo again.

'I was at the funeral. I saw it. Of course she was there; Mr Moriarty was good to her. She said he helped with housing but he also fixed her up with part-time work with his company.'

I look surprised.

'I know because we organized a standing order payment from the company to Carli's credit union account. Padraig told me she was going to help with bookkeeping.'

OMG! A school dropout who never did a bookkeeping course in her life being paid for accounts work by a company Alro suspects is in difficulties. That doesn't make sense.

The Law Society man will be back any minute. I look at my watch in an exaggerated way.

'I interrupted your lunch and you've been so kind. I've remembered I promised to meet someone at two o'clock. I've got to go.'

I scribble my name and phone number on a scrap of paper and rush out asking her to call me if she finds the will in the safe.

So Amy and the solicitor knew each other which helps to explain why she posted on her blog about his being innocent until proved guilty, though it doesn't tell me why she had the contacts with him. Could it simply be to arrange a meeting with his client Carli? Why go through him? She could probably get Carli's number through her PR people though they might want to publicise any meeting. Amy would trust a solicitor's confidentiality. Yes, that could be it, she wanted to meet the young woman who like her had lost a child and suffered at the hands of the media.

And, confirmation of sorts of my suspicion of Mrs Moriarty. A row about money; not necessarily connected with Carli but the secretary had said Moriarty's company was paying money to her for bookkeeping which seems rather unlikely.

It was worth missing lunch for this amount of information.

CHAPTER 29

My next meeting is not in fact until six o'clock so I have four hours to kill. A leisurely late lunch in the Tower Hotel helps pass some time. If only I had my swimming togs with me, I'd have spent the afternoon in the hotel's leisure centre.

But my togs are at home so I decide to revisit Reginald's Tower adjacent to the hotel. I know the Tower from my time in Waterford as a student. I'm a bit of a history buff and I love the Tower and the area around it known as the Viking Triangle. I spend an hour taking in the history of the Tower imagining I am Aoife, daughter of the King of Leinster, who married Strongbow there.

Back in the 'real' world I find an internet café hoping for news from my accountant cousin Brian. He was a bit surprised when I rang him asking him to get the latest Moriarty company accounts from the Companies Office and to give me his thoughts on them.

'Molly, I have the accounts for Moriarty Engineering for 2009 and 2010. The company made a loss in 2009 and 2010 and was just about solvent at the end of 2010. Nothing surprising about that in a recession, but one thing I notice is that Michael Moriarty took out €50,000 as a director's loan in the year ending 30 November 2010 and the election wasn't until February 2011. There's no way of knowing when in the year he took it out.'

Interesting. Brian's briefing continues:

'He'd have a salary as councillor and expenses but that isn't anything like the TD package. He didn't get the ministerial salary until March 2011. The accounts for the year ending

30 November 2011 haven't been filed yet so there's no way of knowing if he repaid the loan in that year.'

Now, nobody knew for sure when the general election would be. I can understand taking out a loan for election expenses but why take it out before you need it and pay interest?

'Molly, one final thing, that solicitor who did a runner, Padraig Mahoney was solicitor to the company.'

I already knew that, but good to have it independently confirmed.

'Thanks Brian, let me know when you've finished looking at the other stuff I sent you. Molly x'

I had dispatched Davina's documents to him for advice since some of them didn't mean a lot to me.

So another mystery. What happened to the €50,000? Could it have gone to Padraig and vanished with him? Could that be the reason why Mrs Moriarty was so upset and mentioned missing money? But why would a loan for election expenses or some other personal expenses be handed over to the company solicitor? That doesn't make sense.

**

Killing time in a café until my appointment with Emer Flynn, I order another coffee and make one of my lists encompassing the information I have gathered today.

What if the loan was to do with Carli Walsh? He was already providing her with a monthly income for apparently doing some work for his company. Now given the unemployment situation when you can get good workers for minimum wage why would he hire Carli with zilch experience as a bookkeeper?

Could the monthly payment be for Tommy rather than for wages? The only way he'd be doing that is if he was the father. OMG. That would explain why Mrs Moriarty hated her.

It might also explain that €50,000. It was taken out of the company at the latest by 30 November 2010 when Carli was just a pub singer with a new baby. Tommy was born that October. Could the money be to do with his future? A solicitor could be needed to draw up documents.

**

It's time for my next meeting almost before I know it. I'd looked in on the Forum while in the internet café resisting the temptation to post, afraid of saying too much. It's been an incredible day so far, but will Emer talk? We've exchanged a lot of Facebook messages since her holiday and I feel I know her. I've arranged to call to her house; she lives quite near to Aunt Bernie and I'd stressed how easy it would be to meet at her home. My intention is to have her relaxed so she will hopefully speak freely. I know from her Facebook page that she likes a particular brand of vodka so I've bought a bottle and some mixer.

Mrs Flynn answers the door and ushers me into the neat living room.

'Emer's been delayed at work but says she should be here in about ten minutes.' So my luck continues; I have some time alone with her mother who may be able to help me. It was the emergency with Mrs Flynn that resulted in Tommy being left alone and taken, if that's what happened but I'm really not sure if it did. She offers tea and has made cakes because I'm coming; very sweet of her.

I ask her if she knows Bernie and we chat about the Irish side of my family. She decides she probably knows Bernie 'to see' and thinks my cousin Sandra was at school with another of her children. This establishes my bona fides which is important. I ask her about Carli and she beams.

'She spent lots of time here because she wasn't very happy after her foster parents took another girl in.'

I comment, 'It's amazing how well she's doing now. If only they could find her baby, wouldn't her life be perfect?'

Mrs Flynn interjects. 'I blame myself for Tommy being gone.'

'You can't blame yourself for being ill.'

'Emer thought I was really bad at the hospital and came to get me instead of Tommy. I didn't know about her collecting him. When I rang her, I exaggerated a bit about how I felt. I'd been waiting around all afternoon in outpatients for blood test results, then they gave me an injection. They found it hard to get a vein and I got a bit upset. I don't like injections. I couldn't face waiting for the bus and then it's quite a walk here from the bus stop. Emer left Carli a message but she didn't get it.'

Mrs Flynn is genuinely upset. I reach across the settee and take her hand.

'Don't blame yourself. You did need help getting home and there was no way you could know about Emer having just agreed to collect Tommy. Carli really should have taken him into the hairdressers.'

She continues as if I haven't said anything. 'I didn't sleep for a month after it happened. The gardai were here. It was dreadful.'

'Have you seen Carli since it happened?'

'Only once, but Emer's in touch with her all the time.'

'I was hoping to meet up with Emer when I came over at New Year but she was away on holiday.'

'She really needed that holiday. She works all the hours she can get and she's resitting some of her Leaving Certificate this summer. She wants to go to college.'

That holiday had puzzled me as Emer's Facebook page had indicated she was broke. Could Carli have paid for it to keep her quiet? Or was it a genuine kindness to a good friend? And Carli was possibly broke herself following the solicitor's actions, though it's not clear whether she had retained some money herself.

'Holidays are important. It must be hard, working and studying.'

'She wants to be a nurse but she didn't do well enough in her exams to get in, so she's trying to get better grades.'

'Being good at exams doesn't make you a good nurse.'

I've struck a cord here. She starts to berate the current nurse training system only to be interrupted by Emer's arrival.

She's very apologetic about being so late.

'Pauline was supposed to work the evening shift and she didn't turn up. We couldn't get an answer from her mobile. Alan, that's my boss, asked me to stay until he sorted out the staffing for the evening.'

Mrs Flynn says worriedly, 'Well I hope he pays you for the extra time. He didn't pay you when it happened before.'

I stand up and shake her hand. She's about the same height as me, and unlike her friend Carli keeps her hair its natural mid brown colour. It's tied back in a high ponytail, and if she's wearing any make-up it's not obvious.

I say, 'Your mum's been looking after me so well. You've rushed back. I'm sure you need a few minutes to change and wind down.'

Emer sends me an appreciative glance and agrees she needs a minute or two to organise herself. She vanishes upstairs while Mrs Flynn pours me another cup of tea.

**

We're sitting drinking the Finlandia vodka I bought. Mrs Flynn has gone to bingo and I'm hoping for more information. Emer has literally let her hair down and changed into leggings and a sloppy jumper.

'Molly you really shouldn't have spent all your money on the vodka.'

I smile and say money is for spending. She agrees. Then she starts asking me questions, which is fair enough as I asked her plenty in the last hour.

'Have you thought about going back to work? I know why you took all the time off. I mean you had to with those injuries but you're better now. Don't you get bored?'

Actually I've never been bored because investigating what happened to the two children has kept me occupied. She knows I'm interested in the case but not how much.

'Didn't I tell you, I went back to work this year? It was really hard getting up early again. It's not so bad now that summer's coming. I'm even thinking of taking up golf.'

Emer giggles, no doubt influenced by the vodka.

'Golf's an old person's game. Don't see you on a golf course, Molly.'

Of course she's only 19, but flattering that she doesn't see 30 something me as an old person.

'What about Rory McIlroy? He's only 22 or so, hardly older than you.'

'I suppose.'

'Was Carli ever into sport, or was it just music?'

'Carli could have been good at anything she tried. She did play hockey in first year then she lost interest. She could have done well at school; I think she regrets that now. She told me she'd see Tommy got a good education.'

I change tack.

'I can't make my mind up about Dave from all the stuff about him in the papers.'

I note a slight frown when I mention his name.

'I don't think she'd have dropped out of school if she hadn't met him. Like I said she can do anything she puts her mind to. He dropped out of school. OK he was working but it was just a crap job, not going anywhere.'

I fill up her glass. She takes a large sip and continues, 'I'm not his biggest fan but I don't think he had anything to do with Tommy going missing. I just wish Carli had asked me in the first place. I was usually the one who helped her. I think he was trying to get back with her then, so she felt she'd give him a chance to help with Tommy. He did love him.'

'I've often thought it would be helpful for Carli to meet up with that English woman who lost her baby a couple of weeks after Tommy went missing.'

'Molly, you must be psychic. Carli met her, think it was about a month ago. She needed a new lawyer. Remember, Padraig did a bunk with her money.'

'That was over four months ago. Why is she just dealing with that now?'

'You see her life has been crazy, and she left it. Her management look after her contracts so it wasn't urgent she got a new solicitor. But I think something happened. The gardai were on her back and she needed advice from someone she could trust who would understand her position. That Amy was a top lawyer and she'd lost her baby and people said bad stuff about her.'

'You mean the gardai suspected Carli?'

'She didn't say exactly but I got the impression they'd found something on her and she couldn't cope with it herself. Now it might have been something to do with that guy Moriarty.'

I'm excited.

'Were they asking about that funeral incident? That was crazy.'

'Carli didn't say much about that but I know she was upset. She was trying to contact him close to the time he died. I know because she was in Waterford in March and we met up. She went outside to make a call but I overheard the message she left because she was angry and shouting. I could work out it was him from the message. He hadn't been returning her calls and she was mad. I know he helped her get the house and I think he gave her some money to get set up there. She had a really angry face when she came in and I didn't dare ask her about it.'

'Yeah, that sounds odd. They didn't find out for certain why he died and there are stories flying around. I can see the gardai might be interested if they knew about those phone calls.'

The vodka is loosening Emer's tongue. Leaning forward she confides, 'I feel Carli's not telling me something about Moriarty. I don't know what it is but it must be important if the gardai are on her back and she has to get help from Amy Blake.'

And I believe her. In *vino veritas* they say, so I suppose in *vodka veritas* is also true.

I walk back to Aunt Bernie's with difficulty and I can't honestly blame that on not being fully recovered from my accident.

CHAPTER 30

Ifeel the need for a holiday when I return home after the hectic Waterford trip. After an affectionate reunion with Pedro, I switch on Carli's blog and there it is, more or less as Emer told me:

'Folks, had to get a new solicitor after that f...er did a bunk with my money. Gave it some thought; not rushing into it this time. Then it was obvious, see if Amy Blake who lost her baby like I did would consider helping me even though she has lots of problems now with her husband's accident.

Carol Jennings the journalist gave me her number; she's interviewed both of us. So I rang her and the housekeeper put me through. Amy was so nice, asked me over to meet her.

And would you believe, Mary the housekeeper and Peter, Amy's son are both fans of mine. And Mary tried to get Barry's tea for me. She thinks Irish people only drink Barry's tea. She was relieved when I said I only drink water now. The beautician says it's the best for my skin.

Had a great day with her. I sang after dinner with Peter on backing vocals. He says the kids at school won't believe it so this is why it's on my blog! Peter has given me his mobile number and is expecting lots of texts. He's in the end of year school show in July and I've promised to try to attend.

Amy's agreed to look after me legally. And her husband's firm will look after financial things for me. We've now had a meeting with Inspector O'Rourke who's leading the team looking for Tommy, and that's cleared up some issues. It's like a weight off my shoulder.'

How I'd love to know for certain what are the 'issues' that meeting cleared up!

**

Amy had also mentioned her new role on her blog but in a more circumspect way. While it's a new role, I know from old Mrs Askworth that it actually started in February, three months ago. Why only mention it now? Hmm is this significant? Has a lot been going on behind the scenes? Amy doesn't say this news is three months old. The blog is cleverly worded giving no defined timescale which I suppose is what you'd expect from a lawyer.

'Carli Walsh has contacted me to ask for legal advice with her new career. While I am continuing my career break from my employers for the foreseeable future, I was happy to agree to help Carli, given our common bond. We met recently and she is a charming young woman. I'm sure she has a great career ahead of her.'

Over to the Forum. Members have clearly been reading the mothers' blogs too.

Missing Children Forum Portal Home Register Log In	 every child matters
June 11 2012 at 6.40 pm OMG the two dodgy mums are now an item	Taxpayer Posts: 219 Join Date: 22.11.2010 Location: London
June 11 2012 at 6.54 pm What do you mean?	Suzy Posts: 93 Join Date: 27.2.2011 Location: Bath
June 11 2012 at 7.01 pm Amy has become Carli's lawyer.	Taxpayer Posts: 220 Join Date: 22.11.2010 Location: London

June 11 2012 at 7.22 pm Yeah, saw that on their blogs. Wonder if the PR people are behind it?	Declan Posts: 575 Join Date: 2.4.2011 Location: Dublin
June 11 2012 at 7.48 pm That's a bit cynical. Carli was let down by that crook who ran off with the money. Makes sense this time she'd want a woman and one who'd empathise with her.	Fairplay Posts: 88 Join Date: 5.5.2011 Location: Ireland
June 11 2012 at 8.01 pm Hi, folks been away doing some research on the cases but can't say too much just now.	Miss Marple Posts: 49 Join Date: 10.9.2011 Location: St Mary Mead

June 11 2012 at 8.21 pm	CoolDude
Then why say anything at all? I don't think you know anything!	Posts: 92 Join Date: 4.7.2011 Location: Bahamas

CoolDude doesn't like me; that's clear from previous posts. I want to tell the Forum what I've discovered but for all I know Emer could look at it, and if I spilled the Waterford beans it would be obvious I was the source. But I must tell them something.

June 11 2012 at 8.29 pm	Miss Marple
OK. About the dead minister, seems he might have had some money problems. His company accounts aren't impressive and he took a €50,000 loan from the company sometime in 2010. He also had the same solicitor as Carli, the one who did the bunk. I heard his wife had a row with the solicitor about money just before he disappeared.	Posts: 50 Join Date: 10.9.2011 Location: St Mary Mead

June 11 2012 at 8.33 pm Might point to suicide, if he had debts. But hang on he was a minister, on the expenses gravy train – that would soon wipe out any debts	CoolDude Posts: 93 Join Date: 4.7.2011 Location: Bahamas
June 11 2012 at 8.41 pm Interesting that the Minister and Carli had the same solicitor. Might mean they knew one another better than we think. But that makes it really strange that Mrs Moriarty acted the way she did at the funeral.	Declan Posts: 576 Join Date: 2.4.2011 Location: Dublin
June 11 2012 at 8.50 pm Look, Mrs Moriarty was bereaved – she'd lost a young husband with a brilliant career in front of him. She was in total shock, and she just reacted irrationally seeing a 'celebrity' at the funeral and was worried there'd be a media scrum disrupting the funeral. In her position any of us could have done the same.	Fairplay Posts: 89 Join Date: 5.5.2011 Location: Ireland

June 11 2012 at 8.59 pm	CoolDude
Not very impressed with your 'revelations' Miss Marple. You haven't moved the investigation on.	Posts: 94 Join Date: 4.7.2011 Location: Bahamas

I'm tempted to post something rude but I resist. Better to prepare an updated list of suspects than waste time on that arsehole.

June 11 2012 at 9.07 pm	Miss Marple
CoolDude, maybe you'd give us your analysis of the leading suspects in both places.	Posts: 51 Join Date: 10.9.2011 Location: St Mary Mead
June 11 2012 at 9.15 pm	Fairplay
Good idea, Miss M, time to step back and look at what we know definitely and who we can rule out and why.	Posts: 90 Join Date: 5.5.2011 Location: Ireland

June 11 2012 at 9.25 pm	CoolDude
OK, here's my thoughts. Tommy and Rose are really twins born to Carli (they look alike according to some members on this Forum) and they were separated at birth. Jimmy Blake bought the girl twin because he really wanted a girl after three boys and Amy didn't want anymore children. Carli was happy to take the money- she'd advertised for a family to buy her unplanned brat, wasn't just going to give them up for adoption – no money in that – twins in a bedsit is no joke. Only baby Rose wasn't the easiest baby and even with nannies Amy couldn't cope. The most likely thing is that she accidentally killed her, hit her too hard or over sedated her; then she had to cover it up. She couldn't let the body be found so she arranges the 'abduction' and probably phoned in the bomb warning too. As for Tommy, most likely it was some drug dealer Dave owed money to. Taken as a warning. He didn't pay up. Tommy could have been killed or sold off to a childless couple – Tommy was young enough for that to be feasible. Miss Marple – there's your connections – the babies are brother and sister and both have unsatisfactory homes and both are probably dead, certainly Rose.	Posts: 95 Join Date: 4.7.2011 Location: Bahamas

OMG. CoolDude is taking the piss. But at least his scenario doesn't get support.

June 11 2012 at 9.43 pm Didn't realise you had such a sense of humour CoolDude or that you agreed the babies are alike. Thought you had dismissed that as rubbish earlier. Now you say they are twins and Carli sold one of them. Why didn't she sell the other one?	Declan Posts: 577 Join Date: 2.4.2011 Location: Dublin
June 11 2012 at 9.51 pm I don't think you're funny CoolDude. It's not a laughing matter.	LegalEagle Posts: 11 Join Date; 20.12.2011 Location: Law Library
June 11 2012 at 9.59 pm Loosen up folks. And maybe Carli and Amy are connected too; maybe Carli is a much younger half sister, the result of a fling her father had?	CoolDude Posts: 96 Join Date: 4.7.2011 Location: Bahamas

June 11 2012 at 10.06 pm I'm going to complain to the moderators about you CoolDude. What you're suggesting is libellous.	LegalEagle Posts: 12 Join Date: 20.12.2011 Location: Law Library

I resist the temptation to join in the slanging match because CoolDude's last post sets off a bell ringing in my head. I know he's joking when he suggests the two mothers are sisters but that new look of Carli's for the song contest final had intrigued me. She had reminded me of someone, and in the six months since I noted that, I haven't been able to work out who it is.

But could it be Amy Blake? She doesn't look like the person pictured today but weren't there lots of family pictures of Amy in the Jennings interview last October? I've kept all the newspaper articles about the case. I root though the cuttings pile. Initially I can't find it. Damn. Finally, I locate it out of order. There's a page of pictures including one of Amy with her parents on her eighteenth birthday.

Eureka!

Why didn't I see it before? I replay the pod cast of Carli's winning performance in Star Search. The resemblance to the young Amy is amazing. Can Carli be the baby she had adopted? That interview came out about six weeks before the final when Carli's look changed weekly and she looked nothing like those pictures. She had that natural look only for the final; I remember critics saying it was to get the granny vote. She changed it again afterwards. People would have thrown out the paper with the Jennings interview ages ago and forgotten those pictures.

I can hardly control my excitement as I search Wikipedia for some dates relating to the two women which may confirm my theory. Liz had said Amy had become pregnant in January of her final year which meant her baby was born sometime in October unless it was very premature and Liz had not mentioned that being the case as you would expect her to do as a gynaecologist.

Wikipedia gives Carli's date of birth as 10 October 1992. That fits exactly. Now for Amy's entry. The entry refers to her missing child and being a solicitor but doesn't say when she graduated with her law degree. Did it give this information in the Jennings interview? I don't think so. I check the text of the interview and there it is mentioned in passing. Not surprising I didn't specifically remember it.

'We drifted apart as you do. We both moved on. He was in a different faculty so after we split, our paths didn't cross really. Medicine is a long course so I graduated in 1992 before he did. I heard later that he qualified. I've no idea where he is now.'

Amy graduated in law in 1992. It fits. The resemblance and the dates may be coincidental but I don't think so.

I always felt the cases were connected, and this surely proves it. Thank you CoolDude!

In fact, if Amy is Carli's mother then the two babies are related, though not twins as CoolDude jokingly suggested.

CHAPTER 31

I don't recognise the handwriting on the envelope which has a local postmark. It's from Davina, enclosing a copy of a reminder letter she has sent to Detective Inspector Hargreaves, and his reply.

By registered post
2 July 2012

Dear Detective Inspector Hargreaves

I write to put on record my dissatisfaction with the lack of communication from you following our meeting on 22 February.

At that meeting I explained the background to the board meeting which resulted in baby Rose Blake being left alone and I handed over to you a number of documents suggesting that serious fraud has taken place in organisations Amy Blake has been connected with.

While appreciating the pressures on the police force, surely the life of a baby and serious fraud is worthy of attention.

I have discussed this with my solicitor who has advised me to send this letter.

Failing some action by the police it is my intention to go to the media in the autumn.

Yours sincerely

Davina Marsden

And his reply sent the next day

3 July 2012

Dear Mrs Marsden

I acknowledge receipt of your letter of 2 July 2012.

The information and documents you provided are being reviewed and I am informed that a decision should be taken by October.

Yours sincerely

DI Colin Hargreaves

The same day my cousin Brian reports back to me on the documents Davina gave me.

His brief email reads:

'*This stinks but experience tells me the police may not be able to prosecute. You're dealing with a lawyer here, one who is a master of procedure. I'd need access to information only the police can normally get to be more specific. But the police will be able to get what they need and presumably they have good forensic accountants on the team. Davina is clearly an astute woman. I can understand why Amy was so uptight about that meeting that her baby was an unwelcome distraction. I don't believe she harmed her child. Keep digging Molly – if anyone can find Rose you can. Brian x*'

How I'd love to be a fly on the wall in the forensic accountants' section.........

CHAPTER 32

Carli is mentioning Amy a lot on her blog; wonder how Amy feels about that? Of course it's not surprising that she talks about her a lot given what I suspect is their real relationship.

'Life's crazy, working on the new album, but when the minders leave me alone, I go up to stay with Amy. I know she's my lawyer but she's becoming like a big sister. And I've been meeting her family. Met her mum last week and she showed me lots of family pictures and told me stories about her childhood.

Dodging the minders is fun! I got to meet up with Dave recently. It was a bit frustrating just texting and tweeting. His leg's fine again and he's studying computers and has plans to start a business. He sees the stuff printed about my 'boyfriends' and he doesn't care because he knows it's rubbish. In fact it's fun answering silly questions from the press. Often they don't realise I'm taking the piss. I tell them about my favourite make-up, what soaps I watch, which footballer I'd date, what I like for breakfast, just any old rubbish.'

Wonder if the PR people would like that last paragraph? I think I'd enjoy that too; telling stupid 'journalists' stuff like that.

On July 14 her blog is sad:

'I always feel depressed on this day because it's the anniversary of the day that driver killed my parents. He must have been drunk. He was on the wrong side of the road on a Sunday morning. But how could somebody be that drunk then? My parents were returning from Mass. How could God allow something like that to happen to good people? I was about ten when the social services told me I was adopted. I

wasn't bothered about it because the only parents I knew died in that crash.'

This is confirmation that she was adopted. The car crash information she had revealed in an earlier interview. She moves on to happier comments:

'Getting to know Amy's son Peter and it's like having a little brother. That nanny who sold her story said he's difficult and he isn't. He's had a terrible time at school since his sister vanished. Some of the mums blame Amy and their kids told him his mum is evil. Then he's had his dad so ill and his dog poisoned. All those bad things in a short time. He's amazing to have survived emotionally. And I've met Jimmy, his dad. He can't speak too well due to the accident but he managed to get over to me that he's a fan.'

I hone in on certain phrases *'like a big sister'*, *'family pictures'* and *'like having a baby brother'*. If I didn't already suspect that the two women are mother and daughter I wouldn't have realised the implications of Carli's coded language in the blog. She can't say that Peter is her brother so she says *'like having a baby brother.'* And she describes Amy as *'like a big sister.'* I wonder when she knew the truth about her parentage; she met Amy back in February though she didn't mention it in her blog until May. Perhaps it was then that Amy told her. Yes, this blog confirms my suspicions.

And then something out of the blue in the blog:

'Some people have been contacting me about the by-election in September; saying I should stand. Thought they were joking TBH. But they weren't. They said I was a friend of Michael Moriarty and he'd helped me. One religious lady said how happy he would be if I took his seat. He'd be smiling in heaven. Now I don't know about that!'

341

Amy's blog as usual is quite conservative.

'Jimmy's back surgery went well and the medical team say he should be able to walk properly in a couple of months. Thank you to everybody for all the cards and kind letters I've been receiving.'

I'd emailed Alro filling him in on my trip. No response but not surprised really. That guy clearly worries about getting caught for leaking the information.

And I've finally got something out of Liz. Her email reads:

'Sorry to be so long in replying but I've been really busy at work. You know mine isn't a nine to five job.'

Indeed, being a gynaecologist isn't that.

'I did ring Amy; she's very hard to get through to as she's working so hard trying to keep Jimmy's business ticking over. She says she's done her own research and is convinced Peter had nothing to do with it, so that's it. She told me she's now advising Carli Walsh – you probably saw that on Amy's blog – she seems to be getting on well with her. I think you should respect her judgement and forget about him as she has done.'

I'm not sure whether I believe Liz or Amy. And can I forget about Peter given my mixed motives in searching for him?

CHAPTER 33

eedless to say I don't give up my search for Dr Peter.
My instincts tell me he is the key which means I accept
the time it takes and the frustrations along the way. I
have to reduce my lengthy short list of 19 doctors all located
outside the UK by late July when I have booked holidays at
work. Colleagues have been asking where I'm going and I fudge.

More long hours of research reduce the list to five names.
More hours gave background on the families they came from
and their interests.

Top of my shortlist is Dr Peter Bennett. It has to be him; he
ticks all the boxes. His surname ties in with what the other
'Dr Peter' told me, that it began with a 'B' and was a relatively
common name. This Peter lives in the Charente Maritime area
in South West France; has spent some years after qualifying
working for an aid agency in the third world and Liz had told
me that Peter was idealistic. And what better way to mend a
broken heart than to take on a challenge like that?

Maybe I'm being silly but I know a psychic has said that
Tommy is alive and living in the sun. The Charente Maritime
region would fit the bill.

And, Emma the estate agent I met in February, told me that
the mystery house viewer had answered a call in French. Now
that could have been a call from his work about a patient. Or a
call from his French wife; I dismiss this inconvenient thought as
it doesn't fit my theory.

I searched the local paper archives of his home area, Richmond
in south west London. His father Graham built up a successful
business from scratch, some sort of engineering concern. At
school he was an outstanding rugby player and the star of

school musicals but he appeared to have given up both soon after he started university. The pictures I located had not really helped me know if he is the student at the charity ball. Some pictures show him in his stage costume while he is wearing a protective helmet in the rugby pictures. His musical ability was one of the reasons I put him top of my list of possibles; Carli's musical talent has to come from somewhere.

My instincts tell me this Peter is the one, but if it isn't, I'll have to follow up the other four. One is in Poland, one in Canada, and two are in the States. All are apparently unmarried which was one of the criteria for making the shortlist. Of course the fact that I can't find any mention of their being married doesn't mean that they are not; they could be in a long-term relationship with children for all I know which would make it very unlikely they would be interested in taking Amy's child after all these years.

I felt that it was hardly believable that the three living outside Europe would travel so far to kidnap a baby hence the doctor in Poland is no.2 on my list. However he too is unlikely as he was speaking at a medical conference on the day Rose vanished and couldn't have got to Amy's house in time to take Rose. He's listed on a conference programme I found on the internet. I suppose it's possible he pulled out of the conference, but unlikely. His surname does begin with 'B'. It's Banaszewski, but that hardly qualifies as a common name.

So it seems logical to start with Peter in France. Unfortunately I haven't been able to get a recent photograph of him anywhere. There's no photograph on his LinkedIn page and he doesn't do Facebook! Not necessarily suspicious as not everybody puts a photograph on their LinkedIn page. Peter's page reveals he works in the A&E Department in Saintes Hospital which reinforces my theory that he is the one. He's idealistic, or at least he was in his student days. That indicates to me that he's unlikely to be a highly paid consultant with private patients.

France is known for its excellent public health service which would attract doctors like him. Yes, I think I'm right to put him top of the list.

Once I finalise my shortlist, thanks to the internet I am able to get flights and accommodation booked quickly. Now I can tell my colleagues where I am going for my holiday if they ask. As they might wonder why a newly 'single' woman would book a gîte in a quiet place in rural France I've a story ready if anyone asks; I'm getting the accommodation free as it's owned by a friend of my mother's and I know people in the area. Nowadays it seems I lie more often than I tell the truth, but it's in a good cause isn't it?

**

I can hardly concentrate on my last day at work before the holiday. Colleagues don't comment on my inefficiency as it's normal to be excited before your annual summer holiday. My neighbours are looking after Pedro and Lidia is coming in one weekend when they are away. She's been such a great support to me since Jeff died. When I had my accident her English was very limited and I hardly ever saw her as she kept our house spotless while Jeff and I were out at work. Since I left hospital, we've had many conversations; limited at first but now we're communicating quite well. In the early days I would cry a lot and Lidia would put her arms round me. I remember one early conversation when she tried to comfort me. She said, 'Molly you beautiful lady.' She so obviously meant it and I'd never thought of myself as even particularly pretty. Funny how that complement lifted my spirits at a horrendous time.

**

My packing is finished. The taxi to Manchester airport is booked for 7 am, but before I retire for the night I log onto the Forum and can't resist posting –

Missing Children Forum Portal Home Register Log In	 every child matters
July 31 2012 at 9.32 pm Hi folks, taking a break from the debate – off on my summer holidays.	Miss Marple Posts: 52 Join Date: 10.9.2011 Location: St Mary Mead
July 31 2012 at 9.39 pm We'll miss you, come back refreshed with new theories.	Declan Posts: 593 Join Date: 2.4.2011 Location: Dublin
July 31 2012 at 9.49 pm I second that. Don't always agree with you Miss Marple but you're never boring.	Sherlock Posts: 129 Join Date: 29.6.2011 Location: Baker Street

How sweet of Declan and Sherlock. I wonder if I'll be able to tell them what I find out, assuming it's not all one big wild goose chase.

PART V

AUGUST 2012
FRANCE

CHAPTER 34

The flight to Bordeaux has been smooth and the satnav in the hired car gets me safely to the gîte I have rented about 90 kilometres from the airport. As I negotiate the endless roundabouts en route I wonder if I am in need of counselling rather than a 'working holiday.' I am paying high season prices on what might be an expensive wild goose chase. But I might find one or both of the missing babies. How can you put a price on that?

I stop at a supermarket on the way and stock up for a few days. After a meal and some local wine and a good night's sleep I'll be ready to start my investigation.

In the morning I stroll the 400 metres into the village and start at the boulangerie.

'Une baguette, s'il vous plaît.'

No problem with that. Then comes the tricky stuff. I summon up my schoolgirl French. To be honest, I did an intensive online course to brush up on the language the week before I came away so it's probably a bit better than that.

'Je crois qu'une amie qui était au collège avec moi habite près d'ici et elle a une bébé qui a deux ans. Est-ce qu'il y a beaucoup des enfants ici?'

'Non, malheuresement, les gens quittent parce qu'il n'y a pas assez de travail ici. L'école locale a fermé parce qu'il n'y a pas d'enfants.'

'Pas d'enfants. Pas du tout?'

Madame smiles.

'Il y a une famille Anglaise qui a deux enfants. La mère est morte mais la grand-mère y habite. Le père travaille à l'hopital local. Madame Bennett, elle achète du pain ici.'

This is what I'd hoped to hear.

'Ma soeur est enceinte de son premier enfant et j'ai besoin d'expérience pour l'aider.'

How good I have become at lying or telling half truths. My sister had her first baby earlier in the year and helping her with it is a little impractical as she doesn't live near me.

Madame smiles again. 'Peut-être vous rencontrerez Madame Bennett et ses petit-enfants.'

'Quand elle arrive ici?' I ask trying to sound casual.

'Ça dépend. En général à midi.'

'Au revoir madame.'

I leave. I daren't ask any more in case she gets suspicious. But at least I know to buy my bread at lunchtime. And I'm shaking with excitement. Madame said there were two children. I had hoped to find one baby but two......

I stroll around the village. In the pharmacie I buy some suntan lotion which I'm definitely going to need; temperatures in August can exceed 30 degrees.

Another chance to use my improved French.

'Vous êtes en vacances?'

'Oui, je suis ici pour le soleil et le vin francais. Cette région est vraiment jolie.'

'Il fait toujours beau en août.'

'Y a t' il quelque chose à faire, peut-être un festival local où......?'

'Si vous allez dix kilometres à Jonzac il y a un bureau de tourisme là.'

'Merci, je le ferai.'

So I go to Jonzac, a very pretty town, and collect lots of leaflets. I expect that Madame Boulangerie and Madame Pharmacie are discussing me over their lunchtime café. Maybe their conversation is like this -

'She seems to be on her own. Maybe she's a writer needing a peaceful setting for a book. She's asking about an old school friend with a baby...'

**

The next day I go to the boulangerie just before noon. While I'm being served an older woman in her mid 60s comes in. She addresses the shopkeeper in fluent French with a slight English accent. I gather the shopkeeper is telling her I am the woman who wanted experience with children.

The woman addresses me in English:

'Madame tells me you are looking forward to becoming an aunt?'

'Yes, my sister is having her first baby in September, and it's the first one in the family for years. She's had lots of gynaecological problems so we're all really anxious for her.'

'You'll probably be godmother and doing lots of babysitting?'

'Yes, I expect so. But my sister's waited so long for this baby that I don't think she'll let anyone else mind it for ages.'

'She's right. You can't be too careful. My grandchildren are with their father today. We don't use babysitters unless we know them very well.'

I nod.

'Yes, babies are so precious. I think people can be very casual with them.'

She clearly likes that remark and tells me about a French case in the Deux-Sevres region; a mother left four children aged two to twelve at home alone for a weekend while she attended an evangelical prayer meeting.

'She told the court she had arranged for someone to mind the children but they didn't turn up. The court was lenient and only gave her a six month suspended sentence.'

'Unbelievable,' I say and I almost blurt out the story of Amy leaving her baby home alone but stop myself in time. I actually know about the case she mentioned as it came up in my research.

I hope she's going to ask me to call round but she doesn't. Shall I take a chance and invite myself? Or would that blow it? I pluck up my courage and explain I'm only 400 metres away and would love her to call and tell me about the area as she's clearly a long term resident. She agrees to come for lunch the next day as her son will be minding the children. I resist the temptation to say bring them too. This is progress, a chance to get to know her. I mustn't blow it.

** **

I hear a car pull up and a knock on the door. I see a car drive off. Who gave her the lift I wonder? She answers my unspoken question herself. It's too hot to walk and her neighbour is going this way. She doesn't want to take the car in case Peter, her son, needs it for the children. Her neighbour will collect her on the way back.

Or I could drop you back, I say. And I add that I'd love to see her grandchildren. Then regret I've said that, but she doesn't seem to have noticed, just responds that Jeanne her neighbour is literally passing here on her way back so she doesn't need to trouble me.

I've prepared a simple lunch in the garden and as she's not driving I plan to loosen her tongue with the help of a chilled bottle of rose wine which I must drink sparingly in case I deviate from my prepared story of the sister with the gynaecological problems and the birth due next month. Actually my sister had her baby six weeks ago. It's about 30 degrees, the sky is cloudless and the setting idyllic. I must remember my cover story about being a tourist who wants to use her local knowledge.

I ask her how long she's lived here and she explains that her family have owned their house for close to forty years, used it most summers and now she lives here permanently. I prompt her.

'I hear this area's full of British people.'

She smiles and agrees.

'You can get property here very cheaply because there's so little work that the young people move to the bigger towns. It's a very mature community here. The French health service is good which is important when you're getting on a bit. The climate is lovely and in the winter it's mild. We grow fruit and vegetables in our garden all year round. In fact you hardly need to learn the language because there are so many British people here. But I made an effort to learn because I think it's disrespectful to the French to move here and not bother to learn their language. They appreciate you making an effort even if you speak it badly.'

I smile and say how madame in the boulangerie did not laugh at my French.

She mentions an outdoor community swimming pool at Archiac only a few kilometres away which is also great for sunbathing if you don't want a long drive to the sea. She tells me she's involved in the local drama society which is mainly composed of expatriates. She obviously loves the pace of life here.

'Where did you live before?'

'Mainly in London because my husband worked there.'

This is the first time she has mentioned a husband. A tear trickles down her cheek.

She continues. 'This is silly, it's over four years since he died and he'd been ill for a while so I was expecting it.'

'That doesn't make it any easier,' I say. A cliché I know but she seems to appreciate it. I fill up her wine glass and she doesn't demur.

'My son kept me going,' she said. 'He's a doctor and he came back from Canada where he was working. He told me the cancer had spread and it was only a matter of time. He was there when Graham died and he was the one who suggested I sell up and move to our French holiday home. Peter was used to spending time here as a child. Over the years we got to know the people here so it wasn't like going to a strange country.'

I ask if Peter ever went back to Canada since he's working and minding his children here.

'He did return for a while,' she said. 'He didn't have the children when he was here those months with his father. He went back to Canada and met their mother. They had twins, a boy and a girl; but she was killed when they were one. A car accident. He stayed there for a while but then he decided to move here and live with me. He can get a job anywhere with his qualifications.'

Am I imagining it, or is she saying well rehearsed lines? She did tell me she's active in the local drama society. I note she doesn't even mention the name of her grandchildren's mother.

'The children are my life. They make up for losing Graham. And having Peter here is wonderful. I never saw much of him when he was studying medicine even though he lived at home. Then after he qualified he worked all over the world, in some really dangerous places with third world charities.'

I realise I mustn't push her too much. If she's hiding something which I strongly suspect, she will get suspicious. She doesn't say that Peter was devastated by the accident that took his wife's life. Perhaps that's being too suspicious. I'm a stranger after all; why should she reveal the details of the family tragedy to me? It's obvious anyone losing a partner in an accident would be upset.

I bring out the brochures I collected from the tourist office and she makes suggestions. Then she asks about me, which is not unreasonable given that I've been quizzing her.

'I'm a widow like yourself. My Jeff died a year ago. I had to take a lot of time off work after it because I had a stupid accident when I was still in a state of shock but I've gone back to work now.'

'What made you choose this area for your holiday?'

'I wanted somewhere quiet and sunny. I'm not into bars and nightclubs. My boss suggested this area.'

This isn't true of course but I've got used to lying after my months on the search for the truth.

'He was here years ago and he thought it would be a great place for me to recharge my batteries after a really difficult year. And I heard a friend from school had married a Frenchman and was in this area; thought it would be nice to look her up.'

'Do you know the name of her husband?'

I had to admit I didn't. Not surprising as the school friend doesn't exist. I blather on about her name being Laura Benson and that a friend of a friend said she now has a two year old son. Anyway this conversation ends when she decides this woman is not in the immediate area or she would know.

'I can't believe you're 35, I'd put you at no more than 28.'

I warm to this woman. But I have to be careful. No more wine for me. I mustn't talk about my Irish connections. Keep it simple; I'm an English widow looking for a quiet sun holiday off the main tourist track. I'm telling her about my voluntary work helping charities and NGOs with their IT problems when we hear a car hoot. For once I'm telling the truth as I've always helped good causes.

'That's Jeanne,' she says getting up and reaching for her bag. We've been getting on like a house on fire. Dare I risk asking her again? But I've played it just right.

'You've been so kind. You must come over to us for lunch and meet the children.'

Trying not to sound overjoyed I say of course I'd like that, and suggest Friday but she says no because Peter is working that day. So we agree on Sunday. As soon as she's gone, I'm on the phone to cousin Brian.

'On Sunday I should know if I'm right.'

Even though he's five years younger than me, he's very protective and insists on getting the exact address of Mrs Bennett's house and that I ring him as soon as I'm home from the lunch on Sunday. He'd tried to persuade me not to go, feeling that I should pass my research to the police.

'Brian, you're going over the top.'

'Molly, these people may have kidnapped one or both children. And if they did, they may have phoned in that bomb warning. And you know I think there was something odd about Jimmy Blake's car accident. I know you don't agree with me about that.'

Indeed I don't agree with him. I had laughed at him and said he was worse than me. After all, Jimmy Blake had had the mother of all rows with his wife when she discovered he was shagging her best enemy. He was totally distracted and that's how the accident must have happened. I just don't buy any conspiracy theory on that one.

Sunday can't come soon enough. In the meantime I must visit some of these tourist places to keep up the cover story.

CHAPTER 35

'You've asked this English woman to lunch. Are you mad?' Peter doesn't normally talk to his mother like that but he's worried.

'What's the harm? She's really nice; does a lot of voluntary work and she's excited about becoming an aunt next month. She'll love the children. She's a widow like me and her husband died last year.'

He realises mother is matchmaking and in a less than subtle way. She has her grandchildren which she always wanted but she also wants a daughter-in-law.

'Well you've asked her now. I'll be polite but we do need to watch what we say. For all we know, she's a journalist.'

'She's definitely not,' his mother says triumphantly. 'I looked her up on the internet. Her name's listed on the company she mentioned and there's a photograph and job title. Senior IT consultant. I rang the company asking for her but the receptionist said she was on holiday for the next month. I also looked at her Facebook account. Can't get in to see her friends but her photo is there, same as the one on her company website. Trust me, she's OK.'

He's relieved to hear this but still has questions. 'Why not go off with girlfriends to a livelier place than here?'

'That wouldn't be her way,' his mother replies. 'She's a thoughtful person. I'd say she wants peace and quiet for a while to help her to move on. And you couldn't have a better place to get away from it all than here.'

His mother has always loved this place. They came here for holidays when he was little. They could have afforded somewhere more expensive or exotic but they usually chose to come here. The odd time they tried something different, they always returned to France the next year.

This was where he came when he had the crisis back in 1992. He had not told his mother about it then even though they were very close.

On balance he decides Mother is probably right. This is a great place to come to get away from it all and someone who works with computers all day needs a break as much as anyone else, but you'd think she'd bring a friend. Is he being paranoid by having this lingering doubt? He's so afraid that something he didn't anticipate may wreck all he has here.

Does he feel guilty about what they have done? He doesn't know. It has been strange watching Sky News which he gets here, postulating who might have taken the babies. They had never intended to take them but that was the way it worked out, and now he is glad they did. But before anyone judges him and his mother, they must understand the context......

**

Back in medical school days he was in love. They were together for almost two years and he'd assumed they'd get married. He never said it, but assumed she knew as he did that they were meant for each other. She was ambitious in a different way to him and in hindsight that was probably why it all went wrong. He was never interested in being rich, and while he could certainly have made serious money as a doctor he wasn't motivated by it. He had planned to spend some years abroad with one of the Aid Agencies before settling down at home. She used to laugh at him wanting to live in discomfort in the Third World. But she was only just winding him up or so he had thought. He'd tell her he didn't want to live in discomfort; being away only meant not having the home comforts he was used to, and that they're not essential.

Lying in bed one weekend she had insisted, 'You'll change when you qualify. After all that hard work you'll want some money in your pocket.' But he hadn't taken her seriously. That was her way. He'd slagged her off too about her ambition. Deep down she was a caring person he was sure.

The crunch came when she was in her final year with her exams two months away. She seemed off form and looked peaky but when he asked what was wrong she said it was exam stress and overwork. He knew she was determined to get a first and accepted her answer. But he'd called to her flat one morning and found her retching in the bathroom. He'd then realised what he should have known before. Crazy that as a medical student he'd not spotted she was pregnant. At first she denied it. He told her it was great news; they would manage until he qualified. But she said no, she had other plans. She had booked an appointment with an abortion clinic and the counselling session she had to have first was a formality to comply with the law. They'd had a blazing row, the worst they'd ever had.

Then another bombshell.

'Peter, I should have said this sooner, but I've been having doubts about us for a few months. I've been thinking we're too different to make a go of things.'

He had screamed at her, 'And you think getting rid of this baby sorts everything?'

He'd pleaded with her.

'Please have our baby; I'll look after it. You take time out to see what you want.'

But she had asked him to leave and accept her decision. He'd had no choice. As he left the flat she had shouted 'I'm not having the baby so don't try anything.'

He had called the next day but she'd already changed the locks. She wouldn't return his calls. A week later he received a letter which he has to this day:

Dear Peter

I know this is tough for you but please accept my decision and don't try to contact me. I've made my decision and I have to live with it. You don't accept it but it's my body. It's not easy for me either. You probably won't believe that.

You'll be qualified soon and you have a great future ahead of you. You'll meet someone who is as idealistic as you. I wasn't and I saw that but you didn't. It wouldn't have worked. I've known that for a while though I put off doing anything. Maybe you knew it too and wouldn't face up to it. Anyway we both have to move on.

I really wish you the best and I'll always love you a little bit.

Amy

He had drunk himself silly that week. She had aborted his baby, told him he'd meet someone new, yet said she'd always love him. What kind of woman was she? He'd spent that summer in his family home in France frantically working in the garden to keep his mind off things. He hadn't trusted anyone again for years which had doomed the few relationships he had tentatively entered.

It's an old cliché that life is strange but it certainly had been in his case.

Normally he wouldn't have been in London when the apparently innocuous letter that was to change everything arrived. He had worked abroad most of the time after he qualified. When his father had been diagnosed with pancreatic cancer he had taken extended leave and returned to the UK to be with him.

That day the consultant had told him and his mother to prepare for the worst. He'd known that anyway but she hadn't. When they got back from the hospital, his mother was fighting back tears so he had ignored the post in the hall until the next day when she was calmer.

He rarely received post at his old home address and when he did it was usually marketing material from old databases. This letter was clearly not in that category; handwritten with the writing vaguely familiar. It was from Andrew, a medical student in his year, informing him of a fifteen year reunion he was organising the following month. He'd banged off an email saying he'd go, expecting quite a liquid evening with his former colleagues probably now consultants and boasting about their earnings and trophy wives. He was curious to see who had gone the money route and who like him had gone the other route or indeed had given up on medicine altogether.

But it hadn't been the way he thought it would be. It was actually a life changing event but he didn't know that then of course. Yes it had been a liquid evening, but that was the only way in which his preconception had been correct.

Andrew had booked a private room with its own bar in a hotel. It gave Peter a funny feeling seeing *Bart's Hospital class of 1993 reunion* flashing on the hotel's notice board. His student days seemed light years away. He was late because

Dad's condition was worsening and he'd almost decided not to go, but his mother had put pressure on him. 'You need a break dear, and I'll be here for your dad.' If the hotel hadn't been only two tube stops away he still mightn't have bothered. So he'd made what turned out to be a fateful decision affecting not only his own life but others.....

**

The room was packed and he didn't recognise all of them. Funny to think they were all pushing forty now and some already with thinning hair and paunches. The women were much better preserved as is always the case. He had recognised Liz. Hard not to, she still had the same striking dark red hair, though her style was completely different now. His mother could have put a price on her understated elegant outfit. He couldn't; he just knew it was expensive. She saw him and waved.

'Hi Peter, you're as handsome as ever.'

She had always flirted with all of them. Amy and herself had got on very well. When he was with Amy she had got to know quite a lot of his medical friends and Liz was as ambitious in her way as Amy was. He had wondered if they still met after Amy left him and whether Liz knew what had happened to her. He really shouldn't ask her. That was in the past now.

He had joined Liz who insisted on getting him a drink. They'd moved into a corner to get some privacy.

'You must be doing well,' he had joked, 'with that outfit and paying the prices in this place.'

She had laughed. 'Yes, I'm a consultant now and the money's great.'

They had chatted for a while, comparing their medical experience after qualification. Then more drinks. He recalled that Amy had joked that Liz fancied him and glanced at her left hand. No rings. She must have noticed his glance and looked at his hand spotting that he too did not wear a wedding ring. She said mischievously, 'I'm still looking for Mr Right, what about you?' Then she apologised immediately. 'Sorry, Amy really hurt you.'

He had taken a large swig of his third whisky. Normally he would not have reacted to a remark like that. He rarely drank but on this occasion he had reacted angrily.

'Yes it did hurt me when she aborted our child which I wanted.'

Liz had looked as though she had just received very bad news. She didn't respond to his angry statement.

'Why do you look like that?' he had asked. 'Weren't you shocked? Aborting a healthy child is wrong. We take an oath to save life and she aborted our baby and wouldn't listen to me.'

'It was a long time ago,' she said obviously very embarrassed. 'She did what she thought was best. She made a choice and you didn't agree with it. Let's talk about you. Where did you get that suntan?'

He wouldn't let her change the subject.

'Did you see Amy after we split up? You two were close.'

'Well a bit,' she had said unconvincingly, 'but not much as she had her finals. I had a couple of letters from her but I haven't heard from her in years.'

Liz was clearly very uncomfortable and longing to change the subject. If they hadn't been in a corner she would have tried to get them into another group to avoid this topic which clearly was a no go area for her.

Why was she being so shifty? The Liz he remembered was an upfront person who always called it how it was. Abortion happened quite often and was easy to get under UK law. Though they were all doctors, he recalled there was no general abhorrence of it among his fellow students. He didn't approve of abortion. How could doctors perform abortions given the Hippocratic Oath? The right to choose brigade, they just don't understand the issues. Amy had booked an appointment with one of those abortion clinics that pretend they provide counselling; they get the paperwork signed and hey presto you have a legal abortion.

But what if Amy had changed her mind? But could she have done that and not told him?

He had grabbed Liz's hand.

'Tell me, did she have the abortion?'

Her face had paled.

'Look, let's not go there. What's done is done.'

'Shit. I can tell from your face you're covering something up!'

He had grabbed her other hand but she didn't respond.

'Look, obviously you promised her you'd never tell me. And you haven't. But I can tell from what you're not saying there was no abortion.'

Liz had nodded, 'She was very confused. She did intend to have one but the counsellor felt she didn't really want that and told her to think about it for 24 hours and come back if she still felt the same. She never went back.'

'But why didn't she tell me?'

'Because she had decided to end it with you and she knew a baby would keep you together for the wrong reasons. She was very ambitious and she didn't want to be bringing up a baby she didn't want, in a relationship she felt had no future.'

'Did her parents know?'

'I don't think they ever did. She was five months pregnant when she took her finals. She went up to see them after the exams very carefully dressed so it wasn't obvious. She told them she had this short term contract for six months in the States which offered fabulous experience. I was actually working there then on a short summer contract and she would send me letters to post to them. I hated being involved but we were friends and I respected her choices. Maybe she told them later but I doubt it. I haven't had any contact for years so I don't know.'

'Tell me about the baby.'

Liz had hesitated obviously feeling she was breaking her promise.

'OK but she must never know I told you.'

He hadn't responded to that.

'Tell me.'

'It was a girl and she called her Catherine. She was adopted when she was only a few days old by a family in London. That's all I know.'

So he had a daughter and she'd be about sixteen now. What kind of parents did she get? Where was she? He'd been satisfied Liz didn't know any more but he was determined to find out more.

'Thanks for telling me.' He had given Liz a hug and moved off to meet some others.

**

He'd intended to start his search for Catherine straight away but his father's health deteriorated and he had to be there to support his mother.

After dad died, he had helped his mother sell up and move to the family place in France. It was on his first night there after selling up when he'd had more than he usually did to drink that he'd told her about Catherine. From that day she became a woman with a mission; to find her granddaughter. He'd tried to say that she mightn't want them to turn up out of the blue, even though he had intended to do exactly that.

He had discovered that the law in Britain enables a third party to get a copy birth certificate once the person concerned is 18. He had applied for Catherine's as soon as he legally could. Liz had told him her date of birth and where she had been born. He completed the online application form and back it came two weeks later; a birth certificate for Catherine Browne, daughter of Amy Browne, father unknown. That had hurt, 'father unknown.' It should read 'Father wanted her very much,' he mused.

His mother had decided to hire a private detective to find out who had adopted her. The report told them that his daughter had been adopted by Cora and Stephen Walsh, a couple with no children living in London. Mrs Walsh was an Irish citizen born in Dublin and the family had moved to Ireland in 1996 when Mr Walsh lost his job. One year later both were killed in a car crash but Catherine survived with minor injuries. Or rather Carli because her name had been changed by then. After that she had been in the care of the state and short-term foster care until she was found a long-term placement in Waterford in the South East of Ireland. And – the bombshell – he had a grandson Tommy who lived with Carli in council accommodation.

She had persuaded him to organise passports for the children against his better judgement. Looking back he saw that they had always intended to take both his grandson Tommy and Amy's daughter Rose, though they had argued the passports were like an insurance policy, something you had, but never hoped to have to use. He could see now that he had taken Rose to replace the daughter he should have seen growing up, and his mother had snatched Tommy because he was her great-grandson and apparently not being cared for properly.

His mother had still been grieving for his father when she'd insisted on getting the passports and it was difficult to reason with her. So he had called in a favour from a man whose life he had saved doing locum work in London in an Accident and Emergency Department while his father's health deteriorated. This man was a well known gangster brought in with gunshot wounds. Peter had saved his life and on his discharge had told Peter to contact him if he needed anything, and he had stressed the anything.

One phone call and a brief meeting with his former patient resulted in two passports arriving the following week.

They had decided to go to Ireland first. They booked a mobile home outside Waterford on a secluded site with a beautiful ambience. They had Carli's address from their private detective. Not an impressive place. A run-down estate which had problem tenants written all over it.

The night before, they had been to the Black Swan pub where she sang. They had sat in the corner and enjoyed her talent. To be honest he couldn't see any resemblance to either Amy or himself but maybe without the heavy make-up for the pub lights and with her hair a more natural colour, he might have felt differently. Carli's hair was streaked dark red and strawberry blonde. He didn't like it, or the barely bum covering skirt she wore. Mum reminded him that both his father and himself had great voices so that was where Carli's talent came from. She obviously had regular fans as the place was packed even though it was a Monday. As he got drinks for mum and himself, a man at the bar beside him said 'She's going to be a big star and do Waterford proud.' He'd nodded fighting the temptation to tell a total stranger that the talented performer was his daughter.

**

From their parked car at the end of Carli's road, they saw her emerge with a buggy. She lifted what must be his grandson into a car seat and folded up the buggy. She seemed to be struggling with it. Had they been nearer they would have heard her bad language as the old buggy always gave her problems. They followed at a safe distance. She drove into the city centre and parked close to a corner in a side street. She had got out without the child and after making a phone call standing by the car she vanished around the corner. He had parked about 50 metres behind her car. After about five minutes Mum got out and looked into the car, then she vanished round the corner for a couple of minutes. She reappeared and was about to try the car door when a woman who had just parked her car behind Carli's said something to her. Afterwards, Mum told him the woman had assumed the car was hers and had asked her politely to move it back from the corner.

Then the act that changed everything.

Afterwards his mother explained why she did it. She had seen Carli sitting in the hairdressers' reception reading a magazine, clearly there for an appointment, with her son left in the car. Her one attempt for the child's safety was to park the car near to the corner! Mum had looked into the car at the sleeping Tommy, the image of her own son at that age. She told him afterwards, 'He was so like you and it was as if there was a voice in my head telling me to protect him, like someone else was taking over my body telling me to save Tommy. So I took him. She hadn't even bothered to lock the car.'

His mother had run back to their car as fast as she could, given that she was carrying a sturdy ten month old baby; climbed into the back seat and shouted drive as though it was a scene in a US crime series. He had done as he was told and they had headed back to the mobile home.

**

Looking back it was like a bad dream; but a dream that became a good one. His respectable middle class mother had kidnapped a child, albeit her own great-grandson. As she told him repeatedly on the journey, Tommy was the image of him at the same age and she had to protect him. They stayed in the mobile home, which they had chosen because it stood alone on a secluded site, for the fortnight booked and until the publicity had died down a bit and then drove to Dublin where they took the car ferry to Liverpool and from there to a self-catering holiday apartment he had booked in Manchester. Lovely and anonymous. And with other families with small children there. He had left mother there enjoying her new role with Tommy whose curls they had cut off. Mum had bought baby clothes in girly colours, mainly pink. Whenever they had met anyone out taking a stroll around the area, they assumed Tommy was a girl. He went to Accrington where Amy now lived on his main mission.

He had researched her current life with the aid of the internet and magazine articles. Her first child had been a boy and she called him Peter. That cannot be a coincidence he had thought. You call your first child after the boyfriend you dumped. In that last letter she had said she would always love him a little bit. She has to regret what she did.

He had watched her minder, a Chinese girl who seemed to love her charge. He chatted to her briefly in Tesco's and was tempted to snatch the baby then as mother had done in Waterford but it was too risky. He'd had a stroke of luck when he discovered browsing on the internet that Amy's house was for sale. He'd rung the agent and made an appointment for a group booking. Ideal. He knew from a magazine article that Amy had a King Charles spaniel. He'd had a dog like that for his 5th birthday. He'd bought some treats from a pet shop and would befriend the dog. There were others viewing the house so he was able to walk round by himself most of the time. Sammy the dog had capitulated to the treats, rolled over and let him tickle his tummy. He had taken a wax impression of the back door key which had been left in the door. Baby Rose's room was impressive; she certainly had better surroundings than Tommy did. But a father who, according to the papers, was not at home much and a mother, who allegedly spent more time on the social scene than with her daughter.

His research had been very thorough. He was able to 'accidentally' bump into one of Amy's committee friends in a bookshop she ran. From her he discovered that there was a meeting on Thursday evening. He planned to visit the house when Amy wasn't there using the key he had made from the wax impression. He wasn't sure what he wanted to do. Did he plan to take Rose to compensate for the daughter who grew up without him? He's never been able to answer that question honestly. He just knew he wanted to be with her daughter.

His mother had helped with the research. She had made a reconnaissance trip, followed Amy's elderly neighbour and joined her table in a café. The neighbour had provided a useful picture of Amy's household and he had felt reasonably confident about the visit he proposed to make. He knew from his mother's research that the au pair was on a day off though he wasn't sure when she would return.

He had parked his hired car in the parking space attached to the playing fields at the back of the three houses in the cul-de-sac where Amy lived. He'd insisted on two top specification child car seats when booking. He had a baby sling and a large loose coat with him so if he succumbed to the temptation to take Rose she'd be well covered up. His was the only car there. A lucky break; presumably the dull gloomy evening had kept people away. He had waited there, and heard her car leave. He had seen Teresa's car there but the neighbour had told his mother that Teresa was a nervous driver and only used it for short local journeys. Surely she must be back as Amy had just driven off. Hopefully she would be watching TV and wouldn't hear him creep up the stairs. He had tried the key in the back door but it was unlocked. He had crept in and realised nobody was there. Sammy appeared from the kitchen, recognised him and happily accepted a treat. Upstairs he gazed at Rose sleeping soundly not believing she was alone in the house. He lifted her up and she snuggled into the baby sling. His coat covered her. Still the only car in the playing field area, he was back with Rose in the apartment in Manchester within an hour. They had put two children on their booking form and fortunately, the porters changed frequently, so nobody noticed they arrived with one child and left with two.

Mum was delighted. As before they stayed for a while until the publicity died down. They had bought a double buggy in Ireland and had taken their 'twins' out. They returned to France on the car ferry from Dover; the officials hardly looked at the children's passports. Mother had told her friends that he was moving to France with his children after the tragic death of their mother. They had no reason to disbelieve her.

They bought British papers and watched the UK channels all available in France. Amy's former nanny sold her story to the papers confirming his impression of Amy. The nice Chinese girl went missing obviously because she was an illegal. His daughter Carli seemed not to care and went on to win the talent competition. Her first record was a No.1 and now she was in demand as a songwriter. The determination she obviously has reminds him so much of her mother. In one way he wants to get to know her but in another way he doesn't.

He sometimes feels bad about Amy but when he does, he thinks about the pain she inflicted on him. Her husband is now in a wheelchair and she's been vilified by the media with limited exceptions, and some of the stuff on the internet is vile. He has to confess to following the various internet blogs on his children as he now think of them. He's been tempted to register and post but decided that would be too risky. Nobody has established the two children are connected. It's been suggested by a few people but other posters don't seem to agree. These posters haven't been able to prove it and hopefully never will. Probably just retired people with nothing better to do.

**

He wishes mother hadn't asked this woman to lunch. He worries that somehow they'll be found out and the children taken away from them. He's so busy now with work and the children that he doesn't need anyone. Mother doesn't agree and says she won't be here forever. The children have shaken her out of the depression that hit her when dad died and she's a new woman. Those children deserved to be rescued but the law won't see it that way. They are very lucky the police have no good leads and their budgets have been cut. It's wrong that budgets are more important than children but at least in this case, it's worked out in the best interests of the children.

Chapter 36

I'm hoping my nerves don't show. I'm wearing a multi-coloured sleeveless dress just above the knee with sunglasses on my head. My suntan is developing nicely and I've just used mascara and lip gloss. I look good but I'm nervous.

Mrs Bennett ushers me in.

'We're having lunch in the garden. Peter and the children are out there.'

She leads me through the house and into the garden. Two suntanned toddlers are playing in a sandpit. Supervising proceedings is Peter who stands up as he sees me.

OMG. I knew there was the possibility that this man might look something like Jeff, if he was the drunken student in the old photograph but I am nonetheless unprepared for the reality. It's like I'm seeing Jeff in front of me. When I open my eyes I'm lying on the couch in the salon and Peter is sitting beside me.

'You gave us a shock. The sun can get to you. We're used to it and mother thinks we should have lunch inside. Or we could take you home if you're not feeling well. The children might be too much for you.'

Without thinking I blurt out, 'You look so like my husband and he died last year.'

He looks stunned.

I apologise for fainting and say I'm fine.

'Well OK,' he says. 'We'll watch you carefully.'

'Can we eat outside? It wasn't the sun. I love the heat, that's one of the reasons I'm here.'

He motions for me to follow him and we go into the garden where the children are still happily in their sandpit now supervised by Mrs Bennett. He introduces them to me.

'This is Anna and her twin Graham. They're nearly two.'

Hmm. Mrs Askworth had said the child with the lady too young to be a grandmother had a name beginning with G she couldn't quite recall.

The children aren't very interested in me as they're having too much fun. They're both blond and slim; they don't have the chubbiness that children of that age tend to have. Maybe it's the healthy French diet. And they don't look anything like the pictures of the missing children that were published.

I pick up a spare bucket and set to work on my own castle. This impresses the children and I have their attention.

Mrs Bennett comments favourably on my sandcastle and says she'll be serving lunch in a few minutes and asks that the children wash their hands. Peter takes Anna and I take Graham to the nearest bathroom where we have a major task in de-sandifying them. I'm feeling calm now and Peter and I are laughing as we try to clean the children up.

I sit next to Graham in his highchair ready to lend a hand if needed with his lunch.

Peter watches me for any further signs of fainting. I suspect he planned to ask me lots of questions to satisfy himself of my bona fides. Now he can't. Equally I feel I can't ask too much in case he decides I'm a journalist. The safest topic of conversation is the children.

'They seem to get on really well,' I say. 'I've a friend with twins (I don't) and they fight all the time.'

Mrs Bennett smiles. 'They're really good and they even share their toys.'

'Perhaps you're a biased granny?'

She denies it.

'Peter was a good baby. We only had him and he never got spoilt and bratty. Graham, he's called after my husband, is really like Peter at his age.'

I'd love to ask about the dead mother of the 'twins' but that would be insensitive as I have to officially believe that story. Will be interesting to see if her name comes up at all.

So I ask about the French education system and their plans for the children. Mrs Bennett explains that children start what the English call primary school at six but they usually go to kindergarten at three which is called nursery maternelle and is generally attached to the primary school.

'Some start at age two in the prematernelle but we think that's too young. Our two have each other so we'll wait until they're three.'

I nod. 'My mother kept us at home until we started school at five. I had my sister and friends next door so there was always plenty of company.

She continues. 'I'm only 64 and I love being a 'grand-mère.' I'll mind them as long as I can.'

Peter chips in. 'Mum has amazing energy and she'll be around for her great-grandchildren.'

She laughs. 'Indeed I will. I would have loved more children but it didn't happen. So when he started school I went back to nursing.'

'Peter, is that why you became a doctor, because your mother was a nurse.'

'Sort of. Money doesn't motivate either of us and we need to feel our work is worth doing.'

'But doctors earn very good money?'

'They can do, but it depends what you do. I spent years working for charities overseas; I had no interest in the big money areas. I was at a med school reunion about three or four years ago and some of my former colleagues were certainly cleaning up. One was in plastic surgery – giving celebs bigger boobs, different noses and more rounded bottoms. An absolute waste of their skills.'

I ask what his area is. I already know from his LinkedIn page but I can't officially know.

'I've moved around. I'm in A & E in the hospital in Saintes and I love it. It's a continual challenge. Some of the problems are relatively trivial but sometimes it's your reaction and skills that saves lives.'

The questioning turns to me.

I explain how being a civil servant just didn't suit me.

He nods understandingly. 'Probably like working in the NHS?'

I laugh and tell him about going to college that bit older.

'I gave up the civil service for college and people thought I was mad to leave a permanent job.'

Peter likes this.

'Too many people value money and security. But nothing in life is secure and money can't buy everything. I'm fortunate. I earn good money but I'd give it up for the children if it was necessary. I understand what you did, and computers are fascinating.'

Then he starts a different line of questioning, but an easy one where I don't have to lie.

'Mum says you're involved with some charities?'

I chat away about the work I've done for deserving causes that can't get adequate funding and Peter nods approvingly.

'You hardly have time to have a life with all this and your day job,' he says.

I agree that my voluntary activities more than give me a full working week. A slight exaggeration; all my spare time since returning to work has been spent on finding out what happened to the missing babies.

Laughing, I say I may have been overdoing it lately but add that my dog keeps me sane and I have to get home at a reasonable hour or there'll be trouble from Pedro.

At the mention of the word dog Anna pricks up her ears.

'I want dog,' she says. Graham chips in, 'Want dog.'

I show them the picture of Pedro on my mobile phone.

'Want dog,' Anna demands meaning my Pedro.

I try to explain that Pedro is in another country but I don't think she understands, so I show her more photos and she's happy. I tell her I ring him every day which is sort of true as I do ring my neighbours to see if he's OK.

Mrs Bennett says it's time for the children's afternoon nap and that she likes to have a nap herself after lunch. She hopes I'll forgive her but she knows Peter will look after me. The children say they want to see more dog pictures. So I show them the same ones again and they're happy and toddle off with her.

Peter and I start to clear away the plates. He seems relaxed now.

He has an easy charm which is endearing. I wonder why Amy decided to dump him. I'd love to know about his relationships since but I daren't ask.

'My mother's matchmaking. I hope she's not embarrassing you going off with the children like that.'

I laugh and explain it happens to me too.

'After I was widowed my family were there for me, but now they say I have to move on as it's over a year since Jeff died. They keep trying to set me up.'

'It's not easy to move on,' he says, 'but you can, believe me.'

'I suppose you didn't have time to grieve.' I said, wondering if I had gone too far.

'No I didn't. The children needed care. They're my life and it's wonderful here.'

'I love it too. The peace. No rat race.'

'How much longer are you here?'

'Two more weeks. I'm going to hate going.'

'I've some leave this week. I'm working tomorrow and Tuesday but would you like me to show you some of the area on Wednesday? Mother will mind the children.'

I accept the invitation. I'm playing it right. I'll have a day with him and be able to draw him out.

I had noticed recent pictures of the children in the salon but no baby pictures. And no wedding photograph of Peter and his late wife. But maybe they never married though I suspect Peter would be conventional about getting married first. I still have pictures of me and Jeff up. But these pictures or rather the lack of wedding ones are only circumstantial evidence. They're not proof that he is the kidnapper.

We've adjourned to the garden after finishing the clear-up and are relaxing in the sunshine. Then out of the blue a killer question, 'You thought I looked like your husband. Am I like him otherwise?'

Why is he asking this? I pause, collecting my thoughts.

'Yes in a way I think, but I've only just met you.'

'Sorry, unfair question,' he apologises. I appreciate his sensitivity and continue to try to answer the question.

'Jeff wasn't money minded and you obviously don't worship money either. He was passionate about sport and he did a lot of voluntary work training local boys from disadvantaged areas in athletics and rugby. That was one of the things I loved about him. The boys from the team he coached were devastated when he died. He actually collapsed training for a charity marathon. I'd no warning. The boys from his team formed a guard of honour at his funeral.'

I start crying and he puts his arm around me.

'Don't be afraid to cry. When you lose the one you love, there's no quick fix. I've been there.'

Mrs Bennett returns as we're like this and she jumps to the wrong conclusions and leaves the garden.

Peter laughs softly.

'Mother thinks her wiles are working.'

I stop snivelling. I like this man. Yet I've come here to bring him to justice and to return the children to their parents. Am I mad?

He releases me.

'Enjoy the sun. I'm going to get some cold beers.'

We chat away as if we've known each other for years.

Then he arranges to pick me up on Wednesday morning.

**

Wednesday takes an age to come. At exactly eleven o'clock as he promised, his car pulls up and I see two blonde heads in the back.

'Change of plan,' he says. 'Mum's feeling tired and they've been asking for you so I thought we'd all go to Jonzac. There's an amazing leisure centre there with facilities for children. They love it.'

It takes me only a minute to fetch my swimming togs. I had already been to Jonzac to collect tourist literature to keep up my role. A pretty town and I had noticed the leisure centre, Les Antilles de Jonzac.

Jonzac is about 10 kilometres away so we're there in no time. The children know the place well and are pulling at the belts in their car seats eager to get in. I take Anna into the ladies changing room.

I'm not the greatest swimmer; I prefer to sunbathe so I'm able to supervise the children on the water chutes while Peter swims in the main pool. Mrs Bennett had packed lunch for us so after our swim we retire to the park. It's a gorgeous day and we really need the sun umbrella in the boot.

Anna asks me if Pedro can swim. He certainly can. She's delighted to hear that I phoned him after I was at their home. She seems very advanced for her age.

The children demolish the healthy lunch full of salad and fruit which Mrs Bennett has packed. I agree to some wine as I'm not driving. I can't believe how relaxed I feel and it's not due to the wine. After lunch we make sleeping places for the children under the huge umbrella and they nod off quickly. I suddenly realise I haven't had a cigarette since I've been in France and I don't want one. It's true that I have cut down my smoking drastically since I was in hospital but I still enjoy the occasional one. Smoking was the only thing I had in common with Carli, and now maybe I don't even have that. Here I am with this adorable child who may be her son. I just don't understand how she could have left him the way she did.

'What are you thinking?' Peter's question brings me out of my daydream.

'I'm thinking I don't want to go back to work.'

'Then don't.'

'That's not practical. You're crazy.'

'I don't mean walk out on your employer. Go back; see what kind of a deal you can do. With your skills you can work from home and that needn't be in Manchester. Sell up, make a few bob and come here. Or rent your house out. You can buy or rent property here for very little, the cost of living is reasonable and the health service is great.'

'You're making sense.'

'Yes, I know I am. I've seen so many people staying in places they didn't want to be in for no good reason. You've no ties apart from Pedro and he can come here. All you have to do is to have him micro chipped and vaccinated thirty days before you travel.'

I protest that I've got friends and family in the UK but he points out that when you live in the sun you get visitors especially with all the cheap flights available. Which I know is probably true.

Peter points out that if I had any close friends surely I'd have them with me on this holiday and I suppose he has a point of sorts.

'Most of my friends are married or in a relationship and weren't available.'

'That's my point,' he retorts. 'You don't have a man in your life to keep you back there.'

Then he looks embarrassed.

'That came out the wrong way. I didn't mean to make you sound like a loser. Oh God I've used another loaded word. Better keep my mouth shut. I mean I'm sure you have lots of admirers.'

I look at him bemused.

'That's a nice thing to say. I'm flattered.'

My heart is pounding.

'I mean it. Life can be wonderful. You turn up in this small place and here we are having a great day and the children love you.'

This is crazy. Of course I didn't turn up out of the blue. It took months of detective work. For what seems like an eternity I'm speechless, and then Graham wakes up and breaks the silence.

'Want drink.'

The atmosphere is broken. His devoted father, or more likely his grandfather, gets him some milk. Then Anna wakes up too, also thirsty. Peter asks Graham if he needs his nappy changed and he indignantly denies it.

'I think you do. Daddy can smell a poo.'

'No poo daddy.'

I agree with Peter. There is a smell obvious even though we are in the open air.

'Graham, my Pedro does lots of poos in my garden and I clean them up.' I show him a picture of Pedro in the garden.

I get his interest.

'Maybe you did a little poo?'

He nods.

Peter also nods to me which I take to be a message to go ahead. I am out of my comfort zone here. But it goes reasonably well. Graham is co-operative and the new nappy is on.

'You did well,' Peter says. 'We'd better head back. I was wondering if you'd be interested in something on here this evening. The local operatic society is having a Gilbert and Sullivan evening and there's a lot of British people in it. The area's full of Brits as you've probably realised. They've been on to me to join but my hours are antisocial and I'd miss rehearsals. I'd like to, because I do sing.'

I know he has musical talent from my research but I clearly have acting skills which have been essential to my research journey.

'I'd love to come,' I say, 'though to be honest I can't tell one note from another.'

'There's a reception after the show and I'm invited. You'll be able to meet some local people.'

**

'I am the captain of the Pinafore and a right good captain to.
I'm very very good and I'd like it understood
That I command a right good crew...'

The words of the operetta bring back happy memories of school when we did that Gilbert and Sullivan show.

We're in the packed auditorium enjoying the evening.

Peter hears me muttering the words under my breath.

'I thought you didn't sing?'

'I don't but we did this one at school and I was a backstage helper. It's amazing how I still remember the words.'

In the interval, he introduces me to people and I feel them wondering who I am. I make polite conversation. My French has improved quite a lot on this trip and I'm able to hold my own with the local French people who make up about fifty percent of the audience. In a quiet moment Peter tells me that most of the British people here have taken early retirement like his mother. He is one of the younger ones and when any single daughters of the retired Brits visit their parents he is always introduced to them.

He laughs.

'It baffles me why parents think a doctor is a good catch. We work unsociable hours. The work can be very stressful and we're as much prone to alcoholism and depression as any other profession, probably more so.'

The second half flies. At the end the audience gives the cast a standing ovation. There's a great buzz at the drinks reception after the show. Some of the cast are still in their costumes and stage make-up. As an outsider, and with the area's most eligible bachelor in tow, everyone wants to meet me.

How long have you known Peter is the standard question and I don't like to say only since Sunday. So I fudge and say it was earlier this year. Peter hears me give one of these answers, squeezes my arm and whispers in my ear – 'You're doing fine. Don't mind them asking.'

One of the cast, Ralph Rackstraw the sailor courting the Captain's daughter Josephine, tells me that Peter has a fine tenor voice but no amount of encouragement can get him into a show; he asks me to persuade him.

I feel I've known him for years, well certainly months. Not surprising when you think of everything I knew about him before we finally met.

In the car returning home Peter is singing songs from the show. I join in. Normally I'd never sing but I'm on a high as if I've taken a mind-altering substance when I've only had two glasses of champagne.

'Are you going to offer me some coffee?' he asks as he pulls up outside my house.

As the coffee is bubbling away in the percolator he says 'I know this house well. It used to be owned by an English family who holidayed here like we did. In fact they had a daughter my age and she was the first girl to break my heart.'

He says it quite lightly so I ask equally lightly if it took a long time to get over her.

'No', he says. 'Her family sold the house and the next year there was another English family with twin daughters my age and they both fancied me. I had a great time.'

I pass him his coffee and while we're both sipping away there's a moment of silence. Then he puts his cup down and kisses me softly on the lips.

'I have to go now or I'll never go. I start early tomorrow. I've some leave due and I'll see if I can get my hours changed while you're here.' He kisses me again and departs blowing another kiss from the door.

A few minutes later, I get a text. 'Home safely. Thinking of you. I'll ring you tomorrow.'

He does.

We spend every possible hour together for the rest of my 'holiday'. I don't want to go home.

I am holding back the tears as we embrace beside my hired car before I set off to the airport.

'I'll phone you the minute I'm back.'

'You'd better, or I'll get on the next plane to see you're OK.'

**

On the plane I try to think logically about my time in France which is not easy. I've solved the mystery of the missing children but I've fallen for their kidnapper. Or have I? He looks like Jeff and I'm vulnerable even allowing for the progress I've made in moving on. What on earth should I do? Pedro can't advise me on this! There's nobody I can confide in given that kidnapping is such a serious offence.

It won't be too long before I see him again as he's coming for a weekend in September. Does Peter have any idea about my real motive for taking a holiday so near him? I have no way of knowing.

PART VI

SEPTEMBER 2012-OCTOBER 2012

CHAPTER 37

A unt Bernie is on the phone the day after I get back from France. After establishing that I've had a great holiday she proceeds to fill me in with the Waterford news.

'Carli Walsh is going for the Dail,' she announces. I have to admit I'm surprised even though she'd mentioned the possibility in her blog in July. I mean she's got what she wanted which is fame. Of course there has to be a by-election after that Minister died but what's in it for Carli I can't imagine.

'I sent you the cutting, didn't you read it?'

I have to admit I haven't yet. Now that I know the truth, media reports don't have the same attraction. And to be honest, I'm asking myself whether it would have been better if I hadn't found out. And sometimes I question whether I did find the missing babies in France or just meet a gorgeous man who has two children by his deceased partner and who happens to look like Jeff and also really likes me? I must stop thinking like this; it's unsettling. I promise Bernie I will read the cutting and end the conversation.

Carli Walsh to stand in Waterford By-Election

Singer-song writer Carli Walsh has announced she is running as an Independent candidate in the Waterford by-election to be held later this month.

The by-election arises from the death of Michael Moriarty, Junior Minister for Transport.

Ms Walsh knew Mr Moriarty from the time he held his constituency clinic in the pub where she sang before she became famous.

'I had no interest in politics before I met Michael. He really believed that young people should get involved and he talked to me a lot about it. Young people in Waterford are demoralised. They think the only answer is emigration. They're not represented and I want to represent them in the Dail.'

Mrs Fiona Moriarty declined to comment when asked if she would be seeking the Fine Gael nomination. She also declined to comment on Ms Walsh's candidacy.

On the Forum, there is considerable interest.

Missing Children Forum Portal Home Register Log In	 every child matters
September 3 2012 at 11.07 am Great publicity stunt from Carli Walsh, she's standing in a by-election	Fairplay Posts: 95 Join Date: 5.5.2011 Location: Ireland

September 3 2012 at 11.56 am Yeah, it's the end of the summer silly season. Papers will print anything	Declan Posts: 601 Join Date: 2.4.2011 Location: Dublin
September 3 2012 at 12.07 pm The politician's wife will stand. They keep it in the family.	Liam Posts: 50 Join Date: 2.8.2011 Location: Belfast
September 3 2012 at 12.44 pm Wish people could be more positive. Like Carli said, young people don't vote. I wish her the best.	Suzy Posts: 101 Join Date: 27.2.2011 Location: Bath

September 3 2012 at 1.19 pm Apparently she's going to mount a big social media campaign. She's got thousands of followers on Twitter and she's going to issue a 'political' tweet every day from now to the election.	Fairplay Posts: 96 Join Date: 5.5.2011 Location: Ireland
September 3 2012 at 2.07 pm But will these tweeting kids actually vote assuming they even live in Waterford?	LegalEagle Posts: 14 Join Date: 20.12.2011 Location: Law Library
September 3 2012 at 3.03 pm More negativity. Would be great if she encouraged young people to vote.	Suzy Posts: 102 Join Date: 27.2.2011 Location: Bath

They move on to a discussion of social media, and then to a recent missing child case.

September 4 2012 at 9.04 am	Noelle
That Tia Sharp case is horrendous. I never believed that she'd run away. When a family says she wouldn't do something like that, I always believe the opposite! I always thought she was dead.	Posts: 68 Join Date: 3.10.2011 Location: Bradford
September 4 2012 at 9.52 am	Pam
Unbelievable what's coming out now. At least the police seem to have got the bastard. That fucker who was living with her gran.	Posts: 33 Join Date: 27.11.2011 Location: York

I'm glad the online conversation has turned to the murdered English schoolgirl because I feel so uneasy after my trip to France. It would be wrong to post. After all I now know that Carli didn't hide her child to raise her profile as many people suspected. And I know that Amy too is innocent. Yet I've done nothing about it. And I've lied to my cousin Brian, the only person who knew the real reason for my 'holiday' in France.

Or would it be more accurate to say that while I strongly suspect that neither of the mothers is guilty and that the children are happy elsewhere, I haven't proved it. Peter and his mother didn't admit to it. I didn't notice any discrepancies in what they said. I could be taking the facts that suit me and making them 'fit' my theories.

**

And Forum members have a new issue – another left in the car story which fortunately doesn't end in tragedy.

September 4 2012 at 10.04 am Saw something last week in the Irish Independent reminding me of Carli. Someone left a 2 year old girl locked in a car for at least an hour. Police called and the mother got the child back when they found her	Fairplay Posts: 97 Join Date: 5.5.2011 Location: Ireland
September 5 2012 at 11.05 am Saw that. Was in the car park at Carrickmines shopping centre and the article said it was a hot sunny day. Shocking. Will they prosecute the mother? At least Carli thought her friend was coming to collect her child...	Liam Posts: 51 Join Date: 2.8.2011 Location: Belfast
September 5 2012 at 1.13 pm Isn't there a crèche in that shopping centre?	Declan Posts: 602 Join Date: 2.4.2011 Location: Dublin

September 5 2012 at 7.12 pm Don't know but this is clear cut neglect. The mother should be prosecuted.	LegalEagle Posts: 15 Join Date: 20.12.2011 Location: Law Library
September 5 2012 at 9.27 pm That mother must have known about Tommy Walsh being taken from a car, and she does this!	Noelle Posts: 69 Join Date: 3.10.2011 Location: Bradford

And so the posts continue in similar vein.

**

It seems that some people are taking Carli's candidacy seriously if the papers are to be believed.

Opinion Poll says Waterford by-election too close to call

Four candidates are polling strongly and any one of them could take the seat according to a new RedC poll out today, one week before the by-election.

Fiona Moriarty (FG) heads the poll with 24% of the first preference vote but Carli Walsh (Ind) and Larry Glynn (Lab) are both on 22%. Seamus Redmond (SF) is on 19% but insiders

*believe his campaign is gaining momentum and he could take
the seat depending on how the transfers go. Joe Boland (FF) is
on 12%.*

*The performance of 19 year old singer Carli Walsh continues
to amaze the pundits. With no political background, her
campaign theme of hope and jobs for young people seems to
have struck a cord; though seasoned political commentators
feel that on the day some young people may not turn out or find
they are not registered.*

*The campaign has become bitter as witnessed by the sharp
exchange on the Frontline Special between FG candidate Fiona
Moriarty and Ms Walsh.*

*Ms Moriarty said her opponent's candidature solely related
to her new album due out around polling day. She said her new
song 'Don't Leave' was a cynical ploy to win votes. When Ms
Walsh responded with some strong language, the presenter had
to move to an advert break.*

**

Every day Carli posts an election blog and updates her
Facebook page.

Yesterday's reads:

*'Folks, our campaign office is manic. Thank God, my best
mate Emer, has been able to take time off work to run it for
me. People are calling in offering to help all the time. So far
we've called to about 75% of the houses in the constituency
and with a week to go, we hope to get to the rest. People who
told me they never voted before say they are going to vote for
me. Amazing. Went back to Hair-I-Am. Kevin has being doing
great work there for me with the clients. It was great to chat to
them and was promised a few No.1 votes.*

*Some of my posters got defaced. I thought all that hate
was over but someone wrote 'child neglecter' on the ones on the
Quays. Local radio discussed it and most of the texts coming
in said it was wrong to do it; why not just vote for another
candidate?*

*The papers are saying I'm in with a chance which is crazy,
crazy, crazy.'*

**

Peter's coming for a long weekend, arriving on the eve of the
Waterford by-election. If I'm right, I'm now an accessory to the
crime and I must have it out with him. The children actually
could be twins, but I'm fooling myself because that's what I
want to believe.

**

We're cuddled up on the sofa watching the election coverage
on TV. Peter's brought me a video of the children and has
promised to take them back one of Pedro.

And the poll is right; it's clearly going to be close as the
morning news reveals:

*'This is Linda Bradley for Sky News at the Waterford By-
Election count where Carli Walsh is seeking to become the
youngest politician in the Irish Parliament. This by-election
follows from the death of Michael Moriarty in March.'*

Studio: 'Linda, have they started counting?'

*'Yes indeed they have. They started at nine this morning
and hope to have the result of the first count by 1 pm.'*

Studio: 'Can you explain to us exactly what that means?'

'In the Irish system you put a number 1 by your favourite candidate, number 2 for your second favourite and so on. By 1 pm they'll know who got the most number ones and they will eliminate the candidate with the lowest vote which is expected to be the Fianna Fail candidate. Then they count his no.2 votes and transfer them to the other candidates, and so on.'

Studio: 'What are the polls saying?'

'There was an exit poll last night and that indicates it'll be very close between four candidates. The turnout is about 71% which is very high for a by-election. We're also hearing that a lot of young people were voting which is not usual.'

Studio: 'And that would favour Carli Walsh?'

'Probably but the Sinn Fein camp is saying they have a lot of support among the young, so you wouldn't know.'

Studio: 'Could a surprise result affect the government?'

'No, the coalition government has a big majority. It would be embarrassing for the government if Mr Moriarty's widow doesn't take the seat. There is a tradition here of relatives being elected when the holder dies. There's no love lost between the Fine Gael camp and Ms Walsh's supporters. Some people are very cynical about Ms Walsh's candidacy but she is from Waterford and well known here as indeed she is in the UK now.'

Studio: 'We'll come back to you at lunch time for the first count.'

**

Studio: 'Linda, is the first count in?'
'They've just announced it and it's going to be a cliffhanger. Four candidates have received over 9,000 No.1 votes and Carli

Walsh has come in second two votes ahead of Fiona Moriarty for Fine Gael. Sinn Fein has topped the poll but as I said it'll be close. Fianna Fail got 14% of the vote but have no chance of getting the seat.'

Studio: 'Any of the candidates there yet?'

Linda: 'Most of them are and I can see Carli Walsh and I'll try and get a word.'

'How does it feel to see all those votes for you Carli?'

Carli: 'Linda it's amazing, amazing. I can't believe it. Thank you Waterford!'

Linda: 'And now back to the studio'

**

I switch off the TV as the main lunchtime news finishes but Peter says he wants to see the results special in the evening. I laugh nervously and say I didn't know he was so interested in Irish politics.

'I want to see how the singer did.'

'Oh Carli Walsh. My Aunt Bernie in Waterford voted for her.'

Then I remember I haven't told him about my Irish relatives in Waterford and wonder if it might start alarm bells ringing. But I'm going to confront him anyway aren't I? Fortunately Pedro jumps on his lap distracting him as if he understands my problem. So the danger passes.

It's a gorgeous late September day so we spend it in the garden. After dinner we're glued to the election special.

'*We're coming to you live from the count centre in Waterford where it looks like the government could lose its first by-election of this Dail term. Labour candidate Larry Glynn was eliminated an hour ago on the 9th count leaving Sinn Fein, Fine Gael and Independent Carli Walsh.*

As Carli Walsh has the least number of votes of the three remaining candidates she will be eliminated next. They've been counting for the last hour and they're close to announcing the distribution of her votes. The tallymen are telling us a lot are going to Sinn Fein. Carli's transfers will decide whether Fine Gael or Sinn Fein take the seat.

Apparently there's no significant transfer to the other woman candidate, Moriarty, as you'd expect, in fact there's virtually none. Carli Walsh was ahead of Moriarty for Fine Gael until Larry Glynn for Labour was eliminated and he transferred to Fine Gael as you'd expect putting Moriarty ahead of her and Redmond for Sinn Fein. The Sinn Fein camp is looking happy. I think they're confident.'

The cameras show the candidates waiting anxiously for the redistribution of Carli's votes. Carli looks radiant and is posing for photographers. Beside her is a woman I recognise. It's Amy Blake. The camera cuts to an interview with Carli who is explaining that Amy has been one of her campaign helpers and looks after her legal affairs. It's like a rugby scrum around her as photographers push to get the best shots.

Back to the announcement. Carli continues to smile while the Fine Gael candidate looks tense.

The Returning officer says.....

The distribution of Walsh's surplus is as follows:

Moriarty   + 124

Redmond   + 3002

I hereby declare Seamus Redmond elected.

The Shinners as they're called are jumping up and down as well they might but I feel sorry for Fiona Moriarty who looks as though she's going to cry. She's lost so much and now a 19 year old pop star with no political pedigree has cost her a seat in the Irish Parliament.

Mrs Moriarty is forced to make a short speech and it's clear that defeat is not something she had contemplated. It's not the most gracious speech I've ever heard. It contrasts with Carli's; she is effusive, thanking everybody and she gives the surprised Sinn Fein candidate a big kiss which the photographers love. They've put the detailed results on the screen and Peter comments that Carli actually beat Mrs Moriarty by two votes on the first count.

'Don't you think it was all a publicity stunt?' I ask.

'Maybe. But it's good to see people voting instead of just complaining. It was a great turnout for a by-election and good to see the government get a shock. The new Irish government has done nothing for the health service even with a doctor as Minister for Health.'

He's seen enough and he switches off. He looks as though he's a lot on his mind.

'What are you thinking?'

He hesitates.

'You know don't you?'

I think he's going to admit everything and do I really want him to do that? I pretend I haven't heard which isn't convincing as the TV isn't even on now.

'Molly, don't pretend you didn't hear me. We must have this out; I've been putting it off because I don't want to spoil what we have.'

I say quietly, 'Some things are better left unsaid.'

'Not this one.'

I can see he's determined to talk.

'You didn't really come out on holiday, did you?' he says in a very gentle tone.

'Well it was a special kind of holiday. I really needed one but I was addicted to the missing babies' cases. I'd lost my own baby and I couldn't understand why those mothers did what they did. Looking into what might have happened helped to take my mind off my situation. It was like therapy.'

It's such a relief to have it out in the open.

'When did you realise I knew?'

He looks confused.

'It's really hard to say. I was suspicious of you initially as I would have been of anyone turning up like you did. Then I put those suspicions out of my mind. Mother had checked you out and everything you said was true. I suppose it was after you left and I had a little time to myself that I wondered if this was too good to be true. There wasn't anything specific but I became convinced that you hadn't been entirely honest. I put off raising it. I could have been wrong and I could have blown what we have. But in the end I just had to.'

I feel like crying. Yes I have lied to him but I do love him so much.

'Why haven't you done anything about it? Gone to the police?'

'I couldn't.'

'Why?'

'Silly question. You know how I feel about you.'

'You've never said.'

'We've been like a couple of lovesick kids more or less since we met.'

'So what are you going to do?'

'I don't know.'

'Can I tell you how it happened? We never planned to take the babies.'

He tells me the whole story and it only makes me more confused. What he and his mother have done is serious and they would face long jail sentences if convicted. I explain how

I found him, about the Forum and meeting with Liz through it, how I prepared a shortlist of doctors and eliminated them one by one. How I hoped to find one missing baby, but actually found two.

'Would you visit me in jail?'

'It would be crazy for you to be in jail. But you could return them so no-one knew it was you. I'd help you do that.'

'You'd be an accessory after the fact. You could go to jail too. Molly, mother wouldn't do it.'

'You have to persuade her.'

'She loves you too, Molly.'

**

The weekend goes too fast. At the airport I say, 'You will think about it. It's the right thing to do.'

He asks, 'But will you accept whatever we decide?'

A tough question.

What's 'right' in this case? What is best for the children? From their blogs I knew that Amy and Carli have met and that Amy is acting in a professional capacity for her. It's not surprising that Amy would be involved in her election campaign but what I don't know is whether Amy has told Carli she is her daughter, and if she has whether she has also revealed who her father is. She's described on her blog how she's met Amy's family and given the impression she's part of the family. But that could be merely PR spin. Carli is young enough to have lots more children. And she has a half-brother, grandparents and a stepfather though she doesn't know this if Amy hasn't told her the truth. There is no right or wrong in this case.

So I answer truthfully, 'I don't know.'

He seems to understand. He kisses me and is gone.

**

Back home I switch on my PC and seek solace in the Missing Children Forum. I hadn't checked in while Peter was staying. Interesting reading the comments on the by-election now, knowing the results.

September 23 2012 at 5.05 pm		Declan
Can't believe the results coming in from Waterford – our favourite child neglecter could be elected.		Posts: 622 Join Date: 2.4.2011
Boland Joe (FF)	7,712	Location:
McDermott Bertie (GP)	2,325	Dublin
Glynn Larry (Lab)	9,432	
Kelly Mattie (PBP)	2,378	
Kelly Michael (Socialist Party)	2,522	
Moriarty Fiona (FG)	9,537	
Redmond Seamus (SF)	9,801	
Sweetman Brendan (Ind)	2,452	
Walsh Carli (Ind)	9,539	

September 23 2012 at 5.16 pm What a nerd you are Dan, typing out all those figures!	CoolDude Posts: 103 Join Date: 4.7.2011 Location: Bahamas
September 23 2012 at 5.22 pm And she'll get her election expenses refunded with that good vote – our taxes!	Taxpayer Posts: 231 Join Date: 22.11.2010 Location: London
September 23 at 5.26 pm It won't be your taxes. You live in London!!!	CoolDude Posts: 104 Join Date: 4.7.2011 Location: Bahamas

September 23 2012 at 9.37 pm	Suzy
Result in – SF took it with Carli's transfers. Amazing! The face on that FG woman was something else.	Posts: 103 Join Date: 27.2.2011 Location: Bath
September 23 2012 at 10.05 pm	Declan
Could be a reason for the sour face. There's a rumour in Waterford that her late husband was the father of Carli's baby	Posts: 623 Join Date: 2.4.2011 Location: Dublin
September 23 2012 at 10.21 pm	Mags
Come on, that's rubbish. How would a middle class guy like him be having an affair with a school drop out half his age!	Posts: 399 Join Date: 2.9.2010 Location: Liverpool

September 23 2012 at 10.25 pm Since when did age matter? Pulling a bird half your age is good for the soul	Liam Posts: 52 Join Date: 2.8.2011 Location: Belfast
September 23 2012 at 11.01 pm This is getting crude. I'm logging off.	Mags Posts: 400 Join Date: 2.9.2010 Location: Liverpool
September 23 2012 at 11.03 pm It's a year since both those kids went missing. It's not looking good. I thought there'd be an outbreak of first anniversary articles in the papers but didn't see anything. There's always an outbreak of McCann stuff on their anniversary	Noelle Posts: 70 Join Date: 3.10.2011 Location: Bradford

September 23 2012 at 11.19 pm It's been good for Carli since her child vanished – hit records, a great performance in Eurovision and to be fair to her she obviously encouraged young people to vote and that has to be good. But we don't hear much about Amy Blake these days.	Fairplay Posts: 98 Join Date: 5.5.2011 Location: Ireland
September 23 2012 at 11.22 pm I heard Amy doing a radio interview recently – she's working hard running the husband's business. He's out of hospital and she hopes he'll go back to work soon. She's really dignified and I have to admire her for getting her marriage back on track after all that happened.	Lucy Posts: 5 Join Date: 21.8.2012 Location: Accrington
September 23 2012 at 11.29 pm Funny, Miss Marple's not around. You'd expect her to have an opinion on this child neglecter almost getting elected. She hasn't posted for ages.	Columbo Posts: 117 Join Date: 6.3.2011 Location: New York

September 23 2012 at 11.31 pm Just heard a radio interview with Fiona Moriarty. Guess what she's claiming now? Carli wasn't entitled to stand because she's not 21. Her age varies depending on what paper you read. Moriarty's claiming Carli's nomination papers must have been incorrect. And she should be prosecuted.	LegalEagle Posts: 16 Join Date; 20.12.2011 Location: Law Library
September 23 2012 at 11.35 pm What a bitch! If you can vote at 18, why can't you stand at 18? And Carli didn't win so even if her nomination was technically invalid so what!	Liam Posts: 53 Join Date: 2.8.2011 Location: Belfast

I switch off the computer and lie awake all night.

CHAPTER 38

Two weeks after Peter's visit I'm still not sleeping. If I can find out what happened then so can the police. For all I know, they could be moving in. Even though I'm really busy at work and exhausted at the end of the day, it's not helping me sleep. I've kept off the Forum but tonight I have to see if anything's happening. It appears there might be.

Missing Children Forum Portal Home Register Log In	every child matters
October 10 2012 at 10.10 am Hey, there's rumours that the police in Waterford are close to a breakthrough in the Tommy Walsh case	Declan Posts: 624 Join Date: 2.4.2011 Location: Dublin
October 10 2012 at 10.15 am Rumours! There's always rumours. Be specific	CoolDude Posts: 105 Join Date: 4.7.2011 Location: Bahamas

October 10 2012 at 10.23 am What I heard was that the appointments book for those hairdressers was being gone through.	Declan Posts: 625 Join Date: 2.4.2011 Location: Dublin
October 10 2012 at 10.32 am Pathetic. They'd have gone through all the appointments for the day Tommy vanished and talked to all the clients in that afternoon.	CoolDude Posts: 106 Join Date: 4.7.2011 Location: Bahamas
October 10 2012 at 10.41 am No, it's more than that. There's a tweet from that guy in the local radio station #check real name of glamourpuss in Carli hairdressers that day.	Declan Posts: 626 Join Date: 2.4.2011 Location: Dublin

October 10 2012 at 10.50 am What the hell does that mean?	CoolDude Posts: 107 Join Date: 4.7.2011 Location: Bahamas
October 10 2012 at 11.19 am Could be just trying to get listener numbers up by cryptic tweets?	Fairplay Posts: 99 Join Date: 5.5.2011 Location: Ireland

Interesting. I haven't a clue who 'glamourpuss' refers to. It doesn't sound dangerous to us but I need to know the story behind this. My only hope of finding out is through my cousin Sandra so next time Aunt Bernie is on the phone I ask her to put me on to Sandra.

Initially, Sandra is baffled.

'I've seen lots of glamorous girls in there. I mean if they do a good job with your hair, you should look good when you leave. There's a few models that go there. They just work locally; they're not top models like Kate Moss.'

She mentions their names, which mean nothing to me. I'll see what I can find out about them. She promises to ring me if she thinks of anything else.

**

Maybe Alro knows something, but it's 24 hours after I emailed him and no response. My research on the local 'models' has come up with nothing. One appears to have gone to the same school as Carli Walsh which is hardly surprising as she's the same age. Another is dating a footballer I've never heard of and the third was the star player in the school camogie team. I'm not sure what camogie is! And, having seen pictures of them on their Facebook pages I don't even think they are particularly glamorous. So is this another false lead? Hopefully it'll take up police time. I just can't stop worrying that the police could swoop before I know what Peter decides.

**

Another local newspaper cutting has arrived from Aunt Bernie. They're few and far between now as the case is effectively on hold. Page 5 is interesting. The headline reads:

'Gardai deny Tommy case Detective resigns after row'

It's a short article accompanied by a picture of an attractive looking man in his late 30s at the christening party of his first child earlier in the year.

'Colleagues were stunned by the resignation of popular Dan O'Rourke after fifteen years service with the gardai. Inspector O'Rourke was in charge of the investigation into the Tommy Walsh case and is believed to have complained bitterly about the lack of resources allocated to it. Waterford has been full of rumours in the past two weeks about a breakthrough in this case and Inspector O'Rourke's resignation at this time is regarded as unusual.'

The article went on to quote colleagues of his.

Ban Garda Orla Reilly said, '*He was so easy to work with and all the team will miss him. We had no idea he planned to leave the gardai. He worked long hours on the baby Tommy case and was determined to find him. He believes he is still alive.*'

She'll probably get into trouble for saying that, I think. But that tells me something is up, or she wouldn't take a risk. Surely only the press office can comment on police matters?

**

Lying awake that night, something is on the tip of my tongue and I don't even know what it is. Sounds daft. I get up, put on my dressing gown and start doodling on a pad at my desk. I've been getting information from Alro in Waterford who has to have connections with the gardai. Who is Alro? Then it hits me.

ALRO. Reverse that and you get ORLA. Could Alro be Ban Garda Orla Reilly, not a 'he' as I assumed? Or is this just a coincidence? Alro hasn't responded to my last email, but might now if I have discovered her identity.

I email Alro again and start the email Dear Orla……..

Though it's 2.01 am, I get an immediate brief reply, giving me a mobile number to ring in the morning between 8.30 and 9.0 am.

**

Nervously I dial the given number.

Before I can speak, a young sounding voice says, 'Miss Marple?'

'Yes, that's me. You must just have come off the night shift?'

'I have. You're as sharp as your namesake. You understand now how careful I've had to be, but I'm furious with the way Dan's been treated.'

'What happened to him?'

'We went over some interview notes with Fiona Moriarty and saw that she said when bitching about Carli Walsh that the hairdressers had no baby ban. She knew this why – because she went to that hairdressers 'sometimes'. We didn't get the significance of that at the time or we'd have asked if she was there on the day Tommy vanished from the car.'

'Now we re-checked the appointments book for the day. We found two Fionas booked in but neither of them with the surname Moriarty. Then I remembered that Fiona Moriarty's maiden name is Kelly and there was a Fiona Kelly booked in at 3.0 pm for highlights cut and blow dry. If she was seen on time that would have her leaving at around the time Carli arrived...'

'But why would she use Kelly?'

'Well she won the Waterford Rose as Fiona Kelly. She wasn't married to him then but I think she keeps her single name for work and uses the married one when she's doing the political wife bit. I've seen her use the name Kelly in fashion and beauty pieces she writes for the local paper. You'd think she would have said she was there that day when we interviewed her if she had nothing to do with it. She'd lost her own child to a cot death and she may have known that her husband had fathered a child with Carli.'

I interrupt.

'I always had a feeling that Dave might not be Tommy's father. I don't know why; just an instinct. Is it definite that Moriarty was the father?'

'We think so. We discovered he was paying her €1000 pm out of his business until Tommy vanished. It was in the system as bookkeeping costs but we don't believe that.'

'Couldn't Moriarty have taken Tommy to stop the financial drain?'

'No, we don't think so. He was on the Ministerial gravy train then and we checked his movements that day. He was in Dublin. That wife may be a looker but she's not popular around here. Full of herself and a real snob. Anyway I went to talk to the salon manager who confirmed that Fiona Kelly was indeed Fiona Moriarty and had been a customer for several years. The appointment had been kept though she couldn't confirm exactly when she left but agreed that she would have been there about an hour and a half. She told me that Mrs Moriarty hadn't been back since, which didn't surprise her as they'd lost a few customers over the missing baby. On the other hand, the salon manager admitted they'd gained more customers than they'd lost from all the publicity.'

'Is Fiona the glamourpuss in the tweet going around?'

'That was one of my colleagues. He's friendly with someone in local radio and he tipped him off. We were all so angry when we weren't allowed to follow this up. The problem was the sensitivity of the situation. I mean she's the widow of a government minister who stood in the by-election to facilitate the government and then she loses. The government owes her one. She had to take a lot of flack on the doorsteps over all the cuts. They say she never wanted to stand but the government thought she was the only person who could hold the seat for them. Well Dan asked the Superintendent for advice and he'd promised to get back to him. A day later Dan was called into the Super's office and Dan said he knew something was wrong when he saw how embarrassed he looked. He'd gone higher up to cover his own back. This is what he was told:

'Look Dan, I don't like this either but I've been told to leave it. The lady is untouchable. The party owes her one for standing in the first place. I mean to be beaten by the Shinners when you never wanted to stand and were trying to get over losing your husband.'

'Dan said he protested but the Super insisted our evidence is circumstantial. He pointed out that I had been in her house and there was no baby there. A bit pathetic. I was only in her living room for a few minutes to ask about the incident at the funeral. Then I was more or less told to leave. I didn't look for a baby there. The Super told Dan that the woman has suffered enough; that it was ridiculous to think she could be involved and that she was to be left alone. That's it, in a nutshell.

'Anyway Dan stormed out and went home. He resigned two days later though we tried to persuade him not to.'

'What'll he do now?'

'Not sure. He had a lot of untaken leave with all his overtime on the case so he got a good cheque when he left. I don't think he'll let this go. All I know is he's taken his wife and baby off for a holiday to think things over. The media got wind that something was up and were ringing him constantly. One even found his home address and tried to get an interview at his front gate. Dan wanted to get away before he said what he shouldn't.'

'So will you and the rest of the team continue?'

'No, that's the only lead we had. We thought we had a lead when that woman came forward last year; the one who saw a woman by Carli's car. But nothing came of that. We think the woman must have been a tourist.'

I thank Orla for being so frank and ask her to keep in touch. She agrees. This is good news for us. Peter's mother is no longer in the frame, and Inspector or rather ex Inspector O'Rourke may go after Fiona Moriarty, who may be an unpleasant woman, but she isn't guilty of taking Carli's baby. Poor Mrs Moriarty. She lost a baby and a husband just like I did. But O'Rourke can't hound her without getting arrested. Or could he be like that Portuguese cop, the one in charge of the Madeleine McCann case? He was taken off the case for some reason then he wrote a best selling book about the case and got sued. No, I wouldn't want a book about the case. Who knows what it might bring out of the woodwork? I must find out the story with the baby Rose team. It seems safe on the Tommy front, for now anyway.

CHAPTER 39

I don't have to wait long to find out what's happening in Accrington.

I'm enjoying my lunchtime sandwich when I think I hear on the radio that police have been called to Amy Blake's house. I almost choke. While I'm coughing the newsreader moves to the next item. Damn. I was taking my lunch at my desk which is a bad habit I have. We have a TV in our staff room so for once my colleagues see me at lunchtime. I switch on Sky News. The ads are on, but scrolling across the bottom of the screen I see the 'police swoop on Amy Blake's home'....

At last the wretched ads cease.

Reporter: '*Police have called to the Accrington home of Amy Blake today. She's been taken to the local police station.*'

Studio: '*Is this a breakthrough? Is she being charged with harming her missing baby? Have they found a body?*'

Reporter: '*No, we're hearing the charge is unrelated to baby Rose who has been missing for over a year now. There's a number of journalists here because rumours were going around all day that something was going to happen. The police have promised us a statement later.*'

Studio: '*Any word of charges against Jimmy Blake?*'

Reporter: '*That's not clear. All we know is that he's back in hospital. He was in hospital for months after the dreadful car crash he was in last year, then he was able to come home. His next door neighbour told us he had to go back to hospital last month with some complication.*'

Studio: 'We'll come back to you for the press conference.'

* *

I've been glued to the TV waiting for the press conference. Fortunately the boss is not in today to witness my total lack of productivity. My colleagues see me as a little eccentric but someone who gets her work done so nobody comments on my taking such a long break in the staff room. It seems like days but the press conference comes an hour after the lunchtime news broke the story.

* *

Reporter (at Accrington police station): Detective Inspector Martin Benson from the Fraud Squad is about to read a statement and he has said he won't take any questions. Here it comes.

'Amy Blake has today been arrested in connection with a number of charges relating to fraud and misappropriation at the St Jude's Hospital and Research Centre. The arrest is the culmination of a six month investigation resulting from information provided to the police. Further arrests in this matter are under consideration.'

I was not expecting that even though I knew Davina had followed up her complaint. She told me she's keeping a bottle of very expensive champagne for when Amy is brought to justice. I presume Davina will get very drunk tonight.

* *

I work frantically for the rest of the day to make up for lost time. It didn't look as though there would be more news today. Amy was released on bail as is usual.

At home I look at Carli's blog and there it is:

'I thought it was a bad dream when I got a call from Amy Blake telling me she is to be arrested. I kept saying 'You didn't take your baby, I know you didn't.' She was only allowed a minute to talk to me. I couldn't work out why she was being arrested if it wasn't about Rose. We've become so close now she's looking after my affairs. I was so upset I had a fag. I've really been trying to cut down because I know it's crazy to smoke as a singer. Amy has helped me so much and I'm going to stand by her. Watch this space. Calling a press conference tomorrow.'

**

And she's as good as her word. Fortunately it's Saturday so I don't have to worry about what colleagues think. Sky News is promoting the press conference with rolling headlines across the screen. It finally starts at 11.30 am. The room is packed which doesn't surprise me. Since Carli did so well in the Eurovision Song Contest, the press lap up any story about her. Sky News has been feeding us titbits telling us this is nothing to do with a new album or a new boyfriend but a really big story.

There's standing room only when Carli gets up to speak. She's wearing a tailored knee-length navy skirt with a lacy cream long-sleeved blouse. Her make-up is subdued. She thanks everybody for coming at short notice and then reads from her prepared script.

'I'm here today to support my mother Amy Blake and to ask you to help me get the ridiculous charges against her dropped.'

The buzz from the audience as she says the words 'my mother' prevents her from continuing.

One of the minders grabs the microphone and asks for order and says Carli is going to explain everything. She has to ask for quiet several times.

Finally Carli can continue. I see the media scribble frantically in their notebooks. When Carli asks if there are any questions, just about every hand goes up..........

**

So Amy had told her the truth as I suspected. She now knows she has grandparents, a half-brother and a stepfather, and I suppose she has been getting to know them over the past weeks. Carli's blog certainly gives that impression. This makes me feel a little less guilty. She has lost her son but has gained a family.

But does she know who her father is?

Carli's bombshell has livened up the Forum:

Missing Children Forum Portal Home Register Log In	every child matters
October 16 2012 at 3.21 pm OMG. You couldn't make this up. Carli is Amy's daughter!!!	CoolDude Posts: 108 Join Date: 4.7.2011 Location: Bahamas

October 16 2012 at 3.29 pm There has to be a connection between the missing babies. Not believable that two from the same family go missing in the same month AREN'T CONNECTED. Miss Marple always felt the cases were linked. Where the hell is she?	Declan Posts: 627 Join Date: 2.4.2011 Location: Dublin
October 16 2012 at 3.31 pm Hey, Amy hasn't been charged with Rose's disappearance. Remember that!	Fairplay Posts: 100 Join Date: 5.5.2011 Location: Ireland
October 16 2012 at 3.39 pm Might all be a set up. Lots of stuff coming out now about police corruption...don't believe Amy needed to defraud anyone. Carli has put lots more stuff up on her blog; it's quite moving when she describes Amy telling her she is her mother	Suzy Posts: 117 Join Date: 27.2.2011 Location: Bath

October 16 2012 at 3.41 pm That's you being naïve again. It's those that have it, that want more. It's called GREED. And Carli will have PR people writing her blog.	Mags Posts; 401 Join Date: 2.9.2010 Location: Liverpool
October 16 2012 at 3.51 pm Interesting times ahead. It's been a bit boring on the Forum recently (with respect to all the regulars!!). Did anyone hear the rumours about a new lead in Waterford?	Sherlock Posts: 141 Join Date: 29.6.2011 Location: Baker Street
October 16 2012 at 4.08 pm The detective in Waterford has resigned I heard. Well, did he resign or was he pushed? Carli mentioned him on her blog – said he was a 'cool guy and tried his best to find Tommy.' Love to know whether she's glad he's gone.	Declan Posts: 628 Join Date: 2.4.2011 Location: Dublin

Hmm. Looks as though there's no imminent danger from the Accrington police. They'll be concentrating on getting a conviction on the fraud charges. They may well believe now that Rose's disappearance was a set-up because of the tricky meeting that night. They'll try to get a conviction on the fraud charges, and hope ultimately to locate Rose that way.

But Carli's revelation has made Forum members feel there must be a link between the cases, and that's worrying. Some of them are really smart.

Please God, I've a breathing space until Peter and his mother decide what to do. I have to check Carli's latest blog that Suzy finds so moving…

It reads:

'*When Amy told me who she really was after she helped me with some police questions I couldn't really take it in so I acted as though it was no big deal. But in the rare moments I'm alone I did ask myself why she gave me away. On reflection I didn't buy her 'to give me the decent life she couldn't have' story. I know it wasn't true because I've met my grandparents now and they would have helped out while Amy established her career. They didn't know about me.*

They've been so nice to me and invited me to stay with them anytime I'm free. Which is rare, but they genuinely mean it. Of course I had read everything I could about Amy before I met her because her child went missing too and she was criticised like I was. I had admired her for being ambitious and wanting to get on. She isn't from a wealthy background, just an ordinary one. She's worked hard for everything she has, like I have. I see similarities between us, we're both ambitious and determined to go as far as possible with the talents we have. Except that I didn't 'lose' Tommy to get publicity as some people still think I did. And I'm sure my mother is innocent too.

I don't blame Amy for my tough life. I blame the driver who killed my lovely adoptive parents.

Jimmy isn't bothered about Amy having me all those years ago. I wasn't worried about his reaction because it was years before he met Amy.

I would like to know about my father but Amy doesn't want to talk about it yet.'

Yes, interesting indeed but I suspect she has her PR people helping with these long blogs. The word 'yet' worries me. Amy doesn't want to talk about it 'yet.' Just when might she tell her and how anxious is Carli to know?

CHAPTER 40

Since Peter returned to France I've been living on my nerves. He hasn't made a decision because his mother understandably wants to leave things as they are. Numerous phone calls don't help.

'Look, the children have been with you longer than they were with their own parents. You've got to consider this from the children's point of view.'

I regret using that argument because he's able to turn it against me.

'Exactly, that means staying with me.'

And given Amy's current situation, I have to admit he has a point.

He's heard about Amy's arrest on October 15th and while she's out on bail pending trial, he points out she could get several years if found guilty and that they'd have to make an example of her as she's a lawyer and was abusing her position at a charity. As Jimmy Blake may have been an accessory, Peter says the chances are he could go to jail too so how could the Blakes raise a young child? I can't really answer that.

Then he starts on Carli. He's ambivalent about her which is not surprising. He admires her talent but he sees a hardness in her like her mother and says her career would come first.

'She can afford a nanny for every day of the week but that isn't the right way to bring up a child.'

You can't argue with that either. I say that it seems from the media that she is back with Dave who might want to be a full-time dad.

He laughs at that.

'You can't believe all the rubbish you read in the papers.'

'It isn't fair of you to punish Carli. She's innocent in all this.'

'That's rich coming for you. You've attacked her for leaving Tommy in the car.'

He puts the phone down on me.

**

After many more tense phone calls Peter promises me a decision by the end of October. I'm not sure I believe him. He doesn't accept that if I could find out the truth, then why can't the police, who have access to channels closed to me? He says meeting Liz on the Forum was an incredible stroke of luck and if that hadn't happened, I might not have found the truth. He seems to think I have an intellect far outreaching that of the police and there's no way they will ever find the children. I just worry that the Irish detective won't let go.

**

I haven't been checking the Forum every day but something tells me switch it on today.

Missing Children Forum	
Portal Home Register Log In	every child matters

October 29 2012 at 1.04 pm	Lucy
Hey folks just got a tweet that they've found a child in the crèche at the Trafford Shopping Centre	Posts: 16 Join Date: 21.8.2012 Location: Accrington

October 29 2012 at 1.09 pm	Suzy
Very funny Lucy, you put children in crèches, might be news if they found an OAP!	Posts: 118 Join Date: 27.2.2011 Location: Bath

October 29 2012 at 1.32 pm	Lucy
No, think the tweet means it's been abandoned there	Posts: 17 Join Date: 21.8.2012 Location: Accrington

October 29 2012 at 1.39pm Hey, Sky News is reporting more than one child...	Declan Posts: 629 Join Date: 2.4.2011 Location: Dublin
October 29 2012 at 1.48 pm This is getting ridiculous. Must be common that parents forget the time when they're shopping and the crèche management gets annoyed. I've used that place when I visit Manchester. Have cousins there. You can only leave kids there for two hours and believe me that's not much time in the Trafford Centre.	Suzy Posts: 119 Join Date: 27.2.2011 Location: Bath
October 29 2012 at 1.52 pm That crèche is fabulous. My kids don't want to leave when I collect them.	Nancy Posts: 16 Join Date: 3.9.2011 Location: Manchester

October 29 2012 at 1.59 pm Anyone know how old these children are?	CoolDude Posts: 121 Join Date: 4.7.2011 Location: Bahamas
October 29 2012 at 2.03 pm Kids have to be at least two to be left there.	Suzy Posts: 120 Join Date: 27.2.2011 Location: Bath
October 29 2012 at 2.10 pm Please God it's one of those missing kids we've been discussing all year	GoodMum Posts: 425 Join Date: 4.1.2011 Location: UK

October 29 2012 at 2.22 pm Sky news saying an 'older' woman left the child and no reply from the bleep they give parents. No reply from the mobile number she gave either.	Declan Posts: 630 Join Date: 2.4.2011 Location: Dublin
October 29 2012 at 2.30 pm Just got another tweet saying it's two children	Lucy Posts: 18 Join Date: 21.8.2012 Location: Accrington
October 29 2012 at 2.32 pm Any advance on two....!	Suzy Posts: 121 Join Date: 27.2.2011 Location: Bath

October 29 2012 at 2.37 pm Got another tweet saying the kids are foreign	Lucy Posts: 19 Join Date: 21.8.2012 Location: Accrington
October 29 2012 at 2.46 pm What do you mean 'foreign?' Is someone taking the piss?	Suzy Posts: 122 Join Date: 27.2.2011 Location: Bath
October 29 2012 at 2.51 pm Actually the tweet said 'black'. Didn't like to put that. LegalEagle might pull me up for being racist.	Lucy Posts: 20 Join Date: 21.8.2012 Location: Accrington

October 29 2012 at 3.07 pm	Declan
Sky News wouldn't be reporting this unless the child or children had been left there well past collection time and there was some other reason why this is newsworthy. Remember the 'older' woman a witness saw standing by Carli's car....?	Posts: 631 Join Date: 2.4.2011 Location: Dublin

I ring Peter. No reply. He promised a decision by the end of this month. I wish he'd reply but he's probably with a patient. It's so frustrating that I crave a fag to calm my nerves. I've none with me as I've almost managed to stop. I get one off a colleague who makes a smart remark about my willpower. I light up not caring if someone comes into my office and catches me smoking. I've something important to finish but I can't concentrate. I keep checking the news on my computer. I leave another message on Peter's mobile. There's nothing new on the Forum so I make an appeal.

October 29 2012 at 4.11 pm	Miss Marple
Lucy, where is your info coming from? This could be significant.	Posts: 53 Join Date: 10.9.2011 Location: St Mary Mead

October 29 2012 at 4.14 pm Hi Miss Marple. Thought you'd moved on to other things. My friend works at the Trafford Centre. Rumours flying around there she says.	Lucy Posts: 21 Join Date: 21.8.2012 Location: Accrington
October 29 2012 at 4.19 pm Were the children black? And how many?	Miss Marple Posts: 54 Join Date: 10.9.2011 Location: St Mary Mead
October 29 2012 at 4.22 pm My friend got a tweet saying they were black but thinks it's a joke. Says so much going around you don't know what to believe. But she saw the policeman in charge of the Rose Blake case heading towards the crèche. She knows it was him because she's seen him on the police appeals for information.	Lucy Posts: 22 Join Date: 21.8.2012 Location: Accrington

It must be serious if Detective Inspector Hargreaves has been called in. I ring Peter again. Still no reply. I'm shaking. I can't believe he's finally persuaded his mother. We had spoken two evenings ago and he had confirmed that a decision was imminent.

My extension rings. The boss is looking for the report I should have had completed this morning and I promise it in thirty minutes. I force myself to concentrate.

I can celebrate this evening.

EPILOGUE

FRANCE
OCTOBER 2013

A year has gone by. Did I do the right thing? Or more to the point did Peter and his mother do the right thing? Depends if you think that the natural mother has inalienable rights or whether you believe a child's rights can sometimes conflict with the mother's.

It's not black and white.

When Peter told me his mother wouldn't return the children and that he supported her decision, I was devastated. It was particularly hard because when I heard about the uncollected children in the Trafford Centre crèche I assumed Mrs Bennett had returned them. I knew that they had stayed near there with Tommy prior to taking Rose. In fact Mrs Bennett had told me she had been shopping in the Centre and had tried to leave Tommy in that crèche but he wasn't old enough then. But as both Tommy and Rose were two when the crèche story broke, I knew they could have been left there.

But it wasn't Tommy and Rose in the crèche. There was an innocent explanation. The children's grandmother, who had signed them in, had collapsed in the Centre while shopping and had been taken to hospital. Their parents were out of the country with their phones switched off so when the crèche rang them as the back-up number she had given, they didn't respond.

We argued and split up for a while. I had a couple of dates with blogger Declan when he came to work in Manchester for a month. A nice man but not for me.

Peter and I reconciled and married at Easter in the French equivalent of a registry office with just Mrs Bennett and a colleague of Peter's as witnesses. I told my family afterwards. Pedro has moved here and is happy in his new home.

We had hoped to have our own child but I knew from tests carried out after my miscarriage that my chances of taking another pregnancy to full term were not good. Peter had known that and would have told his mother. Perhaps it influenced their decision to keep the children. No sign of any pregnancy so far but I keep hoping.

Amy's first trial collapsed on a technicality and there's going to be a retrial. I can see this dragging on for years. Her lawyers are arguing she can't get a fair trial because of all the publicity. She's still running Jimmy's accountancy business and in any case her law firm can't take her back in the circumstances. I heard she has another Chinese au pair but a legal one this time.

As for Carli, she married Dave this summer, sold the pictures to Hello magazine and she gave the fee to children's charities. There are rumours that she's writing a book which will expose the goings-on in some of the children's homes she was in before being placed with long-term foster parents, but that may just be her PR people keeping her profile up.

Neither Peter nor his mother seems to feel any guilt but I do sometimes. And I still worry about somebody finding out. If I could solve the mystery maybe someone else could......Aunt Bernie says the Irish detective has set up his own investigation agency. Suppose Carli, who is now earning big money, hired him to find Tommy. She seemed to like him from the way she blogged about him. If Amy ever tells her about her father, wouldn't she look for him? I've no way of knowing what's in her head; she may believe it's a business enemy who took Rose. She wouldn't want to believe it was Peter. Hopefully she is concentrating on her retrial.

Two magazines are exclusively revealing that Carli's pregnant so maybe she won't hire the Irish detective. I've thought about Dave who tried to be a good dad to Tommy even though as it turned out he wasn't the biological father. If he and Carli are expecting a child then I shall feel less guilty about him.

And Davina, who sends me the occasional text, claims Detective Inspector Hargreaves' wife told a friend of hers in the golf club that he doesn't believe Amy was involved in her daughter's disappearance and will never give up looking. It was Davina who destroyed 'charity queen' Amy as the media dubbed her, so I take notice of what she says.

Yes I do get stressed on occasion. And I still check in on the Forum in case any new theories are being discussed but mainly nowadays they're analysing other cases.

Anna and Graham are so happy, and really isn't this all that matters?

ENID O'DOWD was born in Stratford which is now part of the London Borough of Newham. On Saturdays if the wind was in the right direction she knew when her local football team West Ham United had scored!

She has a degree in History and Politics from Liverpool University, a Higher Diploma in Journalism and after qualifying as a chartered accountant she worked for a while in Australia, New Zealand and the Middle East.

In 1975, while working for the International Planned Parenthood Federation in Beirut, Enid was blown up in an isolated incident before the war proper in the Lebanon commenced, escaping with relatively minor injuries.

She moved to Ireland in 1977. She joined the Green Party and stood as a candidate in the Dublin City Council elections in 1985 coming close to being elected. She became disillusioned and left some years before it became the junior coalition partner in the Irish Government of 2007-2011.

She published her first book *Cancer in a Cold Climate: the Shafting of St Luke's Hospital* in 2010. This explored the political machinations behind the decision to phase out and ultimately close the well-known cancer hospital. She was almost arrested in the Dail (Irish Parliament) when she shouted 'Shame' at the six Green TDs (MPs) as they came into the lobby after voting for the Bill to close the hospital.

She has also written about the outrageous expenses paid to Irish politicians. One article in the Irish Times ruffled many feathers and led to a debate with the Head of Communications at the Dail on Liveline, the main Irish phone-in radio show.

Fateful Decisions is her first fiction book. She now combines writing with lobbying for causes close to her heart like improved health services and integrity in politics. She also runs a financial clinic on a voluntary basis in her local Citizens Information Centre for those who cannot afford the professional services of accountants.

Enid has three adult daughters and lives in Dublin with her husband and two dogs.

www.enidodowd.com

By the same author:

Cancer in a Cold Climate:
the Shafting of St Luke's Hospital
(2010)

Hugh